# PRISONER OF NIGHT AND FOG

# PRISONER *of* NIGHT *and* FOG

ANNE BLANKMAN

BALZER + BRAY
*An Imprint of* HarperCollins*Publishers*

Balzer + Bray is an imprint of HarperCollins Publishers.





---

Library of Congress Cataloging-in-Publication Data
Blankman, Anne.
Prisoner of night and fog / Anne Blankman. — First edition.
pages cm
Summary: In 1930s Munich, the favorite niece of rising political leader Adolf Hitler is torn between duty and love after meeting a fearless and handsome young Jewish reporter.
ISBN 978-0-06-227881-4 (hardback)
1. Hitler, Adolf, 1889–1945—Juvenile fiction. 2. Nazis—Juvenile fiction. [1. Hitler, Adolf, 1889–1945—Fiction. 2. Nazis—Fiction. 3. Jews—Germany—Fiction. 4. Love—Fiction. 5. Munich (Germany)—History—20th century—Fiction. 6. Germany—History—1918–1933—Fiction.] I. Title.
PZ7.B61333Pr 2014 2013043071
[Fic]—dc23 CIP
AC

---

Typography by Michelle Taormina
14 15 16 17 18 LP/RRDH 10 9 8 7 6 5 4 3 2 1
❖
First Edition

*To Mike, who knows why*

# PRISONER OF NIGHT AND FOG

# PART ONE

## A GIRL OF WAX

Nothing is more enjoyable than
educating a young thing—a girl of eighteen
or twenty, as pliable as wax.
—*Adolf Hitler*

# 1

GRETCHEN MÜLLER PEERED THROUGH THE CAR'S rain-spotted windshield. Up ahead, a man was crossing the street, so far away he was little more than a child's cutout stick figure of spindly legs and arms and head. She could tell from his broad-brimmed hat and long coat that he was a member of the Hasidic sect.

"Look at the Jew," her brother, Reinhard, said. He and his comrade Kurt started snickering. Gretchen ignored them and glanced at her best friend sitting beside her in the back. Lights from passing buildings flashed over Eva's powdered face and the lipstick tube she was opening.

"You needn't fuss with your appearance for Uncle Dolf." Gretchen smiled. "You know he always says he's a man of the common people."

Eva reddened her lips with a quick, practiced sweep of her

hand. "Yes, but he's so fascinating. I want to look my best for him."

Gretchen understood. Adolf Hitler might be an old family friend to her, but to Eva, he seemed glamorous and mysterious, the most famous man in Munich. Although Uncle Dolf had never held an elected office—for serving as a mere Reichstag deputy would be beneath him, and he had no interest in local politics—he had set his sights on Berlin, and was campaigning for the presidency. Lately, politics had kept him so busy that his invitation to share dessert and coffee with him was a rare treat.

The car jerked to the left.

"What are you doing?" Gretchen cried.

The engine growled, a sure sign that Kurt had punched the accelerator. The tires skidded across the rain-drenched cobblestones, and Gretchen gripped the front seat so she wouldn't slide into Eva.

Yellow beams from the car's headlamps cut through the darkness, illuminating the Jew for an instant, making his face ghostly as he stood still, staring in shock as the car shot toward him. His mouth opened in a scream, and, dimly, Gretchen heard herself screaming, too, begging Kurt to stop.

The Daimler-Benz careened in the other direction, its back end fishtailing. The abrupt movement shoved Gretchen against Eva so hard she lost her breath. They were going too fast—in seconds they would fly over the curb and plow into a group of ladies in front of a clothing shop—and then there was a harsh grinding of gears and the brakes slammed so hard, she and Eva were thrown back in their seats. The car stopped.

For an instant, no one moved. The engine ticked as it cooled down, a tiny sound in the silence. Gretchen took a deep breath, trying to slow her frantic heartbeat. Then the boys slithered out and started to run, their jackboots thumping on the ground. A small piece of her wanted to cheer them on—after all, Uncle Dolf had explained to her many times how Jews were subhumans, determined to destroy her and other pure-blooded Germans—but part of her hesitated. The man's face had been so frightened.

"I wish they wouldn't bother with him." Eva pouted. "Now we'll be late."

Being late was the least of their problems if Reinhard and Kurt started a brawl. Through the windshield, Gretchen watched the boys launch themselves at the Jew. He barely had time to cry out before they seized his arms and began dragging him toward the alley.

Gretchen scrambled out of the automobile. She knew her brother too well to doubt what would happen next. Just as she knew how furious Hitler would be if Reinhard started a street fight. Uncle Dolf was always complaining that Party members had been branded as a group of brawlers. Dozens of times he had said that if the National Socialists wished to make any electoral progress, they must appear law-abiding. She had to stop her brother.

The wet cobblestones, slick from the recent rainfalls, slipped beneath her feet, but the breeze was dry and it carried the sounds of the boys' shouts. "Filthy Jew!"

From the backseat, Eva sobbed. "Don't leave me alone!"

"I need to stop them."

Gretchen slammed the car door shut. Dusk had fallen early,

painting the jumble of brick and stone buildings along the avenue with stripes of blue and black. Electric streetlamps broke apart the descending darkness, throwing small white circles on the Müncheners walking along the sidewalk—burghers in fine suits strolling to restaurants for a fancy meal, day laborers in stained jackets and patched trousers trudging to beer halls, office girls in flounced frocks striding to their rented rooms, all with their heads down, faces turned away, so they didn't have to watch the two boys pushing the Jew toward the yawning gap between the stone buildings.

Exhaustion slumped their shoulders, and hunger hollowed their cheeks. Rampant unemployment and inflation and starvation had weakened them—that's what Uncle Dolf would say. Germans had become so wrapped up in their lives, in trying to survive by any means they could, that they didn't see the danger creeping closer. This was how the Jew triumphed, a sewer rat slipping into a barrel of apples and spoiling them all, without anyone noticing until the first rancid bite.

Gretchen exhaled a shaky breath. *The Jew is my eternal enemy.* Those words had guided her heart for twelve years, thanks to her honorary "uncle" Dolf. She owed him so much. He had taught her about art and music, all the things that her father hadn't understood and her mother found dull. In gratitude to him, she had to prevent Reinhard from damaging the Party's reputation with another street fight.

The Jew's heels slapped on the cobblestones as Reinhard and Kurt pulled him closer to the alley. Nobody looked toward the struggling boys. Across the Briennerstrasse, a group of men opened the Carleton Tea Room's door, letting out a stream of soft lamplight. They wore the plain brown uniform of the SA—the Sturmabteilung, or storm troopers—the same division within the National Socialist Party to which Reinhard and his friends belonged.

There would be no help from that quarter. If she called out, they would run across the avenue, their fists raised and ready.

"*Please!*" the Jew screamed. The long, harsh sound pushed against her ears, so hard that she wanted to clap her hands over them and block the cries out. What could she do? SA men across the street, and inside the café, Uncle Dolf probably sat with his chauffeur, eating strawberry tarts and waiting for her and the others with growing impatience because he wanted to leave for a musical at the Kammerspiele. She couldn't go to him, not when asking for his assistance would expose Reinhard's part in a street beating, and Mama wanted the Müller family to remain above reproach.

She had to stop the boys.

Her feet smacked into the pavement as she ran into the alley. It was lined with stone, and so dark she had to blink several times for her eyes to adjust. Rubbish bins leaned against a wall, and they were probably stuffed with kitchen waste, judging from the rank stink assailing her nose. And there, at the far end, her brother and Kurt leaned over the man.

He lay on the ground. Between the boys' legs, she caught sight of him: a sliver of his face, pale and smooth; an eye, dark and wide; and the corner of a mouth, red and moving as he shouted, "*Stop!*"

A cry hurled itself from Gretchen's throat before she could snatch it back. "Don't hurt him!"

She froze. What had she done? She had meant to tell the boys to stop their foolish behavior, that Uncle Dolf would be angry—not defend a Jew. But the pain in the man's voice had been more than she could bear.

Reinhard paused. In the shadows, he was a column of darkness, like Kurt, but she recognized the hard line of his shoulders and his massive six-foot-tall frame as it slowly unfolded from its crouching position. Only eighteen, just a year older than her, and he was already a solid wall of muscle. He moved toward her, into the rectangle of light thrown from a window two stories above.

Gretchen's mouth went dry as sand. When she looked at him, she might have been looking at a male reflection of herself, as they had been when they were young children: white-blond hair, cornflower-blue eyes, fair skin, all of the features their uncle Dolf praised as Aryan. While her hair had darkened to honey and her eyes had deepened to navy, however, Reinhard's appearance had stayed the same. He hadn't changed. He had only gotten bigger.

"Go back to the car," Reinhard said. "And make Eva shut her mouth."

Gretchen glanced back. The automobile sat across the avenue, parked cockeyed from its sliding stop. In the backseat, Eva rocked back and forth. Probably crying, but so quietly they couldn't hear. One small blessing, at least. Reinhard detested tears. A few passersby glanced at the car, then shrugged and went on.

"She'll be fine," Gretchen said. She had to speak now, before she lost her nerve. "Reinhard, you shouldn't do this. You know how angry Uncle Dolf would be if he knew—"

His laughter cut into her words. "Kurt! Gretchen thinks the Führer will be angry if he finds out what we're doing."

Kurt laughed, too. "We're defending ourselves, Gretchen. Didn't you see this subhuman walking across the street, right in front of us? Why, I did all I could to avoid hitting the fellow!" He leaned down and grabbed a fistful of the Jew's hair, yanking hard so that the man had to look up. Resignation had stamped itself onto his pale oval face. The slumped set of his mouth told Gretchen that he knew he had no chance of getting away.

"You ought to let him alone," Gretchen said. Inside, she was shaking, but her voice sounded calm to her ears. "This behavior is exactly the sort that Uncle Dolf says makes the SA look like a bunch of brutes."

Reinhard glanced at her, his eyes blank and emotionless. Sometime during the fight, he had taken off his suit jacket. Suspenders formed dark slashes against his white shirt. He had rolled up the sleeves, and she could see the muscular ridges of his forearms.

Familiar knots tied in her stomach. Reinhard wouldn't hit her, she knew; he never did. What he did was far worse. And she was disobeying him, in front of his friend.

She should go back to the car. But the man's eyes fastened on hers with such intensity that she couldn't rip her gaze away. He was younger than she had thought, about twenty-five to her seventeen, and his face looked soft, the chin roughened by a few patches of stubble, as though he couldn't grow a proper beard. He wore the black clothes of the traditional Hasidic Jew: thick trousers, long flapping coat, yarmulke pinned to his brown hair.

His lips moved silently. *Please.*

How could she refuse him, when he lay on the ground, so broken and quiet? How could she walk back to the automobile, knowing the boys' fists were quickly cracking him into pieces? How could she think he was incapable of true feelings, when she had heard him cry out in pain? But he could be pretending. Uncle Dolf always said the Jew assumed whatever disguise suited his purposes best. Especially a victim, if it permitted him to escape.

And yet, the slowness with which the Jew hung his head, clearly giving up on her help, made her decision for her. "Let him alone. Uncle Dolf is waiting for us, and he'll be annoyed if we're late."

"Waiting for us fellows, you mean," Reinhard said. "I think you and Eva have shown you're quite incapable of handling an evening out on the town."

With one hand, he grabbed the Jew by the coat and jerked him into a sitting position. Then he plowed his other fist into the man's face.

"*Stop!*" Gretchen screamed, sickened at the ease with which Reinhard hit him.

With one swift motion, Reinhard wrapped an arm around her waist and pulled her against him. Through the layers of their clothes, she felt heat rolling off him, pushing into her skin. His familiar scent of cheap cologne and cigarettes clogged her nostrils. Each breath she inhaled, she breathed in more of him. Her stomach roiled.

"I told you," he whispered into her ear, "to go back to the car."

"What's the matter here?" A stern male voice boomed down the alley.

Reinhard released her. Gretchen staggered sideways before she slapped a hand against the stone wall for balance. Peering into the alley was a man in a dark green uniform. Lamplight glinted off the metal insignia on his helmet. She sagged with relief. A state policeman.

A small crowd had gathered behind the officer. Some of the men stood on tiptoe, trying to look over the policeman's shoulders.

"Nothing is wrong," Reinhard said. "A misunderstanding, that's all."

"Get along, then," said the policeman. He shrugged. "And look smart about it."

Reinhard and Kurt ambled out of the alley. Gretchen watched them head across the street, toward the café. She could guess what would happen next: The boys would strut to Hitler's table, Reinhard dropping into a chair and smiling away Uncle Dolf's annoyance at their lateness, then casually saying Gretchen and Eva couldn't come. Uncle Dolf would sigh with irritation until Reinhard asked him about one of his favorite topics, music or painting or used cars, and Uncle Dolf would start talking, a shower of words, until he had completely forgotten about the two girls who were supposed to complete their table tonight.

It was safer that way. The fewer people who knew what had happened in the alley, the better. What had she been thinking, defending a Jew? She must be going mad.

But she hadn't been able to stop herself. There must be no more death in the streets. Not after what had happened to her father.

A picture rose in her mind: Papa, facedown on the ground, blood reddening the cobblestones. He had died only a few miles from here, his body pierced by policemen's bullets.

Faintly, she heard someone wheezing for air, and realized it was herself. She stared at the wall, memorizing the pattern of the stones and lines of mortar, until Papa's image slipped away.

The Jewish man limped toward her. He had cupped his hand around his nose. Through his fingers, she saw blood trickling over his lips, onto his chin.

"Is it broken?" she asked.

"No, I don't think so." His voice sounded light and cool, like softly falling snow. "Thank you. A thousand thank-yous, Fräulein."

She didn't know what to say. Gratitude from a Jew was a poisoned gift, Uncle Dolf had told her. They smiled in your face and slid a knife between your ribs. And yet this man looked at her with such clear, thankful eyes. "You'd better get home," she said at last.

On the Briennerstrasse, he limped away in the direction opposite the one her brother and Kurt had taken. By now, the crowd had scattered. All except a lone man, watching her. He stood beyond the streetlamp's illumination, so he remained in shadow.

"You're not at all like the others," he said. The voice was young and quick, with the sharp accent of a Berliner. Not a man, but a boy, perhaps her age or a little older. She wished she could see him. "Are you, Fräulein Müller?"

She started. How did this stranger know her name? And what did he mean, comparing her to Reinhard and Kurt? "Who are you?"

He took a step closer. He wore the plain navy suit and white shirt of an office worker. His eyes seemed so dark, they might have been black. Beneath the slash of his brows, they watched her carefully. Through the shadows, she could barely trace the long sweep of his jawline and the lean shape of his face—a beautiful fine-boned face, but so fierce she instinctively took a step back.

His teeth shone white when he opened his mouth. "You've surprised me, Fräulein Müller. Not an easy feat, I promise you."

"Who the devil—"

Heels clicking on cobblestones interrupted them. Eva hurried toward her, holding her hat on with one hand and clutching her pocketbook in the other. "Gretchen! What in merciful heavens has been going on? Why did you leave me in the car all alone for so long?"

Gretchen hesitated. "Wait a moment." She turned back to the stranger. But the shadows where he had stood only seconds ago were empty.

# 2

"WHAT A WRETCHED EVENING." EVA TUCKED Gretchen's arm under hers, propelling them toward the Carleton Tea Room. "For a moment, I truly thought Kurt was going to hit that man. Thank goodness he managed to swerve away in time."

Swerve *away.* Gretchen cast her mind back. The automobile had jerked to the left, then to the right, before lurching to a sudden halt. Kurt had aimed the car toward the Jew, then lost his nerve and yanked the wheel in the opposite direction. That was the true reason the car had fishtailed and stopped. Not because of the wet cobblestones. A sudden chill sank into her bones, even though the August evening was warm.

Gretchen said nothing as Eva chattered on. There was no reason to frighten her friend about something they couldn't change. "I do think those boys were frightfully rude," Eva said, "going on without us! And after all the trouble I went to, curling my hair and pressing my best blouse! I know Reinhard's your brother, but he can be so beastly sometimes."

Gretchen shuddered. Eva had no idea how right she was.

With an effort, she pulled herself back into the conversation. "Eva, I'm sorry, but Reinhard said we can't go to the café with them. He's upset with me."

Eva stopped walking. "Well, I like that! Who the devil does he think he is?"

That was what Gretchen had wondered so many times about Reinhard. What did he see, when he looked in the glass? Or did he not look at all?

"And I was so anticipating spending time with Herr Hitler." Eva sighed.

Gretchen understood: Uncle Dolf was a rising star in a political party that had limped along on the fringes for years and was finally starting to surge in popularity. Sharing his table meant curious gazes from other diners, and Eva adored attention. After all, missing Hitler himself wasn't that much of a disappointment—Eva worked as a camera apprentice for Heinrich Hoffmann, his favorite photographer, so she often saw Hitler when he dropped by the shop.

"I'm sorry," Gretchen said.

Eva's silvery laugh rang out as clearly as a bell. In the thirteen years they had been friends, Gretchen had never known Eva to be angry for long. "Foolish boys. Well, our absence is their loss. Why don't you come back to my apartment? I've a new stack of film magazines, and a Karl May book I want you to borrow. The bits with the cowboys and Indians are simply thrilling! Only . . ."

The pause pulled between them. Eva bit her lip. "Only you

must promise not to mention Herr Hitler to my father," she said in a rush. "I didn't tell Papa we were supposed to see him tonight."

Gretchen nodded. She knew too well how deeply Herr Braun disapproved of Uncle Dolf, and how he tolerated her and Eva's friendship only because they were girls, and therefore they weren't expected to think about politics. These days, when she went by Eva's apartment, she tried to avoid Herr Braun, knowing if he saw her, he would start grousing about the Austrian upstart politician and saying a young lady like her had no business gallivanting about with a fellow old enough to be her father. As though Uncle Dolf saw her as anything except an honorary niece of sorts, the adored child of the man who had died for him.

But acknowledging Herr Braun's feelings would create a wedge between her and Eva. So she forced herself to smile as they strolled to the streetcar stop, listening to her friend chatter about how wonderful it would be if she could get away from her strict papa and become a famous actress, like Marlene Dietrich, or perhaps a world-renowned photographer, flying off to exotic locations while poor Gretchen toiled at university, studying to become a doctor. Gretchen smiled and said all the right things, and tried not to think about the mysterious stranger, or the Jew in the alley, or her voice screaming at the boys to stop.

But when she glimpsed their reflections in a shop window—both slim and dressed in their best blouses and knee-length pleated skirts, Eva's heart-shaped face surrounded by a cloud of dark-blond hair, her cheeks powdered and rouged so skillfully you only saw the cracks in the cosmetics if you stood close, and her own oval face, tanned and unpainted, her hair pulled back in a shining braid, like a proper National Socialist girl—she wondered at their forced happy tones. As though they were both hiding secrets. How odd. Eva had nothing to conceal from her. And she, Gretchen, had such strange fears about her brother, she wouldn't even admit them to herself.

In the morning, Gretchen lay among her twisted sheets, listening before she dared to move, thinking again about the mysterious stranger from outside the alley. Who *was* he? From the street, bottles clinked as the milkman set his wares on the front steps. Horses clip-clopped over the cobblestones, dragging carts full of vegetables and fruits, fish and bread to the Viktualienmarkt. A distant streetcar's bell clanged, and an automobile's motor hummed, carrying an early driver on his journey. A typical Sunday morning, outside, at least.

Still she didn't sit up. With every ounce of her body, she listened to the boardinghouse settling around her. Down the hall, a toilet flushed. No surprise there, since three elderly ladies with small bladders shared her floor. Someone coughed. Frau Bruckner in the next room, no doubt, who sneaked cigarettes and then splashed herself with violet scent to cover up the unladylike odor of tobacco.

Safe, everyday sounds. Gretchen rolled onto her side. Dawn had painted her tiny box of a room pale gray. Everything looked the same: the battered old armoire in the corner, the writing table with its tidy stacks of library books and school texts, the whitewashed walls covered with cheap postcards of foreign places that she longed to visit, and the desk chair hooked under the doorknob.

Last night, as she always did, she had barricaded herself in her room. Reinhard might have been able to force open the door, but he couldn't have stopped the chair from crashing to the floor and waking her. Since the chair was still upright and she had slept through the night, Reinhard may have already set a booby trap for her elsewhere in the house, as punishment for questioning him in front of Kurt.

She sighed and sat up. Sometimes, she wasn't certain which was worse—falling for one of Reinhard's sadistic tricks, or waiting for him to spring one. Days, perhaps weeks, might pass before he punished her for opposing him in the alley. No one possessed as much patience as her brother.

At her feet, a small cat lay curled like a soft gray pincushion, and despite her unease, she smiled. Darling little Striped Peterl, her father's final gift, given hours before his death. Eight years old and still petite as a kitten.

She nuzzled his fur before getting up. Nerves prickled her skin as she washed in the basin's cold water. Stupid. Hadn't she already checked the room? No one was standing behind her. And she would move carefully once she reached the corridor. She would be fine.

She dressed quickly, pulled the bedclothes back into place, and twisted the lock. Closed doors lined the empty corridor. No dead mouse on the floor, no glue on the knob. But Reinhard wouldn't pull the same old tricks he had pulled before. He preferred surprises.

The windowless stairwell was dark, since Mama didn't permit the wall sconces to be switched on until night, to save on the electric bill. Gripping the banister, Gretchen moved slowly, sliding a foot along each step until she was certain it was secure. She was three-quarters of the way down before her shoe hit something besides the stair.

A string stretched above the step, its ends fastened to the walls with thumb tacks. Only a few stairs from the bottom, so she wouldn't have had a long fall. Not enough to get badly hurt, but enough for a twisted ankle.

Gritting her teeth, she pried the tacks loose and stuffed the string into a skirt pocket. What if one of the older boarders had decided to come down early? A tumble down four steps could break elderly bones. It was a risk Reinhard would have taken, knowing the chances of someone other than Gretchen coming downstairs first were extremely small. She shook her head as she strode into the front parlor, dumped the tacks into a tin inside the desk—waste not, want not, her mother always said—and tossed the string into the basket where the old ladies kept their knitting.

In the kitchen, she opened the stove hatch and raked the coals before lighting them. Once they started burning, she set the coffeepot on the range to percolate and peered into the icebox. No meat, which was hardly a surprise; she couldn't remember the last time she had eaten sausages for breakfast. Maybe at her grandparents' farm in Dachau, but that had to be at least two summers ago.

These days, her stomach was so empty from hunger that only Hitler's words could fill it again: *Work and bread for all. Someday our great Fatherland shall rise again. Carried on the shoulders of her young people.* He had smiled and tugged on her braid. *Because of young people like me, Uncle Dolf?* she had asked, and he had nodded, saying the words she had always wished her own parents would say to her. *You are special.*

And she was recognizable. Perhaps that was why the stranger outside the alley had known her name. Within National Socialist circles she was called "the martyr's daughter," the title granted after her father had jumped in front of Hitler during a long-ago street fight, his body taking the bullets meant for their leader. But what had the stranger meant, she had *surprised* him? The comment made no sense.

Heels clacked on the floorboards. Mama pushed the swinging door open. "You're up early. Have you started the coffee yet?"

"Yes, Mama. There isn't much in the icebox, and the bread has mold on it."

Mama shrugged as she tied her apron strings. "Cut off the green part. And set the table. The nice cutlery, mind, since it's Sunday."

As Gretchen assembled silverware and napkins on a tray, she watched Mama from the corner of her eye. Although her mother wore a plain striped housedress and hadn't painted any color on her face, she was still pretty, with the delicate features of a ballerina and the swelling bust of a cabaret dancer. Long ago, Gretchen had accepted that while she had inherited her mother's fair coloring, she had gotten her father's figure—tall and arrow straight.

Today, Mama's forehead looked smooth, without any worries to wrinkle the soft skin. Maybe she would listen. Words bubbled up Gretchen's throat. *Mama, I saved a Jew last night. And I don't know if it was the right or wrong thing to do.*

Mama shot her a sharp look. "Daydreaming again, Gretl?

Cut the bread, and quickly, too! The boarders ought to be down any minute."

Without replying, Gretchen scraped mold off the stale loaf. She should have known better than to want to talk to her mother. Mama never listened anymore. She was too busy running the boardinghouse: fixing meals, shopping at the market, washing linens, scrubbing toilets, smoothing away petty annoyances among the old ladies. Mama believed only creeping subservience prevented the Müllers from living on the street. In the eight years since Papa had died, she had worked so hard for the family who owned the boardinghouse that she had whittled herself down into someone Gretchen no longer recognized.

They moved about the kitchen in a routine practiced so many times, they didn't need to speak. Coffee was poured into a carafe; cups and cutlery and napkins were carried into the dining room and set on the ancient tablecloth; a poor man's breakfast of rice pudding with sugar and cinnamon was ladled into bowls and brought out to the waiting ladies.

Back in the kitchen, Reinhard lounged at the round table. His pale eyes flicked over Gretchen's legs; he was probably hoping to see her limping. "How are you feeling today?"

"Fine," she said quickly, hoping he would drop the subject.

Muscles tightened along his jaw, only for an instant, before he forced a smile. "Mama, did Gretchen tell you about last night? Your daughter is quite fond of Yids, it seems."

She should have expected this reaction. Fail to punish her one way, make her pay in another. Might as well get it over with. The longer she tried to outwit him, the longer he would toy with her. She sank into a chair. The rice pudding already looked cold, but she wasn't hungry now anyway.

"No, Gretl hasn't told me a thing." Mama nudged Gretchen's plate closer. "Eat up. We haven't much time before Mass."

"Quite a Jew lover, this one." Smiling, Reinhard jerked his chin toward Gretchen. "Wouldn't let me teach a subhuman a lesson he needed to learn."

Gretchen stared at the floor, memorizing the grain in the wooden boards. Something had lodged itself in her chest like a stone, hard and heavy, pressing down. Sometimes, she thought she could stand anything but her mother's quiet disapproval. Which was all she seemed to get.

"What happened?" Mama's voice sounded as clear as a mountain stream. And as cold.

Curse Reinhard and his smug smile! "Mama, you know how Uncle Dolf says the Party needs to be a respectable organization, if he's to be taken seriously as a politician. Street beatings hurt his reputation. I—I was trying to help," she faltered under her mother's quiet, measuring gaze.

For a moment, Mama turned her gold wedding band round and round on her finger, studying it. At last she said, "You must do as Herr Hitler wishes, Reinhard." She gathered the breakfast dishes with shaking hands. "He knows what is best. No more fights, if that is what he says. After what happened to your papa, I'm sure Herr Hitler wishes to be very careful with his supporters."

Gretchen swallowed her disappointment. How like Mama, saying something without any meaning. Both she and Reinhard had memorized the story of Papa's great sacrifice, they had heard it so many times. How the National Socialists had attempted to seize control of Munich back in 1923. How they had marched directly into a waiting cordon of state police troopers, and Papa had flung himself in front of Hitler when the bullets started. How Uncle Dolf had been imprisoned for high treason. How the Party had nearly ripped itself apart, and only Uncle Dolf's leadership had pulled it back together.

As she got up, Reinhard brushed past her. "Are you certain that was the *only* reason, little sister?"

She said nothing. But she heard the laugh in his whisper—he guessed the truth. Her original intention had been to prevent an illegal street beating that might reflect poorly on the Party. Once she had seen the Jew lying on the ground, helpless . . . She had seen a person. Not a monster.

She gathered the dirty dishes in the dining room and went to the back steps, where she scraped the leftovers into the slop bucket. Summer sunlight sprinkled across the courtyard. Somewhere, someone had opened a window, letting classical music from the wireless spill across the warm breeze.

In the backs of the buildings opposite, flags hung from a handful of windows: the yellow hammer and sickle against the red background of the Communists, the dark green of the Social Democrats, the black eagle against the blazing yellow of the Bavarian People's Party, the bloodred rectangle and white circle surrounding the black swastika of the National Socialists. Politics was everywhere these days, it seemed. Automatically, she touched the gold charm on her necklace; the *Hakenkreuz*, the hooked cross, had been last year's birthday present from Uncle Dolf.

Would he think she had betrayed him, and everything the

Party represented, when she had protected the Jew? How could she go on, if the one adult whom she trusted without reservation, the man who had grown into her second father, no longer thought her worthy?

Flies buzzed around the bucket, attracted by the nasty mix of day-old horse meat and rice pudding going bad in the heat. She felt sick.

She knew the answer. Without Hitler's friendship, she could go on. But she might not want to.

# 3

GRETCHEN STEPPED INTO THE KITCHEN'S WELCOME coolness. After church, she had spent the afternoon hanging wet sheets on laundry lines strung across the courtyard and beating carpets on the back steps. As she poured herself a glass of water, she caught a low murmur that she instantly recognized. Uncle Dolf. No one else had such a lovely voice, dark and warm and rich, like melted chocolate. The sound pulled her into the front hall.

"I don't want children," he was saying, "and I think it would be irresponsible to marry when I can't devote enough time to a wife."

"The right woman would understand. Your dedication to the Party must supersede all else." Mama sounded giggly and girlish.

Gretchen put a hand to her overheated face. She must look a fright.

"Is that little Gretl's footsteps I hear?" Hitler asked. "Come in, my sunshine!"

He had called her by that pet name since she was a child. Just hearing the phrase lifted her heart.

Hitler rose and kissed the backs of her hands. Beaming, he stepped back and surveyed her. Somehow, he always remained reassuringly the same.

In the twelve years she had known him, his appearance hadn't altered: his lank brown hair still flopped over his forehead, even though he faithfully combed it flat every morning; his pale blue eyes were still clear and direct above his sharp cheekbones, his mustache still a dark smudge above his thin lips, and his face still angular and half-starved, as though he were continually hungry but didn't care enough for his personal comfort to eat. Today he wore a brown pinstripe suit. The bulges beneath his jacket came from the items he always carried—a pistol and a cartridge belt. His whip lay on the table.

"Helping your mother like a good girl, I see," he said.

Flushing, she slipped the kerchief off her head. "I was cleaning the carpets. Dust gets in my hair if I don't cover it."

"Never be ashamed of an industrious look," Uncle Dolf said. "The true German woman works hard in her home."

The elderly ladies perched on the flowered sofa nodded. All of them were knitting, more scarves for Hitler, probably; Gretchen saw the beginnings of a swastika motif in one of them.

"Won't you stay for tea, Herr Hitler?" Mama asked.

"No, no. An unexpected guest is an unwelcome addition at table." As Hitler glanced at Gretchen, she realized they were face-to-face. Without even noticing, she had grown to match his five feet seven inches. Although she saw him at least once a week, they were usually sitting, chatting at his regular table in a restaurant or lounging in his parlor. How odd it felt, to see eye to eye with this man who always seemed so large that his presence filled a room as soon as he opened his mouth.

"It's no trouble," Mama said. "Feeding a man who appreciates his food is a true pleasure for me. What you need, Herr Hitler, is a wife to look after you. I declare, you are wasting away!"

"I can't have a wife when Germany is my greatest love." Hitler bowed. "As charming as you ladies are, I must excuse myself. I came to invite Gretl to join me at the Alte Pinakothek." He extended his arm for her to take, and Gretchen smiled. He always used such courtly gestures.

"I should love to go to the museum, Uncle Dolf." She didn't even need to look at her mother for permission. No matter how many chores remained, Mama always allowed her to go with him, wherever and whenever he wished.

In the front hall, he waited patiently while she fetched her pocketbook and hat. As they stepped out into the slanting sunshine, he smiled and said, "Few things are as pleasant as a young lady's company."

He had often said those words to her when he talked about music and painting, explaining how a girl's mind was made of wax and needed to be molded into its proper shape. How soft and malleable she felt, sometimes, when his electric-blue eyes pinned her in place and his thundering voice stormed out endless words.

Just as a father would, he had told her. His mind touching hers, forming it into the right sort of brain for her, the National

Socialist girl he always said would someday become a golden, shining example of womanhood for the other German ladies to emulate. She was so proud that he had chosen her to mold into that perfect girl.

As they headed down the front steps, Uncle Dolf tugged on her long braid. "Now, what is this nonsense I heard about you coming to a Jew's aid?" he asked.

Shame heated her face. Who had told him? What could he possibly think of her?

He stood on the bottom step, a half smile pulling at his lips. At the curb, his chauffeur leaned against the red Mercedes, waiting, and farther up the avenue, a trio of middle-aged ladies, strolling in their Sunday best, nudged one another and nodded at Hitler, no doubt recognizing Munich's most famous resident. To passersby, she and Uncle Dolf might have been a father and daughter, out for a pleasant afternoon together. Her dry eyes burned. Not a girl and her dearest idol about to part ways.

"Please don't be upset." Her voice split on the last word. "You said we must be a respectable Party."

"I suspected it must be something like this." Hitler patted her hand. "Yes, the National Socialist Party must appear very respectable; that is true. And I am shocked, simply shocked, when my followers misunderstand my meaning and resort to illegal behavior. You did the right thing, Gretl."

Relief flooded her veins like blood. He still loved her. Her pity for the Jew was an aberration, or a typical reaction from a future medical student who hated seeing anyone in pain. That was all.

"Thank you," she said.

Hitler kissed her hand. His lips felt dry and cool. "Not at all, my sunshine." He smiled. "You are still my favorite child." She smiled back. She had never been anyone else's favorite, and each beat of her heart seemed to say she belonged, she belonged, she belonged.

# 4

WHEN THE SCHOOL DISMISSAL BELL RANG ON Monday afternoon, Gretchen, reluctant to leave, slowly slid her books into her leather satchel. The other girls hurried out, giggling and whispering. Home to their mothers, who would drink tea with them and ask about their day at school. Her heart twisted. To their mothers, who would listen to their answers.

The science classroom's familiar smells of chalk dust and formaldehyde assailed her nose. If only she could stay here, where everything made sense, with the predictable sequence of mathematics and the beautiful logic of science. Without the muddy mess of politics and religion and the questions that tormented her.

As she walked down the narrow hallway, she wished life could be simple and straightforward. She wanted to be so many different puzzle pieces—Uncle Dolf's sunshine, the martyr's daughter, the serious student, the future physician. The last was almost within her grasp. The new school term had started at Easter, so she was already halfway through her final year of Gymnasium, the university preparatory school. The university entrance exam was scheduled in a few months' time. If she did well, soon she would begin studying medicine. Outside, the narrow Tengstrasse thronged with students spilling out of school: classmates from the Gymnasium, laughing and chattering to one another as they milled about on the pavement, and small boys from the primary school, roughhousing and teasing as they streamed down the avenue.

Gretchen joined her circle of friends. The girls were groaning about Frau Huber's announcement—a Latin exam this week, simply cruel after the weekend's assignment on the *Aeneid*, with all those horrible declensions—and Gretchen's gaze moved to the next group of girls, meeting the eyes of Erika Goldberg.

Erika smiled and Gretchen started to smile back, then shame pushed heat into her cheeks and she looked away. She was supposed to despise Erika Goldberg. Erika with the wild corkscrew curls and even wilder laugh. Erika who told funny jokes and could recite the first five stanzas of the *Aeneid* from memory. She was the enemy, Gretchen had to remind herself when they passed each other in the hallway.

But she couldn't. She laughed at Erika's jokes, even though she shouldn't. She admired Erika's grasp of Latin, even though she should sneer. And sometimes, when her classmates gathered at the front steps after school, she wished she could stand with Erika, talking about Frau Huber's ridiculous clothes, or the impossible English exam, or the handsome boys from the Gymnasium the next street over, but she didn't. Whenever she turned in Erika's direction, an invisible string jerked her back.

She looked away from Erika's tentative smile, muttering an excuse about getting back to the boardinghouse to help her mother.

As she walked on alone, hot, dirty air pressed against her face. Up ahead, a low-slung black automobile belched exhaust, and a street vendor scooped scorched-smelling roasted chestnuts into paper bags for schoolboys. Mothers pushed babies in prams, and a woman with a mop tossed a bucket of water onto a flight of front steps. A trio of young men, wearing the SA's plain brown uniform with the swastika brassard on the arm, ambled along, laughing and smoking. The street looked the same as it did every afternoon when she walked home from school. Everything seemed endlessly the same.

The future unrolled before her like a ribbon: sleeping with a chair hooked under the doorknob every night, beating carpets on the back steps, cooking the boarders' breakfast, scrubbing the toilets, changing the linens, pouring fresh water in the basins, haggling with vendors at the Viktualienmarkt, fighting the nightmares about Papa, imagining his bloody body in the street and herself unable to help as his chest stilled and his eyes grew blank.

Tears locked her throat. She hadn't been able to save her father, but she could save other people, someday. She walked faster. Nobody understood her ambitions except Uncle Dolf. He battled his life, as she did, searching for something bigger, something meaningful.

A small boy darted in front of her. "Wait," he said. "I've got something for you."

The child couldn't have been older than seven or eight. She recognized his cheerful, dirty face; he had been one of the schoolboys clustered around the chestnut cart.

"What is it?"

"I don't know, do I?" He sounded indignant. "I don't go reading other folks' love letters. Here." He pulled a white envelope from his leather bag.

"Love letter." She had to laugh. "You must have the wrong girl."

"Nope." He thrust the envelope into her hand. "The gentleman said a pretty girl with a blond braid and a white blouse and a *Hakenkreuz* necklace. You're the only one, so it must be you."

"Wait a minute." She grabbed his spindly arm. "What gentleman?"

"I don't know." He tried to pull his arm back. "Some tall fellow in a dark suit. Must have been rich, though, because he gave me two marks."

Marks, when the boy would have completed the errand for groschen. Not rich, perhaps, but determined.

Unease whispered up her spine. She whipped around. Boys playing jacks, girls walking home, housewives carrying string shopping bags. Nobody suspicious.

The boy scampered off. At the corner, a streetcar trundled to a stop, blue sparks flying from its electric cable, and she climbed up its steps.

No one looked at her as she threaded her way to the back. Leaning against a pole for balance, she ripped open the envelope.

*Monday, 17 August 1931*

*Dear Fräulein Müller,*

*Although you hide it well, it is clear you are nothing like the others, which is why I presume to send you this letter. Last week, I was approached by one of the Nazi Party's original members. He is old now, and his health frail, but his memory is clear. He told me a troubling story that I believe you, as Klaus Müller's daughter, deserve to hear. Your father did not die a martyr to the Nazi cause, and your family's precarious position within Hitler's party is predicated on a lie.*

*I beg you give me a chance to explain, and I shall meet you directly outside your home this evening at half past six o'clock.*

*A Friend*

The paper rustled in her shaking hand. How dare anyone make up such lies? She knew Papa had been shot to death trying to protect Uncle Dolf, just as she knew the ocean's waves would endlessly roll on the shore, each slap of water eroding the sand a little more. It was one of life's truths.

And no one—certainly not an anonymous stranger who signed his despicable lies with the appellation *A Friend*—could be allowed to question her father's sacrifice. He had died so Hitler might live. No one must be permitted to forget his final, heroic act. Or question it.

She glanced out the window at the long city streets winding past. The summer sun hung like a bright coin in the sky. Hours left before this mysterious *friend* showed up at the boardinghouse. She would meet with him, of course—Uncle Dolf always said the only way to deal with a perceived threat was to attack first—but she must have a means of protecting herself, in case the stranger was dangerous.

The streetcar jerked around a corner. She grabbed a canvas ceiling strap to steady herself. And she thought of the knives in the kitchen drawer—long and shining and sharp.

# 5

THE HARD BLUE LIGHT OF EARLY EVENING SPREAD across the Königinstrasse. Gretchen waited in a narrow passage between the stone houses. Nerves tightened her grip on the knife's hilt. Motionless, she let the alley's shadows wrap around her like a cloak. Only the glint of her eyes and the knife in her hand, she knew, might betray her.

But he wouldn't be looking for her. He would be scanning the houses, searching for hers.

Across the avenue, the massive Englischer Garten stretched its manicured lawns in both directions. Along the pavement, working-class men in rough jackets trudged to their rented rooms, grumbling about low wages, and she was reminded of Uncle Dolf's laugh when he said the crippling depression was the best thing that could have happened to him or the Party. People were desperate for saviors, for change that put food in their bellies and coins in their pockets. For any kind of stability. And that was precisely what Hitler promised to provide.

A few feet away, a group of girls played, their jump rope smacking into the sidewalk, and a rangy dog shot out of a front garden, its owner shouting about a mess on the carpet while the animal darted into traffic, dodging the private automobiles, buses, bicycles, and pushcarts that choked the Königinstrasse at half past six.

Ordinary.

But nothing was ordinary for her now, all the familiar sights rendered strange by the letter. She felt it burning through her skirt pocket.

And then she saw him.

There was no mistaking the man, although they hadn't met. He was what she had expected—a solitary figure walking through the descending dusk, stopping occasionally to check the building numbers. Tall and lean, with a quick, long stride, as though he were in a hurry. She clutched the knife handle more tightly.

As the man grew closer, recognition arrowed through her. A fedora was pulled low over his face, leaving only an impression of olive-tinted skin and a sharp jaw. But she knew the shape of that wide mouth, and the curve of those broad shoulders.

It was the stranger from outside the alley.

He wasn't a man, then, but a boy hovering on the brink of adulthood, perhaps eighteen or nineteen to her seventeen.

She darted from the shadows. On the sidewalk, the boy paused, glancing at the number on the skinny stone boardinghouse. She moved so close only an inch of space remained between their bodies, and his scent of oranges and soap washed over her. Before she could lose her nerve, she pressed the knife's tip into the small of his back, just hard enough that he could feel the prick of metal through his clothes.

"You wrote Gretchen Müller a letter," she said. Her voice sounded strong and low, almost as if it were a stranger's.

"Yes."

He started to turn around, but she said, "Across the street. Into the Englischer Garten. We can speak there."

"I had hoped we could speak like civilized people in the beer hall down the street." The boy sounded half-amused, as though he wasn't taking her seriously. His sharp Berlin accent laced each word.

She could only imagine what the other diners might say if they recognized Uncle Dolf's favorite pet sitting with someone who was an enemy of the Party. "No. Into the park."

The boy heaved a sigh, as though he found all this tiresome, but he didn't argue. They ran as the neighbor's dog had, zigzagging between the automobiles and buses and horse-drawn carts. By the time Gretchen reached the sidewalk, she had lost track of the boy. Panic seized her heart. He had gotten away.

But then she saw him, waiting at the park entrance. He had pushed the fedora back, so she could see his face clearly for the first time. A handsome face, but she had been right—there was something dangerous about it. His eyes weren't black, as she had thought, but dark brown, the irises encircled by gold.

"We mustn't speak here, out in the open," she said.

His hard expression didn't change. "Very well."

They walked quickly, stepping onto one of the flower-scented paths that wound through the Englischer Garten. She hid her hand among her skirt's folds, concealing the knife. Its sharp hilt dug into her palm, but she was too nervous to put it away.

At this hour, the paths were crowded with workers returning home, their faces exhausted, their pockets jingling with the stingy groschen they had been lucky enough to earn today. When Gretchen and the boy reached a cluster of pine trees, by silent accord, they moved off the path. Needles sighed underfoot as they walked deeper into the dark woods. The trees' tops bent closely together, partially blocking out the sun's fading rays, enclosing Gretchen and the boy in a pocket of green-tinted shadow.

His face was all angles and planes: a strong jaw, high cheekbones, a razor-sharp nose. There was nothing soft about him, but his eyes, when they met hers, seemed kind and earnest.

"How about an exchange of information?" he proposed. "I'll tell you what I know about your father's death, and you tell me why you found it necessary to greet me with a knife."

An unfair trade. His side would contain lies, and hers, memories no outsider could understand. Papa's death protected her family. If he had died during the Great War, or from influenza, his widow and children would have been quickly forgotten. Bundled off to Mama's parents' farm in Dachau, perhaps, to live in creeping poverty.

Instead, they were protected. An old Party comrade had found Mama the boardinghouse manager position. Another had paid for Gretchen's piano lessons. At Christmas, she and Reinhard received dozens of boxes of chocolates, and when she was a child, she had gotten a china doll whose eyes opened and closed, and

Reinhard had gotten a set of charcoal pencils and a sketch pad with exquisitely thin paper. After Party speeches, society ladies kissed her cheeks, and when she sat beside Hitler at his regular table at Café Heck, SA men clasped her hand in gratitude.

Best of all, Uncle Dolf had remained their beloved family friend. Sometimes, when he was in one of his nostalgic moods, he talked about sturdy, dependable old Müller. How his trusted lieutenant had known that he, Hitler, was destined for great things, and had laid down his life so Hitler could accomplish them.

There could be no trade. "Who are you?" she asked.

"I'm a reporter," he said. "I came to you because this is a critical time for the Nazi Party—"

"National Socialist," she corrected automatically. She hated the way some people said "Nazi" so casually, as though they didn't even realize it was Bavarian slang for "country bumpkin."

"I beg your pardon." He smiled slightly, then turned serious. "Fräulein Müller, Hitler's campaigning for the presidency as we speak. His party is poised to become the most powerful political force in the country. And it mustn't happen."

"Mustn't happen?" Irritation inched into her voice, although she tried to hold it back. Had this boy made up a story about Papa, luring her to this meeting, so he could pour out his political beliefs, knowing she was one of Hitler's favorites and might repeat his concerns to the Führer? Uncle Dolf had warned her about such interlopers.

Now, more than ever, the Party had to guard itself against its enemies. In the last elections, the National Socialists had increased their presence in the Reichstag from twelve to one hundred seven deputies, and they were quickly becoming the most popular party in the country. They had, as Uncle Dolf often said, reached the tipping point in their political movement.

"The National Socialist Party is the best thing that could ever happen to Germany!" Gretchen said. "Herr Hitler is committed to reducing unemployment and creating more jobs."

The boy's gaze moved over her face, and she shifted uncomfortably. There was an unblinking fierceness in his gaze. She couldn't recall the last time someone had looked at her so intently.

"I see you truly believe that," he said at last. "But why wouldn't you? You've lived in Hitler's shadow for as long as you can remember."

She brushed his words aside. "Why did you send me a letter?"

"Nothing matters more than exposing a lie." He moved closer, the pine needles sighing under his feet. "And because you're Klaus Müller's daughter. I thought that you, more than anyone else, would want to know what happened to him."

Confusion blanked her mind. "I already know. He died protecting Herr Hitler."

"He was murdered."

She rolled her eyes. "Of course he was. The state policemen shot him and let him bleed to death in the street."

What a waste of time. She started to push past him, but he grabbed her arm. His fingers felt hot against her bare skin.

"I'm sorry, Fräulein Müller, but they didn't." The boy's dark eyes locked on hers. "An old Party member—disillusioned by Hitler's politics—came to me with information that he believes proves your father wasn't killed by police at all, but by a National Socialist comrade. Your father wasn't a martyr, Fräulein Müller; he was murdered. I aim to find out who did it."

The trees tilted and blurred, skinny black trunks and green-leaved branches swirling together like a child's experiment with finger paints. From far away, she felt the boy's hand slide from her arm, then his fingers gripping both of her shoulders, steadying her.

A cruel joke. That's all it was. Finally, she found her voice. "You're wrong."

In the greenish-black light, she saw the grim set of the boy's mouth. It wasn't a joke. While Gretchen, stunned into silence, stared at him, his hands fell to his sides, but her shoulders still burned from his touch.

"I have proof," he said quietly. "I'll get to the truth behind your father's death, and once I do, everyone else in Munich will know it, too."

He tipped his hat. "If you decide to do right by your father's memory, you can find me at the Golden Phoenix nightclub tomorrow night."

He strode away, a tall figure rapidly darkening with distance until he was part of the shadows descending on the park.

Ludicrous lies, an attempt by an overly ambitious reporter to dig up dirt on Uncle Dolf—that must be it. She gripped the knife harder. Her fingers dug into the carved wooden handle, the almost painful sensation grounding her in this moment. Her family's special relationship with Hitler meant they were targets, too.

Uncle Dolf had warned she must constantly be on her guard against the Party's myriad enemies. He had said his opponents were flung across every corner of the city, barely discernible, like a spiderweb—until you tossed water on the gossamer net and there your opponents were, glistening like diamonds, brilliantly bright and unmistakable.

He would want to know about this strange conversation. She hesitated. Something about the boy held her back. The kindness in his voice, perhaps.

A sudden, sharp pain sliced through her thoughts. The knife had slipped. Thin lines of blood ran between her fingers. In the twilight, they looked black. She wound a handkerchief around the stinging pain. Then she stepped out from the trees and started walking.

Even in the deepening shadows, the boardinghouse appeared tired and dingy, like an aging theater actress who looked old and faded beneath the thick layers of makeup. Soot streaked the stone in places, last week's rainfall dotted the windows, and the cheap smells of lung soup and horse meat wafted through the open door.

In the front hall, Gretchen snatched up the telephone's earpiece. She dialed the apartment house at 93 Hohenzollernstrasse, turning toward the wall and hunching her shoulders, as though she could curl into herself and become invisible. Her heart slowed in relief when someone answered the building's communal telephone and promised to fetch Eva.

As she waited, her eyes traced the garish red-and-purple flowered wallpaper. Across the hall, the ladies gossiped in the parlor. Supper was over; she hadn't shown up to help Mama with the cooking and cleaning. What would her mother say? Gretchen swallowed hard. Nothing her mother could come up with would be worse than what the boy had said.

"Hello!" Eva's crystalline voice echoed down the telephone wires. "Thank heavens you rang! I've been stuck here, reading film magazines, because naturally my father won't let me go out, and I've been trying not to think about cream pie—"

"Eva," Gretchen broke in, "something strange has happened." Out of habit, she glanced around the empty hall, although she knew she was alone. "Can I come by the shop tomorrow? I must talk to you."

"Are you all right?" Eva asked. "Gretchen, you sound . . . I don't know . . . as if you can't breathe."

"No, I'm not all right." The words tumbled out before she could stop them. "There's a man—a boy, really—and he's told me a horrible story about my father—"

She stopped as a light, feathery shuffle sounded from the staircase. One of the boarders was coming down. "I must go."

She dropped the earpiece onto its handle and went into the kitchen. Her mother stood at the sink, scrubbing dishes. Even the tight set of her shoulders looked annoyed as she snapped, "Why weren't you here to help with the boarders' supper?"

"I'm sorry, Mama. I lost track of time."

"We're losing more than that." Her mother shoved a dripping plate into her hands. "It's the bills, Gretl. I can't pay them."

Although the building owners paid for electricity and coal, all residents were charged for rent and food. Gretchen's family paid a reduced amount, and Mama received small payments for her work as the boardinghouse manager, but her salary barely covered their housing and meal costs. Extras such as clothing had to be budgeted for carefully.

"Can we ask Uncle Dolf for a loan?"

Her mother plunged her hands into the sudsy water. "The Party is perpetually low on funds, at least that's what they say. Besides, we're in the same hole every month, just sinking deeper." She pushed another plate at her, and Gretchen realized she hadn't dried the first one yet. "You need to get a job. A real job, Gretl." Mama didn't look at her. "You'll have to give up your schooling."

"*What?*" She couldn't have heard correctly. Not her education, the single rope she held to climb out of the dark hole of drudgery Mama expected her to live in. Not her dreams of becoming a doctor. Not when she had only a few months left before graduation. She was so close.

Slowly, Gretchen set the still-wet dish onto the stack on the counter. The sound of china plates clinking together seemed loud in the quiet kitchen.

"You heard me." Mama pulled the plug, and water gurgled down the drain. "We can begin looking for a suitable position in the morning. There won't be many available, but I'm sure Herr Hitler will put in a good word for you somewhere."

Gretchen felt as though she had stepped into a freezing lake. "Please, Mama, I must go back. I'm in my last year of Gymnasium."

"I know, and you wish to be a doctor and heal everyone and do all sorts of splendid things." Her mother sounded annoyed as she scrubbed the counter. "But it's impossible. You'd best go upstairs and press your white blouse to wear tomorrow when you go looking for work. No one will hire a slovenly girl."

Gretchen opened her mouth to protest, then shut it. Talking back was not permitted. Not by any family; she didn't have a single friend who dared to argue with her parents. The decision had been made. There could be no pleas or tears; they wouldn't make any difference. Blindly, Gretchen walked into the hall, nearly knocking into the man peering at one of the cheaply framed prints of wildflowers.

"Excuse me," she murmured, catching only a momentary impression of black hair, gold-rimmed spectacles, and a flurry of apologies in muddled, schoolboy German before she threw herself out the front door and pounded down the steps, running faster and faster until she thought her lungs would burst.

There was only one person she could go to for help, but Uncle Dolf was due to deliver a speech at the Circus Krone in less than an hour. She would have to hurry.

# 6

THE CIRCUS KRONE WAS A CAVERNOUS HALL LINED with dozens of rows of wooden benches. Gretchen paused at the entrance. Hundreds of people packed the seats: burghers in suits beside laborers in tattered jackets, housewives in flowered dresses next to society ladies in silk, even theater folks in vivid makeup rubbing shoulders with street toughs in black, everyone jumbled together without regard to class distinctions, as Hitler always instructed.

Different classes, but the same tension tightened their shoulders and the same desperation hooded their eyes. They needed a savior to pull them out of this dark hole—the hole of inflation and high unemployment and gnawing hunger and a progression of shoddily built governments that kept collapsing. Gretchen heard the word *Heiland* on nearly everyone's lips. A savior, a healer. The man they needed Hitler to be. It was no coincidence they greeted him with *Heil*s. He had come to deliver them all.

The podium was still empty; he hadn't arrived yet. But she mustn't search him out now. Disturbing him before a speech would only annoy him.

The air was hazy with tobacco smoke drifting lazily to the high ceiling. The crowd's voices swelled and sank like the tide, washing over her, and suddenly the chattering rose to a dull roar. *"Sieg Heil! Sieg Heil!"*

That was the signal that Uncle Dolf was coming. She caught sight of his half niece in the front row. Geli Raubal had turned in her seat. Her eyes widened when they met Gretchen's, and she waved, mouthing, *Sit with me! Hurry!*

Gretchen rushed down the center aisle. Geli pulled her close, whispering, "How marvelous to see you! Now I needn't be bored silly." She jerked her head toward the thirtyish man sitting beside her. Gretchen recognized the florid face and icy eyes; they belonged to one of Hitler's many adjutants, who sometimes acted as Geli's chaperone.

The crowd cheered again, saving Gretchen from having to reply. She often didn't know how to respond to Geli's saucy comments. Unlike the National Socialists who kowtowed to Hitler, Geli often teased her uncle Alf, and even accomplished the rare feat of making him laugh at himself. When Geli had moved to Munich four years ago, Gretchen had expected their ages to wedge them apart—after all, Geli was six years older—but her merry, easy manner had made them friends. They often sat together at Café Heck, or shopped along the Maximilianstrasse, Gretchen watching as Geli tried on hat after hat until she giggled and said she couldn't decide and would have to buy them all and to please send her uncle the bill.

The crowd roared. Gretchen stood with them, peering through the crush of bodies and the swirling cigarette smoke. Along the walls and beneath the raised podium stood uniformed SA troops. Their heads swiveled as they studied the audience; their bodies were ready to spring forward to drag away hecklers.

She spotted Reinhard among them, a tower in a brown uniform. He stood with his arms clasped behind his back, feet wide apart, poised to attack.

Quickly she looked away from him, glad he hadn't noticed her. Even as relief flooded her veins like blood, she felt embarrassed. She could never tell anyone how much she feared her own brother, or how Reinhard secretly punished her for a cross word or an ill-timed laugh by playing nasty tricks: her library book left on the front stoop on a rainy night although she could have sworn she'd placed it in her satchel, her best blouse balled up beneath her bed even though she had searched there five times already. There was no one else it could be, although he hadn't confessed and she hadn't had the nerve to confront him.

The shouts of *Sieg Heil* filled the air as Hitler strode down the center aisle, his face set in tight lines, his arms swinging purposefully. Tonight he wore the blue serge suit he was so proud of, and a sheen of perspiration already coated his forehead.

Like the others, Gretchen had turned to watch Hitler approach. The audience members raised their arms in the National Socialist salute, united in their identical pose.

But there was someone, standing near the back, who was not saluting or applauding. In the dim light, she could barely see him—a tall figure, arms folded over a broad chest. When he moved, the pale lamplight washing him with gold, she nearly gasped aloud. It was the boy from the park.

He was watching her. When their eyes met, he doffed his hat. For the first time, she saw the dark fall of his hair, the chestnut-brown strands gilded by the lamplight.

Unable to stop herself, she nudged Geli. "Do you know that boy? The one standing near the back with his arms crossed?"

Geli looked and then laughed, the sound drowned by another wave of applause as Hitler reached the platform. Her brown bobbed hair brushed Gretchen's cheek as she leaned closer to whisper. "Handsome fellow, isn't he? That's Daniel Cohen, my dear. The newest reporter at the Poison Kitchen. And a Jew."

*The Poison Kitchen.* Gretchen had heard of it, of course: the local Socialist newspaper called the *Munich Post*, one of a dwindling number of publications opposed to the Party. Uncle Dolf called the reporters a bunch of charlatans who cooked up vicious lies about him, and he had christened them with their nickname. In Uncle Dolf's opinion, calling someone a poisoner was the worst insult possible, for that meant he was a race defiler, a polluter of blood.

And a *Jew*. She had liked the boy's eyes; she had thought they were beautiful. And the sharp planes of his face, and his deep, quick voice.

A sudden commotion shattered her thoughts. At the back of the hall, a group of brownshirts had surrounded an elderly man. He looked as weathered and frail as a twig, but he was putting up a good fight, kicking and hitting at his assailants. The crowd laughed and jeered as the SA fellows struggled to restrain the old man. One of them lost his balance, staggering backward into a heavyset man in SA brown.

Even from the back, Gretchen recognized his wide, squat figure. Strong and muscular once, perhaps, but now rapidly melting into fat. It was SA-Stabschef Ernst Röhm, the head of the SA and Reinhard's superior.

Röhm pushed the boy away, shouting angrily. He whirled on Reinhard, who stood apart, expressionless. Jabbing his finger at Reinhard's face, he shouted something.

Then Reinhard stepped forward into the mass of flailing bodies, shoving his comrades aside until he reached the old man. The fellow shrank back, his hands coming up in surrender, but Reinhard ignored the conciliatory gesture. He whipped an arm around the old man's waist, hefting him as easily as a sack of grain, and carried him outside, the man screaming for help all the way.

She wouldn't have thought anything of it, for audience members were frequently dragged away by the brownshirts, but she caught sight of Cohen running toward the exit, too. He looked terrified.

After the speech ended, Uncle Dolf walked out as the music was still playing, his usual trick to avoid the mobs of followers. While the others stood about in little clumps, discussing Hitler's proposals about creating more jobs through road- and housing-construction projects, Gretchen said her good-nights to Geli and her chaperone and then hurried through the crowd into the warm, starlit evening.

Hitler's red Mercedes sat at the curb, its engine running. His chauffeur was opening the back door for him as she raced toward them, calling his name.

Uncle Dolf turned. He looked tired, his skin pale and paper-thin. Sweat had darkened the hair at his temples, turning the brown strands to black. "Ah, Gretl. Shouldn't you be home, helping your mama like a good girl?"

"Please, Uncle Dolf." Her chest felt tight from running so hard. "Something awful has happened. Mama says I can't return to school."

"Is that all?" He chuckled. "Why, I would imagine most girls your age would be eager to leave school behind and settle on a fine young man instead." He patted her cheek. "But I suppose you wish to continue in your schooling, my good little future doctor. Why does your mama propose leaving your studies?"

"Herr Hitler," the chauffeur said quietly, "the audience should be leaving any moment."

Hitler grunted. "Always, they want to hunt me down after a speech and haggle over every point." He waggled a finger. "Don't give anyone a chance to challenge your ideas!"

"Please, Uncle Dolf, I just need a moment." Desperation tightened her voice into something she barely recognized. "Mama says we can't afford it. She says I need to find a job, but there is so little work, and I want so much to be a doctor, and I'm certain there's something you can do—"

"Hanfstaengl," Uncle Dolf interrupted, "weren't you complaining the other day that your office isn't adequately staffed?"

For the first time, Gretchen noticed the tall man lounging against the lamppost a few feet away. Ernst Hanfstaengl was the NSDAP foreign-press chief, a bear of a man with an immense lantern jaw and wiry dark hair. "I've done more than complain about it, Herr Hitler; I've practically shouted it from the rooftops. And I've been shut up in a tiny office where nobody can ever find me—"

"Yes, yes, we really must improve your situation, Hanfstaengl," Hitler said hastily. "Fräulein Müller shall be your new assistant. She can help your secretary, whenever you get around to hiring one. She'll start the day after tomorrow, which should afford you enough time to find her a desk."

Gretchen wanted to object. Hadn't he understood when she said she didn't want a job but to continue her schooling? Still, she said nothing. No one refused a favor from Hitler.

Hanfstaengl shot a resigned glance at Gretchen. "I don't suppose you have any secretarial experience, do you?"

"Well, I help my mother at the boardinghouse—"

"In other words, no." He rolled his eyes.

"Hanfstaengl," Hitler snapped, "surely hiring the daughter of one of our fallen comrades isn't too much to ask?"

Hanfstaengl swallowed a sigh, his massive shoulders practically shaking from the effort. "Of course not."

"Her father made the ultimate sacrifice for the good of the Party." Hitler's voice grew louder. Behind them, Gretchen heard the clatter of footsteps; the crowds were leaving the Circus Krone. "If it had not been for Klaus Müller and his daring act, I would not be here. But Providence had other plans for me."

"Herr Hitler," the chauffeur said, "we really must be going!"

"Yes, yes." Uncle Dolf kissed Gretchen's hands. "Don't look so downhearted, my child; it is all arranged."

*But* hovered on her lips though she didn't dare say it.

Hitler and Hanfstaengl got into the Mercedes. As the car

drove away, she watched its taillights turn into ruby-red pinpricks.

He hadn't understood. That was all. Once she had a chance to explain the problem to him properly, he would talk to Mama. He would find a way for her to continue her schooling. Hadn't he arranged for Geli to begin medical studies at the university, and when she tired of them, found a music instructor so she could begin a singing career? Surely he could do the same for her.

The tramp of footsteps cut into her thoughts. Marching toward her was a group of young men, dressed identically in black shirts and red bow ties. Her legs locked her in place. *Communists.* Of the dozens of warring political parties that had sprung up in Munich after the Great War, this group was the only one she feared. Uncle Dolf called Communism a plague sweeping down from the Russian steppes and infecting so many European countries, an ideology formed solely to promote Jewish interests and destroy all non-Jewish nations.

And they were carrying truncheons.

"We heard an ugly rumor that there was a Nazi gathering tonight," one of them called. He looked her up and down. "I see the ugly part was wrong."

Frantically, she scanned the narrow street. Nobody else up ahead. Behind, audience members slowly meandered out of the Circus Krone, chattering with one another. They were a few yards away. Not close enough if the Communists decided she was worth attacking. She'd heard of girls involved in street fights between National Socialists and Communists; one girl had even died in Berlin last year. There was nowhere to run.

"You're mistaken." She willed her voice not to shake. "I'm

walking home, that's all."

"A likely story." One of the men nudged another. "Look at her necklace."

The *Hakenkreuz*! Her fingers closed over the charm. She'd forgotten she was wearing it. She might as well string a placard around her neck, proclaiming she was one of Hitler's favorites.

"You don't want to hurt a girl," she said.

"No," the same man said. "But I'm happy to take you as a hostage."

And he leapt at her.

# 7

FOR A HORRIBLE INSTANT, THE MAN WAS SUSPENDED in midair. Gretchen watched him coming toward her, his body lowering, lowering—

Then a dark blur knocked the man sideways. The two grappled on the pavement, swearing at each other. She heard the sickening sound of fists meeting flesh. The dark blur scrambled to his feet, glancing at her. It was Kurt. A cut under his eye dripped blood.

"Get out of here!" he shouted, and she turned and ran.

Behind her, she heard the Communists' feet thundering on the sidewalk. Ahead, she saw Reinhard and a group of SA fellows, standing in a bunch, laughing and talking, then turning, their faces slackening in surprise when they saw her.

"Communists!" she screamed. "Help!"

They rushed past her. She kept running, but someone

grabbed her arm, and she nearly snatched it back before she saw who it was.

SA chief Röhm. He had lost his cap, so she could see how his hair had been shaved so close to the scalp that his pale skin showed, a fresh-scrubbed pink like a pig's hide. His small eyes focused on hers. Pockmarks disfigured his broad face. From shrapnel, she'd heard, but she didn't know if the injuries had occurred during the Great War or while he had lived as a mercenary soldier in Bolivia during the twenties. The deep gouges had always unsettled her, ever since she'd seen him again in April, after Hitler summoned him back to Munich to take over the SA.

"Fräulein Müller, this is no place for you." His voice sounded as rough as pieces of sandpaper rubbing together. "Come."

His grip was tight on her wrist as he pulled her along. Stumbling, she broke into a light jog to match his pace. Ahead, the avenue stretched out like a gray ribbon before it fell into darkness, and behind, the men's cries and grunts started to fade.

"Don't look so frightened, Fräulein." Röhm stopped, his heavy chest rising and falling with labored breaths. He grinned, startling her. "Street fights are to be celebrated, not feared. That's one of the many things the Führer and I argue about. The trouble with you is the same trouble with most Germans: Our countrymen have forgotten how to hate." He ran a broad hand over his brown tunic, smoothing out the wrinkles. "Your brother understands."

She recalled Reinhard's blank eyes meeting hers across the kitchen table as he casually told their mother how much Gretchen must like Yids. She shuddered. Yes, he understood hatred. Sometimes she even wondered if he hated *her*. Or if he thought his tricks were a bizarre form of brotherly teasing—

The shrill blast of police whistles pierced the air. Röhm cursed. "I must get the men to scatter. I'll send Kurt to ferry you home."

"No! That's not necessary!" But she was speaking to his back; he was already jogging back to the melee. More men ran from the direction of the Circus Krone to join the fight. Thirty or forty men now spilled across the street, punching and shouting.

A few yards away, Reinhard smashed his fist into a man's face, watching emotionlessly as the man crumpled to the ground. Another man flung himself onto Reinhard's back, but the added weight barely moved her brother. With one quick motion, he reached back, seizing his attacker's arms before flipping him overhead and throwing him down to the pavement.

Gretchen couldn't look away. He made it look so *easy*, crushing men with a few well-aimed punches. As he stepped into the golden light of a streetlamp, she saw how calm and impassive his face looked; his eyes flicked back and forth, searching for a possible threat, and his jaw clenched, but no anger tightened his expression, no fear contorted his features. And yet . . . Gretchen scanned the other men. All of them looked furious or scared, sometimes both. Reinhard was the only one who appeared untouched.

More police whistles sounded. The men broke apart, racing into the shadows. As quickly as it had begun, the fight seemed over. Gretchen released the breath she hadn't realized she'd been holding. Shaking, she turned away.

"Gretchen!" Kurt called behind her.

So Röhm hadn't forgotten his promise to find her a chauffeur. The thought of getting back into Kurt's car was more than she could bear. She remembered the Daimler-Benz skidding across the cobblestones, its headlamps illuminating the Jew's face, frozen with shock, for one terrifying second before the car spun in the other direction. But there was no reason she could refuse a ride. She would have to go with him.

"A rough bunch tonight," Kurt said as he caught up to her. "A few more minutes and we would have had the best of them. We'd better get out of here before the police arrive."

They ran onto a side street. At this late hour, it was deserted, the lights in the office buildings extinguished. Halfway down the block, Kurt's auto sat at the curb. As he began to drive, Gretchen stared through the smeary windshield, listening to the tires rumble over the cobbles, wondering what she could possibly say to fill the silence. The old man! Cautiously, she watched Kurt from the corner of her eye. He leaned over the steering wheel, frowning, peering hard at the street.

"I *knew* I should have washed the windshield," he muttered.

Ahead, a few men weaved drunkenly along the sidewalk. Somewhere, a door opened and closed, letting out a quick blare of music.

"Kurt," Gretchen said, "who was that old man? The one you fellows removed from the Circus Krone tonight?"

"Hmm? Oh, just a half-dead Party crank." Kurt's frown deepened. The drunks had spotted them, and one of them had started to unbutton his trousers, leering at Gretchen. "Fools!" Kurt stuck his head out the open car window. "Nobody wants to see your pitiful excuse for manhood!" *Must he fight with everyone?* Gretchen bit back a sigh.

After a quick glance for traffic, Kurt jammed the accelerator, speeding the car through an intersection. "Boss's orders," he added. "Röhm said the man's to be dragged out of every meeting he attends."

The response seemed strange. Gretchen suppressed a shiver. What interest could Röhm have in an elderly, infirm Party comrade?

"What happened to him?" she asked.

"I don't know." Kurt patted his pocket, probably searching for cigarettes. "We taught the fellow a lesson and then he staggered off with some boy. Weeping like a child." He grinned and held up a pack. "Hurrah, cigarettes!"

"Why does SA-Stabschef Röhm care about the old man?"

Kurt slammed on the brake, so hard that she had to fling out her hands so she didn't fly into the gearbox. "Idiot drivers." He gestured at the Opel crawling in front of them. "The fellow's been hanging around Party headquarters and attending the Führer's speeches. Asking all sorts of questions about the putsch."

*The putsch.* Her heart beat faster. The event that had ended in the street shoot-out that had killed her father.

"Questions?" She hoped she sounded casual. "What did he want to know?"

Fumbling in his pocket for a lighter, Kurt steered one-handed along a quiet street. When the lighter flared into life, its tiny orange flame illuminated his face for an instant, revealing his fair eyebrows and jade-green eyes. "All manner of nonsense. The position of the men in the front line. Powder burns. Stupid old man's probably going senile."

She froze. A dull roaring filled her ears. *Your father did not die a martyr to the Nazi cause, and your family's precarious position within Hitler's party is predicated on a lie.* An old Party comrade, who had known her father during the early years of struggle, who might have marched alongside her father during the final minutes of his life . . . "Yes, nonsense," she managed to say. "He must be losing his mind."

When Gretchen finally got back to the boardinghouse, closing the door in Kurt's face as he leaned in for a kiss, which struck her as ludicrous, she hurried up the stairs, skipping the creaking steps. As she did every night, she locked the door, slid the chair under the knob, and untied the heavy curtains. Alone, at last.

She found Striped Peterl in her armoire, curled on the toes of her winter galoshes. She carried him over to the bed and stretched across the chenille coverlet, letting the cat lie on her chest, rumbling, as she petted him and thought.

The old man had asked about the men's positions in the front line. He must have meant the march on the Residenzstrasse. Eight years ago, after failing to take over the city in the putsch, the National Socialists had paraded through Munich, right into a waiting cadre of police officers. Her father had walked with Uncle Dolf in the front. When the shooting started, Papa had jumped in front of Hitler, his body jolting as bullets bit into his chest. Taking the shots intended for his leader.

The familiar band tightened around her chest, cutting off her breathing. *Calm, calm.* She closed her eyes and focused on the flow of oxygen in and out of her lungs. Three deep breaths, the old trick Hitler had taught her. Feeling the air flow into her nostrils, her chest filling.

The method worked, as it always did. She opened her eyes. The men in the front line—a famous Great War general, a former flying ace, an army colonel, a prominent National Socialist from Russia, the Munich SA leader, Hitler's personal bodyguard, Hitler himself, and her father, Hitler's old friend from the war.

*Papa shot* . . . Memories swamped her—the tickle of his mustache on her cheek when he kissed her, and the warm roughness of his hands as they patted her face.

They had been sitting on the kitchen floor, which was the only room they could afford to heat during the miserably cold November of 1923. Her father wore his Great War uniform and an armband decorated with a swastika, and they huddled beside the stove as he placed a kitten in her hands.

"It's for you," Papa said. "I've already named it Striped Peterl."

"Papa, I love it!" She stroked its soft fur. "But what if it runs away, too? Like Little Franzl?"

A strange expression twisted her father's face; for an instant, he looked afraid. But that was ridiculous; her big, strong father was afraid of nothing, and certainly not of the family cat that had disappeared a month earlier.

"You must be very careful with it," he finally said. "Don't let anyone else play with it. The cat is just for you, do you understand?"

"Yes, Papa. Thank you." When she kissed him, she felt a sudden wetness on her cheeks and knew it came from his tears, and she cried, too, because Papa had promised by tomorrow night the National Socialist flags would fly from City Hall. But what he had to do first would be very dangerous.

And now, eight years later, in another house, in another part of the city, in another stage of her life, she felt like that nine-year-old child again, alone and mourning the father who would never return.

She kept his uniform on the armoire's top shelf. When Mama had come home from the city morgue with Papa's things, she had wanted to burn it, and toss out the battered shoes, the blood-stained woolen long johns. But Gretchen had begged to keep the shirt, the ruined cloth she had embraced over and over, sobbing because it hadn't protected Papa at all, needing it because it had been the last garment to touch his skin.

The shirt had been folded into a small square, and she shook it out, running her fingers over the bullet holes. So many holes, she couldn't count them all, although she had tried. Gunpowder and dried blood, faint gray and rusty red, everywhere. Tears burned her eyes, and she started to fold it, freezing when she saw the tear in its back.

Her breath caught. A hole, on the back of the shirt, where her father's shoulder blades would have been. A bullet hole. Gray powder had been ground into the cloth around the hole's edges. Confused, she ran her fingers over the ragged circle, stiff with dried blood, discolored from a gun blast. Powder burns, the old man had said.

She knew the shape bullets made when they tore into something, and the grayish powder they sprayed if you fired at a close target. Uncle Dolf had taught her long ago, when she was a small child. He was one of the best marksmen in the city and believed everyone ought to know how to handle a weapon.

On Sunday afternoons, after he stopped by for tea, he and

Papa would take her and Reinhard to the Englischer Garten, to a copse of beeches far from the paths, so no one would see them practice shooting at the trees. At first, the recoil shoved her back a few steps, into Uncle Dolf's legs. He laughed and showed her how to dig her heels into the dirt, so she could brace herself.

She stared at Papa's shirt. If the hole had been formed by a bullet's exit, there wouldn't have been powder burns. Only blood. But she could *see* it, a messy circle of grayish dust and dried blood.

Someone had shot her father in the back. State police troopers had stood in front of him. Only other National Socialists had been behind him.

*The Jew was right.*

# 8

THE NEXT NIGHT, GRETCHEN WALKED INTO THE Golden Phoenix dance hall and stopped short to stare. Blue-and-gold designs papered the walls, turning the enormous space into a glittering Easter egg. A glorious sound, pulsing with sinuous energy, cascaded from the orchestra stand. Small tables had been arranged along the room's edges, where couples in evening dress lounged over drinks.

The dance floor dominated the room's center; it was a massive wooden rectangle where men in tuxedos and women in short satin frocks danced a peculiar routine Gretchen had seen in films. The Charleston, she thought it was called, a popular dance from America. She couldn't help feeling a burst of excitement. How beautiful and glamorous everything seemed.

"That music," said a voice behind her, "is American swing."

She turned. Daniel Cohen leaned against the bar. Tonight

he wore a black suit. At some point, his bow tie had come undone and the shirt's top button had popped open, exposing his collarbones. She could see the pulse beating in his throat, a rapid tattoo beneath the skin, and the sight relieved her. He was nervous, too.

"Swing music is degenerate." She forced the words out.

He studied her with watchful eyes. "Do you like it?"

Yes. But she wasn't supposed to. "I've never heard anything like it before," she evaded.

Cohen spoke a few words to the bartender. Gretchen leaned against the counter, trying to appear as though she knew how to act. This was madness. She glanced toward the exit. Maybe she should leave. But then she wouldn't know what had happened to Papa.

She didn't move.

Cohen pressed a glass into her hand. "You National Socialists clean up well."

She flushed and resisted the urge to look down. Geli had given her the dress last summer, after she'd tired of it. The short black cocktail dress glittered with thousands of sequins. Gretchen had untied her usual braid and let her long hair ripple halfway down her back. A beaded band with a dyed-black ostrich feather encircled her head. The dress was a perfect fit for Geli's curves, but on Gretchen's smaller frame the bodice dipped lower than she liked, and she kept yanking the neckline up.

"Thank you." She tried to hand the glass back, but he didn't take it. "I can't accept a gift from you—"

His mouth twisted. "From a Jew, you mean? You certainly do march to your Hitler's drum, don't you?" He grabbed the glass, setting it down so hard on the bar that liquid sloshed over the edge. "Will sitting with me offend your delicate sensibilities or must we stay standing?"

She had angered him. She wasn't sure what surprised her more—that she was sorry for it, or that he was bothered by her. Somehow he had struck her as the sort who would never permit someone else to make him feel uncomfortable.

"I'm sorry," she said, but he waved her off.

"Forget it. Let's sit down."

They found a tiny table against a wall. Gretchen watched the men and women at the bar, laughing too hard over their drinks, and the dancers, moving too fast, as though trying to forget their troubles for one night.

"Why do you keep looking about?" Cohen asked. "You needn't worry about being caught with me. I doubt any of your NSDAP friends would come into a place like this."

"No, it's just I've never been to a nightclub before."

Surprise widened his eyes. "How is it I've lived in this city for only a month and I suspect I've seen more of it than you have?"

"I'm not allowed." She spoke defiantly, to hide her embarrassment. How babyish she must appear, a child who wasn't permitted to go out to nightclubs or listen to popular music.

"Then how did you get here tonight, if it's forbidden?"

She shifted uncomfortably. "I snuck out."

He laughed. The unexpected mirth transformed his face, softening its strong angles. She caught her breath and had to look away.

"Really?" Cohen said. "Maybe there's hope for you yet. There's a city hidden beneath the one your National Socialists want you to see—music and culture and art and dancing, all the things they're trying to blind you to."

His approving tone shamed her. She couldn't imagine Uncle Dolf's reaction if he found out.

"I don't need your advice," she said. "I snuck out so I could speak with you again. I need you to explain this story you seem to think you've uncovered about my father."

She spoke softly, so he couldn't hear how badly her voice shook. *Never show your enemies how much you care*, Papa had taught, *because then they have power over you.*

All traces of merriment fled from the reporter's features. He leaned across the table, the dim lamplight touching his cheeks. "You set those brownshirt thugs on Dearstyne, didn't you?" His gaze clapped onto hers. "You were afraid he could damage your family's precious favored position in the Party. No one else could have done it. I've kept him a secret from everyone except my editor."

She didn't know why the anger in his voice surprised her; Uncle Dolf had warned her that Jews were vipers in the grass, ready to turn and strike at any second. "I didn't tell anyone. And who's Dearstyne? The old man from the Circus Krone last night?"

"Yes, Stefan Dearstyne." He sounded bitter. "Your brother and his mates beat him and kicked him when he was on his hands and knees, looking for his knocked-out teeth." An image of Reinhard, bending over the defenseless elderly man, his arm raised in mid-strike, flashed before her. She felt sick. "We're not here to talk about them, but my father—"

Cohen surged to his feet. "I can't listen to your evasions. Not even for the best scoop of my career. Good-bye, Fräulein Müller."

"Wait!"

She hurried after him. Her arm flashed out, her fingers closing around his wrist. He stopped and looked down at her hand, as if the sight disgusted him. "Are you sure you want to do that?" he asked. "Touch a Jew? Isn't that against the rules?"

"I don't care about the rules right now!" She pitched her voice low, but the people at the surrounding tables turned to look at them. "People are staring at us."

He pulled away without replying, moving quickly across the dance floor. She mustn't let him leave, not until she knew Herr Dearstyne's story. She darted in front of him and seized his hands. Revulsion roiled her stomach. But she *must* know the truth about Papa.

"Please," she whispered.

Herr Cohen stared down at her, his eyes hard, his expression unreadable. "I can't figure you out," he said, so quietly he might have been speaking to himself. "Every time I think I understand who you are, you seem to change."

What he thought of her didn't matter. Nothing mattered except for the small, circular hole in the back of Papa's Great War tunic.

"Please," she said again. "I swear to you, I haven't told a soul about your letter. I only told my dearest friend that I was coming here tonight, nothing about you. One of the SA boys said they'd received orders from SA-Stabschef Röhm to throw the old man out on sight, but that's all he knew."

His expression didn't soften, but he pulled her into his arms. When she started to jerk away, he said, sounding annoyed, "We'd better dance, if we want people to stop staring at us."

Uncertainty froze her in place. But she sensed the others' curious gazes. Reluctantly, she placed her hands on Cohen's shoulders. Beneath her fingers, his tightly corded muscles flexed. Tense and hard, as though he were barely holding himself together. His hand fit into the curve of her waist; his fingers felt warm through her dress's thin fabric. The orchestra slid into a slow number, and they began to waltz.

Their eyes were only inches apart. As their bodies moved together, repeating the same box step, she watched his pupils, waiting for them to enlarge and swallow the brown-and-gold irises, to turn into black pools as Uncle Dolf had promised.

But nothing happened. And the sour stink of sweat and decay she had expected, she didn't smell. Only a light scent of soap and cologne. The fingers holding hers felt smooth and soft, not rough with tangled hair.

Could she have been wrong about him?

He twirled her around. She spun across the dance floor, the other couples blurring into a whirl of blacks and reds and greens and blues. He drew her close to him again. His hand, at the small of her back, gripped her too hard. As though he hated having to touch her.

"We can be useful to each other," he said, his breath a warm flutter on her neck. "I tell you what I know, and you use your connections to get me the information I want."

Nerves prickled the back of her neck. She could easily imagine Uncle Dolf's disappointment if he learned she had worked with a Jew. Then she thought of the bullet hole in her father's shirt, and everything else fell away. "Explain to me why Herr

Dearstyne is so curious about my father's death."

"Dearstyne started wondering about the street shoot-out after he read his late brother's diary," Cohen said, his hand relaxing on her waist as they swayed back and forth. "And before I tell you anything else, I think you need to share something, too. What convinced you to search me out here tonight?"

"I remembered something. About the clothes my father was wearing when he died." She took a deep breath, like a swimmer bracing herself before diving into icy water. "There were powder burns on the back of his shirt."

Cohen's eyes widened. "Then I was right! I knew it! I—" He broke off with a curse. "What's your brother doing here?"

She twisted in his arms. Standing near the nightclub's entrance, washed by the golden chandelier lights, stood two familiar figures. Reinhard and Eva. And it was obvious from the way their heads turned, surveying the milling crowd, that they were looking for someone. It had to be her.

Hastily, she pulled away from Cohen. "Get out of here! Go, go!"

"Why, Fräulein Müller," he said, sounding sarcastic, "I might almost believe you care about me."

"Just go! My brother probably outweighs you by fifty pounds. He could crush you in an instant."

Cohen laughed. "Fräulein Müller, don't you know it's rude to insult a man's ability to fight?"

The unexpected flash of humor startled her.

She watched as he cast a speculative look toward the entrance. How could he be so reckless with his own safety? Or did he think other things mattered more than his well-being?

She couldn't figure him out.

"Please, Herr Cohen." She touched his shoulder, nudging him forward. "I don't want anyone to get hurt. We can meet some other time."

His head snapped back so he could stare at her. "You wish to see me again?"

"Yes. I—" The words stuck in her throat. "I need your help. And you said you need mine. We can work together."

He nodded, his expression wary, as though he wasn't sure if he believed her. "A Jew and a National Socialist, joining forces. I never thought I'd see it. Very well. I accept your proposal. I shall contact you soon. Watch for my message."

"Yes, but *go*!"

To her relief, he turned away. He had barely taken two steps into the whirling mass of dancing bodies when Reinhard reached her.

"Who was that?" he demanded.

"Nobody." She twined her fingers together so her brother wouldn't notice that they were shaking. "Nobody," she repeated, and Reinhard watched her with his blank eyes, a muscle twitching in his jaw, before turning and heading toward the bar for a drink.

# 9

"HOW COULD YOU BETRAY ME?" GRETCHEN SAID to Eva as they walked into the powder room. Her friend wore a short beaded dress with a dropped waist, and she'd curled her hair into tiny ringlets. She looked like the American flappers in the film magazines she loved to read.

*"What?"* Eva sounded scandalized. "Gretchen, I would never—"

"Wait." Gretchen glanced under the wooden stalls—no feet—and peered into the adjacent lounge, where a couple of fraying upholstered chairs sat—empty. The mirror reflected the room back to them, a mix of wood and gilt that should have looked rich but seemed tired in the harsh lighting. The patterned paper had begun to strip from the wall; the sink basins were chipped, the wooden stalls splintered. It looked like everything else in Munich, beautiful once but slowly decaying. Only Hitler could reverse this gradual rot, he had promised so many times.

"You told Reinhard where I would be tonight," she said. "I didn't mention it to anyone but you."

"He rang me up, looking for you. I didn't realize it was a secret—"

"I should have thought it was obvious! You knew I was sneaking out to come here—"

"Yes, but this was your *brother* telephoning me! I would hardly expect you to hide things from him."

Gretchen rested her head against the mirror. The glass felt smooth and cool. Eva didn't understand. She never would, for how could she possibly comprehend the fear that welled within Gretchen whenever her brother came near? The way Reinhard treated her was her most shameful secret.

"I'm sorry," she said at last. "I shouldn't have shouted at you."

"That's all right." Eva touched Gretchen's shoulder. "You never told me why you wanted to come here. Is it a boy?"

"Yes. In a way." Although she yearned to tell Eva everything, she said nothing more, fearing that someone might come in and overhear. Or that Reinhard, waiting in the dance hall, would grow impatient and demand to know why they had taken so long.

Eva leaned close to the mirror, smoothing the rouge on her cheeks with her fingertips. "I suppose we girls must have our secrets." Her high giggle sounded unnatural, and Gretchen frowned, thinking how different Eva sometimes seemed since coming home from the convent school two years ago—concealing her face beneath layers of cosmetics and wanting to bleach her hair, as though she yearned to turn into someone else. Eva added, "What a darling frock. Wherever did you get it?"

The black dress sparkled back at Gretchen in the glass. "From Geli Raubal. You know how she likes to hand off clothes she's grown tired of."

"Oh," Eva said flatly. "Her."

Gretchen watched Eva redden her lips. She had never understood why Eva disliked Geli. The two girls hadn't even met—Geli revolved within Hitler's elite inner circle, while Eva was merely a tiny fixture on the outer rings of the Party, since she knew Hitler only through casual conversations at the photography shop. Once, Gretchen had suggested introducing the girls, but Eva had refused, muttering that they were probably too different to get along.

When Eva was done, they went down the curving corridor toward the dance hall. With each step, the music swelled louder and louder, and Gretchen had to bring her lips to Eva's ear to be heard.

"Just out of curiosity . . . How did Reinhard act when you said that I'd come here?"

"Oh, you know Reinhard." Eva giggled. "He said we ought to meet you and have some fun ourselves. He wasn't angry," she reassured Gretchen. "He never is."

That was almost true. Which was strange, Gretchen knew after observing the three Braun sisters together. Siblings were *supposed* to grate on one another's nerves. The continual rubbing together of their lives, the daily irritations of sharing homes and parents, should have ensured that she and Reinhard sometimes squabbled. But they never fought.

She followed Eva into the dance hall, the music washing over them like the sea. And as she watched Eva, grinning as she swept by in Reinhard's arms, she could almost pretend she was happy.

⁂

The boardinghouse's front door was locked at half past nine every night. Residents were given a key and told not to switch on the lights if they got home late, to save on the electric bill. But not Gretchen or Reinhard, and Gretchen suspected that this was their mother's way of ensuring they stayed in their rooms all night.

The tactic certainly hadn't stopped Reinhard. For years, Gretchen had heard him scaling the neighbor's back wall and jumping into the courtyard, sometimes with a muffled curse if he landed on a broken bit of flagstone. Although Mama fastened the back door, the mechanism was old and unreliable, and some patient twisting was enough to jiggle the lock out of place. Or so Reinhard had boasted. Gretchen had never tried it.

She stood now in the neighbor's back garden, studying the stone wall. Not terribly high. She tossed her pocketbook and high-heeled shoes over, listening as they landed with soft thumps. She leapt as hard as she could. Her fingers grasped the ledge and she pulled herself up.

Below, the courtyard was a narrow black rectangle in the darkness. The flagstones looked farther away than she had anticipated. But she couldn't lower herself down; the walnut trees clustered against the wall, impeding any attempt to get down that way. She would have to jump.

She flung herself into open air. Something shifted in the darkness below her. A man's head, turning to look at her, the whites of his eyes shining—

She swallowed a scream. When she landed, air rushed out of her lungs. Gasping, she scrabbled upright as the shape separated from the shadows and came toward her. Its fuzzy lines sharpened, becoming the hulking figure she knew so well. Reinhard.

He was laughing. "You should have seen your face!"

Her hands clenched, ready to shove at him. But she didn't. There was no beating Reinhard at his games; she had learned that rule long ago. So she picked up her shoes and pocketbook and walked to the back steps, Reinhard loping along beside her.

"Where've you been?" he asked. "It took you longer to get home than I expected."

His words sent a shiver along her spine. "You're spying on me," she gasped.

Reinhard laughed in his easy, careless way. "This city can be a rough place at night. What sort of brother would I be, if I wasn't watching out for my little sister?"

It was true Munich could be dangerous, as street fights often erupted between political parties. But Reinhard had never expressed concern for her safety before. Which meant he suspected something. That was why he had smiled and refused, when Gretchen and Eva asked if he wanted to take a streetcar back with them. Somehow, he had gotten here first. So he could wait for her. To time how long it took her to return, to determine if she had gone elsewhere first. To see if she returned alone.

Shaking, Gretchen fiddled with the doorknob. If Reinhard guessed she had met with a Jew tonight . . . She could not imagine what he would do to her.

The door creaked open. Reinhard ushered her in with a flourish. "After you, Sister."

She hated having to walk in front of him. She darted inside, pressing her back against the wall as he lumbered into the unlit kitchen.

Her brother's footsteps thudded as he crossed the room, and then he knelt to open the icebox. He made a face. "There's never anything decent to eat." He reached for an apple from the fruit bowl and polished it on his shirt. "I heard you're starting at the Braunes Haus tomorrow."

Gretchen nodded. The Braunes Haus, or Brown House, was the new National Socialist Party headquarters, and where Hanfstaengl maintained his office. "I'll be helping in the foreign-press department."

As Reinhard chewed, she saw the large muscles in his neck moving, forcing the bits of apple down. For some reason, the sight made her sick.

"Good." His teeth shone white as he grinned. "Working is better for girls than studying anyway. Besides, you wouldn't want to show me up by getting more schooling than me, would you?"

Comprehension blazed through Gretchen's brain as Reinhard went into the hall. Standing stock-still, Gretchen listened to his feet on the stairs, the wood groaning beneath his weight. In her mind, she traced his route in the twisting stairwell, then down the second floor's corridor to his bedroom, beside their mother's.

She hoped she was wrong.

Mama kept her account ledger locked in a kitchen cupboard. The key was hidden in an empty sugar tin in the pantry. It took Gretchen less than a minute to skim the last three pages and realize her mother had lied to her. Next to each Müller family account were the words *paid in full* in her mother's tidy handwriting.

They could easily afford to continue her schooling. Every single one of their bills was paid, and there was an excess of nearly two hundred marks, which her mother had noted "for emergencies" in her round script. They could have paid the 2.70 marks for her school field trips, too, but Mama had always said the amount was too high, and Gretchen had to stay home instead, feigning illness on those days.

They could afford to send her to university.

The truth was obvious: Reinhard hadn't wanted her to graduate. He hadn't wanted her to become a doctor. He hadn't wanted her to rise above him. He had never finished vocational school, and his job in a butcher's shop was menial and backbreaking. He spent his days hacking apart meat and came home with his work overalls splattered with guts and blood.

Gretchen shoved the ledger back into the cupboard. Mama had lied to her. Because maintaining an uneasy peace with Reinhard was more important than Gretchen's happiness and future success. Because Reinhard had always mattered more.

She wanted to yank open her mother's bedroom door and demand an explanation. She wanted Mama to sob and apologize, arms outstretched for forgiveness.

But it was no use. They wouldn't speak about it, not tonight or in the morning. The decision had been made. Reinhard had gotten his way, as he always did; they were forced to circle around him like dying planets, and he, the sun whose magnetic pull directed their rotation, was the glowing orb that might blaze into uncontrollable brightness at any instant.

Moving like a sleepwalker, Gretchen headed for the stairs, stopping when she saw a dark shape looming on the landing. The outline was unfamiliar: a bowler hat, slim shoulders, small build. The shape shifted and moonlight from the window slid across it, and she recognized the man she had nearly knocked down in the front hall last night. He must be the new boarder her mother had mentioned while they were washing up after breakfast. An Englishman, Mama had added, and she didn't know what he was doing in Germany, but as he had paid two months' lodging in advance, she didn't care either.

He made an awkward bow. "I beg your pardon, Fräulein," he said in slow, careful German. "It was not my intention to eavesdrop on the conversation, but I couldn't help hearing your voices as I climbed the stairs."

*My God, what now?* "That's all right, Herr . . ."

"Please, permit me to give you my card." He handed her a square of pasteboard. Although it was in English, she could read enough of it to know he was Alfred Whitestone and the address was somewhere in Oxford. "My name," he went on in the same halting, stilted German, "is Whitestone. I am a doctor, but perhaps not of the sort you are accustomed to."

"I'm pleased to meet you, Herr Doktor Whitestone." Habit forced her to smile politely. "I hope your stay will be pleasant."

"'Pleasant' is immaterial to me," he said. Behind his spectacles, his eyes were sharp. "What I aim for is an informative visit."

She was tired of playing verbal games with everyone she spoke to tonight. "I'm sure it will be. Now, if you'll excuse me, Herr Doktor Whitestone, I must go to bed."

She climbed the stairs to her room. Once she had locked the door and wedged the chair beneath the handle, she stood for a moment, listening. But it was several long minutes before she heard him move again and walk upstairs and into the room beside hers.

# 10

THE BRAUNES HAUS WASN'T A BROWN HOUSE AT all, but a former palace of pale stone. Huge swastika flags dripped down the front of the large building. Gretchen heard the bloodred rectangles snapping in the summer breeze as she locked her father's decrepit bicycle to an iron railing.

Two black-uniformed SS men guarded the enormous bronze front doors, and they stepped back to let her enter the massive lobby, whose walls were carved with thousands of swastikas. Inside, uniformed men moved quickly, intent on their destinations. A couple of the younger ones eyed her curiously, and she realized what an odd picture she must make—she was the only female in the lobby, and the only person not wearing a uniform.

Although it had been months since she had last visited the Braunes Haus, she remembered the plaque's location. Even as she told herself not to look for it because she couldn't afford tears on her first day, her feet turned toward the wall.

The plaque listed the names of the sixteen National Socialists who had died during the failed putsch. Her father's was etched there, and she resisted the almost overwhelming urge to run her fingers over the smooth grooves forming the letters KLAUS MÜLLER.

She glanced over the other names: Max Scheubner-Richter, Lars Dearstyne . . . *Dearstyne.* The same surname as the old man, Stefan, who had been dragged from the Circus Krone. Cohen had said that Stefan had been troubled after reading his late brother's diary. This must be his brother, who had perished during the putsch. What upsetting discovery had Stefan made? And what did it have to do with her father?

She felt the curious stares of the adjutants passing through the lobby. As if from far off, she heard air rasping in her throat. Quickly, she wiped her face clean of emotion. She couldn't think about this here.

The grand staircase loomed at the lobby's far end. As she climbed the steps, she passed more adjutants, some in SA brown, some in SS black and brown. She didn't recognize any of the men belonging to the new, racially elite Schutzstaffel unit.

The SA men grinned at her, a few saying "*Heil Hitler*," but the SS members only nodded at her sharply without breaking stride. The SS men moved quickly, not a movement wasted. All of them dressed identically in brown shirts and black trousers. Lightning zigzags in silver thread shone on their collars. None wore a weapon, which seemed so strange. She didn't know a single SA man who didn't carry a knife or a pistol.

From below, she heard the name "Müller," and she turned, thinking someone was calling to her. Two SA fellows climbed the stairs, talking quietly to each other—Kurt and an older man with graying hair whom she had never seen before. When they saw her standing on the landing, they nudged each other and fell silent, doffing their caps as they passed, and continued along the second-floor corridor.

They had been talking about her. She sensed it, from the way their gazes had skittered away from her.

As she watched, they slipped into one of the offices lining the hallway, leaving the door ajar. She glanced at her wristwatch. Ten minutes to nine. She was still early. And the hallway was empty.

She darted down the corridor. She vaguely remembered the rooms' positions: Hitler and his personal secretary Rudolf Hess's offices were housed on this floor, and the Senators' Chamber was the room Kurt and his companion had entered.

Its heavy door was open an inch. Scarcely daring to breathe, she placed her eye against the door's crack.

Kurt and the older man stood beside a shining wooden table surrounded by dozens of red leather chairs. She remembered Uncle Dolf talking proudly about those chairs, purchased to commemorate the Party's recent election of additional members to the Reichstag. Marble and mosaic decorated the walls. Deep-pile rugs woven with swastika symbols covered the floor. The older man was pacing, his footsteps whispering against the carpet. "What's this about?" he demanded. "I haven't much time, Herr Jaeger."

"It's Reinhard Müller," Kurt said. While the first fellow's voice had sounded strained and weak, Kurt's was young and polished, a stone rubbed smooth by a river. "He has been approached and has accepted."

"Müller? The son of that dead shoemaker?"

Gretchen couldn't stop a little sound of distress. The SA men stopped speaking. She didn't dare move away.

But nothing happened. Cautiously, she peered through the sliver of open door.

Apparently satisfied the noise had been nothing, the SA fellows had picked up their conversation.

"The very same," Kurt said. "But he's a different sort from his father. Reinhard has ice instead of blood. We shan't have any problems with him."

"Good. I'm depending on your judgment, Jaeger." The man barked out a sudden laugh. "The sainted, dead Müller. He was the sorriest excuse for a fighter I ever saw."

Gretchen stared at the carpet. She felt the roughness of Papa's beard against her face when he kissed her, the warmth of his arms holding her until the last icy grip of a nightmare melted away. He had been more than all the labels he had garnered in death: the martyr, the sainted Müller, the heroic shoemaker. He had been a husband, a father, a soldier who came back from the war with tremors in his hands and an occasional blankness in his eyes, as though the battles had scooped out something inside him.

The swastikas woven into the rug blurred together, and she had to blink several times before they came into focus again. He had been someone she was only beginning to get to know when he died.

"Then it's agreed," Kurt said. "Reinhard Müller can receive his first assignment."

The inevitable *Heil*s and clicking of heels followed. They were turning to leave. Gretchen stepped back, horrified when her shoe sounded on the floor. She couldn't get away. They would hear her.

A group of SS men poured into the corridor from the grand staircase, their boots tramping loudly. *Thank God.* She hurried toward them, pasting on a smile, waving without stopping. They tipped their caps, greeting her in their quiet, respectful manner as she took to the staircase, heading for the third floor and trying not to break into a run.

Below, she heard the rumble of their voices, but she couldn't separate out the smooth strand of Kurt's. Maybe he hadn't left the Senators' Chamber yet. It didn't matter. She was gone, and she doubted any of the SS men would mention her appearance in the hall.

As she climbed the steps, she ran a hand over her blouse, smoothing out the wrinkles and hoping she looked presentable on her first day. What sort of assignment had Kurt and his companion meant? Reinhard was an SA street tough, the sort that Uncle Dolf depended on to provide protection during speeches and muscle during fights. Hardly the type to get asked to do anything important for the Party.

And insulting her father . . . She had reached the third floor. The corridor was deserted, so she closed her eyes and counted—another of Uncle Dolf's old calming tricks. They hadn't known Papa. They could be forgiven for their ugly comments. Steadier, she continued along the corridor.

She rapped on Herr Hanfstaengl's door. A brusque "Come in!" summoned her into the tiny office.

Hanfstaengl was hanging up a telephone receiver, his massive frame contorted to fit behind the small desk. He looked like an adult forced to use child-size furniture. Impatience jutted out his jaw in an expression she recognized after seeing it so many times over the years. "You're a clever girl, Gretchen, and I shan't waste your time." He started to pace. "I have nothing for you to do. There's no end of work in this confounded office, but Herr Hitler won't let me get anything accomplished!"

He aimed a swift kick at the wastebasket. Unsure whether to laugh or back away, Gretchen decided the wisest thing to do was nothing.

"He sticks me in this small office on the third floor so foreign correspondents must wander about this whole place, searching for me and stumbling across God-knows-what information we're trying to suppress in the meantime." Hanfstaengl threw up his ham-size hands. "It's all I can do to convince him to be interviewed for a foreign paper, and most of the time he doesn't show up for the reporter, and I have to search the whole city until I find him looking at used cars or holding court at Café Heck.

"Don't look so alarmed, child," he continued, curling into his desk chair. "Sit down, and we shall find something you can do."

"If this is an inconvenience, Herr Hanfstaengl, I can find a position elsewhere."

"Of course it's an inconvenience, and no, you certainly can't find a job elsewhere. Why, *I* can't get a full-time position in my own family's art-reproduction business; that's the sort of desperate straits Germany is in. We all must go begging these days." He smiled, although there was anger in it. "How's your mother?" he asked so abruptly it took her a second to answer.

"She's well, Herr Hanfstaengl. She thanks you very much for the job."

"Liesel's a fine woman. I must tell my wife to call on her soon. They got on famously in the old days."

*The old days . . .* Those three words were enough to pull up the past for Gretchen. Once again she was a little girl, sitting on the parlor floor of their shabby apartment in the Schwabing district while her mother and Hanfstaengl's elegant American wife sipped tea and chatted about poetry and art, and Reinhard played toy soldiers with the Hanfstaengls' toddler, Egon. Snow swirled past the window, and somewhere, out in the white-blanketed city, her father and Herr Hanfstaengl sat in a beer hall, stamping their feet to keep warm and cheering as Uncle Dolf took the podium.

A lump lodged in her throat. "It all seems so long ago."

"Yes." He spoke softly, and she guessed he was remembering his little daughter Hertha, dead two years now. She thought of her father's grave, the tiny stone square that said so little: KLAUS MÜLLER 17 SEPTEMBER 1892—9 NOVEMBER 1923. It said nothing about the fact that he had been a husband, a father, a gifted shoemaker, a soldier.

"Herr Hanfstaengl," she said, "what do you know about my father's death? I mean," she added when his eyebrows drew down in surprise, "I know he was a hero, but no one has ever told me very much about what happened. And now that I'm older, I'd like to know."

"It isn't a pleasant story," he said. Concern lined his long face. "And I don't know all the details."

She thought of what her history teacher always used to say—history depends upon one's perspective. Perhaps if she gathered others' recollections of her father's death, she could piece together what had happened during those frantic sixteen hours, beginning when her father entered the beer hall with Uncle Dolf and ending with his death in the street.

"Please," she said. "Tell me what you do know."

"Very well." He leaned back in the chair. "It isn't as though we have very much work to do anyway," he added sarcastically, and he began.

# 11

"IN THE EARLY YEARS AFTER GERMANY LOST THE Great War, Munich teemed with plots and attempted takeovers," Hanfstaengl said. "Everyone was desperate."

Gretchen nodded. She remembered waking with ice crystals sparkling on the walls, because they couldn't afford to buy coal. Falling asleep on her makeshift bed, the divan in the parlor she shared with Reinhard, her stomach cramping from hunger. Papa kicking a chair across the room, sobbing, because he had missed a streetcar, and had arrived at the bank fifteen minutes later than he had expected, to exchange his pay from the shoe shop for foreign currency or gold marks, as everyone else tried to do. Fifteen minutes, and the value of his paper money had fallen by a quarter. The postwar inflation was quickly strangling and starving them all.

"So," Hanfstaengl said, "it wasn't unexpected when Hitler

decided it was time for the National Socialist Party to seize power by force. We knew that most of the city's top leaders and citizens would be attending a meeting at the Bürgerbräukeller."

Gretchen knew this part of the story well. The plan was simple: A contingent of SA men would storm the beer hall and take the city's leaders hostage. Hitler would convince the hostages to hand over power to the National Socialists, and by the next day, control would have smoothly shifted into the hands of the NSDAP.

"I saw your father when he arrived at the beer hall, at around eight o'clock," Hanfstaengl said. "Police had roped off the area—somehow they'd gotten wind that something important was going to happen that night—and I was standing outside, arguing that the journalists and I ought to be allowed inside. Then Hitler's automobile pulled up. He came out, followed by Graf, Rosenberg, Amann, and your father."

Gretchen leaned forward on her chair, concentrating. *Graf* . . . that would be Uncle Dolf's bodyguard, who would be gravely shot the following morning during the shoot-out. *Rosenberg* . . . clearly Alfred Rosenberg, as such a Jewish-sounding name was peculiar in a high-ranking NSDAP man. The name Amann sounded familiar, though she couldn't place it. Shaking the thought off, she focused on Hanfstaengl's story. Plenty of time for questions later.

"Your father looked upset," Hanfstaengl went on, leaning back and lacing his fingers across his chest. "Nerves, I assumed, for we were all on edge. Hitler had warned us we would be either victorious or dead by dawn.

"Fortunately, Hitler told the police guard to let me in, and I hustled my journalist colleagues inside as well. Even that ridiculous fellow Gerlich, the one who's become such a pebble in our shoe. He was fairly bubbling over with excitement, saying he was about to witness history."

*History* . . . Gretchen nodded hard. How wrong they had been. The putsch hadn't been a triumphant revolution, but an amateurish farce. Sixteen hours of fumbling that had ended with sixteen National Socialists and four policemen dead in the street.

"Most of Munich's elite were squeezed into the Bürgerbräukeller's main room," Hanfstaengl went on. "I was nodding off in boredom to a speech when the SA brownshirts burst in, brandishing their pistols and machine guns. The whole place became a madhouse."

The next part of the story was embroidered on Gretchen's brain, for she had heard it so many times. By the next morning, the attempted revolution was unraveling like a ripped tapestry. The police had formed an immense cordon around the beer hall, and the Reichswehr, the National Defense soldiers, had been called out to assist the state police troopers. The putschists knew most of them had only hours, maybe minutes, of freedom left before they were arrested.

"The Reichswehr soldiers flooded the streets like cockroaches fleeing a fire." Hanfstaengl still sounded bitter. "I ran to my apartment to pack. I hoped I could escape over the border into Austria. Then my sister rang me to say the men were on the march."

This was the hardest part for Gretchen to hear. She curled her hands, fingernails cutting into her palms. Papa was walking to his death. The brownshirts had decided to save Ernst Röhm.

During the night, he and his SA troops had taken over the Reichswehr headquarters but were now besieged from all sides. The Reichswehr had closed off most of the access points to their headquarters, except for the Residenzstrasse, the narrow street that spilled into the Odeonsplatz.

"I was running when a great swarm of people surged up the street from the Odeonsplatz," Hanfstaengl said. He started pacing again. His legs were so long, he could only take a few steps in the tiny office before he had to spin around. "One of them was Lars Dearstyne. I recognized him as a first-aid man in an SA brigade. He'd been shot twice, in the shoulder and the side."

*Lars Dearstyne!* Gretchen started. The name she'd seen on the martyr plaque in the great hall minutes ago. Cohen had said that Stefan Dearstyne had wondered about Papa's death after reading his brother's diary. . . . She waited for Hanfstaengl to go on.

"Dearstyne told me the Reichswehr had opened fire with machine guns. He'd seen your father leap in front of Hitler to take a bullet. Then Dearstyne collapsed. I half carried, half dragged the poor fellow until we came across his elder brother. Stefan, I think his name was."

Gretchen was shaking inside. All these different pieces, nothing fastened together yet, all floating apart . . .

"The rest you know," Hanfstaengl said. "I escaped to Austria; Hitler made it to my country house in Uffing before he was arrested for treason and imprisoned; and Dearstyne succumbed to his injuries a few days later."

He paused while Gretchen's thoughts spun out in all directions. Something was wrong about Hanfstaengl's story, but she couldn't snatch hold of it.

"Yet see how far we've come in eight short years!" Hanfstaengl said, then spread his arms wide to encompass the small room. "Now let's make ourselves worthy of our pitiful salaries."

He pushed a stack of newspapers across the desk. The tidy lines of type seemed to jump about on the pages. She didn't know how she would ever settle down to accomplish any work.

"Today's morning editions," Hanfstaengl said. "Clip any articles mentioning the Party. I have a meeting with an English correspondent at the Regina Hotel and won't be back in today, so feel free to let yourself out when you've finished."

"Yes, Herr Hanfstaengl. Thank you."

She tried to read the papers while he collected his hat and stick. The sentences jumbled together. Unemployment reaching as high as 14 percent, massive floods in China, a first-ever constitution for Ethiopia. She couldn't concentrate. For nearly an hour, she skimmed the pages, half of her thoughts on the task, half running over Hanfstaengl's story again and again.

It reminded her of a song played in the wrong key. It almost sounded right, but there was something slightly off about it. She had to reread the articles because her mind insisted on swerving out of her control.

And then she realized. The timing was wrong.

Lars Dearstyne had said her father had leapt in front of Uncle Dolf when the bullets started. She'd heard the story so many times that she had never questioned it, but now she saw it didn't make sense.

Her father had worn his war uniform. Although he had decided to join the SA, he hadn't formally done so yet. Therefore, he should have been marching in the rear with the rest of the tagalongs, with two thousand men separating him from the front line.

But he had been right there next to Uncle Dolf, close enough to shield him when the gunfire erupted. He had flung his body in front of Hitler's, the bullets riddling his chest and killing him quickly. That fact was incontrovertible. She had heard it from dozens of lips; she had heard it from Uncle Dolf himself. Papa may have been shot in the back—a mistake in all the confusion, she hoped—but he had also served as a human shield for the Führer.

But what had her father been doing alongside Hitler in the first place? There was no chance he would have marched with Hitler simply because they were friends—Uncle Dolf adored order and would have insisted that everyone march in his proper section.

The shoot-out had been over in thirty seconds. There had been no time for her father to charge up from the rear unit. He must have marched with Hitler in the same line. But why had her father been there at all?

She shoved her chair back. There was no decision to make; there were no options to consider. She knew what she must do. If anyone saw her leave, she would say she was getting a breath of fresh air. She couldn't risk using the Braunes Haus telephone switchboard, so she snuck into a hotel lobby down the street.

A voice she already recognized answered on the second ring. *"Munich Post."*

"Herr Cohen," she said, "it's Fräulein Müller."

There was a pause. "Have you rung to make good on our agreement? A National Socialist who keeps her word—what an oddity you are, Fräulein Müller."

How she hated his condescending tone. "Never mind what I am, Herr Cohen. Yes, I'm ready to fulfill my promise, provided you tell me about the dead man's diary."

"The Diana Temple," Cohen said. "Eight o'clock tonight. Come alone or the deal's off."

The church bells chimed six as Gretchen left the Braunes Haus. She was unlocking her bicycle when a hand clamped over her wrist. "Say nothing," a voice whispered in her ear. "I'm revising the favor you owe me. You must come with me right now, for we haven't much time."

It was the Jewish reporter. He had tipped his fedora low over his face, so she could scarcely see him. Today he wore a blue suit, its fabric softened by many washings, its cuffs hemmed in mismatched thread. The combination of navy and sky-blue threads looked strange. Everyone knew Jews were wealthy. Surely Herr Cohen could afford new suit jackets instead of stitching up old ones?

"I'm glad to see you have some sense." He pulled her bicycle back from the iron railing. "Other NSDAP pets would no doubt be screaming at the sight of me."

A pet, a stupid mindless creature—that's how he saw her, this Jew who looked down at her. Anger and surprise stole her voice.

Together, they moved past the old stone palace, he wheeling the bicycle. All around them, shopgirls in smart dresses and businessmen in dark suits strode home. Across the street, a cluster of young men in SS uniforms laughed and loped along, probably on their way to supper in a noisy beer hall. No one guessed she was walking with a Jew.

Slowly, she felt the muscles in her stomach unclench. But when his eyes fastened upon hers, they were so sharp with intelligence and intensity that it took all of her self-control not to squirm. He looked at her as if he knew precisely what she thought about him and he didn't care because there were other things that mattered far more.

Nobody had ever looked at her in such a dismissive manner. Not even Reinhard. Although Cohen couldn't have been more than four or five inches taller than she was, she felt impossibly small walking beside him.

"I must talk quickly, and there is no time to ask questions," he said. Although his Berliner dialect altered the sound of the words, she understood him easily. "Stefan Dearstyne rang me as I was closing up the *Munich Post* offices a few minutes ago. He said Röhm and his men were following him, and he would rather die by his own hands than by theirs. He was using one of the public telephones at the train station, and he said that as soon as we hung up he would fling himself in front of an oncoming train."

He ignored Gretchen's startled gasp. "Most likely, he's already dead. But his brother's diary is in his apartment, and we must, at all costs, prevent Röhm and his men from finding it. The diary is the only proof I have that your father was murdered. I need it, and you're going to help me get it."

She felt like she stood on shifting sand. All the perfectly smoothed edges of her old existence seemed jagged now. What he proposed was impossible. "I—I can't."

They had reached the curb. Traffic curled around the corner, a black Mercedes, then a white Horch. Across the street, a tired-looking old horse pulled a cart. The driver lashed his whip across the beast's back.

Even as Gretchen watched, the animal's skin split apart. Three long red welts marred its matted brown hair. The horse kept walking, its head hanging, its slender legs moving more and more slowly. Sweat gleamed on its neck, from the strain of pulling such a heavy load, and its white eyes rolled when the driver cracked the whip across its back again.

She swallowed hard. Had she become that horse—beaten and bloodied but still serving its master without question? A beast of burden. An easily dismissed pet.

Someone who was so scared, she would choose the familiar lies over the truth? Papa deserved better than that. And so did she.

"I'll do it."

"Good." Cohen was nervous now; she could see it in the way he scanned the street, his eyes narrowing at the cluster of SS men, still laughing, digging in their pockets, probably looking for cigarettes or change. "We must leave straightaway. Röhm and his men may be heading toward Dearstyne's apartment even now. Get on the handlebars."

She said nothing more as she clambered on. She felt the bicycle shift as Cohen straddled it; felt his breath on the back of her neck as he pushed off the pavement with his foot; felt his arm brush hers as he leaned forward to pedal. She flinched. What would Uncle Dolf say, if he saw her now?

She should move away. She *must*.

But when she twisted her neck, she looked into Cohen's eyes, dark and clear and determined, focused on the street ahead. She saw the smooth curve of his cheek. And she couldn't fear him.

So, even though she knew she should move away, she stayed still, leaving her arm where it was, lightly touching his.

# PART TWO

## THE GREAT MAGICIAN

Great liars are also great magicians.

—*Adolf Hitler*

# 12

STEFAN DEARSTYNE'S APARTMENT WAS IN A narrow brick building on a side street by the central train station. The front door wasn't locked. The lobby, a depressing box whose walls might have been white once, years ago, was lit by a dying light fixture flickering off and on.

"Third floor," Cohen said. It was the first time he had spoken since they had left the Braunes Haus on her bicycle. The glimmering light gilded his face for an instant, and even though she knew she shouldn't, Gretchen couldn't help looking at him.

In profile, she saw things about his features she hadn't noticed before: the straightness of his nose, the full shape of his lips, the sharp point of his chin. Why couldn't he appear the way he was supposed to? The human shape of his face, the human smell of him—all combined to make it difficult to remember he was a subhuman.

"We must be quick." Cohen dashed across the lobby, making for the ancient linoleum-covered stairs. She raced after him.

Their jagged breathing and pounding footsteps mingled in the quiet. When they reached the third-floor corridor and Cohen whipped a tool out of his pocket, forcing it into the nearest door lock, she hung back for an instant. Her heart kicked against her ribs like a recalcitrant mule.

She was about to break into a stranger's apartment with a Jew as her accomplice. While her brother's boss and his comrades raced through the city toward them. She stepped closer to the stairs. She couldn't do this.

Cohen crouched on the floor, frowning at the lock. "Why won't it open?" he muttered to himself, then glanced at Gretchen. "Going somewhere?"

"I—I can't do this," she faltered, and he threw his tool down in frustration.

"Neither can I." He surged to his feet. "Maybe I can break the door down."

"Wait!" She grabbed his arm to stop him. "Röhm and his men will certainly notice a destroyed door! And do you want to bring all the neighbors running because of the racket?" She picked up the tool. It was a slender pick with a needle-sharp point. Gently, she fitted it into the lock, twisting with feather-light fingers until she heard a satisfying click. She turned the knob and the door swung open.

Cohen let out a low whistle. "Impressive. How'd you learn to do that?"

"My father taught me." She didn't add that Papa had instructed her how to pick locks so they could sneak into their apartment building's cellar and steal coal for their stove. It hadn't been his fault—the postwar inflation had been slowly killing everyone—but she didn't want to say anything about Papa that a stranger might misinterpret.

"Your father . . ." Cohen sounded amused. "What interesting lessons you National Socialist children are taught. My upbringing must seem boring to you—my father only taught me more prosaic things, like how to read and tie my shoelaces. Never mind," he added when she glared at him.

They stepped into the room. Walking inside felt like walking into a black night unrelieved by stars. Shutters had been fastened across the solitary window, leaving only slivers of light showing. Gretchen ran a hand over the wall, searching for a light switch, but there wasn't one.

When Cohen flung the shutters back, she saw the window was the old-fashioned sort, without any glass, just a rectangle cut into the wall. Street sounds rushed into the room: pigeons crying, shoes tramping on cobblestones, schoolchildren shouting at one another.

Dearstyne's home was nothing more than a small, cramped room: a sagging sofa that clearly doubled as a bed, for there was no mattress anywhere; a long countertop where an iron ring constituted a stingy stove; a scarred bureau under the window that must hold most of his possessions, because there was no armoire; and a couple of cardboard boxes filled with odds and ends. A single photograph lay on a low table.

Cohen dove for the boxes. Gretchen headed toward the bureau, but something about the photograph trapped her eye.

The paper was rough and yellowed. Not a photograph, but

a snapshot that had been neatly clipped out of a newspaper. It had been snipped without a caption or accompanying text, and it showed five men shoving their way through a massive crowd. A young-faced Uncle Dolf walked in the lead, wearing his belted trench coat, with his slouch hat pulled low, which always made Mama roll her eyes and mutter that he looked like a gangster. Following him were four other men. Alfred Rosenberg, grim-faced beneath a dark hat, then Ulrich Graf, Hitler's old bodyguard.

The next man seemed vaguely familiar. He was squat and barrel-chested, like a boxer, but so short that he resembled a dwarf. The top of his head barely reached the other men's shoulders. She thought she had seen him before, but perhaps only at the important Party functions everyone attended, a minor cog on the wheel circling far away from the center of the NSDAP machine.

A few steps behind, her father was frozen in midstride. He must have been cold, for he wore no coat over his Great War uniform, but his expression betrayed no physical discomfort. His face looked bewildered and unhappy as he stared at Uncle Dolf's back, and Gretchen could almost hear him saying, *Adi, what have I done wrong?*

She thought back to Hanfstaengl's story of the putsch. This photo must have been snapped as the men made their way into the Bürgerbräukeller while Hanfstaengl and members of the press milled about outside. Within thirty minutes, the SA troops would storm the beer hall and Hitler would rush to the podium, waving a pistol and shouting that the national revolution had begun. In sixteen hours, Uncle Dolf and Graf would be gravely wounded, her father dead. It must have been the last photograph taken of Papa, and he looked more miserable in that moment than she had ever known him. She had thought he would feel triumphant, certain that power was almost within the Party's grasp.

"What are you doing?" Cohen cried. "Hurry! Röhm might be here any minute!"

She dropped the clipping and hurried to the bureau beneath the window. She yanked open a drawer and pulled out three graying undershirts. Their rank smell hit her in the face like a fist. Quickly, she went through the bureau's pitiful contents: woolen long johns with holes in both knees, a sweater with an unraveling collar, two pairs of badly darned socks, broken bootlaces, handkerchiefs so old the fabric had turned transparent—

"Nothing!" Cohen kicked a box in disgust. "Do you see any other boxes, Fräulein Müller?"

As she turned to answer, she spotted something in the street. At the dinner hour, the narrow avenue writhed with people: day laborers in stained jackets, schoolchildren in checked dresses or shirtsleeves, all hurrying home for their supper, and, in the midst of them, a brown circle, moving steadily.

She froze. The men's heads were down, their faces obscured by their caps, but their distinctive brown uniforms identified them instantly. And Röhm was unmistakable—the quick, deliberate walk and the squat, heavy frame.

"It's Röhm," she said. "He's on his way."

If Röhm found her, here, in this old Party crank's apartment, helping a Jew—

Cohen cursed. "We can't leave without the diary."

Her heart swung like a hammer in her chest. The muscles in her legs tensed, ready to run. *Get out, get out, get out.* But she had to know more about Papa's death.

She glanced about the room. A moth-eaten sofa whose cushions had been tossed aside; a bureau whose drawers hung open drunkenly, their contents spilled across the floor; a few shirts and trousers and socks; a counter with a white porcelain teapot . . .

She stared at it. So clean, when everything else in the apartment was dirty and dingy.

Cohen followed her gaze. In two strides, he had reached the teapot and ripped off its top. He grinned. "Well done, Fräulein Müller." He pulled out a hammered metal box, barely bigger than his hand.

"Let's clean up this mess," he said, slipping the box into his pocket. "Or else they'll know someone else was here first."

"No, they won't." They must get away *now*. "For all they know, Dearstyne was a lousy housekeeper—let's go!"

"Almost done." Cohen snatched up the pile of papers and threw them into the box. Outside, Gretchen heard the low rumble of a man's voice, still so distant she couldn't separate the sound into words. *Röhm*, she thought as Cohen reached for the sofa cushions on the floor.

"Forget the cushions!" She snatched up his hand and ran, pulling on him so hard that he bumped into her. They rocketed into the hallway. Footsteps echoed from the stairwell; another moment and the SA men would be upon them.

The back stairs were their only chance. Still clutching the boy's hand, she ran down the corridor, away from the main staircase. Together, they reached the closed door at the end of the hall, skidding to a stop. He twisted the knob, and then they were hurtling down the back stairs in the darkness. All of the overhead bulbs must have burned out, but it didn't matter, for she could move by feel: the slippery linoleum steps, the metal railing beneath her hand, Cohen's fingers clamped on hers.

They shot off the bottom step together. There was light shining around the edges of a door, where it hadn't been fitted properly into its frame, and she raced toward it. Her hands fumbled for the doorknob, closing for an instant around the boy's, and she heard his shuddering breath in the darkness as the knob slipped around in their sweaty fingers, and then he was turning it and they flung themselves outside.

A narrow alley, lined with brick. Here the buildings leaned toward each other so precariously, they blotted out the little bit of sunlight left. Cohen ran toward the opposite building's wall, where he had chained the bicycle to one of the barred windows. He hopped astride; then she climbed onto the handlebars and they rode off into the encroaching night.

# 13

DUSK HAD BEGUN TO STRETCH ACROSS THE CITY when they reached the Diana Temple in the Hofgarten. The manicured gardens feathered out in all directions, bushes and flowers fading into blurs in the blue-black twilight. Gretchen felt the warm exhalation of Cohen's breath on the back of her neck. Sitting so close to him on the bicycle should seem wrong, but it didn't. His proximity should disgust her, but it only confused her.

Sometimes she had seen boys in the street wearing yarmulkes, or heard them speaking Yiddish when she rode a streetcar. She had always turned away, so she could avoid them. An easy task, since many of the city's Jews lived in the southern part of the city, far from her. At school, she tried to ignore the four Jewish girls in her class. That, too, had been easy, for their surnames placed them at opposite ends of their alphabetically arranged seats, and she sat in the middle. Obeying her father's instructions to stay away from Jews had been simple. She had barely had to try.

Until she had seen the Hasidic man in the alley, she hadn't looked at a Jewish male, not really looked at him, long enough to see the planes of his face, the expression in his eyes. Until that night, she had never spoken to a male Jew before.

They were nothing like she had been taught.

A dull buzzing sounded in her ears. If she and her people were mistaken about the Jews, then they were mistaken about everything. Without that screw, the entire machine would eventually break down. She felt a sob rise in her throat, and had to swallow it down. Uncle Dolf and Papa couldn't be wrong. Could they?

If they were wrong, nothing made sense anymore. The box she had carefully constructed about herself would fall apart. And she didn't know if she could bear standing out in the open, in the harsh wind, without the comforting warmth of those walls she had built to shut out everything she didn't like or understand.

The bicycle coasted to a stop. Gretchen clambered off the handlebars, accepting Cohen's outstretched hand before remembering they shouldn't touch. And she had taken *his* hand, back in Dearstyne's apartment.

She ripped her fingers from his grasp. For a moment, he looked startled, his face pale in the thickening gloom. Gretchen folded her trembling arms across her chest.

"I see," he said softly, "you have remembered yourself."

His shoulders rose and fell with a sigh, but he didn't make a sound. Then he turned away, striding down the path toward the Diana Temple, leaving her with the bicycle. The downward tilt of his head looked lonely.

She had hurt him. The thing she had always thought was

impossible—wounding a Jew's heart—had happened. The boy hadn't been pretending; she had seen the injury in his eyes before he'd walked away.

She walked slowly after him, the bicycle's tires rumbling over the sidewalk. He was waiting inside the Diana Temple. He didn't look at her as she neared the small stone building that stood in the center of a set of converging paths. Archways as large as doors spanned the curved walls, so she could see him standing inside, leaning against the wall, head down, dark hair hanging and hiding his expression. The metal box gleamed dully in his hands.

He said nothing when she entered. He didn't look at her until she touched his hand, hesitantly, her fingers light, barely skimming his warm skin. But she heard the breath catch in his throat. He recognized what she was doing—touching him deliberately.

"Thank you for helping me off the bicycle," she said.

His head lifted. He didn't smile. But something changed in his face—a loosening of clenched muscles in his jaw, perhaps—transforming him from formidable and intimidating to quiet and grave. "You're welcome."

They sat together on the floor. Cohen fiddled with the lock for several minutes. Finally, he pulled off his shoe and smashed it onto the box with such force that Gretchen started. The broken lock dangled in two pieces. Inside the box lay a worn leather book, no bigger than her palm. Cohen flipped through it, pausing at a page before pressing it into her hand.

"Read it," he said. "And you'll start to understand, as I have."

She carried the diary to one of the arches, where the purple gleam of twilight still filtered strongly enough through the opening for her to see the page.

*10 November 1923,* she read.

*I am dying. I must write this down before it is too late. The tall shoemaker Müller marched in the front line, a few feet ahead of me. When we reached the Residenzstrasse, the street was too narrow for him to walk with the others, so he continued on ahead of them. I think he was hit first. I saw his body jerk once. Then he stumbled in front of Herr Hitler, his body acting as a shield, absorbing the bullets meant for our leader. He was dead in an instant.*

*Then I was shot and on the pavement, too. I dragged myself forward on my elbows, trying to get to Hitler. He had fallen, too, maybe shot. But Müller's corpse lay between us. There were powder burns on his back. I knew at once what those marks meant—someone had shot him at close range. It must have been one of our men, but I can't imagine who. I wanted to tell Hitler, but he was already scrambling up, helped by two other comrades, and they were hustling him away, and I tried to run, too, toward the center of the city with everyone else—*

She stopped, staring at the white page without seeing it. In her mind's eye, she saw her father marching in the softly falling snow, proud and tall in his Great War uniform. She saw him knocked sideways by a bullet's blast, then his body convulsing again and again.

Taking a shaky breath, she pressed the heels of her hands into her eyes, willing the image away. Powder burns on his back. A bullet hole, encircled with dried blood and gray dust, on his tunic between his shoulder blades.

Someone had pressed a pistol against her father's body and fired. The shot's proximity sprayed powder onto his coat, and the bullet's blast knocked him sideways in front of Hitler.

Everything Cohen had said was true. Someone had murdered her father.

Tears burned her eyes.

The powder burns meant the shot had been fired too close to her father's body for it to have been a mistake. She couldn't deny or explain away the truth anymore, not now that she had seen the same doubts as hers in someone else's journal.

She opened her eyes and stared at the blurred floor. Her father had not been a hero; he had not leapt in front of Hitler to protect him from a barrage of bullets. He had stumbled sideways, protecting Hitler with his body, because he had already been shot. The bullet's impact in his back had thrown him in front of Hitler. He hadn't intended to sacrifice himself for the Führer at all.

Her hands tightened into fists. He had been murdered, and whoever had killed him needed to pay.

Daniel spoke, his voice gentle. "I'm sorry. This must be hard for you."

She didn't bother replying; there was no real answer. "How did you find out about the diary?" she asked.

She watched him as he answered. How steadily he kept his eyes on hers, as though he had nothing to hide. As much as she wanted not to, she believed everything he said. "Stefan Dearstyne came to the *Munich Post* offices last week, late at night. I was the only reporter still there.

"Stefan had recently found the diary, and was deeply troubled by what it revealed. He had known nothing about his brother's suspicions, and Lars had died the day after writing that entry. Apparently, Stefan had been asking questions at NSDAP meetings and speeches, but he wasn't getting anywhere. I agreed to help him investigate in return for an exclusive scoop."

She braced her hand on the archway frame, the stone rough under her palms. Papa's reputation had kept her and her family safe and cared for. But it had all been built on a lie. A National Socialist had murdered her father. And for the first time in her life, she had a problem she couldn't present to Uncle Dolf and wait for his solution. Without knowing who was involved, how could she drag Uncle Dolf into a dangerous investigation, especially when the Party was strengthening into the most powerful political force in Germany? He needed to focus on the Party's goals, not on an eight-year-old crime.

She felt Papa's hands rubbing her back after she woke crying from a nightmare. She felt his warmth curling around her when she sat on his lap and smelled his scents of tobacco and shoe polish and snow-dampened wool. She heard his voice, deep and slow, like that of a dove, nothing like Uncle Dolf's wood-thrush voice, which was melodious and smooth but flowed so fast that sometimes she couldn't hang on to his words long enough to puzzle them out. She tasted Papa's lumpy potato pancakes—the one food he could cook—too tough in places and too soft in others, and remembered how she ate every bite, even when Reinhard pushed away his plate and Mama said she should have saved the potatoes for soup instead. And she saw his bullet-ripped and bloodied uniform.

"I need to know what happened." She sounded so harsh, she scarcely recognized herself.

"Even if it means your family loses its privileged status?"

She turned away from the archway, her palms stinging. She had gripped the frame so tightly, the stone had scraped her skin. But she didn't mind the pain. She welcomed it. The sensation was something to cling to; anything was better than this gut-churning fear. "Even then, Herr Cohen."

"Very well." His eyes held hers for a long moment. "You realize it's very likely that whoever killed your father is a high-ranking National Socialist, for he would have been marching in the front lines. And whatever we uncover will create a scandal within the Party."

"You'd like that, wouldn't you?" She tried to sound scornful, but her voice was shaking too badly.

"No." He spoke quietly, without a trace of the anger or condescension she expected. "I want what I suspect you want, although you may not wish to admit it. The truth." He hesitated. "No matter what it costs."

# 14

LIKE EVERYONE ELSE IN A BOARDINGHOUSE, Reinhard kept his door locked, though a few twists with Gretchen's hairpin solved the problem. She stepped into the gloom, drawing the door closed. In the heavy silence, her ragged breaths sounded thunderous. *My God*, she thought, *I must be going mad, taking a chance like this.*

Since meeting with Cohen yesterday, she had felt a subtle shifting of the ground beneath her feet. It moved and buckled continuously. She had to walk carefully, speak slowly, or she feared she might betray her new imbalance. Her new fears.

This morning, Gretchen had helped Mama prepare the boarders' breakfast, she and her mother speaking like strangers as they moved about the kitchen in their well-practiced routine. At the Braunes Haus, she had answered telephones, filed papers, skimmed newspapers for stories about the NSDAP; she had listened when Uncle Dolf stopped by the office to complain to Hanfstaengl about a foreign reporter's unflattering article; and she had smiled when he kissed her hands farewell in his old-fashioned manner.

After work, she had bicycled back to the boardinghouse, arriving at half past six, just in time to dish out supper: a shoulder roast, stewed in beer with apples and cabbage in a Dutch oven, and, for dessert, a pear cake studded with walnuts. Sugar and fruit and nuts—clearly, the household accounts weren't as dire as Mama had said.

She scrubbed the dishes and then fixed a meal for Reinhard, ham-and-cheese sandwiches and apples, tucked with a red checked cloth into a tin lunch box, and she said nothing as he grinned, boasting he was going on a train journey and wouldn't be back until tomorrow night at the latest. She listened to the front door bang shut behind him, wondering where he could be going. But one never asked Reinhard questions.

And then she turned her gaze toward the stairs. She hadn't been permitted inside her brother's room for about three years, since she had dusted his writing table and accidentally broken a tiny glass bird, a present for his twelfth birthday from Uncle Dolf.

Her heart beat faster. After Papa's death, Mama had given many of his possessions to Reinhard, saying a man's only son should inherit his things. Quickly, Gretchen mounted the stairs. She didn't know when she would have the chance again to search her brother's room.

She wasn't certain what she had expected: piles of dirty laundry on the floor, perhaps, or a stack of girlie magazines hidden beneath the bed, or maybe some records by the big band orchestras he enjoyed. What she hadn't expected was nothing at all.

The room was a blank canvas, leaving no hints of its resident's personality. Her bedroom burst with color: the lavender pillowcases her grandmother had sewn; the postcards of Paris and London, Madrid and Zurich pinned to the wall; the stack of library books on the desk; the red curtains she had stitched together last summer.

Reinhard's room was practically empty: the narrow bed covered with a fraying chenille spread, a spotless writing table, a hooked rug on the varnished floorboards, the furnishings the color of milk, the wood a pale maple, all color washed away.

There was nothing on the walls: no pictures, no books, no records. Neatly hung brownshirt uniforms in the armoire and a wet washcloth hanging over the chipped basin's lip were the only indications anyone had been in here recently.

The room was a void.

Papa's old shoemaking tools lay at the bottom of the armoire, behind Reinhard's winter galoshes and storm trooper boots. The iron shoe repair stand, the heavy old scissors, the thick thread, the patches of leather. She had to blink back tears.

Her father had been so proud of his cobbler skills. Like men of every trade, he had been required to complete a *Wanderschaft*—three years spent traveling throughout Bavaria, studying under different shoemakers before submitting his work to the guild and receiving the title of master, which meant he could open his own business.

He had loved to tell her about those years, walking from town to town carrying a knapsack containing his only possessions, his tools and an extra set of clothes and a tin drinking cup, sleeping in fields when he couldn't find an apprenticeship and stealing fruit from orchards when he was hungry. Finally, after receiving the coveted master title and returning home to Dachau, he had proposed to Mama and, after their marriage, had headed for the big city, Munich, to start his own shop.

But then the war had come, and the shells had blasted away something within Papa, so the man who returned was blank-eyed and unpredictable. Sometimes, he smiled the same wide smile she had seen in old photographs, and talked with the easy charm she imagined had won her mother's heart. Sometimes, he sobbed uncontrollably for hours, crouched in the bedroom, and Mama whispered they must all speak softly so they didn't upset him.

Maybe the old Papa, the good-natured, smiling man in the photos, could have found his way through the twisting corridors Germany had become after her defeat. But not this new man who shifted so readily between sunlight and shadows.

This father lost his business and had to work for another cobbler, settling for a far smaller income. This father moved his family into a shabby two-room apartment in Schwabing, and often they didn't have enough money to buy groceries, so Gretchen and her brother went to bed hungry almost every night.

Sighing, she shook her head. If only she could erase most of her memories of those days, saving only little pockets of them instead. Papa taking her to the zoo, and laughing when she squealed in fear at the lions. Papa smiling when she danced in the kitchen, and scolding Mama for snapping at Gretchen to get out of the way because she had to make supper.

She closed the armoire. There was nothing here to tell her why he had died, only reminders of how he had lived.

She was leaving in defeat when a floorboard sank an inch beneath her weight.

Had Reinhard hidden something here? Why would he go to such trouble? She dropped to her knees and pulled at the board, her pulse throbbing. All of the nails had been removed and the board lifted easily. A stack of newspaper clippings and an index card with her brother's leftward-slanting writing lay in the opening.

She snatched them up. The clippings came from the *Munich Post*. Peculiar. Reinhard rarely read newspapers, but when he did, he flipped through the Party's *Völkischer Beobachter* or *Der Stürmer*. Not the local Socialist paper that Uncle Dolf despised so much he called it the Poison Kitchen. What possible reason could Reinhard have for cutting out articles from a newspaper he likely didn't read?

She was starting to skim the first clipping, dated about two months ago, when a quiet, male voice came from the hall. "Fräulein Müller? Your mother is coming up the stairs."

Her heartbeat pounded in her ears. There was no way she could explain away her presence in Reinhard's room to Mama. Quickly, she laid the clippings and card down, then slid the floorboard into place. She slapped the light switch off and stepped into the hallway just as her mother appeared at the top of the stairs. The Englishman Whitestone stood across the corridor.

"Gretchen?" Mama asked. "Are you looking for me?"

"No. I—I thought you were in bed." She was glad the hallway was dim, for she felt a blush heating her face.

"Fräulein Müller was advising me on the best gardens to visit in Munich," the Englishman cut in. "She has been most helpful."

"Gardens now!" Mama's smile looked forced. "First it is all the places popular in the city with National Socialists, then it is Herr Hitler's favorite restaurants! You will know Munich as well as any local by the end of your visit, Herr Doktor Whitestone." She glanced at Gretchen. "Good night. I've already locked up, and all the chores are finished."

"All right, Mama. Good night."

When her mother didn't move into her room, Gretchen reluctantly climbed the stairs. She would have to return to her brother's room during the night, to make sure she had replaced everything exactly and to lock the door. She heard the steps groaning as Herr Doktor Whitestone followed.

She waited to speak to the Englishman until they had reached their corridor. The single overhead lamp threw most of the hallway into shadow, so she could scarcely see his face.

"Thank you for warning me," she said, wondering how he had known that she wasn't supposed to be in her brother's room.

"I must speak plainly." Whitestone hesitated. "I came to Munich on sabbatical to observe Adolf Hitler. He's a fascinating psychological puzzle. Other psychoanalysts have written about him, and I hope by studying him at close quarters I can gain a deeper understanding of him than they have. I chose your boardinghouse because of your family's well-known closeness to Hitler. But I have seen something here that troubles me."

He looked at her, his expression unreadable. "I overheard your brother on the telephone the other night, speaking to one of your friends. He was most insistent that she tell him where you had gone. And he charmed the answers out of her so cunningly . . ." Whitestone shook his head. "It's probably nothing," he murmured. "The actions of a protective older brother."

Her fingers closed around the doorknob, ready to turn it and dart into her room. "What are you saying?"

"I'm sorry. I shouldn't have spoken." He looked embarrassed. "One of the hazards of my profession is seeing darkness where there may only be light. I'm sure I must be mistaken."

Confused, she nodded as he bid her a good night, and she went into her room. Even though Reinhard was somewhere else tonight, she locked the door and leaned the chair under the knob. Then she stood still, listening to the sounds in the room next door. Splashing water, washing his face in the basin most likely. The rustle of a mattress. Good. He was settling in for the night. As she undressed, she wondered who this new boarder truly was. And what his concerns were about her brother.

Morning sunlight had lightened her red curtains to pale pink before Gretchen woke to insistent knocking and her mother's voice saying she had better hurry downstairs to help with the breakfast or the boarders would be cross.

She shot up in bed. *No.* She had fallen asleep before she could sneak back to her brother's room to lock up.

As fast as she could, she put on stockings and a white dress and shoved her feet into espadrilles. She could lock Reinhard's door on her way downstairs. He would never know what she had done.

But when she opened her bedroom door, her mother was waiting for her in the hallway, glaring. It would have to wait until after breakfast.

Gretchen was still drying dishes when the doorbell rang. Geli stood on the front steps, powdering her cheeks. She snapped her compact shut and smiled at Gretchen. As usual, she wore simple clothes: a sundress in soft green, a broad-brimmed straw hat, and espadrilles.

"Gretchen!" Geli beamed. "I'm so glad to have caught you at home. I'm inviting you on my little escape—a picnic on the Chiemsee with Uncle Alf and some of the old dears. Won't you come along with us?"

"I'm afraid I have to go to work today—"

"With Herr Hanfstaengl? Why, he's sitting out in the car right now."

Gretchen peered over Geli's shoulder. Hitler's red Mercedes was parked at the curb, its engine running. The chauffeur sat behind the wheel, with Hitler beside him. Eva's boss, Heinrich Hoffmann, sat in the jump seat, and Hanfstaengl was in the back with Hoffmann's pretty teenage daughter Henny, her head covered with one of the tight-fitting caps—brown leather in the winter, white linen in the summer—that Hitler kept in the glove box to protect the women's hair. Everyone waved.

There was no way to refuse politely. "Thanks, I'd love to," she said, wishing she meant it. But now she looked at the smiling men and wondered if any of them had been involved in her father's death.

The drive out of the city went quickly. The soot-choked air became a bracing mountain breeze; the cobbled streets became wide green fields, the waving grasses shimmering with gold. Trees cut a jagged line along the horizon—towering pines that seemed to pierce the sky's bright blue canopy.

When the Mercedes encountered another car on the long, lonely roads, Uncle Dolf urged the chauffeur to drive faster. "We mustn't let them beat us!" he shouted, and Geli clapped her hands with delight.

Everyone except Hitler sang songs from Viennese operettas to pass the time. Hanfstaengl waved his arms, conducting an invisible orchestra.

Gretchen looked away from the fields rolling past. Uncle Dolf had twisted around in the front seat to gaze at her. Had he guessed that she suspected someone had murdered her father? That she believed someone within Hitler's beloved Party had been been involved in Papa's death? Uncle Dolf's face flushed when their eyes met, and he turned away quickly, as though he had been caught looking at something he shouldn't.

Confusion prickled her skin. He didn't suspect anything, not if he was embarrassed. But why should he be? She studied the back of his head: the familiar fall of dark hair, the strip of pale skin above his shirt collar, the slender seashell shape of his ears. Somehow, he looked different, though he was supposed never to change but to remain her beloved Uncle Dolf forever. Instinctively, she sensed that something had altered between them. But she couldn't guess what it was, or why it seemed to matter so much.

# 15

THEY PICNICKED BETWEEN THE WOODS AND THE lake. It was his favorite spot, Uncle Dolf said as they spread woolen rugs on the grass and the women unpacked the baskets of food: cheese and salami sandwiches, roast chicken in wax paper, apple tarts, flasks of coffee and tea, and, for Hitler, a bottle of mineral water.

The talk drifted like the gently lapping lake waters, soft and dreamlike. Gretchen barely heard a word because she couldn't stop staring at the surroundings. It had been nearly two years since she had last left Munich, after the stock-market crash had sucked away any spare pfennigs for train tickets. Besides, her grandparents insisted on motoring the thirteen miles from Dachau to Munich in their old car. They said they preferred to visit the big city, but she had overhead them, once, telling Mama that Reinhard would no longer be welcome in their house, not after they had caught him stealing eggs from the henhouse and throwing them on the ground—a costly waste they couldn't afford.

Gretchen pushed the memory away. It didn't matter now; Reinhard wasn't here to ruin things for her. She took a deep breath of the tree-bark-scented air. She had almost forgotten what a forest looked like, dark with pines, so beautiful she stared, the sandwich lying neglected on her lap.

Finally, the others were finished, the baskets packed, the rugs rolled up. They sat on the soft white sand, listening to Uncle Dolf talk about what he would do when he was elected president. A motorway would run from Munich to Salzburg, and a large restaurant would overlook the lakeshore.

Uncle Dolf drew in the sand with a stick, sketching the modern university he wanted to build, with a yachting school, a heated swimming pool, and first-rate sporting facilities.

Lovely dreams. Somehow, though, when Gretchen listened to Uncle Dolf, she forgot how fantastical his ideas sounded. They were no longer dreams, but a reality just out of reach. A glorious, golden future that seemed so sweet after the years of scraping along, the years of shame and want after Germany's defeat in the war. When she heard him talk about how great their empire had been, and how great it would be again, she felt almost giddy with relief. Soon it would be over, this miserable existence of soot-stained alleyways, gnawing bellies, her brother's footsteps on the stairs. Soon, if Uncle Dolf was right, everything would change. Somehow, she would be free.

Geli stood, dusting sand from her hands. "Come, ladies, it's time for swimming."

As she followed Geli along the curving shoreline, Gretchen

glanced back at the men, still sitting on the sand, Uncle Dolf talking on and on. His strident tone and his quiet expression were so at odds, she wondered if he spoke of matters completely different from the ones in his head. His skinny, awkward face had softened into something she had never seen before: He looked, for all the world, like a man in love.

And he was watching Geli.

*Impossible.* She hurried to keep up with the women, her mind spinning. Uncle Dolf didn't have lady friends. In the twelve years she had known him, she had never heard of him taking a lady to the cinema or a play, or dining with a pretty girl or walking in the park with a woman. Instead, he had always surrounded himself with men.

Her espadrilles sank in the sand. Papa had occasionally teased Uncle Dolf, calling him a monk, but she had been too young to understand the word's significance. A man who didn't notice the swell of a woman's bust, or the slender lines of her legs. A man who had shut all the doors of his heart to love or desire. What sort of substance made up such a man's soul?

But he looked at Geli as though he loved her, his face relaxed, his eyes gentle. With such open longing, it nearly took Gretchen's breath away.

Henny nudged her shoulder. "Are you ill? You've gone so pale."

"No." Somehow, she managed to lift each foot, push it forward across the fine white sand. Geli had gone on ahead and already slipped into a clump of trees. "Uncle Dolf—he looked at Geli so oddly—"

"You've caught him mooning after her, I suppose," Henny

said. "Don't tell me you didn't know! Herr Hitler is in love with her."

Henny was eighteen, a mere year older than Gretchen, but something had always separated them as solidly as a wall. It wasn't politics—both of their fathers had joined the Party in its early days—but something running far deeper than that, like the currents moving along the ocean floor, unseen but felt. It was something that embarrassed Gretchen, but as she followed Henny along the curving shoreline, she admitted its source to herself—it was class.

So she didn't dare ask Henny what she meant about Uncle Dolf and Geli. It was absurd, of course, a middle-aged bachelor in love with his nearly twenty-years-younger half niece.

Still, she turned and looked at the men. Hanfstaengl and Hoffmann lolled in the sand, their shirtsleeves rolled up, the sun beating on their faces, while Uncle Dolf and his chauffeur skipped stones along the water's surface. Even from this distance, she heard Hitler's shout. "Twelve jumps! What an excellent throw."

Today he wore traditional Bavarian clothes: leather shorts, a white linen shirt, a pale blue linen jacket with horn buttons. He waded into the water, his knobby-kneed, pasty legs disturbing the crystalline surface, creating small ripples that widened with distance until finally they reached her, yards away.

Geli's laugh cut into her thoughts, and Gretchen hurried to join the girls.

They stood in a thicket of sloe trees along the shore. Sunlight slanted through the branches, gilding the girls' skin with gold as they slipped out of their clothes.

"The water looks divine!" Henny rushed into the lake, her slender legs churning up the water.

But Geli hesitated and glanced back at the men. "My uncle's watching me again," she murmured, so quietly that Gretchen had to strain to hear. "He's always watching me."

Gretchen looked, but Uncle Dolf was peering in the opposite direction, up to his ankles in the water, his hands clasped behind his back. The bottom of his shorts was wet, as though he had turned away so quickly he had splashed himself.

"He isn't watching now."

"Never mind. It doesn't matter," Geli muttered. "Nothing does." Her fingertips brushed Gretchen's bare shoulder, her touch light and cool. "You're so young, perhaps you don't know about love yet. Loving someone is one thing, and being loved is another, but being loved by the one you love—that's paradise. And I don't think I shall ever have it. Some men aren't capable of loving you back."

Geli's lips firmed, as though she wished she could pull her words back inside. But she said nothing more and raced into the lake after Henny. Gretchen stood stock-still, her hands gripping a tree branch, the rough bark cutting into her palms.

What had Geli meant? Unease whispered up Gretchen's spine. Gretchen must be mistaken—but Geli had almost sounded as though she loved her uncle romantically. Even though she complained about his rigid rules and his possessive behavior, a part of her cared for him. And he didn't love her in return, not in the way she needed.

Gretchen stared straight ahead, at the sun-drenched water where Geli and Henny splashed. *My bride must be Germany, my only love the Fatherland*, Uncle Dolf had said so many times. Until now, she had believed him.

Gretchen stepped out from the trees' protection. Ahead, the lake's surface glittered as though thousands of diamonds skipped across it. The men's voices reached her from where they stood along the shore, their forms so darkened by distance that they were mere silhouettes against the sand.

Naked, she ran across the shore. She let the water pull her, sinking like a stone beneath the surface and down toward the doubts that threatened to drown her.

The sun was falling into a pool of oranges and reds by the time Gretchen reached the boardinghouse. Although her stomach protested because she had missed supper, she decided to change out of her sandy clothes before digging through the icebox for whatever scraps she could find. She darted across the front hall, praying the old ladies sitting in the parlor wouldn't call to her, and none did.

Breathing a sigh of relief—that obstacle past, at least—she fitted a key into the lock on her door, frowning when the tumblers didn't click. Perhaps she had forgotten to lock it; she had been in a rush this morning to help Mama with breakfast.

Inside, the curtains had been drawn. She thought she had left them open; she always did, so Striped Peterl could look outside. Something else she must have forgotten, and now the air felt hot and stifling.

"Sorry, Striped Peterl." She nudged the door shut. "It must have been boring for you all day, with nothing to look at."

She tossed her pocketbook onto the bed and reached for

Striped Peterl lying on her pillow. But he didn't move when she stroked him, and his head sagged to one side. Panic seized her heart. Even as her fingers fumbled to find a pulse, she knew there wouldn't be one. The cat's neck had been broken.

# 16

A HARSH CRY BURST FROM HER THROAT. *DEAD*. SHE laid him on the bed, running shaking hands over his body, as if she could somehow resurrect him with her touch. His neck, twisted at such a horribly unnatural angle, and his rib cage, no longer moving, and his eyes, mercifully closed, and his white paws and belly and striped fur, all the tiny parts of him she had loved so much. She heard herself sobbing, great gasping sobs, but they sounded far away, as though someone in the next room were crying.

Striped Peterl's body was still warm and soft. He must have died only a short time ago. As she cradled him against her chest, she felt herself splitting in two—the girl standing in her bedroom, holding her dead cat, shaking, and the girl standing to the side, watching, the two entities separated by the haze of shock.

Memories shot through her head: reading in bed with Striped

Peterl stretched across her feet, his purr rumbling into her toes; dangling a ribbon and giggling while he batted it; crying over one of Reinhard's nasty tricks while Striped Peterl nudged his wet nose against her hand, concerned in his feline way; and sitting on the kitchen floor with Papa, cuddling the last gift he had ever given her. *Don't let anyone else play with it*, he had said. *The cat is just for you, do you understand?*

Now she did. Awareness crackled through her mind like an electrical current. She knew who had snapped Striped Peterl's neck.

Rage filled her, so red and so thick that she couldn't contain it. Gently, she set her cat back on the pillow. Then she ripped the door open and ran down the stairs. All the second-story doors were closed, but she didn't care. She flung Reinhard's door open without bothering to knock and wait to be admitted.

Her brother lay on his bed, flipping through a magazine. The curtains had been shut, and only a small desk lamp burned, leaving most of the room in shadow and his face hidden. Only the whites of his eyes shone in the darkness. Slowly, he sat up, tossing his magazine aside. "What is it? Don't you know you're supposed to knock?"

"*Knock?*" she cried. "Don't you know you aren't supposed to kill poor, defenseless animals?"

He sighed and stood, the mattress whispering from the release of his weight. Quickly, he reached around her to close the door. He wore only an undershirt and trousers. Standing so close, she felt heat pumping off his body and smelled the sharp bite of his cologne. "Keep your voice down. Do you want to disturb Mama and the boarders?"

"Don't pretend you care about them. You've never cared about anyone but yourself." She couldn't stop tears from blurring her eyes. "Why did you do it, Reinhard? He was only a cat. Striped Peterl never bothered anyone. Why did you have to do it?"

Reinhard leaned against the wall, crossing his arms over his chest. In the dimness, he looked bored. "I'm tired from my trip, Gretchen, so if you're only going to repeat yourself and grow more hysterical, I'll ask you to leave."

"Why did you do it?" she cried again and raised her hand, with the foolish notion she could seize hold of him and force him up the stairs to her room, so he could see what he had done. But he must have interpreted her movement as an attempt to hit him, for he caught her wrist in his hand and twisted her arm behind her back.

"Don't try to attack me," he said. "Tonight can go one of two directions for you, so be careful which you choose. Why were you in my room?"

"I wasn't in your room, Reinhard." She was nearly bent over now, as he pressed harder on her pinned arm.

Her heart knocked against her ribs so frantically, she feared she might pass out. She sucked in a great gulp of air. She mustn't faint, for there was no telling what he might do if she lay helpless on his floor.

"Don't lie to me." He spoke calmly. "Why were you in my room?"

"I wasn't, Reinhard, I wouldn't sneak into your room—" She couldn't keep the hysteria from her voice. Each word rose higher until she was practically screaming.

He released her, then pushed her shoulder blades so hard that she stumbled forward several steps before she managed to catch her balance. She swung around to face him; he stood between her and the door, and the single lamp illuminated the far corner of the room, leaving him in shadow. "*Stop lying to me*. Why were you in my room?"

She was sobbing now, even though she hated herself for it. "Why did you kill Striped Peterl? He was only a cat who never did anything at all to you—"

He drew his arm back, then cracked her across the face. White-hot pain exploded in her jaw. She staggered sideways. Only his grip on her arm held her upright.

"Why were you in my room?"

"Please—stop, Reinhard, please—"

He pushed her against the wall, pressing his forearm so tightly on her throat that she could barely gasp for air. His face shoved against hers, so close their eyes were only inches apart. She couldn't look away from him. The bored expression in his eyes chilled her. *He doesn't care, not at all*, she thought desperately. He could hurt her in any way he wished, and not hear the smallest whisper from his conscience. In that instant, she realized her brother wasn't the ice-hearted trickster she had always thought. He was dangerous.

"Why were you in my room?" He spoke in the same bland tone, but sweat beaded his forehead. His pale eyes watched her. "Don't lie to me again, Gretchen. I came home this afternoon from important Party business to find my room unlocked. And you needn't blame it on any of the other residents. That bunch of boring old ladies wouldn't think of breaking into my private space, and Mama wouldn't either."

He pressed harder, and she heard her last lungful of air escape in a shallow gasp. Black spread across the periphery of her vision, the sides of the room collapsing into darkness. "That leaves you. *Why were you in my room?*"

He released her so suddenly that she fell. On her hands and knees, she gulped in air, the blackness softening to gray. Her throat felt raw; every breath scraped against the damaged tissue.

"Please, Reinhard," she managed, "I didn't mean any harm. I—I was curious. It's been so long since I've seen your room. It isn't normal. I'm your sister."

He considered her. For a long moment, Gretchen remained crouched on the floor, frozen in place, as though the slightest movement might upset her brother. *Don't move, don't move*, she repeated in her head, and then he reached for her.

"I don't believe you," he said, and yanked her upright. Before she could throw up her arms for protection, he slapped her face.

An ache flared in her cheek. She reeled backward, smacking into the wall. Blood welled in her mouth, its copper taste gagging her. She curled her arms over her face, and though she wanted to close her eyes and block out the sight of him walking closer, she couldn't. She watched his arm rear back, winding up for another blow, and she tensed, then felt the sudden agony as his fist plowed into her stomach.

She couldn't breathe. She staggered, falling forward, but Reinhard seized her by the arms, jerking her upright. She couldn't suck in any air, and she felt herself sinking down. She looked up to see Reinhard's hand descending again, and a sudden wall of darkness fell as he punched her eye.

For an instant, her vision went black, then it flooded back, dotted with gray. She saw Reinhard, a collection of black and white and gray, saw him reaching for her again—

"Please stop," she begged. The words were hard to say; she was trying to talk around the blood filling her mouth. "Reinhard, please."

He tossed her to the floor, as easily as though she were a doll. When she flung out her arms to break the fall, her palms slapped hard on the floorboards. Pain jolted through her wrists, radiating up to her shoulders.

"Reinhard, stop!" she cried. The slurred words sprayed a fine mist of blood on the floor. "I'll tell Uncle Dolf!"

He stood over her, shoulders rising and falling from loud, angry breaths. "He won't care."

"Yes, he will!" She wanted to say, *He'll care and he'll make you stop; he'll make you go far away so you can't hurt me and Mama ever again*, but moving her mouth sent waves of agony pulsing from her jaw throughout her skull.

Reinhard crouched down, then cupped her chin with his hand, forcing her to look up at him. She saw him through a film of tears and sweat. His figure had begun to blur around the edges, and she wondered frantically if he had damaged her eyesight. The room seemed to grow dimmer, as though someone were slowly turning down a gaslight.

His eyes were flat and emotionless. "Gretchen, you're so stupid."

Then he rose and crossed the room, the floorboards groaning under his weight. He opened the door. "Get out. And get rid of that cat's body. We don't want it stinking up the place."

Fear made her move quickly. She got to her feet and stumbled through the open door. The corridor looked misty, as though she wore rain-streaked spectacles. No one was out there, but they all must have heard.

Something blurred her vision; it might have been blood or sweat, but right now she didn't care which. She wiped it off with the back of her hand and stumbled to her mother's room next door.

# 17

MAMA OPENED THE DOOR ON THE FIRST KNOCK. Her face tightened and she pulled Gretchen into the room, closing the door behind them.

"My God, Gretchen, what has happened?"

"Reinhard," she said, and had to spit blood onto the floor before she could go on. More blood immediately welled up, so the words came out slurred. Her lips felt thick and clumsy. "Mama, Reinhard did this."

Her mother sighed. "Sit down, Gretl. If we wipe off the blood, we can see how bad it is."

She didn't know what she had expected, but it wasn't this quiet, matter-of-fact acceptance. "Mama, didn't you hear me?"

Her mother looked ghostly, a lightbulb flickering in and out of life. She hurried about the room in her white nightgown, gathering salve and bandages from the armoire's top shelf.

Gretchen squinted, trying to bring the room into focus. What was wrong with her sight? Gingerly, she touched her eyes, feeling the bulging curve of her left eye. It had already swollen closed.

Bile streamed up her throat. As she started retching, her mother whipped a water pitcher under her mouth. She vomited into it. The acidic liquid burned her throat.

Exhausted, she sank back onto her mother's bed. Her entire body had started shaking uncontrollably. But her body seemed to belong to another person; her mind was floating somewhere near the ceiling.

"I'm sure Reinhard didn't mean to hurt you." Mama put the pitcher on the nightstand, then busied herself at the bureau, dipping a washcloth into the water basin. "He doesn't understand things as we do, Gretchen. I shall have a talk with him."

Gretchen froze. Surely she couldn't have heard correctly. "Mama, don't you see *what he did to me*?"

"He's always been an impulsive boy who doesn't know his own strength." Mama dabbed Gretchen's face with the washcloth. "I'll make him understand his behavior was unacceptable."

Gretchen's good eye widened. Mama was taking his side. Again. Even when she, Gretchen, sat in front of her, bruised and broken and bloodied. With Reinhard still in the next room. She could hear the rustle of paper. He was reading his magazine again.

"No!" She had to force the words past her already swelling lips. "Make him go, Mama. He can't stay here."

"This is his home. Why do you think we never moved to Dachau, to stay with my parents, after Papa died? They didn't want Reinhard. I can no more choose between my children than

I can choose which limb to cut off." She reached for Gretchen with the washcloth. "You and Reinhard shall have to work out your differences."

"Our differences?" Gretchen choked out. Panic locked her throat. Nothing was ever going to change. She had to get out. She pushed her mother's hands away.

"Gretchen—" Mama started to say, but Gretchen staggered out of the room. Her heart hammered when she glanced at Reinhard's door. Closed. Every nerve in her body screamed to get away from him. She forced her aching body up the stairs, back to her room, as fast as she could. There was no one in the hallway, and she half ran, half fell into her room.

She pushed the chair into its nighttime position, blocking the door. Then she rested her back against the wall, closing her eyes and breathing deeply. Gradually, she felt her body beginning to burn with new pains: stinging mouth, throbbing palms, a pulsing eye, wrenched arm sockets, aching back.

She dipped a washcloth into the basin. Slowly, carefully, she cleaned her face, trying not to notice as the water turned pale pink, then red. The washcloth, though it was soft from years of use, felt rough on her raw skin. When she had finished, she inspected herself in the mirror.

It wasn't nearly as bad as she had expected. Her mouth was split and puffy but—she ran her tongue experimentally along her gums—that seemed to be the worst of it. None of her teeth were loose. Her left eye was swollen and already sealed shut. By morning, it would probably be blackened, but there was nothing she could do about it now. Her hands and knees were scraped from her fall, but soon the skin would heal. Within a week, maybe two, she should look presentable.

She had no luggage, and Papa's ancient valise was somewhere in the cellar. All she could find was an old burlap sack she used for the market, but it would have to do. Two blouses, a skirt, a nightgown, and some underclothes went into it, along with her life's savings—twelve marks, pitiful.

She placed Daniel Cohen's letter in her bag, too. She wrapped Striped Peterl's body in an ancient woolen sweater she had outgrown, and laid him on top.

Her banged-up fingers protested when she drew the curtain aside. The first stars had winked into life. The hour was earlier than she would have liked, but if she waited, she would lose her nerve. It had to be now.

As she crept down the stairs, each wooden creak jolted her heart. What if Reinhard heard, and came out, and . . . She couldn't finish the thought. She couldn't imagine what else he could possibly do to her.

The steps groaned. Someone was coming up. She shrank against the wall, trying to hear over the sound of her hammering heart. A light footfall. Not Reinhard.

Whitestone rounded the curving staircase, reaching the landing where she waited. His spectacles gleamed in the darkness. Behind his glasses, his eyes grew wide.

He said something in English she didn't understand before switching to German. "My God, you've been badly hurt." He shook his head, looking furious. "Your brother. Curse my reticence! I should have warned you. Are you all right—"

"I must go," she said, and rushed past him. Down the steps as fast as she could, her already aching legs screaming with every step. From the parlor, the old ladies called to her, but she ignored them and went straight to the empty kitchen. She snatched her mother's soup ladle from a drawer and fetched her father's ancient bicycle from the back steps, wheeling it through the front hallway to the street outside.

Balancing the bundle on her lap, she bicycled across the broad avenue into the Englischer Garten. At this late hour, the place was nearly empty.

As she cycled along the twisting path, she passed the occasional couple kissing in the shadows, and a solitary man wending his way home after a long day's work. In the distance, voices chattered from the beer garden around the Chinese Tower, and far off, streetcars clanged. But she felt alone, as though a protective invisible bubble separated her from everyone and everything else.

Soon she reached a cluster of trees near the Monopteros Temple. She wheeled the bicycle off the path and stopped under a towering chestnut. It had been her father's favorite tree. When she was quite small, they sometimes picnicked here on Sunday afternoons. Once they had eaten, her father would stretch himself out on the grass and she would rest her head on his chest and feel very special because he would tell her stories, memories of his childhood in Dachau and proposing to her mother, and moving to Munich to find his fortune, and his kindly parents who had died during the great influenza outbreak of 1919.

Other fathers didn't share those stories with their daughters; they told them to their sons. But Papa rarely talked to Reinhard, instead circling him warily, like a man confronting a wild animal, striking out whenever Reinhard's peculiar behavior unsettled his own precarious grip on his temper. Such as the time Reinhard pushed a neighborhood girl down the front steps because he wanted to see if she would cry. Or the time Reinhard used a magnifying glass to burn ants crawling across a sidewalk, because he wanted to time how long it took them to die.

Those days, Papa didn't bother using his belt, as he usually did; he beat Reinhard with his fists, crying the whole time until, finally, he sagged against the wall, muttering to Mama, "Liesel, something's broken inside this boy, and not even my discipline can fix him." And all the while, Reinhard watched them—curled in the corner, his arms clutched around his bruised body, his eyes dry, his face cold.

Gretchen started to dig the heels of her hands into her eyes, to scrub the image away, but the shooting pain in her left eye socket stopped her. She focused on her task. Living from instant to instant would keep her sane.

The soup ladle made a decent shovel, and soon she had a large enough hole for Striped Peterl. Gently, she lowered him into the ground. The thought of his body decomposing, becoming one with the rich earth, steadied her. She had given him a good resting place, beneath the sky he had loved watching from her bedroom window. She patted the earth back into place, trying not to listen to the soft dirt raining down on his body, covering him forever. Finished, she stared down at the mound of dirt and grass.

Tears sparked her eyes. No, she mustn't stop; she mustn't think or she would be paralyzed. She brushed off the ladle, dropped it back into the bag, and eased her weeping body onto the bicycle. There was only one person she could go to now, the man who had always loved her and who had promised to protect the Müller family after Papa died.

She turned southeast, in the direction of the Prinzregentenstrasse. Uncle Dolf would still be awake.

# 18

HITLER LIVED IN THE PRINZREGENTENPLATZ, ONE of Munich's most fashionable squares, in a large gray building surrounded by tall trees. Some windows were open, their lace curtains snapping in the nighttime breeze. The house was reminiscent of sun-filled summer days, of sands bleached white and waves crashing on a quiet shore, and of pale linen dresses. It was a house, Gretchen thought as she hopped off her bicycle and wheeled it toward the foyer, for those who took things for granted.

She dragged the bicycle up the curved tile staircase to the second floor. When Hitler's housekeeper answered the knock, she raised her eyebrows but said nothing, and Gretchen was suddenly conscious of her bruised and bloodied face, her torn dress and ragged breathing, and the battered old bicycle resting against the wall.

"Fräulein Müller," said Frau Reichert, "good evening. Have you come to call upon Herr Hitler?"

"Yes. I—I've run into some trouble." The words came out awkwardly through her swollen lips. She sounded like a drunkard. Flushing, she put a hand to her sweat-streaked hair. She could only imagine how she looked to the proper middle-aged lady.

"It appears so." Frau Reichert moved back, gesturing for Gretchen to enter, and when she hesitated, the housekeeper added, "You needn't worry about appearances here, Fräulein Müller. Herr Hitler is a man of the people."

"Thank you," Gretchen said.

They walked into a large parlor filled with massive furniture, dark wood that gleamed with polish, and walls as white as eggshells. The entire room had been drained of color; the only bright spots came from Geli, lounging in red on an enormous sofa, and Uncle Dolf and Herr Hanfstaengl, in dark blue suits, sitting on matching chairs and laughing heartily over some shared joke. They must have changed for dinner after getting home from the picnic, for they wore fresh, formal clothes.

They froze when they saw her.

"Fräulein Gretchen Müller," Frau Reichert announced, unnecessarily, and retreated, her footsteps fading into the quiet that always seemed to coat the apartment like a layer of paint, muffling every sound.

Both men rose. Uncle Dolf stretched out his hand. "Gretchen?" he said uncertainly, as though he didn't recognize her.

His hand, reaching toward her, was enough to break her.

"Uncle Dolf," she choked out, all her pains forgotten as she ran to him and flung her arms around his shoulders, dropping her burlap sack on the floor. "Please help me! Mama and I can't take it any longer. We need you—"

"Tut, tut, what is all this?" He stepped backward, out of her embrace, his gaze scraping over her bloodied and blackened face before it focused on a far point on the opposite wall.

She couldn't hold the words back any longer. "Reinhard did this." Her jaw throbbed, but she forced herself to go on. "I made him angry, and he beat me." She waved a hand across her face, letting the bruises speak. "My mother and I live in constant fear of him. He isn't like other people. He—" She paused, struggling as her voice careened out of control. "He's a monster—"

She broke off, realizing how silent the room had become. Uncle Dolf continued staring at some far-off point, his eyes never meeting hers. Hanfstaengl looked at his huge hands, braced on his knees. Geli sat on the edge of a sofa cushion, her eyes trained on Gretchen's face, her fingers twisting a handkerchief into a rope.

Gretchen recognized Hitler's expression—he was uncomfortable. She had embarrassed him. He had been enjoying an evening at home, laughing and telling stories with a guest and a relative, and she had shoved herself into his apartment, babbling tearfully.

Slowly, she took several deep breaths, concentrating on the whoosh of air in and out of her lungs. Uncle Dolf's old calming trick worked; she felt far steadier. She had to maintain her self-control. Uncle Dolf couldn't stand hysterical females.

"I apologize," she said. "I shouldn't have burst in like this." She held her hands out, cupping them like bowls and moving them in tempo with her words, as Uncle Dolf had taught her to do when she wanted to sway others' opinions. "I came to you for help, Uncle Dolf, because I can't live with my brother any longer. He's malicious and cruel. The smallest things make him go mad. Tonight, he strangled my cat and attacked me because I angered him. He's found secret ways to punish me and my mother for years and then pretended to be innocent so convincingly that we thought we were losing our minds—"

Uncle Dolf interrupted. "What did you do to anger him?"

She must have misheard. "I beg your pardon?"

"You did something to anger him," Uncle Dolf said, his eyes finally focusing on hers. His eyelids had slid to half mast, a sure signal he was grappling with a strong emotion. "What was it?"

"I—I went into his room without his permission. But—"

"Reinhard is the man of the house." The forbidding expression smoothed itself out. Uncle Dolf sat down, straightening his suit jacket with a quick jerk of his hand. "A man must discipline his family as he sees fit."

*Discipline?* She ran a hand over her face, touching the tender bulge of her closing and blackening eye and the puffy outline of her split lips. She felt, rather than saw, Hanfstaengl guide her down onto the overstuffed couch beside Geli.

Uncle Dolf couldn't be saying these things. Not the kindly friend who taught her about art and let her play his piano and tugged her braid. Not the beloved uncle who had visited her family the day after he was released from prison, with Christmas gifts of chocolates and tea, and who had told them, with tears in his eyes, he would never forget his dear comrade Klaus Müller's sacrifice. He had promised he would protect them.

She folded her hands in her lap, tightly, to stop their trembling. For the first time, she noticed dots of blood on her dress, little red circles against the white. A dull roaring filled her ears. She feared she would be sick, right here, on his parlor floor.

"Unless you change your ways," Uncle Dolf said sternly, "you'll be an unwelcome challenge for a man, a hindrance rather than a tonic, an opponent rather than a pleasure."

He stopped, clearly waiting for her to say something. All of her felt numb but her lips, which ached when she said, "Yes, Uncle Dolf."

She couldn't look at him. Instead she stared at the table, reflected lamplight glowing in the polished wood. It was such a beautiful table. In a luxurious apartment, filled with fine furniture and paintings—unusual choices for a man who professed to want nothing for his own comfort. She had never noticed before how little Uncle Dolf's apartment seemed to mirror his stated preferences.

Narrowing her good eye, she raised her head and stared at him. He had leaned back in his chair, waving his right hand as he spoke, the image of a genial, good-natured host. Smiling like a kindly schoolmaster lecturing his students. Talking at them without waiting for their responses. Had he ever asked for her opinion? She couldn't remember.

Beaming, Hitler nodded. "Very good, my sunshine. It's time for you to consider marriage. Every girl ought to; if she waits too long before having children, she will become sick and hysterical. I suppose there's a handsome, strapping fellow waiting in the wings for you?"

She shook her head. "No, there is no one." *No one at all.*

He waggled a finger mischievously. "That shall soon change. I'll find someone suitable for you. An SS chap, so he's sure to be racially pure. It's very important, to me and to the Party, for you to marry the right sort. A young fellow who's destined to become a leader within the NSDAP. Think what a fine couple you would make, a shining example to the others of your generation! Of course, you're young yet. But you should marry soon; every German man and woman should. Though not me, of course. Germany is my great love."

She opened her mouth to speak, but there was nothing to say.

Footsteps sounded from the corridor. Frau Reichert appeared, carrying a tray laden with drinks: mineral water for Hitler, beer for Hanfstaengl, and a pot of weak tea for Gretchen and Geli.

Once the tea had been poured, Hitler turned to Geli, inquiring about yesterday's singing lesson, and Gretchen realized the previous conversation was over. Uncle Dolf had said all he wished to say on the subject, and they would now move on to more pleasant topics.

So she sat, holding the cup of tea and listening to the talk swirl about her like a creek's current, and she the stone breaking the water's flow. All of her aches started to awaken again.

The realization sank in: She wasn't safe. She had always assumed Uncle Dolf would save her and Mama; once he knew the truth, he would punish Reinhard or send him away.

But he hadn't. He wouldn't.

And now Reinhard would find out she had gone to Uncle Dolf for help and been refused; he would know she had risked damaging his reputation and dirtying his name.

There was nowhere she could go, no one she could ask for protection. She was trapped.

"Singing class was deadly dull today, Uncle Alf," Geli said.

Her hand brushed against Gretchen's knee as she reached for the sugar bowl, and she murmured, "You're breathing quite fast. Try to calm yourself."

Brightly, she went on. "But the pistol lesson was such a lark! Gretchen, my uncle's arranged for Henny and me to have weapons training. We practice shooting at a rifle range just outside the city. Yesterday, Uncle Alf, they taught us how to clean Walthers. We took them completely apart and put them back together again. We felt like characters out of a Western film!"

Uncle Dolf laughed heartily, then grew serious. "These lessons are not meant to be larks, Geli. Every moment, I must guard against assassination. The danger is real. Always, always"—he slammed a fist into an open palm for emphasis—"we must watch for the enemy."

Geli rolled her eyes. "Honestly, Uncle Alf, nobody wants to kill me—"

"*Ach*, there you are wrong. I have many opponents, and most would not hesitate to murder me and, by extension, you. You must never forget that. Already I have survived at least ten assassination attempts this year. They shall not succeed, naturally, as the good hand of Providence protects me. But others' safety is not guaranteed." He turned to Hanfstaengl. "My nerves are bad tonight."

"Shall I be the performing monkey this evening?" Hanfstaengl's smile was mocking, but he crossed to the grand piano and stretched his long fingers over the keys. "My piano playing always soothes you, Herr Hitler. Shall it be Wagner?"

"Always, always Wagner." Hitler settled back into his chair, closing his eyes in anticipation.

The music seemed to go on and on, a violent cascade of notes. Gretchen sat motionless, trying not to think or feel. Suddenly the utter ridiculousness of the situation struck her: Here she was, sitting in Hitler's parlor wearing a ripped, bloodied dress and gripping a teacup with battered hands, listening politely while the music swelled and others sipped their drinks. They looked like a painting, and she, the figure who had been sketched in by mistake.

Geli leaned close, sending a wash of lilac perfume wafting across Gretchen's face.

"Don't worry," she whispered. "You can bunk with me. You shouldn't go home tonight. As for this"—she glanced at Uncle Dolf, nodding in his armchair, one hand conducting an invisible orchestra—"this could go on for hours."

Geli was right; it was nearly two in the morning when Hitler rose. Gretchen was so exhausted, she could scarcely sit upright. Hitler thanked Hanfstaengl for his excellent piano playing, then glanced at her.

"And Gretchen . . . ," he said, clearly at a loss, when Geli spoke up.

"She shall spend the night here, naturally, Uncle Alf. It's too late for her to travel home."

"And I'm afraid she won't fit on my handlebars," Hanfstaengl added.

"When will you ever get a car, Hanfstaengl?" Uncle Dolf demanded.

"When people start buying art again." He looked irritated.

"It is this foul Communism!" Uncle Dolf exclaimed. "Its goal is the destruction of all non-Jewish national states. Communism plans to systemically hand the world over to the Jews. Everywhere we see its loathsome effects—"

"Please, Uncle Alf," Geli cut in, "anything but politics at two in the morning."

He looked annoyed. But then she smiled and looped her arm through his, and he laughed. "Very well, Geli." He patted her cheek. "I know this sort of talk is dull for you girls."

"Good night." Hanfstaengl ambled toward the corridor. "I'll see myself out. Gretchen, a word, please."

She followed him toward the foyer. In the dim light, she noticed the chair in the corner, where Uncle Dolf always deposited the three things he never left his apartment without: his whip, pistol, and cartridge belt. For the first time, she noticed how odd they appeared, resting on a wooden chair in a finely appointed foyer.

Hanfstaengl swung round to face her. All the laughter and merriment had fled from his features. Looming above her in the darkness, he was such a massive figure she took an instinctive step back. But when he spoke, his voice was so gentle she scarcely recognized it.

"You needn't come into work until your face is healed. I shan't let anyone know so you can receive your full pay."

The gesture was so kind and unexpected she only managed a surprised thank-you.

"Good night," he said, and she echoed the words before walking back into the dark parlor.

Geli slept in a corner bedroom beside Hitler's, hers the only room in the apartment with any color. Its pale green walls were dotted with watercolors. One was a Belgian landscape her uncle had painted during the Great War, Geli said as they changed into their nightgowns.

"It's lovely," Gretchen said mechanically. She felt like a machine that was breaking down, all of her movements automatic but painfully slow. "Your room is the finest I've ever seen," she added.

It was true. Of all her friends' bedchambers, Geli's was by far the most beautiful: delicate wooden furniture, embroidered bedsheets, a vanity table crowded with bottles and pots, a bureau where necklaces lay heaped together, a *Hakenkreuz*, the twin of Gretchen's, gleaming at the top.

"I call it my pastel prison." Geli smiled crookedly. "Oh, I'm sorry, you mustn't mind me; it's *you* that we must concentrate on tonight. You've had a beastly time of it, but a good night's rest will do marvels." She guided Gretchen into a chair. "You poor dear! Having to sit for hours when you haven't even had a proper wash. Isn't that just like Uncle Alf, not to pay attention to anyone else when Herr Hanfstaengl starts with his wretched piano playing! I declare, if I have to hear anything of Wagner's again, I shall throw a fit."

As she spoke, she washed Gretchen's face gently. The cloth was made of such fine cotton, it scarcely scraped Gretchen's skin at all. Gretchen closed her good eye, feeling tears leak out. Such simple kindness seemed incredible after the night she had had.

Geli made soothing, sympathetic sounds as she spread salve across Gretchen's burning hands and knees and bandaged them. "There, there," she murmured. "You'll take a headache powder, too."

She took a small, paper-wrapped packet from her vanity table and dissolved its contents in a glass of water. "Drink up, poor thing. This will blunt the worst of the pain."

The tears came faster now, sliding down in silence. Somehow, she had been able to bear everything except for Geli's gentle goodness. "Thank you," she whispered. "You've helped me so much."

"Nonsense. Any half-decent person would do the same. Men can be such monsters." An emotion Gretchen couldn't identify tightened Geli's round face for an instant. "Let's get you into bed, shall we?"

Geli pulled back the sheets. A big feather bed, soft as a cloud—Gretchen had never slept on one before. It took her two tries to clamber onto the mattress, because her aching legs screamed each time she tried to lift them. Embarrassment burned her already inflamed face, and she was glad when Geli snapped off the lamp, plunging the room into darkness.

"Uncle Alf is an insomniac," Geli said, the mattress sighing as she settled herself on her side. "He wanders the hallway for hours at night, so you mustn't be frightened if you hear him walking up and down the corridor. Good night," she added.

They sank into silence. Soon Geli's breathing deepened into the slow, regular rhythm of the slumbering. The whisper of footsteps in the corridor started. Uncle Dolf, pacing. Gretchen yearned for the oblivion of sleep. How much she longed to fall down its dark well, far from the pains and fears keeping her awake.

For a long time, she stared at the ceiling, listening to Uncle Dolf's soft footsteps. With her injured eye swollen shut, her sight had sharpened again. The thought relieved her enormously. If she could see, even if it was with only one eye, she could protect herself. She wouldn't be caught off-guard again. She would attack first.

Uncle Dolf's footfalls sounded in the corridor, the muted padding of slippered feet. If she could speak to him alone, without an audience for whom he had to wear a stern face, she was certain he would help her. She slipped from the bed. With an unsteady hand, she reached for the doorknob.

He stood at the far end of the corridor. In the shadows, he was little more than a dark wall.

"Uncle Dolf?" she whispered.

When he didn't respond, she walked toward him. With each step, he grew clearer, and she saw he wore striped pajamas and a belted bathrobe. His face was impassive, his hair mussed and hanging over his forehead.

"Gretchen, you should be asleep." He shook his head, smiling lightly, like a parent exasperated with a favorite child.

"I couldn't sleep. I needed to speak with you again." Only hours ago, she would have embraced him as she had as a little girl—throwing herself into his arms and imagining he could shield her from all the world's wrongs. Now she didn't touch him. "Please, Uncle Dolf, there is only one person whom Reinhard would possibly listen to and that is you. If you could speak to him about his behavior, he would change—"

"Stop this foolishness." His voice was so angry, she instinctively took a step back. "Gretchen, I have no wish to become entangled in your family's petty domestic squabbles. We shan't speak of this again."

The fury seemed to pump off his body in waves; she practically felt it, as though his emotion were a physical presence. She opened her mouth to protest, but the iciness of his eyes stopped her. She bowed her head and whispered, "Yes, Uncle Dolf."

He brushed past her. She heard his door click open and shut; she was alone.

Moving with the dazed gait of a sleepwalker, Gretchen went back into Geli's room and stood at the window. She twitched aside the curtain and looked down at the slumbering city. Somewhere, on the wall's other side, a few feet away from her, was Uncle Dolf, perhaps trying to sleep or standing at his window, staring at the houses' jagged outline against the moonlit sky. Only a few feet away, and yet it might have been miles.

She stood on the edge of night, that sliver of gray between darkness and dawn, that razor-thin line separating the first part of her life and whatever lay ahead.

There were only a few hours left before sunrise. She couldn't return home; she had no allies, no beloved family friend to help her, no money to leave the city, no means to escape from her brother. She had to figure out how to get away from Reinhard. Forever.

# 19

DAWN BROKE, PALE GRAY AND RINGED WITH SOOT. From the bed, Gretchen watched the shadows on the ceiling grow thinner as the sun rose. Around three, she had crawled back onto the mattress and tried to sleep, finally managing to slide into a dreamless dozing. At seven, when Geli rose, Gretchen's right eye felt gritty from exhaustion, and her blackened left eye beat with a constant throbbing.

All of the aches had swum beneath her skin, settling into her bones, and the effort required to stand and dress seemed substantial. Geli had to help button her blouse. When Gretchen saw the ruined white dress, crumpled in a corner, spotted with rust-colored blood, her stomach lurched. She was glad she had brought extra clothes; the thought of putting the white sundress on again made her bruised skin want to crawl right off her bones.

They ate in the dining room without Uncle Dolf. He wouldn't

rise until ten or eleven, Geli said as she heaped strawberry marmalade onto her toast. So they had hours to fill any way they chose, and perhaps Gretchen would like to join her in shopping along the Maximilianstrasse, Geli's treat.

After everything Gretchen had been through last night, the notion of strolling Munich's most fashionable street, ducking into boutiques to try on hats as Geli always insisted on doing, struck her as so foreign that she had to struggle not to burst into hysterical laughter. Somehow, she managed to murmur, no, she couldn't impose further. Embarrassment heated her cheeks when Geli glanced at her, apologizing and adding quietly that naturally Gretchen wouldn't wish to be seen until she healed.

Gretchen concentrated on the potato pancakes and sausages. Each bite hurt, but she forced the mouthfuls down. She didn't know when she would eat so well, or so much, again, for she couldn't imagine going back to the boardinghouse.

After breakfast, she thanked Geli, gathered her burlap sack, and wheeled her bicycle down the staircase. When she opened the front door and stuck her head out, peering around the square, her heart hammered.

Businessmen left beautiful old buildings for work, sleek automobiles slid away from the curb, and a trio of doves fluttered around the statue of Hitler's favorite composer, Richard Wagner. No Reinhard. No flash of brown uniforms, no tramp of boots on the pavement. None of his SA comrades. Either they didn't know where she was, or they didn't care.

The church bells were chiming eight when she reached the Hohenzollernstrasse. Herr Braun answered the apartment door, dressed in shirtsleeves and trousers and carrying a cup of coffee in one hand. His eyes traveled over her battered face, his mouth slackening in shock.

"Gretchen? Whatever has happened, poor child? Was it an automobile accident?"

"Not exactly." She couldn't tell him the truth; most likely he would be horrified and embarrassed, muttering about dirty laundry best kept within the family. She would expect such a reaction from the strict Herr Braun.

But not from her beloved Uncle Dolf. Tears rose in her throat. She had to swallow several times before she could go on. "May I speak to Eva, please?"

He stepped into the hall, pulling the door halfway closed. "I must be frank with you, Gretchen. I know you've been gallivanting about with this fellow Hitler, and he's not a suitable companion for girls your age. He thinks he sucked in wisdom with his mother's milk. I fear he is a bad influence on you . . . so I really must insist you leave my daughter alone for a time."

She must have heard wrong. Herr Braun had complained about Hitler for a long time, but had always accepted her and Eva's friendship. "I beg your pardon?"

He shifted uncomfortably. "I know our families have been friends for years, but I don't like the change in my Eva's behavior and I am sure it's the effect of this Austrian upstart. Until you distance yourself from him, I must ask you to stay away from Eva."

She had hoped for tears and embraces, not this quiet dismissal.

"Papa?" Eva's voice came from within the apartment. "Who's at the door?"

Herr Braun's eyes met Gretchen's. "No one."

She couldn't speak. She didn't think she could move, but

somehow she turned and started walking. Pain radiated up her legs with every step. She was halfway down the hallway when she heard Herr Braun close the door.

Thirteen years of friendship brushed aside in an instant. Thirteen years, and she didn't matter.

Sadness weighed heavily, like a chain around her neck. She mustn't think or she wouldn't be able to keep moving.

The avenue widened. Suddenly, she was surrounded: throngs of Müncheners marching along the pavement, automobiles and pushcarts and bicycles and streetcars choking the street. She was merely part of the scene, an anonymous girl astride a decrepit bicycle.

No, not anonymous. Maybe she didn't matter enough to the Brauns, certainly not enough to her mother and Uncle Dolf, and definitely not at all to Reinhard. But she mattered to herself. And that was all that needed to be true. She would figure something out.

In that instant, as she pedaled along, she wondered about her father's expression in his final photograph—the whipped-puppy look as he followed Hitler and the others into the Bürgerbräukeller. In those last hours of his life, had he somehow been hurt and betrayed by his dearest friend, as she had been hurt and betrayed by the same man last night? As she had been hurt and betrayed by everyone she thought mattered?

Again, she imagined her father falling in the snow, his body accidentally shielding Uncle Dolf's, his blood darkening the cobblestones. She saw him kneeling with her in the kitchen, smiling as she cuddled Striped Peterl; she felt his lips brush her cheek in a final kiss. And she knew what she had to do.

# 20

ALTHEIMER ECK WAS A SHORT, CRESCENT-SHAPED street lined with a jumble of stucco and stone buildings. Gretchen coasted to a stop before number 19, which housed the offices of the *Munich Post*. A plain structure, with nothing about its unremarkable appearance to announce that the reporters whom Uncle Dolf despised most in the world worked behind those heavy walls.

A warm breeze kicked up. Even its light pressure burned against her scraped skin. Her heart had clambered into her throat, and she could scarcely breathe around it.

What she was about to do should seem wrong. It broke every single rule her parents had taught her. And once she stepped forward—once she asked Herr Cohen to help her, when no one else had been willing—she would cut every rope tying her to her old life.

And she knew it.

She took a deep breath, preparing to count to three. She got to two before she remembered that the calming trick was one of Uncle Dolf's. She'd rather hyperventilate than owe him anything.

She started to wheel the cycle across the empty street. Number 19's front door opened and Daniel Cohen stepped out. He was reading a newspaper and eating an apple as he walked down the front steps.

"Herr Cohen!" she called.

She knew the instant he recognized her. He stiffened, his entire body stilling. Then, with deliberate movements, he pitched the apple core into a waste bin, folded the newspaper into a rectangle and slipped it into a back pocket, and waited, watching her.

Her legs felt rubbery as she walked the bicycle toward him.

His gaze flickered over her face. His expression didn't change, but remained hard and focused. "Who did this to you?"

She wouldn't lie to him anymore; she wouldn't lie ever again. "My brother."

"Why did he do it?"

The old familiar excuses jumped into her mouth—*because I made him angry; because he's troubled and needs our understanding; because he's the man of the house*—but she swallowed them all. "Because he's cruel."

His face didn't soften, as she had hoped, and he didn't offer soothing platitudes, as she had half expected. Instead he nodded, as though she had passed an important test. "Why'd you come to me?"

"Because I have no one else to go to." Admitting such a thing to a Jew should have shamed her. But she had no feelings left. "Herr Cohen, I wouldn't blame you if you told me to leave you alone and never speak to you again. But I need help. Please."

For a long moment, his eyes held hers. There was no warmth in his, no sympathy or kindness, just a measuring gaze. "You look ready to collapse," he said at last. He placed his hands over her bandaged ones. "Let me wheel this to the nearest streetcar stop."

"Where are we going?" She fell into step beside him.

"The last place any of your National Socialist friends would look for you."

The northeast section of Munich belonged to the Communists. Small storefronts with wooden shutters and Cyrillic letters painted on the doors lined the streets. The signs of faded blue and red and gold looked so different from the Bavarian banners of blue and white that Gretchen was accustomed to seeing flying from cafés.

A group of Communist students, instantly recognizable in their black shirts and red bow ties, marched along the Kaiserstrasse. She might have been in Russia, and she understood now why Reinhard had forbidden her to visit this part of the city.

Cohen led her inside a shabby, two-story stone building. Unfamiliar Russian letters covered a hand-lettered sign on the nearest door in the lobby. Inside, a few folding chairs sat against the wall of a small room. A woman sitting at a desk, typing laboriously with two fingers, looked up when they came in. She said something in Russian to Cohen, and he nodded, jerking his head at Gretchen. She folded her arms protectively across her chest. What was this place?

"Come," the woman said in German, rising and motioning for Gretchen to follow.

She dug panicked fingers into Cohen's arm. "Where are we?"

"A doctor's office," he said. "On the streetcar, all you would say was a friend had bandaged you up. Those injuries look serious, Fräulein Müller. You need to have them looked at."

Out of all the people she had gone to for help, he was the only one who had suggested taking her to a doctor. Tears welled in her good eye. He was the only one who had cared enough. A Jew, caring for her. *A travesty or a lie*, Uncle Dolf would say.

It was a miracle.

She found her voice. "Thank you." Suddenly she felt so humbled by Cohen's decency, she couldn't look at him. "Please, will you come with me?" The thought of being alone with a strange doctor while he examined her humiliating injuries seemed intolerable.

"I can't."

"Please," she said again. "I trust you."

Only yesterday, the words would have cut her ears. Today, they felt comfortable and right.

Cohen shot her a glance, looking startled. Then he half smiled, and said something in Russian to the receptionist. She answered sharply. For a moment, they argued, then the woman gave up with a shrug and beckoned them down a dingy hallway.

"I didn't know you spoke Russian," Gretchen said. The comment sounded so inane, she ducked her head.

He grinned. "Just enough to get into bar fights."

They were ushered into a tiny office. The doctor, a middle-aged man with thinning hair, spoke no German, and as he tried to communicate with Cohen, she realized the boy hadn't been lying—he knew very little Russian. They resorted to pantomime, and the doctor motioned for her to hop onto the examining table.

"It's just my face and hands and legs," she said when the doctor mimed taking off his shirt. Heat pushed into her cheeks. "There's no need for me to remove my clothes."

She waved a wrapped hand around her face and knees until the doctor seemed to understand. Cohen shoved his hands in his pockets, rocking back on his heels, the image of insouciance. Pink colored the tips of his ears.

If Gretchen could have smiled, she would have. He was embarrassed, too. Somehow, knowing he could be embarrassed about nakedness made him seem even more normal, more human.

"The fellow doesn't speak a word of German," Cohen said, still studying the brownish water stains on the ceiling. "Do you think you can manage to tell me what happened? He won't understand what you're saying."

She winced as the doctor unwound the bandage covering her knee. The bleeding had stopped long ago, but the skin still looked raw.

Cohen must have taken her silence for uncertainty, for he bent slightly so his dark eyes met her good one. "Fräulein Müller," he said softly, "why did your brother dare to put his hands on you?"

His gentle voice and quiet face loosened the lump in her chest. As the doctor inspected her injuries, she told Cohen everything that had happened—finding her cat dead, confronting Reinhard, surviving his beating, being turned away by everyone she thought would help. The story came out haltingly. Several times, she had to stop to compose herself.

He didn't interrupt once. When she finished, the doctor was wrapping fresh gauze around her hands. He spoke quietly to Cohen, who translated.

"The doctor says the worst of your injuries is to your eye. Ice should help. Morphine would help with the pain, too, but he doesn't have any at the moment, so he says headache powders can give you some relief. The eye should clear up within two weeks, one if you're fortunate. You'll need to change the dressings on your knees and hands for the next two days, but after that, they should be fine." The boy hesitated. "He says you were lucky. Whoever did this to you is very strong."

The image of Reinhard, looming above her, eyes and teeth gleaming in the darkness, flashed through her head. Revulsion twisted her stomach. *Lucky.* In a strange way, she had been. The beating could have been much worse.

And now she knew whom she could trust.

"Thank you," she said to the doctor. "How much do I owe?" She fumbled with her pocketbook. Only twelve marks—how could she possibly pay this doctor and stretch her money toward the expense of a rooming house?

"I'll deal with the payment." Cohen brushed aside her protests. "I'm the one who insisted on your seeing a doctor, so I'll handle it. Why don't you go on to the waiting room?"

In the small room, the receptionist pressed a scribbled note into her hand. "Is church address," she said in stilted German. "For hiding from bad man who hurt you."

This woman's willingness to help her, a stranger, humbled Gretchen. She was thanking her when Cohen came in. Together, they went out into the summer sunlight.

Skinny, hollow-cheeked men stood at the corner, smoking, a bucket of water at their feet, rags in their hands, ready to leap forward to wash a stopped car's windshield for a few pfennigs. Cafés' red-and-black banners snapped in the breeze.

Alone with Cohen, Gretchen found that shyness silenced her tongue. What must he think of her, with a monster for a brother, and so unloved that all of her friends had abandoned her? How could she have laid herself bare before him, when she still knew almost nothing about his life?

Maybe he was already mentally writing an article about her.

"I—I should go," she stammered. "Thank you very much for paying the doctor. Once I've settled somewhere and saved up a bit, I shall repay you."

"Where are you planning on going?"

The sky's bright blueness hurt her wounded eye. Protectively, she curled her hand over the battered eye socket, conscious of the curious looks of passersby. What a sight she must present: blackened eye, bandaged hands and knees, the imprint of her brother's hand still pink on her cheek. She wished she could crawl into a darkened room and never come out.

"I don't know. Somewhere. I can't go back. I'll find a rooming house somewhere, I suppose. Herr Hanfstaengl said I could return to the Braunes Haus as soon as I was well, but I might bump into Reinhard there. . . ." Her voice started to shake.

"You can stay with me," Cohen said.

She stopped walking. Stay with a Jew. In the same apartment, under the same roof, bound by the same walls. She couldn't. She saw Uncle Dolf's face last night, cold and distant, his eyes fastened on the wall while she stood before him in her bloodied dress.

She knew how he thought. Now it was her turn to figure out her own mind.

Cohen was smiling at her. "I can't promise the food will be very good, or even edible, depending on whose turn it is to cook, but it'll be hot. I share an apartment with my cousins," he added. "One of whom is a girl, which would lend the whole arrangement an air of respectability. The setup could work to our advantage if you could teach any of us to cook. We're rather hopeless in the kitchen, I'm afraid."

To her surprise, she laughed. The movement tugged on her sore mouth, but she didn't care. How had he disarmed her so completely with a few casual words and a smile?

She considered the boy beside her. A breeze had kicked up, ruffling the brown strands that had escaped from the newsboy cap he was wearing today and hung over his forehead. His clear, dark eyes met hers without hesitation, as though he had nothing to hide. He was nothing like the monster she had been taught about. He was *human*.

Once the thought would have terrified her. Now she felt it lifting her heart up, back to where it belonged.

She couldn't force her battered lips into a smile. But she hoped he knew she would smile if she could. "Thank you," she said. She kept her voice light, as he had. "With such an appetizing endorsement, how could I refuse? And yes, I can cook, and quite well. You can't be brought up preparing meals every day in a boardinghouse without learning how."

"Splendid. That's settled, then."

They fell into step again, Cohen wheeling the bicycle between them. Up ahead, a streetcar trundled along the avenue, and he started to hurry to catch it before glancing back at her and slowing his pace. She was grateful for his consideration, since each step pulled on her throbbing knees.

Overhead, pigeons tilted in a bright blue sky, and somewhere, church bells rang the hour, twelve long, low notes reverberating in the warm air. Finally, Cohen spoke again. "Once you throw in your lot with me, you can't go back. I need to know: Are you certain you want to go home with me?"

She didn't need to think it over. The one time she had asked something substantial of Hitler, he had pushed her away in disgust and embarrassment. "I'm certain. And my choice isn't because of my brother. I saw something in Uncle Dolf last night, a coldness I didn't expect. If he could turn me aside so easily, when I needed him so badly, what else is he capable of?"

He nodded, but didn't comment. "Since you're coming to my home, shall we drop all this *Fräulein* and *Herr* business? It gets a bit cumbersome."

Heat rushed into her already burning face. She understood what he was proposing. She felt her head nodding yes, even as her heart lurched.

"Good." He glanced at her. "Gretchen."

The sound of her name from his lips seemed so intimate. Shyness forced her gaze to the sidewalk, but she was determined not to be afraid of him, not ever again. "Daniel," she said. His name should have tasted like ash in her mouth, but it was smooth and sweet as honey.

He walked along with that quick, loping stride she already

recognized as distinctively Daniel's. Although the cap shaded his eyes, she somehow knew their expression when he glanced at her—quietly appraising, as if trying to decide whether she was strong enough for whatever loomed before them.

"You realize once you've been to my home, you're dividing yourself from the Party. You won't be able to turn back."

"I know." She raised her chin, feigning a confidence she didn't feel. "You needn't keep giving me chances to back out; I've made my decision."

"Very well, then." Daniel grinned. "Welcome to the other side."

# PART THREE

## IN DESPERATE DEFIANCE

One can try to re-create the world,
to build up in its stead another world
in which its most unbearable features are
eliminated and replaced by others that
are in conformity with one's wishes.
But whoever, in desperate defiance, sets out
upon this path to happiness will as a rule
attain nothing. Reality is too strong for him.
He becomes a madman.

*—Sigmund Freud,*
CIVILIZATION AND ITS DISCONTENTS, *1930*

# 21

DANIEL LIVED ON A SIDE STREET IN THE ISARVORSTADT district. Gretchen's steps faltered when she saw the narrow avenue, crowded with shoddily constructed stone buildings crammed so tightly together that if walls needed to breathe, these would have suffocated years ago.

Although she had spent all of her seventeen years in Munich, she had never walked Isavorstadt's streets, or entered its homes, or frequented its shops. This was where the Eastern European immigrants, mainly Jews, lived.

*Wait*, she wanted to say, but then Daniel's eyes met hers—challenging, as though he knew why she moved more and more slowly—and she raised her head and walked faster, even though her aching legs protested.

The shabby fourth-floor walk-up looked nothing like what Gretchen had expected. She had anticipated vast, luxurious rooms and thick Turkish carpets. But the room she stood in was small and plain, with threadbare furniture and worn pine floors.

"Just because I'm Jewish doesn't mean I'm rich," Daniel said, sounding amused, and Gretchen flushed, turning away from the plain white walls dotted with family photographs and cheap watercolor prints.

"Your home is very nice."

"No, it isn't." He grinned. "It's a hole. But it's fine for me and my cousins."

Confusion hampered her tongue. "You—you shouldn't have paid the doctor." She had assumed he could easily afford the physician's fee, but now, looking about, she knew better.

Daniel smiled easily at her, unaware of her traitorous thoughts. "The fellow owed me a favor, so he wouldn't accept payment anyway. I got wind of some SA men planning to vandalize his office, and warned him. When the SA showed up, they found the good doctor and twenty of his strongest Communist comrades waiting for them." He laughed. "I'm told it was quite a street fight, but the man's office was unharmed, so he's grateful toward me.

"Here, sit for a minute while I hunt my cousins down. Aaron! Ruth!" He moved along the cramped corridor leading to what she presumed were the bedrooms.

The room Gretchen stood in clearly doubled as kitchen and parlor: a small rectangle crowded with a sagging sofa, a scarred round table, and four mismatched chairs. Stacks of books looking ready to topple over covered every surface—the sofa cushions, the table, the narrow strip of kitchen counter. The smell of something spicy wafted from the pot on the tiny stove, and Gretchen was glad for the approaching footsteps that covered her stomach's rumbling.

"These are my cousins, Ruth and Aaron Pearlman. They're students at the university," Daniel said. Two petite teenagers stood with him. They had such lustrous black hair and pale, even features they might have been Snow White and her twin brother brought to life. Both stared at her.

"Aaron, Ruth, this is Fräulein Gretchen Mül—" Daniel started to say when Ruth interrupted.

"I know who she is." Ruth's voice was so filled with venom that Gretchen stepped back. "This is the Nazi you've told us about. What is she doing here?"

"She needs help—" Daniel began.

"A Nazi needs help from Jews? That's rich." Ruth pushed past them toward the stove, where she ladled steaming soup into three bowls. "I don't know what silly sob story you've spun for my cousin, Fräulein, but I promise it won't work on me. You're not welcome here."

This reaction was the one she had half expected. "I'm sorry," Gretchen said. "I didn't mean to cause trouble for you, Daniel—"

*"Daniel?"* Ruth spun around. "She calls you by your first name? Are you actually friends with her?"

"She isn't like the others, Ruth," Daniel said. "Give her a chance."

Ruth tossed the dishtowel onto the counter. "Give the Nazi a chance when her kind is trying to exterminate all of us? I never would have taken you for a fool."

*Exterminate?* Gretchen froze. What the devil was Ruth talking about?

"Ruth, can't you see she's been hurt?" Aaron asked.

"I don't care if she's dying. We know what Hitler is trying to do to us, and if you insist on sheltering her, I'm leaving."

"Ruth, she has nowhere to go."

The truth of Daniel's words hit Gretchen like a punch. He was right; she was alone. Not even the Jews wanted her.

"That's a lie if I ever heard one!" Ruth cried. "Haven't we heard her name bandied about by the Nazis at university often enough, or seen her about town on Hitler's arm? She's his darling golden girl. She must have dozens—no, *hundreds*—of Nazis eager to take her in, in the hopes of getting into Hitler's good graces."

Gretchen flinched. How wrong Ruth was.

"Those bruises you see," Daniel said, "were put there by her brother. When she went to Hitler for help, he turned her away. None of her acquaintances would dare to help her now."

Ruth's gaze flickered over Gretchen again. Gretchen couldn't guess what she was thinking, but finally she said, "Sit down. I'll fix another bowl."

They ate at the tiny table, surrounded by books. The meal was simple—vegetable soup, crusty bread, and beer—but Gretchen found herself as anxious as if she sat at a five-star restaurant and didn't know which fork to use.

Aaron and Ruth said little—they were probably afraid to say much in front of her—but Daniel talked readily. Somehow, he must have sensed her discomfort, sitting in the apartment of people she scarcely knew, and Jews to boot, for he filled the silence, telling her about his life in Berlin.

His childhood had been an easy, comfortable one: He had

grown up in the Waidmannslust district, in a small white house surrounded by cherry and apple trees. He spent hours in the study, reading old fairy tales, classics, foreign authors like Ernest Hemingway and E. M. Forster, and German writers like Thomas Mann and Hermann Hesse. In the evening, he and his three sisters gathered at the kitchen table, the four siblings teasing one another as they finished their homework and their mother cooked dinner and hummed along to the wireless.

His father was an electrician at the Berlin Electric and Power Company, his mother a seamstress, and they had been furious when he graduated from Gymnasium this past spring and announced he wouldn't get a university education after all but would become a reporter. He wanted adventure and action, not classrooms and textbooks, and when he reminded his parents they had taught him to question his beliefs but never himself, they were forced to let him go.

His boyhood sounded like a fairy tale. Gretchen listened, rapt, grateful she didn't have to fumble for conversation. Every bite hurt. Her mouth was so swollen she could scarcely chew, and her throat so sore that each swallow ached.

When the meal was over, Gretchen helped Ruth carry the bowls and cups into the kitchen area. She was filling the sink with a pot of hot water heated on the stove when Ruth left, returning with a bar of soap and a towel.

"Here." Ruth thrust them at her. "I expect a bath will make you feel better."

Gretchen stammered her thanks.

Ruth turned away and started scrubbing the spoons. Her slender back looked stick straight. "Just basic decency." She aimed an annoyed look over her shoulder. *"Would you hurry up!"*

"Yes. Thank you." Gretchen fled.

By the time she returned to the parlor, Ruth and Aaron had already left. "I hope I haven't made you late for work," she said, alarmed when she saw Daniel sitting alone on the sofa, reading.

He smiled and placed a bookmark between the pages. "Do you always worry about everyone else before yourself?"

"I don't know. I suppose."

"It's a miserable habit. You ought to put yourself first sometimes. And no, I'm not late for work; I have a meeting with a potential source, but not for another half hour." Now he looked at her. "I see my cousin's idea of a bath seems to have agreed with you."

She flushed. She knew how improper she must look—her hair wet and holding the tracks of the comb, her legs bare because she had forgotten to pack her other pair of stockings and the ones she had been wearing had been torn when Reinhard threw her to the floor. "It was kind of you and your cousins to have me for luncheon. I shall always be grateful for your hospitality."

He lifted one eyebrow—a trick Gretchen had tried to master as a child but had never managed. "That sounds suspiciously like a farewell speech."

"I was thinking in the bath. . . . There's no way I can stay. Your cousins wouldn't be happy and—"

"That isn't the reason." He watched her steadily. "You've had time to think things over, and the prospect of staying in a Jew's apartment is more than you can stomach, isn't it?"

She felt flustered. "No. Honestly," she added when he looked unconvinced. "I don't want to cause trouble between you and your cousins. I saw Fräulein Pearlman's reaction to me—"

"Ruth reacted that way because the Nazis want to exterminate us."

There was that terrifying word again. "What do you mean?"

He snatched his satchel off the floor and swung it over his shoulder. "You needn't put on a naive act with me, Gretchen. You're far too smart to carry it off. Don't you listen to any of your Hitler's speeches? What do you think he means when he says the Jews must be removed from the Fatherland, like cutting out a cancer to make a person well again?"

"Resettlement in the east, of course. That's what he's always told me." She shrank back when he spun around and glared at her.

"You sound like most of the Müncheners I talk to. What nobody seems to understand about Hitler is he usually says what he means. Everybody thinks he's exaggerating to make a point, but he's not. They grab on to his words about resettlement in the east, because his other suggestions are so outlandish they seem impossible. Listen to what he says, read his book, and you'll understand what he's truly proposing."

She didn't know what she could say to combat the desperate anger in his eyes. She stood before him, twisting the damp towel with her battered hands, weighing his words in her mind. Resettlement in the east—those were the plans she had always heard. Uncle Dolf had promised their enemies would vanish into the night and the fog. Just as in Goethe's famous poem "Der Erlkönig," "The Alder King."

She had recited the poem to Uncle Dolf as they sat in the

parlor together last year, sipping apple-peel tea while the old ladies knitted, and he had smiled, for he loved the tale about the supernatural being who attacked a boy held in his father's arms as they rode on horseback through the night-darkened countryside.

> *"My son, why do you hide your face so anxiously?"*
> *"Father, do you not see the Alder King?*
> *The Alder King with crown and train."*
> *"My son, it's a wisp of fog."*

Uncle Dolf's bright blue eyes had watched her above the rim of his teacup as she recited the rest of the poem, telling of the little boy's growing fear as the Alder King tried to enchant him away from his ordinary life with promises of games and of lovely maidens rocking him to sleep, and then the boy's screams as the Alder King seized him and the father saw nothing but shadows, and the father riding on to the farmhouse, cradling his dead son in his arms.

How Hitler had smiled when he set his drained cup down. *The boy's life snuffed out by the night and the fog, while his father watches but sees nothing.* He'd laughed. *This is how we shall make our enemies disappear, too, one day.* She had fallen silent, unease clenching her stomach.

Fairy tales and discontented dreams, that's all it was, she had thought. Nobody had the power to make someone else vanish into smoke, leaving behind no trace that he had ever lived. Foolish daydreams, and nothing else. She had asked Hitler about the opera he had seen the night before, and he had launched into a detailed dissection of the tenor's performance, and the moment was forgotten.

Until now.

Fear squeezed her heart. Night and fog, disappearing into the darkness, loading Jews onto locomotives that would carry them far out of the Fatherland. Cutting Jews out of Germany like a cancer, so there would be no indication they had ever lived here at all. Extermination. What exactly *did* Hitler intend for his despised enemies?

"You may be right—" she started to say, but Daniel was gone, banging out the door and leaving her alone, locked in, with nowhere to go and only her tortured thoughts for companionship.

Sleep had dragged her like a stone to the bottom of a lake. A hand shaking her shoulder pulled her to the surface, and she opened her eyes to find Daniel's face inches from hers, his expression serious.

"Get up," he said. "We haven't much time, and you should eat something to keep up your strength."

"But what's happening . . . ?" Hastily, she wiped away a line of drool from her mouth, hoping Daniel hadn't noticed, but he was already striding back into the kitchen. The windows were deep blue, darkening to black; it was nearly night. She must have slept for most of the afternoon.

"What's happening?" she asked again, sitting up. Aaron and Ruth were setting plates on the table. Exhaustion must have plugged her ears so completely she hadn't heard them come in or make supper. The aroma of onions, cabbage, turnips, and potatoes carried across the room, and her stomach contracted with hunger.

"I've arranged for us to meet with someone important." Daniel carried glasses to the table. He didn't look at her, and every curve of his body seemed tight and controlled, but whether it was from anger or nerves, she couldn't tell. "You'd better hurry and eat, for if we're late I doubt he will wait for us."

She sat down and tried to smile a greeting at Ruth and Aaron, but her lips were still too swollen. The cousins ignored her anyway. "Who is it?"

Finally Daniel looked at her. "The man Hitler hates more than anyone else in Munich."

Mist rolled off the river. Gretchen and Daniel stood by the banks of the Isar, waiting. The water looked swollen and black in the night—a gigantic snake whose skin glistened from rain. It streamed past in a thundering rush, so loudly that Gretchen had to put her lips against Daniel's ear when she spoke.

"I don't think he's coming."

"He's coming." Daniel's face remained calm; only the fingers drumming on his leg betrayed his nerves. "He said he was coming, so he'll be here."

Gretchen wrapped her arms around herself and shivered. Although the night was warm, the air was heavy with damp. She glanced at Daniel's wristwatch. The glass face was cracked—broken when he'd been dragged out of one of Hitler's speeches for heckling, he had said with a rueful grin at luncheon—but she could read the numbers clearly enough by the lighted windows in the apartment building behind them. Nine o'clock. Only twenty-four hours ago she had been bicycling through the night to Uncle Dolf's apartment, and now she stood in the Isarvorstadt district, surrounded by the people she had always thought were her country's greatest enemy.

"Tell me again what you know about this Fritz Gerlich," she said.

"He isn't a liberal, dishonest scandalmonger, as you've probably been told," Daniel said. "First of all, Gerlich is a highly respected journalist and historian. Today he works at the Bavarian National Archives, but for several years in the twenties he was the editor in chief of the *Münchner Neueste Nachrichten.* And he's a conservative."

Gretchen shook her head. Everybody knew the liberals and the Communists despised Hitler, but many of the conservatives adored him. "That's . . ." And then she remembered sitting beside Uncle Dolf in Café Heck, sipping coffee, bored, while he thundered: *Only by eliminating the Jewish menace shall we regain our health.*

In her mind, she heard Daniel saying she ought to see a doctor, and she saw Ruth thrusting a towel and soap into her hand. She turned and looked at the shabby rows of apartment buildings behind them, full of ordinary people eating, drinking, sleeping, finishing schoolwork, sewing, holding babies. Not subhumans. Not carriers of a virus insidiously infecting the Fatherland.

Perhaps Uncle Dolf was wrong about his opponents, too. *Or lying,* her brain whispered, but she tried to ignore it.

"All I know about Herr Gerlich," Gretchen said, "is he's one of the NSDAP's fiercest enemies."

"Yes. And he was present during the putsch. If he saw

something, he won't be afraid to say it."

The sound of footsteps on cobblestones silenced them. As one, they turned to watch the man walking along the embankment toward them. He was a perfectly ordinary-looking fellow: mid-forties, dark hair slicked back from an oval face, quiet eyes behind round metal spectacles. Gretchen could have passed him a thousand times on the street and never noticed him, and she felt vaguely disappointed at his common appearance. Surely one of the men whom Uncle Dolf despised most in all of Munich should seem more menacing.

When he reached them, he glanced around, the quick, jerking movement of his head reminding Gretchen of a bird. "So this is the Fräulein Müller I have heard so much of for the past several years." His voice was soft and deliberate, as though he weighed each word carefully on an invisible scale. "Fräulein, I was distressed to hear from Herr Cohen that you had been injured, but it gives me great pleasure to meet you in such surroundings, for this tells me you have parted ways with—what do you call him?—your uncle Dolf, I believe."

She didn't dare confirm anything to a stranger, so she said nothing.

"I wish I could say 'good for you,' but I see by your expression you won't believe that sentiment yet. No mind. You will." He turned to Daniel. "And Herr Cohen. I read your newspaper with great interest. Yours is one of the last lights in the growing darkness, I'm afraid.

"Now, on the telephone, you said you wished to ask me about the putsch. Ask away, but I request that we walk, for it is damp by the river."

They fell into step together. The street was nearly deserted; only a few men hurried past, their shoulders hunched, their heads down. Lights shone from the apartment buildings. Shapes moved behind the glass: a woman holding a baby, another sitting down to sew, two boys bending over books, a man packing tobacco into a pipe. The busy indoor activity should have looked normal, and yet it didn't, for there was barely anyone on the street, even though it was only nine.

"It's so quiet," Gretchen said.

"Of course it is." Daniel shook his head. "These are *Jews*, Gretchen."

Her face turned to flame. *I'm sorry*, she wanted to say, because her people were the reason few Jews ventured out at night anymore. She stared down at the dirty cobblestones, grateful when Daniel said to Gerlich, "Please, anything you can tell us about that night would be helpful. We're anxious to learn all we can about Gretchen's father's death."

"Are you now? I should have thought it was a matter long forgotten, but I suppose it never will be by the man's children. What would you like to know?"

"Anything you can remember about my father from that night," Gretchen said. "Did you see him?"

"Yes, briefly." Gerlich hunched his shoulders against the night air. "I had only been in the Bürgerbräukeller for a few minutes when your father came over to the bar where I stood with the other reporters."

"What time was this?"

"About eight, half past, I suppose."

Gretchen thought. Her father would have just arrived at the

beer hall. The SA troops hadn't yet stormed the Bürgerbräukeller; Uncle Dolf hadn't pushed his way to the stage and shot into the ceiling, shouting that the national revolution had begun. Everyone was still seated, listening to the politician's speech.

"How did he seem?" she asked Gerlich.

"Miserable. I remember his attitude surprised me so much that I made a joke, something to the effect of, was this what a revolution felt like. He said it felt like a funeral. The statement was so peculiar, I've never forgotten it."

Daniel glanced at Gerlich. "And a peculiar thing to say to a reporter."

"It was different in those days." Lamplight from a nearby window crossed Gerlich's face. In the sudden wash of gold, Gretchen saw how tired he looked. "We all knew one another; the National Socialist Party was young. Munich teetered on the edge of anarchy. We were all desperate for a strong leader to pull us out of the despair and economic ruin we had felt since the Great War ended. Why, I myself had hoped Hitler might be the man we needed. But when I saw him try to take over the city that night, I knew he couldn't be trusted."

*Trusted.* Gretchen touched her split lips.

"A reporter wouldn't have let my father get away with making such a cryptic remark," she said.

Gerlich laughed. "I see you've spent enough time around Herr Cohen to understand how we operate! No, naturally I questioned the poor fellow until finally he muttered something about upsetting his friend but he'd find a way to make it right. He said he ought to concentrate tonight on his party's goal, not his old wartime memories. And that," he added as Gretchen started to speak, "is all I know, for just then the SA troops burst through the back doors. There was such a commotion, pushing and shouting, chairs falling over and women fainting, that I quite forgot about your father until I heard the next morning that he had been shot."

They walked for a moment in silence. What had her father meant? Why would his wartime recollections bother him at such a crucial time, when he and his comrades were planning to overthrow the government? Determining which memory had troubled him would be difficult, if not impossible; he had spoken little of his war experiences, and those had centered on Uncle Dolf. They had fought in the same regiment, sitting in the trenches, marching across scorched French fields, surviving the same gas attack in the war's final days.

They had reached the end of the street, and Gerlich stopped walking. "Your father may have been mistaken in his beliefs, but he was a good man." He glanced at Daniel. "Herr Cohen, may I speak privately to Fräulein Müller?"

"Of course." Daniel stepped back as they continued on without him.

The street curved and turned into another, this one as narrow and shabby and silent as the previous one. Only the lighted windows broke the gloom. Mist moved in patches across the avenue, and the air was so damp that moisture pushed right through Gretchen's clothes into her skin. She tried not to shiver.

"Fräulein Müller," Gerlich said, "I have heard a little of you through the gossip circles over the years. I'll assume the rumors were true and so shall speak plainly. You are said to be a clever girl. I hope eventually you will understand what Hitler's party truly stands for. National Socialism means tyranny internally and war externally."

His words took her breath away. They contradicted everything she had been taught. And without those familiar ropes to cling to, she felt herself falling through empty air.

Automatically, she started defending the Party. "Herr Hitler says he would only advocate war if other countries insisted on it." Each word came out more slowly as she listened to what she was saying. How could she protect Uncle Dolf's reputation when she already knew he was untrustworthy? Defending him had become a habit she couldn't break.

"I see Hitler's poison is still in your system." When Gerlich smiled at her, Gretchen felt tears burn her eyes because she couldn't remember the last time anyone had looked at her so gently. A few drops fell from her good one, others squeezing more slowly from beneath her closed, blackened eyelid before sliding down her cheek. "For your sake," Gerlich went on, "I hope you rid yourself of it quickly." Then he tipped his hat and strode off into the night, the mist swirling around him, tinting him gray until he was gone.

# 22

THE OTHERS HAD ALREADY LEFT WHEN GRETCHEN woke the next morning. The thoughts moving about in her brain had somehow taken shape while she slept, and she knew what she must do. She fetched Daniel's cheap copy of *Mein Kampf* from the little bookcase next to the sofa and, over a bowl of watery porridge, started reading.

She had always heard *Mein Kampf* referred to as Hitler's autobiography, which he had written in prison while serving his sentence for high treason after the putsch, so she had expected a long retelling of his life, but most of the book consisted of his political theories, the personal section a mere handful of pages. She had hoped for a glimpse into his early years, but all the doors remained firmly closed.

And yet they weren't. At first, as she trudged through the pages, she felt as though she were reading a longer and less eloquent version of Machiavelli's *The Prince*, one dull political diatribe after the next, but slowly she realized what Hitler was saying. Stripped of his voice's magnetic power, the words assumed a darker shade than they would in one of his speeches.

*War*. She set the book down and stared out the window at the street below. He was advocating war. The man who insisted Germany would go to war only if she was thrust into it; the man who proclaimed that other nations' traitorous and cowardly actions after the Great War would push them into battle—he *wanted* war. And Uncle Dolf had created an enemy to fight. He had seized upon the oldest and most convenient scapegoats of all. The Jews.

She remembered the speeches she had heard, the dinnertime conversations, the torrents of words flowing as fast and musically as a stream. All of Germany's perceived enemies—the Communists, the liberals, the money-hungry bankers, the countries that had tried to cripple Germans with the overly harsh Versailles Treaty after the Great War—all had been rolled into one ominous shape, the black-caftaned, hook-nosed, earlocked Jew whom Hitler described with such hatred as the first Jew he had ever seen on the streets of Vienna.

She felt sick. Everything she had ever been taught, everything she had believed, was wrong. The Jews weren't evil.

She thought of Daniel's stories about his parents and sisters, doing schoolwork in the kitchen, listening to the wireless, reading books, picking apples from the tree in their backyard. Erika Goldberg from school, smiling at her across the classroom because they both liked the *Aeneid*. The Jew in the alley, his voice like melting snow. All of them ordinary. Human.

The Jews were an enemy of convenience. Uncle Dolf had practically admitted it when he wrote that a great leader could manipulate his people into focusing on one group as a single opponent. The Jews were an easy target, a means to power; that was all.

Hitler was a liar.

And she was a fool.

She leaned out the window and looked at the street spread out below her. When she was younger, her father had said Isarvorstadt was dangerous. Dirty people and a dirty place, he told her. She had understood the reasoning—the Jews were supposed to be as filthy as rats, and the district was a swampy, low-lying area to the west of the Isar River.

But it was beautiful now.

The river gleamed like a silver ribbon. The higgledy-piggledy houses stood crammed together; figures moved behind the windows, and children skipped rope on the pavement. Somewhere, classical music spilled into the afternoon through an open window, and the smells of cabbage stew carried on the breeze.

Ordinary and simple and not frightening at all, and she was a part of it.

And Hitler wanted all the Jews in Isarvorstadt—all the Jews in Germany—to disappear.

Below, a little boy and his father walked hand in hand, and down the avenue mothers gathered on a building's front steps, watching a group of small girls playing with a dog. All of them, gone, swept away by the night and the fog, as if they had never been, like the child in the poem.

Her heart ached so badly she didn't know if she could bear

it. For so long, she had believed in Hitler's lies, seeing shadows where there should have been light.

Not anymore. Not ever again.

Her fingers were steady as she scribbled a quick note of thanks to Daniel, leaving it on the kitchen table. Fear twisted knots in her stomach. She knew what she had to do. Two nights ago, when Reinhard had thrown her to the floor, the danger had been unexpected. Now she would knowingly walk back into it.

But there was nothing else she could do. No other options if she wanted to learn at last the truth of her father's death. And stop living surrounded by lies.

She was halfway across the downstairs foyer when Daniel and his cousins came through the front door, their faces flushed with late summer heat. Ruth was saying, "I don't care if she's had a change of heart, Daniel. She isn't staying in our apartment any longer and that's final."

"That's right. I won't be." Gretchen tried to sound nonchalant as her fingers curled tight on her bicycle's handlebars. "But I wish to thank all of you for your hospitality."

She looked at Daniel. The swelling in her left eye had gone down a little. The puffy eyelids had separated slightly, and she saw a whole Daniel with her good eye and a sliver of him with the other. The effect was dizzying, and she had to place a bandaged hand on the wall for balance. She felt his dark eyes trace her hand's shape, then travel along her trembling arm, up to her face. His concerned expression said she hadn't fooled him; he knew how weak she still felt.

"I've read a good part of the book," she told him, gripping the handlebars again and trying to appear sure-footed, "and I understand much more now. Thank you."

"Gretchen." He covered her hands with his. Somehow the sight of his smooth, tanned fingers against her white gauze wrappings pulled a lump into her throat. She had wanted to hate those hands once.

"You needn't leave because of Ruth," Daniel said. Warmth pushed through his fingers and her wrappings, into her skin. *Infection*, a tiny part of her brain whispered, but she threw the old thought away.

She looked up, into Daniel's face, studying its sharp planes, committing each of its features to memory. Even with one eye swollen and partially closed, she saw him clearly today. Not a monster. But a boy, blood and muscle and bone, real and breathing before her, watching her with those sharp, intelligent eyes that saw so much.

She liked him. The knowledge paused her heart for a beat, then sped its rate so quickly she swore she could feel the blood coursing through her veins. She cared for him. Ambitious, confident, fierce, clever Daniel.

And she smiled. Even though the motion pulled at her cracked, aching lips.

"Thank you," she said to Daniel. *Thank you, thank you, thank you.*

"You mustn't go," he said, clearly oblivious to the explosions inside her heart. "Ruth will come around," he went on, ignoring Ruth's mutinous whisper that she wouldn't. "Gretchen, you haven't anyplace to go. Please, you mustn't leave. It isn't safe for you out there."

"I'm going back to the boardinghouse. I *must* go," she said when he tried to protest. "It's the only way, don't you see? I've thought it over and I'm fairly certain I'll be safe. The only people I told about what Reinhard did to me aren't likely to repeat it to anyone else. Uncle Dolf certainly won't mention it, since he prefers to ignore anything unpleasant, and Mama won't want anyone to know. Reinhard shan't have any idea I've tattled on him. He'll either be kind to me or ignore me for a few days."

"Your brother's dangerous—"

"I know." Fear sharpened her tongue. "But I *must* risk it. If I ever want to discover the truth about my father, then I have to go back."

He looked down. Even though he stood motionless, she sensed a battle warring inside him. Ruth and Aaron stood nearby, silent.

"Yes," Daniel said finally. "But I hate the thought of you returning to that place—I refuse to call it your home."

He understood. He couldn't call the boardinghouse her home either. She'd been right about Daniel; he saw *through* things that other people never even noticed.

"I'll be fine."

"When can I see you again?" His eyes scraped over her face, and she nearly shivered under the penetrating gaze. For the first time in her life, she knew she had met someone from whom she could hide nothing.

"I don't know. It isn't wise for us to meet in public. But I'll telephone you at the newspaper office as soon as I can."

"Gretchen." He raised his hand, as if he might touch her face, but she saw Ruth's disapproving expression and stepped back.

"I'll telephone you," she said again and hurried outside, into a street turned orange and gold by the setting sun. Daniel caught up to her before she had wheeled the bicycle off the curb.

"Be safe," he said.

"I will," she promised, even though she knew she should promise him nothing.

Now he did touch her face—a feather-light pressure as he laid his hand on her cheek. Everything within her yearned to turn her face into his hand, touch her lips to his palm. But she didn't dare.

He stepped back. "Stay alive."

A few days ago, she would have laughed at the words, chiding him for sounding so melodramatic. Today, she knew better. "You, too." Before she could think herself out of it, she hopped astride the bicycle and started pedaling back into the prison of her life.

# 23

IN THE KITCHEN, MAMA LEANED OVER THE SUDS-filled sink, scrubbing dishes, her unpinned hair curtaining her face. The soft sound of her sobs echoed throughout the small room, and Gretchen paused, her hand on the doorknob, her brain reeling.

Mama never cried. Not since Papa's death, and even those had been angry tears, spilled while she cursed him for his foolish incompetence in allowing himself to get shot. She certainly had never wept over Gretchen.

When she stepped into the room, Mama's head snapped up. Her blue eyes were rimmed with red. Blotches discolored her fair skin. "Gretl," she gasped, and rushed forward, flinging her damp arms around Gretchen.

For a moment, Gretchen stood stiffly in the embrace, unmoving. Tears burned her eyes, but her blackened eyelid couldn't blink them away. With the heel of her hand, she swiped under her eyes, hoping her mother hadn't noticed. For so long, she had yearned for an embrace from Mama, or praise for her good school marks, or approval about her future goals—any sort of attention. Now she didn't even want Mama to touch her.

Finally, her mother seemed to notice and stepped back, her arms falling awkwardly to her sides.

"Have you eaten?" Mama asked. "We had chops for supper. I've saved you one."

She moved toward the icebox, stopping when Gretchen said, "No, I can't eat anything that requires so much chewing."

"Oh. Of course." Her mother flushed. "Perhaps soup. That should go down easily. Why don't you sit while I fix it?"

"No, thank you. I would rather lie down." She felt almost painfully polite with her mother. "Good night."

"I know your accident was very upsetting." Mama's eyes were riveted on Gretchen's battered face. "You'll see, with time, everything will seem better." Her voice held a pleading note.

An *accident*. Naturally that was the story Mama would tell. Exhaustion weighed so heavily on Gretchen's aching body, she couldn't even summon the energy for anger. She headed for the front hall.

"I'll bring soup to your room," Mama called after her. "Get some rest, darling."

"Yes, Mama."

She wanted the copy of *Mein Kampf* in the communal bookcase. She had expected to find the usual cluster of ladies knitting in the parlor, but two men sat on the ancient chintz sofa instead, their forms turned to flame by the setting sun streaming through the window. Her heart froze for an instant, then started pounding so hard she could scarcely hear them talking. It was her brother and Ernst Röhm.

Reinhard didn't look at her; she might have been a stranger passing on the street. With unsteady steps, she moved into the parlor, keeping to the shadows. The bookcase stood against the wall, directly beside the doorway.

As she bent down, her knees screamed, and she let out a tiny gasp of pain before she could stop herself. A quick glance at the sofa told her the men hadn't noticed.

Her scraped-up hands whined as she forced them to grasp *Mein Kampf* and pull it from the shelf. Moving gingerly, like an old woman, she rose and started toward the hall.

"Ah, Fräulein Müller." Röhm's rough voice reached after her. "Come back, won't you?"

Dread settled like a stone in her stomach. What could he possibly want with her? Slowly, she turned.

"*Grüss Gott*," she said.

Röhm waggled his finger teasingly. Sunlight from the window glistened off his scalp. "Come now, Fräulein Müller," he said, "I should have expected a proper salutation from you." He rose and saluted. *"Heil Hitler."*

*"Heil Hitler."* She couldn't look at either of them. Instead, she stared at her feet, indecently bare in her falling-apart espadrilles.

"Yes, Gretchen, you ought to know better," Reinhard said. His mocking tone forced bile into her throat. Her fingers curled into the book's spine, the aching knuckles protesting.

From the corner of her eye, she watched Reinhard's handsome face split into a careless grin. "Herr Röhm, I'd say I've caught you up on everything I did for the Party on my trip. I'd best be going, as I have a date in a few minutes."

"Far be it from me to stand in the way of young love." They both laughed, and Reinhard loped from the room, ruffling Gretchen's hair as he passed.

Her muscles tensed as she willed herself not to flinch. She heard him whistling as he headed down the front hall, then banged the front door shut. How could he feel nothing at all? He had smiled at her so blankly, as though he didn't remember what he'd done two days ago.

"Walk me out, dear child," Röhm said.

As they stepped into the brightly illuminated front hall, he started.

"Fräulein Müller, what the devil has happened to you?" His small, hard eyes focused on her. "I couldn't see your injuries in the parlor, but now, in this light . . . Were you in an automobile accident?"

Irritation surged through her. Anyone who had been involved in as many fights as Ernst Röhm had should recognize the telltale marks of fists.

"It was very painful." She sidestepped the questions. "I wonder if I could ask you something, Herr Röhm."

He inclined his head, waiting.

"There was an old man taken out of the Circus Krone during Herr Hitler's speech the other day," she began, wondering how best to ask without raising any suspicions.

Röhm was already shaking his head. "Stefan Dearstyne. One of the old hangers-on from the early days. He'd been skulking about the Braunes Haus, asking impertinent questions about the putsch—as if anyone cares about such ancient history! Raking up that old disaster is embarrassing for the Führer, so I had him removed from the speech. Then he did us all a favor by dying."

He barked out a laugh and she tried to smile, but her sore lips couldn't manage it. Röhm winced sympathetically, advising her to drink plenty of warm brandy until the pain was past; then he tipped his cap and was gone.

She headed up the stairs, thinking. Röhm couldn't be involved in her father's murder. That much she knew. Every account she had heard of the putsch placed him at the Reichswehr, or National Defense, headquarters. Along with his minions, he had seized control of the same place where he had once worked, but by late morning state troopers had surrounded the building.

Freeing Röhm and his men had been the original reason for the march through Munich, she recalled as she stepped into her bedroom. The men who were still huddled at the Bürgerbräukeller, growing more anxious and despondent by the moment, knowing the revolution had failed, had pounced on a chance to do something.

Within minutes of the first rallying cry, they were sweeping through the city, intent on rescuing Röhm and his men from the police. A ragged parade that had been stopped in the narrow Residenzstrasse by a shower of bullets.

*Bullets.* Gretchen frowned, letting the burlap sack slide off her shoulder onto the floor. Another part of the story no one knew about—who had fired the first shot? Some said an overeager state trooper, but most said the bullet came from the National Socialists' side and had struck a policeman.

There were too many questions; she was no nearer to an

answer than when she had first begun. Soon she would make a time line of those crucial sixteen hours, but now she yearned only for sleep.

After dragging the chair into its usual position, she fell onto the bed, still in her clothes, and sank into a gray and dreamless slumber.

It might have been minutes or hours later—at first she wasn't sure which—when her empty stomach jerked her awake. She discovered that Mama had left a dinner tray for her outside the door, and she was grateful for the soup, even though it had gone cold.

When she had finished eating, she checked her watch—midnight, she had slept for nearly four hours—and was flipping to the next chapter in *Mein Kampf* when she recognized a light step on the stair. Herr Doktor Whitestone.

Carefully she dabbed her still-tender face with a washcloth; then she ran a comb through her disheveled hair and tucked Hitler's book under her arm. It was time. While she was sleeping, her thoughts had ordered themselves together, and now she knew her next step.

Whitestone was already in his room by the time she entered the hallway, but he answered the door after only one knock. Fatigue or concern had formed dark shadows beneath his eyes. White strands she hadn't noticed before wove through his thick, dark hair.

"Fräulein Müller," he said, "are you all right? I have been so worried—"

"I'll be fine," she said, feeling for the first time that it was actually true. She held up *Mein Kampf.* "I've been reading this today and I have many questions for you, Herr Doktor Whitestone, if you have the time to speak to me now."

"Of course, of course." He ushered her into the tiny bed-sitting room. Two days ago, she might have hesitated, knowing it wasn't proper for a young, unaccompanied girl to enter an older man's private quarters, but she no longer cared.

There were only two places to sit, so he chose the bed, she the chair. "How can I help you, Fräulein Müller?"

She took a bracing breath. "You said you came to Munich to study Herr Hitler."

"Yes." Whitestone smiled a little. "Back in England, I run a very respectable, but very dull clinic. I hope by writing a psychological profile on Hitler, I can earn a position at a hospital in London."

"Have you learned much about him?"

"More than I expected, actually. Watching him in his favorite cafés, holding court for hours, has been quite informative."

"Good," she said. "Herr Doktor, I'd like you to teach me everything you know about him. From a psychoanalytical standpoint," she added as he sat back in surprise. She was expressing herself badly, and she tried again. "I've been so disturbed by his behavior over the past few days. I've begun reading his book, and I believe I'm starting to see a part of him I never noticed before."

"I don't know how much help I can be." He opened a silver tin and offered her a cigarette. Impatient, she shook her head and watched as he puffed away, the smoke curling in a thin plume around his face. "I don't understand him," he said. "I doubt anyone does, not fully. He cloaks his past in secrecy. But there are small clues that give parts of him away."

Whitestone looked at her sharply. "I'm not sure this is the

wisest course to take, Fräulein Müller. I assume you've been beaten by your brother—you needn't look ashamed, child, it wasn't your fault—but you *must* accept you've undergone significant trauma. It would be best if you sought out help for yourself."

"This is how I'll help myself." The mention of Reinhard tightened her stomach into knots. For a second, she wasn't sure she could continue talking, but somehow she shoved the words out of her battered mouth. "Until my injuries heal, I can't go anywhere. There's nothing for me to do but sit in my room. I must do something meaningful with my time, and I want to understand Herr Hitler."

Whitestone lifted his eyebrows but refrained from comment. "Very well," he said, and began.

# 24

AUGUST SLIPPED INTO SEPTEMBER, A MERE TEN days as the green rains of summer hardened into the red-gold of autumn. In the mornings, Gretchen helped her mother prepare breakfast for the boarders, and in the afternoons she stayed in her room, poring over *Mein Kampf* and the books on psychoanalysis Herr Doktor Whitestone had lent her. Geli rang to invite her on a trip to Hitler's mountain home in two weeks' time, and twice Daniel called her on the common telephone in the downstairs hallway—and twice she whispered he mustn't contact her at the boardinghouse, in case her brother answered. But she couldn't stop the burst of warmth she felt when Daniel replied he was worried about her and had needed to know she was all right.

The second night she was back, Eva had burst into her room, sobbing, her voice wobbly as she declared, *My father had no right to keep me from the friend I cherish most in the world and what on earth has happened to you, Gretchen, turn on the light and let me see your face!*

When Gretchen clicked on the lamp, Eva stared for a moment, then wrapped her arms about Gretchen and cried. Eva didn't ask again what had happened; it was obvious from her expression that she knew, and she promised they would always be friends, always, and someday she, Eva, would have some real power and she would send that beast far away from Munich.

As Eva cried on the bed, Gretchen stared at her reflection. Bruises circled her now-open left eye. Her still-swollen mouth had started to lose its puffy, misshapen appearance, and the cracks in her lips had begun to knit themselves together. The red imprint of Reinhard's hand on her cheek had faded to pale pink. Bandages still covered her hands and knees. Except for the long blond braid shining down her back, she looked so little like Uncle Dolf's golden pet.

She wouldn't be that girl, not ever again.

She seized her sewing kit from the armoire's top shelf. And even as Eva gasped, "What are you doing, Gretl?" she grabbed the scissors and cut through the braid with one hard *thwack*.

She shook her head, enjoying the sudden lightness. Her hair barely reached her jawline. Freed from the heavy length, the strands had already started to curl. She looked like the flappers she saw sometimes on the streets, or in the American film magazines she and Eva liked to read: modern and daring and completely different.

Nothing like a proper National Socialist girl.

She barely heard as Eva started exclaiming over how sophisticated she looked, and insisting she sit down and let her trim and polish up the haircut. Dazed, she sat while Eva fussed and played with her hair, but she couldn't rip her gaze from the glass. Different and new and completely herself—for the first time.

After Gretchen returned to work at the Braunes Haus, the next six days settled into a strange new rhythm. No one seemed to have noticed her absence—or if they had, they knew better than to say anything. When she left the office, she looked for Daniel in the street, but she never saw him. Perhaps he had understood when she had told him on the telephone that she needed to proceed cautiously. She couldn't risk attracting her brother's attention again.

In the evenings, once supper was over and the dishes washed, Gretchen sneaked into Whitestone's room. She listened quietly while he taught her all he could. First, he said, she must gain a basic understanding of psychoanalytic theory. She learned about hysteria and irrational fears masking real ones and the mysteries locked within dreams.

Only a year ago, Whitestone told her while they sat in his room, lit by a single candle, their voices low as they listened with one ear for Reinhard's footstep, Sigmund Freud had published an important work titled *Civilization and Its Discontents*. In it, he had tried to answer the timeless question "Why are people unhappy?" and he had concluded that one way people try to lessen their unhappiness is by finding a group to hate.

In her mind's eye, she saw the passage from *Mein Kampf* that she had read again and again. *The art of leadership . . . consists in consolidating the attention of the people against a single adversary.* She recognized the man trying to destroy this world and create another in its place.

❦

The next Tuesday evening, as she was heading to the kitchen to fetch a glass of water, she nearly smacked into a shadow in the front hall. The lights were off, to save on the electric bill, but she knew the broad shoulders hidden beneath brown fabric, and the muscular neck encircled by a plain khaki collar. Reinhard.

"Hello, Gretl," Reinhard said in his careless way. "I'm heading to Osteria Bavaria to hear Uncle Dolf speak. You ought to come. Holing up in this house like a hermit's bound to make anyone go mad." He grinned while she stared at him. *It's your fault I've been holed up here, you monster.*

"Fine," she said, surprised by how cool she sounded. "I'd love to go." Some of the men from the Residenzstrasse march might be there. If she was clever, she could question them about the putsch.

"Good." Reinhard ruffled her hair—in precisely the way she had always hated. As she fetched a hat and pocketbook from her room, checking in the mirror that the bruises lingering around her eye were concealed with powder, a tiny part of her wondered if this was Reinhard's way of apologizing.

No. Reinhard was incapable of feeling sorry. There was still so much about psychoanalytic theory she didn't understand, but Whitestone had promised he would start explaining Hitler and Reinhard to her, now that he had taught her the fundamentals.

His voice had been soft when he added, *There is one thing you must understand about people like Reinhard—in some ways, they're all the same. They are utterly incapable of forming natural attachments to others, such as friendships. In the purest sense of the word, they are alone.*

She reached the front door. Together, she and her brother went out into the soft September night.

Osteria Bavaria was one of Hitler's favorite restaurants. The owner kept a side room reserved for him, a long, dark space, the walls decorated with paintings of hunts and pastoral scenes. Typically, the same men occupied the table, laughing and droning on under the heavy iron chandeliers.

Tonight was no different. Some of the usual companions sat with him at his regular table: Hanfstaengl, Eva's boss Heinrich Hoffmann, Hitler's secretary Rudolf Hess, and several others.

A crowd had swelled to fill the room so tightly that Gretchen almost expected the walls to bow out from the pressure. The typical SA and SS fellows ranged about the room, leaning against the walls and keeping an eye out for any unwelcome guests. There were no women and none of the prosperous burghers or society folks who had flocked to hear Hitler at the Circus Krone.

She had expected to stand in the shadows, but Uncle Dolf saw her immediately and motioned her over, while Reinhard stayed back to talk with Herr Röhm. Dread weighted her feet, and every one of her muscles wanted to turn and run. Feeling Uncle Dolf's watchful eyes tracking her progress, she threaded her way through the crowded room.

He smiled when she reached him and kissed the backs of her hands. All, apparently, was forgotten. She shouldn't have felt surprised. She knew Hitler's method of dealing with people he found unpleasant or embarrassing; he either froze them out or acted as though nothing bad had ever happened between them. He seemed to have chosen the second approach for her.

"My sunshine," he said. "Your hair! You are quite changed; I shouldn't have known you! What a lovely young thing you are becoming. Surely the boys are crowding around your door these days."

Daniel's image flashed in her mind, and her heart lurched. If Hitler only suspected the boy she couldn't keep from her thoughts . . .

"No beaux," she said, trying to sound like her old playful self. "I think the boys worry about impressing you, and so they keep their distance."

He laughed, slapping his thigh delightedly. "Yes, I am quite the protective papa bear, am I not? Go, sit, eat something, my child. The cauliflower cheese is excellent tonight."

"Thank you, Uncle Dolf."

She wove herself through the mass of men again, finding a seat at the table's far end, beside Rudolf Hess. He gave her one of his shy, close-mouthed smiles.

He was so unlike the raucous, back-slapping, brawling and beer-swilling sort who liked to cluster around Hitler. A quiet, brown-haired man from the gentleman class who rarely spoke and seemed to blend into the walls so effectively that she often forgot he was in the room. She glanced at him now. He was one of the earliest Party members. Perhaps he had known Stefan Dearstyne. . . .

"A wretched time," he said after they had reminisced about the old days for a few minutes and she screwed up her courage to ask him about the putsch. "I took two ministers hostage at the Bürgerbräukeller and forced them into a car. The plan was to take them to a hideout high in the mountains, so they could be used as leverage if our revolution failed. I was still driving in the mountains when I got word that the putsch had ended in a shoot-out.

"All my dreams were destroyed in that instant," he continued, staring into his foam-topped beer stein. Around them, men laughed and talked loudly, and Gretchen leaned closer to Hess, straining to hear him. "I escaped along a mountain trail into Austria and lived there for a while in exile. But when I heard the Führer had been found guilty of high treason, I knew I must return and take my rightful place beside him. I was sentenced to eighteen months and, in captivity with the Führer, began to work with him on *Mein Kampf.* What do you know about energy currents?"

The abrupt change in conversation forced Gretchen to bite her lip so she wouldn't burst into nervous laughter. Energy currents and vegetarian diets were two of Hess's favorite topics. His alibi would be easy to check. She could cross him off the list.

A voice cut into her thoughts. "Have you heard the news about Amann?" an SA fellow asked Hess. "Poor dwarf's lost his arm in a hunting accident."

Dwarf? Gretchen remembered the photograph in Dearstyne's apartment of her father, Uncle Dolf, and three other men heading into the beer hall minutes before they launched the putsch. One of them had been dwarflike. Was it possible he knew what had happened during the automobile ride to upset her father? She didn't dare ask Uncle Dolf, not after he had turned her aside so easily when she'd needed him. Ulrich Graf was still unwell, after being shot during the putsch, and she avoided Alfred Rosenberg and his endless ramblings about the Jews and Communists if she could. Perhaps, though, this Amann could tell her something.

"Who's Amann?" she asked Hess, but he put a finger to his lips.

Hitler strode to the front of the room. "The question of the Jews," he began, "is a question of race, not religion."

All chatter stopped.

The room was so quiet, Gretchen could hear the men around her breathing. "Some may believe that the Jews can convert to Christianity and shed their true nature," Hitler went on. "But they will never be like us. Their polluted blood marks them for all time. Judaism is in their souls."

The same angry words she had heard for years. But she had never listened—truly listened—before. She looked at her hands, folded demurely in her lap, pale fingers intertwined, blood coursing beneath the skin. Blood that Hitler had told her she should cherish because it was pure. Aryan. And she thought of Daniel's blood, as blue as hers in his veins, and surely as red as hers when exposed to the air.

How had she swallowed all of the lies so easily, without question? She had been so young, a mere girl of five when Papa first brought his old war comrade Adi to their apartment. She hadn't had a proper chance to form her own opinions. She looked away from Hitler's reddening face.

Another roar went up, and Hitler lifted a hand to silence the crowd.

"The internal purification of the Jewish spirit is not possible," Hitler said. "For the Jewish spirit is the product of the Jewish person. Unless we expel the Jews soon, they will have polluted our people within a very short time."

The men shouted again, a harsh, guttural cry filling the room. Gretchen glanced at Reinhard, who stood with others along the wall, his face cold. Why was he here, if he didn't care? Why did nothing seem to touch him at all?

"But surely," shouted a man to be heard above the din, "what you propose, Herr Hitler, is barbaric? Are we not a civilized nation, and as such, do we not offer equal protection to all our citizens?"

"Who said that?" Hitler demanded. "Who spoke?"

A man stepped forward from the clumps along the walls. It was Fritz Gerlich. He looked like a schoolmaster, standing among the mostly uniformed crowd in his plain suit and round wire spectacles. Gretchen looked away, hoping he wouldn't let on if he recognized her. There was a sudden hush, and every man turned toward Hitler, waiting to see what he would do.

"*Ach*, Gerlich." Hitler shook his head, like a weary father scolding a naughty child. "Barbaric, you say? Wars are necessarily barbaric. Make no mistake—we are engaged in a mighty battle with the Jews for our lives, for our souls, for our Fatherland! And Gerlich"—he almost smiled—"I suggest you make your exit quickly."

Gerlich shot him a look of such open disgust that Gretchen wondered at his daring. Then he strode out of the restaurant, into the night. There was some muttering as he left and a few men started to follow him, but Hitler called out.

"Must I remind you that we have a far more dangerous enemy than Gerlich? And they are in our very midst, insinuating themselves into every crevice of our society, poisoning us from within." He smacked his fist into his palm for emphasis.

"We are more than just a political party!" Hitler shouted. "Can there be anything greater or more all-encompassing than our National Socialist beliefs?"

He was practically screaming now, his tone so high-pitched and frantic Gretchen could scarcely bear to listen to him. He had become a stranger. "National Socialism is the desire to create a new and better mankind!"

"*Heil!*" the crowd shouted, their arms extended in the National Socialist salute. Gretchen felt stares drilling into her back. Some of the men must be wondering why she hadn't gotten to her feet yet. Hurriedly, she rose, whipping her arm out. The movement must have caught Hitler's eye, for he glanced at her. Sweat streamed down his flushed face. She barely recognized him.

"My fellow Germans," Hitler screamed, turning back to the crowd, "you know what you must do!"

*"Heil! Heil!"*

Hitler snatched his hat off the table, jammed it on his head, and strode from the room, his usual companions trailing after him. Slowly, Gretchen let her arm fall to her side.

Behind her, the room seemed to explode into sound. The men were shouting, clapping one another on the back, finishing off their steins and smacking them down on the table. "Death to the Jews!" several of them cried.

The men might begin pouring into the street in another instant, eager to begin another night of Jew hunting. *Daniel.* His friends in Isarvorstadt. She must get word to him, straightaway.

The crowd surged like an ocean wave toward the doors, and she let herself be pulled by its current, keeping her head down so no one would be tempted to call to her and offer to escort Hitler's little pet home. As long as nobody noticed her, she could warn Daniel in time.

Once she reached the street, she raced to the nearest café, just a few buildings down the Schellingstrasse. There was a public telephone near the restrooms, in the back. She dialed the exchange for the communal phone in Daniel's building. When a woman answered, Gretchen asked for Herr Cohen and waited anxiously until she heard his voice. "Hello?"

"Daniel, it's Gretchen."

"Gretchen! At last! Is it finally safe for us to meet?"

"Listen to me," she said urgently. "I've just come from Osteria Bavaria, where Herr Hitler gave a speech. All of you in Isarvorstadt are in danger. He's whipped up the crowd. There's no telling what they might do tonight. The men were shouting 'Death to the Jews' when I left." She took a quick breath. "Promise you won't go out again tonight, Daniel. Tell your cousins, tell your friends, lock your doors and windows, don't leave your homes. *Please*."

Silence hovered over the line for an instant. In her mind, she begged for him to believe her. But she knew she wouldn't blame him if he thought she was lying.

"All right, I'll stay home. But I must ring off so I can start telephoning other buildings and send out the alarm."

Relief made her sink onto a stool beside the telephone box. He had believed her. He trusted her. "And the police," she said. "I'll ring up the central station on Ettstrasse and warn them."

"Gretchen, you know the police will do nothing."

"But they must. They *should*—"

"Of course they should," Daniel snapped. "But Munich is rapidly becoming one man's city and they haven't tried to stop him yet. I must ring off. And Gretchen"—his voice deepened, warming—"thank you." He hung up.

Slowly, she replaced the receiver. She saw the truth now.

The man she had loved as a father was a fraud. He kissed the backs of her hands and advocated war; he ruffled her hair and preached death; he had played with her on the carpet with toy soldiers, and all along he had been planning the extinction of an entire people.

There would be no resettlement in the east. No carefully orchestrated exodus of Jews from Germany, no trains wending through the mountains, carrying Jews to another home in another country. There would be no peaceful expulsion. It was obvious now; Hitler had said it himself tonight. *The internal purification of the Jewish spirit is not possible.*

She understood. In Hitler's Germany, the Jews would have no place at all.

# 25

THE NEXT AFTERNOON, GRETCHEN PACED OUTside Herr Hoffmann's photography shop on the Amalienstrasse, screwing up her courage to go inside. A fine autumn rain pattered softly on the sidewalk, but she barely felt the damp. Her reflection in the display windows followed her, superimposed on the bouquets and apples in bowls on the left, and the parade of pictures of Hitler on the right.

As Hitler's personal photographer, Hoffmann maintained a huge cache of photos of his best client, and today, Uncle Dolf looked sternly at Gretchen from a large studio portrait, his usually untidy hair combed neatly against his skull, a formal black suit substituted for his favorite blue serge. Her pale face wavered over his images in the glass, mixing their features, and she jerked away.

Inside the shop was dim and cool. A camera apprentice waved her on, saying Eva was in the back with the boss. She followed the sound of voices down a corridor, into Herr Hoffmann's office. He sat at his desk, talking with Eva and Uncle Dolf.

Panic seized her heart. He wasn't supposed to be here.

Back at the Braunes Haus this morning, Hanfstaengl had grumbled about Hitler wandering off to an art gallery just as an important industrialist was supposed to come by and discuss donating a sizable amount to their presidential campaign. *So typical of Hitler, with his bohemian airs and total inability to follow a timetable,* Hanfstaengl had muttered before dismissing her for luncheon, and she had rushed to the nearest public telephone exchange to ring the *Munich Post*.

But no one had answered—they must all be out, tracking down potential stories, and Daniel was fine, she had promised herself, even as nerves prickled her skin—and she had raced to catch the nearest streetcar. She would have to be quick, if she wanted to return before her luncheon break was over.

Not that Herr Hanfstaengl would probably notice. The Braunes Haus was run in such a slapdash fashion, she doubted anyone would take note if she disappeared for a two-hour lunch. As she had ridden the streetcar toward the Amalienstrasse, though, every muscle in her body cried *go, go*.

If only she knew what had happened to Daniel after they'd spoken last night. When she'd arrived at work this morning, none of the other employees had mentioned Jew hunting in Isarvorstadt, and asking the young adjutants in the visitors' room had netted her blank looks.

Just as Herr Hoffmann was looking at her now, a thin line of confusion marring his forehead. He and Hitler rose, bowing slightly.

"Ah, Fräulein Müller, what an unexpected pleasure," Hoffmann said. His usual scent of alcohol washed over her, and red rimmed his pale eyes. She had always been surprised that Hitler tolerated Hoffmann's drinking, but he had confided once that Hoffmann had been much cut up by his wife's death and they really must make allowances for the poor fellow. A kind gesture, she had thought at the time, but now it reeked of hypocrisy.

"I apologize for interrupting," she said.

"Not at all," Hoffmann replied. "Herr Hitler and I were discussing our next campaign trip to Nuremberg. I have no doubt he'll capture the presidency at the upcoming elections."

Uncle Dolf nodded, sitting again. "I go the way that Providence dictates with the assurance of a sleepwalker," he said. "All is coming to pass precisely as I intend."

Eva beamed. Odd, as Eva didn't care a pfennig for politics, but her cheeks had gone pink and her hands fussed with her skirt's hem, a sure sign she was excited.

"Fräulein Müller, you must come around to the studio soon," Hoffmann said. When he sat, she heard the sloshing of liquid in a flask, probably concealed beneath his suit jacket. "I would like to photograph you and Henny for more propaganda pictures—you know the sort we like, healthy, lovely young people."

"I would be delighted." She and Hoffmann's daughter had served as models many times in the past, sometimes in Hoffmann's studio, sometimes in the little garden behind his villa in the Bogenhausen suburb. Once they had flitted between the trees in the garden while Hoffmann ran a cine-camera and Uncle Dolf and Hanfstaengl lay in the grass in their shirtsleeves, eating cake and watching them. "I wonder if I might borrow Eva for a few minutes? For luncheon," she added, although she had no intention of eating.

"Of course!" Hoffmann became charming and expansive, making shooing motions with his hands at Eva. "All this talk of politics must be dull for Fräulein Braun! Go, and have a pleasant time."

Uncle Dolf stood and kissed the backs of their hands, teasing them with compliments as he always did. "Such a pretty pair! The boys won't know whom to look at first." He made one of his funny, awkward bows toward Eva. "Until we see each other again, my little siren from Hoffmann's." He patted Gretchen's head. "And you, my sunshine. But that hair! I declare, I shan't grow accustomed to it. Isn't that like a woman, changing her hairstyle constantly, just when I have become used to it!"

Gretchen and Eva said their good-byes and hurried out, stopping only for Eva to snatch up her hat and pocketbook. Outside, Eva dissolved into giggles. "His lovely siren from Hoffmann's! I've never met a man who gives such old-fashioned compliments. But he *is* awfully nice."

Gretchen barely heard the words. She seized her best friend's hands. She knew she would need Eva's steady, reassuring presence to help her cope with whatever she might find out today. "I have to go to the police. And I want you to come with me."

Munich's central police station stretched along the Ettstrasse. The multistoried connected stone structures reminded Gretchen of the castles she had read about in fairy tales: massive, forbidding, labyrinthine. As she and Eva hurried up the steep flight of steps, she heard the snorting of horses, presumably coming from the police stables, and the rumble of the force's motorized wagons starting up.

The front door groaned shut behind Gretchen and Eva. They found themselves in a narrow, high-ceilinged room with scuffed pine floors. A uniformed officer sat behind a desk, filling out papers. He didn't look up as they approached.

"Yes? Do you have a crime to report?"

"No. I need to learn about a mur—a death." Gretchen clutched Eva's hand so hard, her friend flinched. But she squeezed back, and Gretchen relaxed a little. Her best friend was on her side. During the streetcar ride, Gretchen had explained as much as she dared, without mentioning Daniel. Although Eva didn't care about the Jews one way or the other, it seemed safest to keep him a secret.

The officer glanced up from his papers. "Is this some sort of trick?" he snapped. "I haven't time to play games."

"My father was killed on November ninth, 1923." Gretchen waited for recognition to sharpen the officer's eyes before continuing. "We were told he was shot by the state police, but I should like to see the autopsy report."

The middle-aged man sighed heavily and went back to his papers. "That's private police business, Fräulein."

She slapped a gold ring onto the desk. It had been Papa's mother's wedding band, and had been one of the few pieces of jewelry he hadn't had the heart to pawn, but had given to her instead, to keep for her own. She ignored Eva's shocked gasp. "It's real gold. Now please show me the autopsy report. Klaus Müller. November ninth, 1923."

The policeman pocketed the ring, his expression never changing. "Follow me, and not a word."

He led them down a whitewashed corridor whose walls flickered with the light from old-fashioned gas wall sconces. A supply closet, filled with reams of paper and ink bottles and official-looking forms, stood near the hallway's end. Saying nothing, Gretchen and Eva stepped inside and waited as he swung the door shut, enclosing them in the darkness.

"Gretl!" Eva fumbled for her hand. "This is madness!"

"Shh! He'll be back any minute."

They waited, listening to footsteps tramping by outside. Finally, the door opened again, the policeman thrusting a thick book at them. He pulled a string attached to a lightbulb hanging from the ceiling. The bulb's illumination was barely enough to read by.

Gretchen opened the book at random and scanned a page. Lists of names. She watched as the policeman came into the closet, shutting the door. "This isn't the autopsy report."

"There isn't one." He shrugged under her disbelieving stare. "An ordinary oversight, Fräulein. The morgue was overwhelmed with dead that day, as I'm sure you can imagine. The staff was terribly overworked. Besides, the cause of death would have been quite obvious. An autopsy would have been superfluous." He nodded at the book. "All the information you need is written there, in the death book."

*The death book.* She tried not to shudder. A tidy collection of the names of the dead, on neatly lined pages. Beside each name was written an age, an address, and the cause of death. She flipped through October 1923. The space of three weeks filled one page, the reasons ranging from "old age" to "weak heart" to "self-murder."

She reached November 9. One day covered an entire page.

Under the "cause" heading, beside each name someone had printed, in dark ink, "bullet wound."

Slowly, she closed the book. Now she understood why no one had questioned her father's injuries. She handed the book to the policeman. Why the coroner hadn't wondered why her father had been shot in the back, too. Riots sweeping the streets, an exhausted and overwhelmed staff at the police morgue, a starving public who cared more about bread. Papa's murder had been easy to overlook.

"Thank you," she said to the policeman. With slow steps, she retraced her route down the corridor, Eva trailing and whispering her name nervously. Someone, somewhere, had spent the last eight years congratulating himself on his good fortune. Faster now, the worn pine floor flying beneath her feet. Bureaucratic incompetence, laziness, luck—all had combined to shield her father's killer.

Faster and faster. She burst out the front door, pounding down the steps, Eva calling after her. Police scooters streamed down the street, heading off for patrol duty, their riders' faces concealed behind heavy driving goggles. Her throat tightened. Off they went to protect Munich's citizens. But no one had protected Papa. In death, he had been abandoned.

Eva grabbed her arm. "Gretchen! What the devil is going on?"

"I don't know," Gretchen said. The sheer hopelessness of the situation struck her, and she cried out, "*I don't know!*"

As Eva drew an arm around her shoulders, guiding her down the sidewalk, whispering they mustn't make a scene, Gretchen felt herself sinking into misery. Maybe Papa hadn't deserved protection. When he died, he had been committing a crime. If he had lived, he would have been imprisoned for high treason, along with Uncle Dolf and Rudolf Hess and all the rest of his friends.

Eva chattered on, but Gretchen didn't hear a word. Uncle Dolf and his friends . . . Uncle Dolf arriving at the beer hall, with a group of companions. Including her father and Amann, the dwarfish man she'd heard about at Osteria Bavaria, the man who'd just lost his arm. In last night's confusion, she'd forgotten about him. She climbed up the streetcar's steps after Eva, her movements automatic, her thoughts spinning. What had happened during that automobile ride to upset her father? And how could she find Amann and trick him into telling her?

# 26

"MAX AMANN," DANIEL CONFIRMED. THEY STOOD beneath the shade of a towering chestnut. All around them, daylight was slowly dying. Trees clustered tightly together, their interlocking branches and lacy leaves blocking out the fading rays of the orange-pink sunset, enclosing Gretchen and Daniel in a well of shadows. Although she heard Müncheners walking the nearby paths that curved through the Englischer Garten, Gretchen felt as if she and Daniel had stepped into a private world.

"The fellow you've described in the photograph can't be anyone but Amann," Daniel said. In the slanting shadows, his face was a pale oval. "He went to the beer hall with Hitler that night, and he's just lost his arm in a hunting accident. He's an old Party comrade, I believe, who fought with Hitler and your father during the war."

That made sense. Only those closest to Hitler would have

been granted the honor of riding with him to the beer hall. She glanced at Daniel. The sight of him, whole and unhurt, gladdened her heart.

This evening, after she had somehow managed to get through an afternoon at the Braunes Haus following her trip to the police station, she had rung Daniel at the newspaper, her hands shaking with relief when he answered and she knew for certain that he hadn't been attacked last night by Hitler's men. This was the first time they had seen each other since she had left his apartment to return to the boardinghouse. Seventeen days, and she already felt so different. She wondered what he thought of her now.

He had said little about her improved wounds, only murmuring she had healed well. But she had felt his gaze, steady and probing, as it moved over her, lingering on her left eye socket and shorter hair.

"Amann used to be the NSDAP treasurer," Daniel continued. "Now he runs the Party's publishing business. And there are rumors he's Hitler's personal banker. Imagine the sorts of secrets he must know. I can start looking into him tomorrow."

He leaned against a tree trunk; he was only a foot away, and yet it might have been a mile. Gretchen yearned to step into the circle of his arms, lay her head on his chest so she could hear the reassuring beating of his heart against her ear.

Heat flushed her face. What a foolish, inexperienced child she was. He had shown her decency and kindness, but he hadn't treated her as though she meant anything to him. And yet she felt as drawn to him as to a magnet.

"I must go," Daniel said. "I've an important appointment to keep."

"With a girl?" The words streamed out before she could snatch them back.

Daniel shot her a startled look. "A confidential source has given me a tip, and I must follow up on it. If he's right, I shall be uncovering a big story the NSDAP is desperate to hide."

"Let me help. Please," she added when his eyebrows rose. "You've done so much for me. I'd like to do anything I can, to help you and your newspaper expose Hitler as a fraud."

For a moment, he was silent, and she couldn't guess what he might be thinking. "Won't your mother grow suspicious, if you're not at the boardinghouse to help with supper?"

Even the mention of Mama was painful. "No. Not after—not after what Reinhard did. She lets me do as I please now."

She didn't tell him how her mother's gaze followed her nervously, as though Mama was unsure what Gretchen might do next. Or how Mama rushed about the kitchen, serving her breakfast, saving the best pieces of bread for her, and a lump of sugar for her tea. As though she could sweep aside the past with pampering.

Daniel's eyes flickered over her face.

"It might be dangerous."

"I'm not afraid of getting hurt. Not anymore."

"No," he said. His voice was surprisingly gentle. "I suppose you wouldn't be, after everything you've already been through." He held up the nearest branches, so she wouldn't get scratched as she walked out. "Come," he said, and they walked out of the woods together.

In silence, they followed the long, straight main boulevards, finally turning into the twisting side streets until they reached a little lane where the patches of lawn in front of the houses were nothing more than congealed mud. Three- and four-story buildings lined the avenue, their wooden siding nearly stripped of paint. Chimneys poked up from the old-fashioned thatched roofs, but no smoke belched into the pewter-colored sky. The residents either couldn't afford the coal for their stoves or wouldn't waste it on a cool autumn night.

"Once we're inside, don't say a word," Daniel said. His face was so grim, she scarcely recognized him.

The sagging wooden steps sank lower under their combined weight. The front door was unlocked, and they stepped inside.

Gretchen had expected an apartment lobby—a collection of tidy wall mailboxes, perhaps, or a line of buzzers for the residents' apartments. Instead, a man sat behind a curved wooden desk, picking his teeth with a pocket knife. The windows were shuttered, so the space was dark, lit by a single kerosene lantern on the desk.

"One hour?" the man asked, setting the pocket knife down and reaching for one of the dozen keys hanging on the wall behind him.

"We were sent to observe," Daniel said. He slid a handful of coins across the desk.

The man picked up the knife and resumed picking. When he spoke, he could barely move his lips or risk being cut, so his words came out slurred. "Next floor. First door on the left."

"Thank you."

Daniel motioned for her to follow, and they started up the stairs. The rotted wood nearly gave way under their feet, and she had to grip the banister tightly in case the steps broke. On the landing, she heard mice squeaking and nearly cried out.

"Steady," Daniel whispered. His hand found hers in the darkness. Warmth flooded her body. If only he would touch her because he wanted to, not just to reassure her.

Four closed doors lined the corridor. The first one opened into a small, bare room. A worn duvet covered the narrow bed, and a side table held a guttering candle and a washing basin.

"This is a cigarette house," she gasped.

"Yes." Daniel ushered her inside, closing the door behind them.

She had never seen a cigarette house before, at least not knowingly. They were notorious as fronts for prostitution businesses—places where men and women grappled in dim, dank rented rooms, paid for in hour or minute increments.

Embarrassment forced her gaze to the floor. In this place with Daniel, smelling the warmth of his skin, feeling his arm brush hers as he closed the door, while her heart beat madly—

Footsteps creaked on the steps. Daniel cursed softly. "I thought we had more time, so I could explain." He bent down, his eyes locking on hers. "Do you trust me?"

Never had she trusted anyone so completely. She nodded.

"Good," he whispered. "Under the bed, and not a word, *please*."

Footfalls echoed along the corridor. Together, Gretchen and Daniel dove under the bed. She pressed her cheek against the cold wood floor, trying not to sneeze at the dust tickling her nose. The bed's frame sat so low, she felt its metal rack pressing into her back. Beside her, Daniel turned his head, too, resting his cheek on the floor, his face only inches from hers.

To her shock, he grinned. "You keep surprising me," he whispered. "I've never met a girl like you."

Something warm and golden spread through her. He liked her, the girl he must have once despised.

The door opened. Daniel nudged her shoulder with his, signaling her to remain quiet. She nodded, peering through the space between the bed and the floor. Two pairs of black jackboots. Only SA or SS men wore shoes like that.

"A cigarette house?" A man snorted. "What sort of bloody meeting place is this?"

"It's private, isn't it?" The other man sounded defensive. Age had roughened his voice, turning it into bits of gravel rubbing together. "Stop your complaining and listen. Orders have come through. The boss has decided on a strategy for dealing with the Jews within Germany."

*The boss!* Gretchen's heartbeat quickened. The term could apply to so many men within the NSDAP: Hitler, Röhm, SS head Heinrich Himmler, Munich's *Gauleiter*, the National Socialist district leader. She listened.

"What is it?" The bed groaned as the men sat.

"It's top secret," the other cautioned. "We can't discuss it in public because the boss is afraid it'll have a poor effect on foreign relations."

"Out with it," the younger man growled. "These rooms are expensive."

The bed sagged lower. Gretchen bit her lip so she wouldn't make a sound.

"Once we're in power, we'll seize Jewish businesses and property," the older man said. "We'll bar Jews from civil service and professional posts and limit who they can marry. The Führer also proposes using the Jews for slave labor or swamp cultivation."

Gretchen's eyes met Daniel's. His were unblinking and hard, as though he had retreated deep within himself.

Anger filled her mind, staining it red. What these men proposed was monstrous. Efficiently ripping away the rights anchoring Jews in society, until they had nothing left. Pulling them out of their jobs, stealing their possessions, breaking up their marriages, and finally forcing them into slavery in the swamplands.

And the man she had loved as a father was behind it all.

Only Uncle Dolf was referred to as "the Führer." A title she had once smiled at, thinking it was a bit presumptuous for a man who wasn't even in an elected office yet to call himself "the Leader." An indulgent bit of vanity on his part, she had thought. The overreaching aim of the megalomaniac, she knew now.

Silently, she lay next to Daniel as the men talked for another moment, snickering about the looks on the Jews' faces when they finally figured out what was happening to them. She listened to the floorboards moan under their boots. The door opened and closed; the stairs creaked as the men walked down.

Daniel slid out from under the bed, and she followed him. The candle had burned out, leaving the shabby room in shadow. Through the thin curtains, she saw the silvery sheen of the new moon, hanging low in the sky.

In the half light, Daniel looked angrier than she had ever seen him. There was nothing she could say to him—no words she could think of that might help. Together, they left the cigarette house, walking down the narrow lane until they had left the muddy lawns and rickety wooden houses behind.

Gradually, the street widened. The buildings now were made of stone. Lights glowed from the windows of nightclubs and restaurants. Up ahead, a cluster of men, talking loudly, entered a beer hall, and across the avenue, a door opened and shut, releasing a burst of laughter from a cabaret. Bluesy jazz music cascaded from a nightclub, and men in fancy suits and women in satin frocks strolled the street, arm in arm, smiling, out for a night on the town. Everywhere the city was alive, all these sweet, simple lives twining together. How blind everyone was, rushing into the restaurants, laughing at the comedians' jokes, smoking and dancing and singing. Without the slightest inkling of what Hitler and his men were planning.

Beside her, Daniel walked quickly, head down, hands in his pockets. The sight of him tore at her heart. Suddenly, she stopped walking. He halted, looking at her with despairing eyes.

"How can we stop them when no one will listen to us, when no one pays attention to my newspaper's articles?" He waved a hand toward the street. "They're all too busy trying to enjoy their lives, and I can't even blame them. The truth is so shocking and cruel, it hardly seems real. I can understand why they don't believe me and the other reporters."

She stepped toward him. "*I* believe."

For a moment, he looked at her intently, in a way no one had ever looked at her before. He stood so close she could smell the scents clinging to his skin, soap and oranges and boy, and she heard the nerves in his voice when he said her name, and she knew what he was about to do, and her heart started pounding.

He kissed her.

His lips felt soft and warm on hers. And feather light, the barest pressure, like a whisper or a sigh, so gentle she might have imagined it.

Breathless, they separated and stared at each other. In that instant, she was more aware of Daniel than she had ever been of anyone in her life: the high cheekbones beneath his olive skin, the flecks of gold in his brown eyes, the tiny shaving nick that meant he had bothered with his appearance for her. His expression was so unlike his usual sarcastic grin she almost didn't recognize him. He didn't smile but kept his eyes steady on hers.

She stepped closer. Their ragged breathing, and the far-off sounds of laughter and music from a nightclub pushed against her ears. But the whole world fell away when she placed her hands on his shoulders, feeling the corded muscle beneath her fingers, and stood on tiptoe so she could reach him. He smiled.

"Am I still surprising you?" she asked.

"Yes," he said. "And I've never been gladder of anything in my life."

Then he cradled her face, touching her so tenderly she could scarcely breathe, and brought his face to hers until their lips met in a kiss that burned her mouth.

# 27

HOURS LATER, A SINGLE, NAGGING THOUGHT wormed itself into Gretchen's mind until she finally woke. Her father's old wartime memories had been bothering him while he milled about the Bürgerbräukeller, at a time when he should have been concerned only with the putsch. She slid into her robe, her mind spinning.

Why hadn't she remembered Fritz Gerlich's remark until now? The former journalist, the fellow who had spoken to her father moments before the SA storm troopers burst into the beer hall. Foolish. She should have listened more closely.

Perhaps something Herr Doktor Whitestone had said earlier tonight had pulled Gerlich's comment to the front of her consciousness. After Daniel had walked her back to the boardinghouse, and watched from across the street until she went inside, she had gone to the Englishman's room and found him packing his things, preparing to catch a late-night train out of Munich, to begin his long journey back to Oxford. Her heart had twisted in her chest. She had forgotten he would be leaving tonight.

And then he had seen her and had smiled in his gentle way and ushered her inside. *I was ready to miss my train because I was determined to speak to you before I left,* he had said. *I want you to understand how your brother thinks, so you can be on your guard against him.*

The grandfather clock in the front hall sounded two long, low notes as she crept down the stairs, her bare feet soundless on the floorboards.

*Permit me to list some characteristics,* Herr Doktor Whitestone had said, *and you nod at each that sounds like Reinhard. Charming at times, moody and unapproachable at others, unable to keep friends or a job. Cannot comprehend emotions such as guilt or shame, and cannot form close bonds with others. Prone to violent outbursts.*

She had nodded at each one. *How do you know all this? Who told you so much about Reinhard?*

The cellar was cold and dark as pitch. She found the old lantern and book of matches sitting on the top step. The tiny orb of light was all the illumination she needed to creep down the stairs.

*No one had to tell me, Fräulein Müller. All of the characteristics I've listed are typical of a certain type of personality. This type treats life as a chess match and is always eight moves ahead of anyone else. He looks at others as opponents or victims, never as friends or lovers.*

She clutched the stairway railing for balance. Below, the cellar yawned—a black hole.

*I hesitate to diagnose your brother because I've never met with him as a patient, and the only reason I speak frankly to you is because I fear for your safety. But you must know the truth. Your brother may be a psychopath.*

The strange word had sounded familiar; she had felt a vague rustling in her mind, as though her thoughts were stretching back into the distant past, but the sensation fell away before she could snatch hold of it.

The cellar's packed dirt floor felt cool and soft beneath her bare feet. The lantern's light barely touched the darkness, turning the vegetable bins along the opposite wall into shadows.

*Psychopaths are distinguished primarily by their utter lack of conscience and lack of remorse for misdeeds,* Whitestone had said, *and their inability to bond properly with family and friends. They care for no one but themselves.*

*What you're describing sounds like a monster.*

*Not a monster, but someone who is deeply, profoundly ill.*

The boarders' trunks and boxes sat in the far corner. For a fee, residents could store their extra belongings in the cellar. The one she wanted was stamped HARTMANN—her mother's maiden name—along its curved top.

*Have you ever noticed the similiarities between your brother and Herr Hitler?* Whitestone had asked. *They are, perhaps, sides of the same coin, or distorted reflections of each other.*

*You mean . . . they are both psychopaths. But that can't be right! They're so different.*

*In many ways, all psychopaths are identical.*

She knelt before her mother's trunk. The hinges squealed when she opened it. An old photograph of her father and Uncle Dolf stared at her from the top of the piles of junk. They stood in a field, dressed in their Great War uniforms, a small white terrier at their feet. The war comrades, so young it made her heart ache, thin and haggard from meager rations, Uncle Dolf nearly unrecognizable behind a drooping mustache, like a Spanish desperado. His old wartime memories were troubling him, Papa had said to Herr Gerlich, only sixteen hours before he was killed. . . .

*Herr Doktor Whitestone, surely psychopaths are rare. Two residing in the same city, with such interconnected lives, would strain the limits of credulity.*

Even the flat black-and-white image couldn't soften the magnetic pull of Hitler's gaze. Shuddering, she flipped the photograph over.

*What I have witnessed may be hard to believe. But the NSDAP leadership seems to contain an extraordinarily high number of mentally diseased men. Narcissists, psychopaths, lovers of violence and death—something about National Socialism appeals to them on an elemental level.*

There were stacks of loose papers—letters, her report cards and Reinhard's, a lavender-colored book of pressed wildflowers, an album full of dusty daguerreotypes of people she didn't recognize, an old-looking report from a doctor's visit—and finally, near the bottom, what she had been looking for, a stack of envelopes jumbled together.

*I wish you weren't going back to England,* she had said when Whitestone closed the suitcase.

*You still have my card, don't you?*

*Yes. I shall write to you, Herr Doktor, if it is agreeable to you.*

He had smiled then and patted her hand. *I am expressing myself poorly. The card is an invitation to come to my home. Anytime. I would be honored if you would like to stay with my family.* His smile had widened at her obvious amazement. *You are a remarkable young woman, Fräulein Müller. If you were ever to have need of my assistance, I would be glad to do all in my power to help you.*

It was more than she had ever expected or dared to hope for. Tears had closed her throat, so all she could do was nod and smile her thanks. He had taken her face in his hands and kissed both of her cheeks, as her father had.

In that instant, realization had blazed across her mind like a tongue of flame. She knew what she was meant to do. She wouldn't be a doctor and heal sick people's bodies; she would be a psychoanalyst and heal their minds. Somehow, she would find a way to pay for her schooling, and she would do for others what she had always wanted someone to do for her family—release the illness trapped within people's brains.

Now she flipped through the envelopes. It was all wrong. She thumbed through them twice before she could accept the truth. None were addressed to Mama in her father's hand; they were a motley collection of letters, some from her grandparents, others from her mother's younger sister, still others from old school friends. None were from her father. All of the letters she had watched Mama pack away after Papa's death—all of the letters he had written to his wife during the Great War, and she had held together with a faded pink ribbon—were gone.

"Gone?" Mama repeated as she spooned porridge into bowls for the boarders' breakfast. "I haven't had those letters for years, Gretl."

Gretchen placed the bowls on a tray, listening for Reinhard's heavy tramp on the stair. Nothing yet. She still had time to question her mother. "Did you throw them away—"

"Of course not." Her mother sounded impatient. Her movements were jerky as she poured coffee. "Herr Hess offered to take them for me. For safekeeping, he said, and I was grateful for his kindness because one's possessions are not always secure in a boardinghouse."

Gretchen placed a handful of checked cloth napkins on the tray. "Herr Hess took Papa's old letters?"

"That's right." Her mother wiped the counter. "Considerate, wasn't it?"

What possible use could Rudolf Hess have for her father's old wartime correspondence? She lifted the tray with trembling hands. *Something was in those letters.* A secret Hess didn't want anyone to know.

Herr Hess had a reputation as a peculiar, but always exceptionally polite and devoted, follower of Hitler. He would do anything for his beloved Führer. Including, perhaps, hide an important secret from Hitler's past.

But, in his own way, Hess was a man of honor. During evenings at Café Heck, while other men boasted about their exploits and wheedled for better jobs within the Party, Hess sat quietly, sipping beer, his gaze trained on Hitler. He cared nothing for his own advancement within the Party. He cared only for his Führer. He wouldn't destroy something that didn't belong to him. Which meant those letters still existed somewhere.

Hastily, she dumped the tray on the dining room table, barely hearing the old ladies' twitters. The hour was nearly eight; Daniel might still be home. If she rang him now, she might catch him before he left for work.

Nerves wound in her stomach as she handed out bowls of porridge. There was only one place Hess would possibly think was safe enough to hide the letters—his office at the Braunes Haus.

Which meant she needed to break in.

The next night, Gretchen crouched in Hanfstaengl's office, listening to the building settling all around her. Nothing. No footsteps, no doors opening or closing. During the day, the place seemed as busy as a beehive at the height of pollination season. Tonight, it was as silent as a grave.

Slowly, she uncurled from her hiding position behind Hanfstaengl's desk. For the past three hours, since the six o'clock end of the workday, she had waited.

Around nine o'clock, she heard the bronze front doors bang closed. Perhaps the two front guards locking up and leaving for the night. Schedules at the Braunes Haus were unpredictable at best, and she had heard that Hitler sometimes liked to conduct business late at night.

With careful fingers, she seized the door handle and pulled the door open. An empty, darkened corridor stretched out in either direction. No one. And Hitler wouldn't come back this evening. He was the guest of honor at an NSDAP dinner party, one of those fund-raising events designed to wring coins and tears from old ladies. Which was why she had waited an entire day before attempting to get into Hess's office. Hitler was gone until morning, luncheon probably, judging by his late rising habits. She wouldn't chance running into him. She was safe.

But her legs shook as she crept down the stairs. All of the lights in the front hall had been extinguished, transforming it into a pocket of shifting shadows. For an instant, she paused on the bottom stair, listening, holding her breath. Still nothing. It must be now.

She darted across the hall. The enormous front door groaned when she shoved it open. A lone figure stood on the sidewalk, its back to her. *Daniel.* He had come, as he had sworn he would.

When she had rung him up yesterday morning, whispering her newest suspicions and her plans to sneak into Hess's office, he had insisted on accompanying her. *You mustn't be alone,* he had said. *I want to help you.* And she couldn't stop the warmth flooding her heart. He *cared.*

"All clear," she whispered.

He sprang up the steps and, together, they ran up the grand staircase. A long corridor lined with closed doors spread the length of the second story. Hess's office stood beside Hitler's. Locked, but a few seconds' work with Daniel's pick solved that problem.

The curtains hadn't been drawn, so silvery starlight sprinkled across the room. A desk, a few chairs, a couple of filing cabinets: an ordinary-looking office.

Daniel yanked open a drawer. "A stack of envelopes tied with a pink ribbon, right?"

"Yes. They were all written by my father to my mother, so they'll be addressed to Liesel." She darted a glance at the door. Still no sound. Hitler's office was only a few feet away. . . . She might never have another chance.

"Go," Daniel said. With rapid fingers, he flipped through the papers in the drawer, then eased it shut and opened another. He didn't stop searching to look at her, saying only, "Hess is a methodical man. If the letters are here, it shouldn't take me long to find them. And you mightn't have another opportunity to go through Hitler's office."

How could he understand her so completely? She barely had time to wonder, just nodded in gratitude and rushed out.

The door to Hitler's anteroom was unlocked.

She hurried into his office. She'd been in here so many times, playing the part of prattling pet whenever Hitler was in a poor mood and needed cheering up.

The room looked different in the moonlight. Quieter, less ostentatious. The highly polished wood and brass gleamed. Across the room stood his desk, small, plain, a flat table with several drawers. Overhead, a chandelier hung darkly, its unlit bulbs covered by miniature green lampshades. Formal red upholstered chairs lined the walls. A bouquet of yellow roses in a cut glass vase sat on a round table. On the wall opposite hung a portrait of Hitler's idol, Frederick the Great.

She rushed to the desk. The drawers opened easily. But the memorandums and copies of official letters she had expected weren't there. A fountain pen, a razor-sharp letter opener, a handful of thumbtacks. Nothing hinting at the desk owner's personality. Her breath caught. A blank canvas. Like Reinhard's room . . .

She closed the drawer and opened another, filled with receipts from an auto garage. Details of repairs to Hitler's precious red Mercedes. Scribbled notes about used cars he was interested in buying . . . She tidied them and slid them back in the drawer.

A thick manila folder lay inside the last drawer. More car

receipts, most likely, or some other meaningless papers. She opened it and froze.

A smudged charcoal drawing . . . of *her*. Although the portrait was clumsily done, she recognized the high curve of her forehead, the length of her nose, the wide shape of her mouth, the childish braid.

Shock blanked her mind. Like an automaton, she looked through the drawings. All head portraits, done in charcoal or pencil, without a trace of color. Pictures of her, laughing, smiling, frowning pensively. Two pictures of her and Eva, her oval face close to Eva's round one, as though she were confiding a secret. And a dozen portraits of Geli. Gazing down, eyes shadowed, dark curls dusting her shoulders, or staring off into the distance. Never looking directly at the artist.

She closed the folder. Somehow, she felt as though she had seen something indecent. As though she had pushed open a door into Hitler's mind, one that he wanted to keep closed. But she couldn't understand what lay beyond the door.

Why had these drawings been concealed in his desk, and why had he never confided that he had drawn her portrait so many times? He always said he had wished to become an artist, but the Academy of Arts in Vienna had been against him. Was he somehow ashamed of his sketches? At their lack of fine skill? Or was art now beneath him, since he had become a well-known politician?

Somewhere, a door opened and closed. *Please, let that be Daniel.* Her shaking hands placed the folder back in the drawer and closed it.

She hurried out. Daniel was stepping into the anteroom as

she entered. He held a pack of white envelopes tied with a pale pink ribbon. "You found them."

"Yes." Daniel looked grave. "We should leave."

Together, they checked the offices a final time, making sure everything had been put back precisely, then jiggled the locks back into place. They raced down the stairs and outside, into the still-warm night. At this late hour, no cars cruised the avenue and no pedestrians walked its sidewalks. Gretchen's heart throbbed against her ribs. *They had done it.*

They said nothing until they had walked several side streets and reached a streetcar stop. No one else waited on the corner with them, and only the lighted windows in the nearby buildings' top floors indicated anyone else was awake in the city.

Then Daniel grabbed her shoulders, grinning widely. "You were amazing! I've never met anyone as brave as you."

She opened her mouth to say he was more courageous than any boy she had known, but he leaned down, pressing his lips on hers, capturing her half-gasped-out breath of surprise at his abruptness.

She had been kissed before: flat pecks on the backs of her hands, quick caresses against her cheek, an awkward series of fumbles last summer when one of the SA boys walked her home from the cinema, the soft pressure of Daniel's lips two nights ago.

But she had never been kissed like this. His mouth, warm and insistent, and his arms, wrapping around her so tightly she could feel his heartbeat pounding through his clothes, and his body shaking as though he stood in a windstorm, and the blood roaring through her veins, and the sudden desire to feel his bare skin on hers. The world narrowed to a single point, his lips on hers, and she wound her arms around his neck, letting the soft strands of his hair brush her fingers, sharing a breath she never wanted to end.

# 28

THE STREETCAR CARRIED GRETCHEN AND DANIEL to the Englischer Garten, where they moved quickly along the winding pathways. Ahead, the Chinese Tower rose into the night sky, a hulking shadow spearing up from the grassy clearing. A massive pagoda-shaped structure, it looked more like a foreign temple than like one of the city's most popular beer gardens.

Daniel drew her down onto a park bench. The scent of summer flowers had faded long ago, and now all she smelled was rich, damp earth, tinged with the bite of decay. Overhead, the moon hung low in the sky, and up ahead, Müncheners laughed and drank at tables clustered around the Chinese Tower. None turned to peer at them.

Still, she didn't feel safe. She imagined Uncle Dolf's gaze drilling between her shoulder blades, his eyes focused on her with the same power and heat as a car's electric headlamps. In her mind, she still heard the men from the cigarette house, laughing about their plans for the Jews. Her father could have been one of those men. He had told her Jews were maggots and kissed her good night. He had followed Hitler's teachings and danced with her in the kitchen. How could he have been so blind? Or had he not been the man she remembered? She had known a small sliver of him, the father part. Perhaps, to others, he had been someone else entirely.

Sadness, heavy as a rock, lay on her chest. Maybe the father she had loved and worshipped hadn't existed at all.

Silently, Daniel slipped the packet of envelopes from his suit coat pocket. The first five letters Gretchen skimmed quickly before handing them over to Daniel, passing over the descriptions of bad food, long marches, and streaming rain. The sixth, though, she read twice. It dated from November 1914, when the war was still new enough to be exciting, and Private Klaus Müller still naive enough to believe that Germany would emerge victorious before the new year.

*My dearest Liesel,* she read,

> *You complained in your letter that I scarcely tell you anything about my comrades and my new daily life in the 16th Bavarian Reserve Infantry Regiment, so I shall satisfy your curiosity. Most of the men are dependable, steady fellows from Munich, but there's one man in our midst who is a definite oddity—a funny little Austrian called Adi Hitler who had been living in Munich before war broke out.*
>
> *He's a courier, so, as you can imagine, he takes tremendous risks to deliver messages when our company lines to command*

*and battalion posts are knocked out by artillery fire. He's a peculiar fellow—skinny, sloppy, bombastically pro-German and patriotic, but generally well liked. He never abandons a wounded comrade and frequently sketches amusing caricatures of the other soldiers.*

*He is quite alone in the world, I gather, for he never speaks of his family or, indeed, his background at all, and he receives no care packages from home. You know how hungry I would be if I could not count on the food you send me!*

*I write these words sitting beneath some trees in the countryside outside Messines. I keep hearing the scream of the exploding shells, although now there is comfortable quiet all around me. It makes me wonder if my mind is beginning to fail me. . . .*

The letter went on, but there was no further mention of Hitler, so Gretchen pressed it into Daniel's waiting hand. She hurried through three more months of letters: rain-soaked trenches, decreasing food rations, forests thick with smoke. Occasionally, her father mentioned Hitler: He had adopted a white terrier that had leapt into their trench; he drew cartoons of the other soldiers; he survived dangerous messenger runs while other couriers died all around them, which made some of the soldiers say he must lead a charmed life or a higher power was protecting him.

The wartime years rushed past: skirmishes in the French countryside, days hunched in the muddy trenches, shells and smoke and screams.

And then she came to the last letter, written in a shaky hand she could scarcely read, let alone recognize as her father's.

*9 November 1918*

*Pasewalk, Pomerania*

*My dearest Liesel,*

*An elderly pastor came to our hospital today to break the news. Germany has become a republic, and our surrender is imminent. Corporal Hitler—the Austrian soldier I have written you about—cried that everything had gone black again before his eyes and staggered back to the dormitory, where he flung himself onto his bunk and begged me to leave him alone. But I couldn't, for we are the only soldiers from our regiment who have been sent here and are quite alone otherwise, so I tried to make him listen to reason.*

Gretchen looked at Daniel, who was reading over her shoulder. He sat so close she could smell the mint of his shaving cream. "This is odd. Why were my father and Uncle Dolf the only ones from their regiment at this hospital?"

"Were they the only ones injured?"

She shook her head. Papa had rarely talked about the war, but he had told her bits and pieces about his last battle. "Their regiment suffered a gas attack in France in mid-October. Some men died instantly, but the rest were blinded—all but one, who could still see faintly and led them to a first-aid station. Why go to the expense of separating my father and Uncle Dolf from the others and sending them all the way to Pomerania when there must have been several closer hospitals in Belgium?"

"Perhaps he explains later on," Daniel suggested, and they returned to the letter.

*Adi sobbed that his eyes burned like coals and all was black. He became hysterical, and finally, in desperation, I searched for Herr Doktor Forster, a consulting specialist from Berlin, who has been most helpful in my recovery. I found the doctor in a nearby corridor, and when I mentioned Adi's name, he quickened his step toward our dormitories.*

*"Herr Müller, wait a moment," he said when we came across another doctor in the hallway, and I moved back several paces as the two men consulted. Their low murmurs reached me, but only a few words were intelligible.*

*And yet, they weren't. I am not an educated man, and perhaps I flatter myself by thinking I am as clever as most, but the two words I caught have perplexed me. I can guess at their meaning, and yet I cannot believe they refer to Adi, this small, intense, peculiar, and yet kindly fellow whom I have fought alongside for four long years.*

*I shall not write them down; to do so is a disservice to a comrade.*

*Herr Doktor Forster went to the dormitories and calmed Adi and is, I believe, planning some sort of new treatment for him. Once we have returned to Munich, I shall take Adi under my wing, and I shall ask you to do the same, Liesel. Time and again, I have seen him risk his life to deliver a message along the front lines. He does not lack courage, and now he shall not lack a friend.*

*I shall return to you as soon as I am able, dearest Liesel. Kiss the children for me.*

*Your loving Klaus*

Gretchen set the paper down. Confusion had turned her mind a blank, empty white. She had expected something monumental, not an overheard conversation in a corridor.

"I don't understand," Daniel said. "What could Herr Doktor Forster have said that was so awful?"

"I don't know. None of it makes sense." Nearby, a sudden shout of laughter sounded from the Chinese Tower. A few men wove drunkenly down the steps toward the trestle tables, their beer steins held aloft so they wouldn't spill a drop. "There's only one person we can ask."

Daniel nodded. "The doctor. He could be anywhere after all this time, perhaps even dead. But we must do all we can to find him."

# 29

THE NEXT EVENING, GRETCHEN WAS WALKING back from work along the Königinstrasse and had almost reached the boardinghouse when a car slid to a stop beside her and Reinhard's voice called, "Gretchen!"

He sat in the passenger seat of Kurt's Daimler-Benz, beside his friend. Both wore brownshirt uniforms. Reinhard's arm rested on the open window frame, the swastika armband wrinkling as he tapped his fingers.

What could they possibly want with her? She bent down to the car window. "What is it, Reinhard?"

"A special invitation to dinner at the Führer's apartment. Get in." When she hesitated, he added, "Mama already knows, so she isn't expecting us back anytime soon."

The thought of going anywhere with Reinhard made her flesh crawl. But they both knew she couldn't say no; nobody refused the rare honor of dinner at Uncle Dolf's home. She climbed into the backseat. As the car pulled away into traffic, she watched the boardinghouse grow smaller and smaller until they turned a corner and it was lost from view.

They drove for a few minutes in silence. Fatigue had settled into Gretchen's bones, and she watched without interest as the buildings trundled past. It had been midnight when Daniel had finally escorted her back to the boardinghouse last night, and she had risen at six to help with breakfast.

During the workday in Hanfstaengl's office, she had started every time an adjutant knocked on the door or the telephone rang. Each interruption might mean Uncle Dolf or Rudolf Hess had discovered someone had gone through his desk. But the day had passed without incident.

The automobile rumbled over the Isar River and past the Prinzregentenstrasse. She finally spoke. "You missed Herr Hitler's home."

The two boys exchanged a glance. "We didn't miss it," Reinhard said. "We have an errand to complete on the way."

She shrugged and looked out the window, watching the houses wind by. Quickly, the buildings changed from old apartment buildings to family homes fronted by tidy gardens. Why had the boys driven here, to a suburb? Kurt lived in the central part of the city, and the only person she knew here was Herr Hoffmann. But they never went to his villa, unless she had been invited for a photography session. . . .

Finally, the car ground to a halt before an apricot-colored stone house on a tree-lined street.

"Wait here." Reinhard and Kurt left the car and hurried up

the front walk. Rather than ringing the bell, as she had expected, they walked right inside. Whoever lived there must be expecting them.

The minutes stretched on. Twilight stretched bluish-black fingers across the street. Somewhere, a dog barked over and over, and a Horch auto glided past. A pair of little girls in matching pink frocks skipped by. What could the boys be doing inside that house? She slipped out of the car. Reinhard would beat her if he discovered her, but she would take the chance. She had to know what they were doing.

She crept across the garden. A bow window bulged from the front of the house. A gap showed between the curtains, just wide enough for her to see through. She stepped over the rhododendron bushes and pressed her face against the glass.

Reinhard and Kurt stood in a large parlor. Sitting on the sofa was an elderly, white-haired man. The small fellow wore only dark trousers, suspenders, and a white shirt, as though he had been interrupted at home when he wasn't expecting visitors.

"Please," he was saying, his words muffled by the window, "don't hurt my wife. Kill me if you must, but don't harm my family."

Gretchen recoiled. *Kill?*

"You should have thought of them before you entered politics." Reinhard reached into his jacket. With one smooth movement, he whipped out a gun, aimed it at the gasping man's head, and cocked the trigger. "This is courtesy of Cell G."

He fired and the old man fell back against the cushions, then slithered to the floor, leaving a trail of blood on the sofa. He didn't move again. Somewhere, someone started screaming.

Gretchen staggered back from the window. *No.* Trapped air burned in her chest. She couldn't push the oxygen out, could only gasp for breath as she moved away, and then she tripped over the rhododendron bushes and fell on the grass.

Somehow, she scrambled up and sprinted across the lawn. She thought she heard the squeak of a doorknob turning—another second and Reinhard would see her—and she jerked open the car door and flung herself inside.

*Breathe, breathe.* She sat bolt upright so she wouldn't curl into a ball. She tried to force air into her straining lungs and coughed hard, her throat turning to fire, tears wetting her eyes. Reinhard and Kurt ran across the lawn. They yanked open the car doors and got in.

"*Go,*" Reinhard said, and Kurt sped away from the sidewalk with a grinding of gears just as a woman burst out of the house screaming, "Murder! Murder!"

Her brother glanced at her in the backseat. "Don't pay any mind, Gretl. She's a crazy old woman," he said, and she nodded, not trusting herself to speak. Hastily, she wiped at her eyes. Her throat still burned, but she resisted the urge to cough. She must make no sound. She must not give Reinhard a reason to look at her.

The ride through the streets was silent. Gretchen watched the houses roll past. Everything looked too sharp, too clear, as though she wore spectacles she didn't need. Dimly, in a back corner of her mind, she remembered Whitestone's teachings about trauma. She was in shock.

Kurt dropped them off at the Prinzregentenplatz, by the statue of Wagner surrounded by thick trees and cooing doves.

Reinhard took her arm as they walked toward number 16. His hand felt warm and rough on her elbow. The hand that only minutes ago had pulled a trigger. Every nerve in her body screamed to pull herself free and run from him. Somehow, she lifted her feet, pushed them forward, across the sidewalk, into the cool front lobby.

"Mama said that Fräulein Raubal has invited you to the Führer's mountain home." Reinhard's eyes were flat and pale.

She had to swallow twice before she could speak. "Yes. I leave in the morning."

They started up the tiled staircase. "Being invited there is an honor. Make a good impression."

They had reached the second story, and Reinhard raised his hand to knock on Hitler's front door.

"Yes, Reinhard," she whispered. "I promise."

Supper at Hitler's apartment was the same as always: one of his favorite dishes, spaghetti this time, with beer for the guests and mineral water for him.

Tonight there were no other guests, and Gretchen sat between Reinhard and Geli, listening to Uncle Dolf drone on about music. He was in a bad mood because he had seen an opera in which he didn't like the soprano, and he spent nearly an hour dissecting the singer's performance and humming entire sections to them. Probably note for note, as he was a gifted mimic.

Unbidden, what she had seen through the gap between the curtains of the apricot-colored stone house rushed back to her, over and over: Reinhard raising the pistol, his face emotionless, his voice matter-of-fact. Reinhard running across the lawn, no trace of fear or regret, only a relentless determination to get away. Untouched, as always.

With a fork, she pushed around the strands of spaghetti on her plate. The sauce looked red as blood. Bile rose in her throat. Murmuring her excuses, she hurried to the washroom and rested her burning forehead against the glass, begging the images to vanish.

*Psychopaths.* She washed her face in cold water. Unaffected by ordinary human emotions, Herr Doktor Whitestone had said. Unable to feel remorse or sadness. Or love. Locked within themselves, untouched by anyone or anything.

She stared at herself in the glass, pale-faced, eyes haunted. How could Hitler adapt himself so skillfully to every situation, disappearing into the shouting, rabble-rousing public speaker in the Circus Krone, into the hard-faced leader inspecting his SA men before a street demonstration, into the tuxedo-clad honored guest at high-society dinners? He altered himself so perfectly to fit each role, she wondered if he was real at all. Perhaps he was one long, continuous facade. An illusion. He had been the kindly uncle because that was what she had wanted from him, and he knew it.

He had manipulated her as deliberately as he had everyone else.

Tears streamed into her eyes, but she blinked them back. He wasn't worth them.

Back in the dining room, the dishes were being cleared, and she followed voices into the parlor. Reinhard was putting on his hat, saying something about going to a cabaret, and Uncle Dolf was chuckling, calling him a skirt-chasing scoundrel. Hitler's housekeeper hovered nearby, clearly waiting to speak. On the sofa, Geli slumped on the overstuffed cushions, fingers fiddling with a ring, head down.

Uncle Dolf turned to Frau Reichert. "Yes, what is it?"

"Herr Amann is on the telephone and wishes to speak to you," she said. "Something about going over the account books."

Gretchen started. *Max Amann.* The dwarfish man from the photograph taken outside the beer hall, who had recently lost his arm in a hunting accident. The same man who might know what had happened to disturb her father during that long-ago automobile ride.

Uncle Dolf looked startled. "What the devil is Amann thinking, calling from his sickbed? Only a fool doesn't care about his health. Tell him the accounts can wait. If he protests, remind him how completely I trust him." He smiled at Reinhard, adding, "No one has such a clever head for business as Amann."

Gretchen knew Amann managed the NSDAP publishing business, the Eher Verlag. And he was Hitler's personal banker, Daniel had said. What a powerful position for a man so lacking in the Party's physical ideals, who looked nothing like the Aryan type Uncle Dolf preferred. She thought again of her father's final car ride. *What might Amann know?*

She might never again have the chance to talk to him. She slipped out of the room after Frau Reichert while Uncle Dolf and Reinhard chuckled together.

"Frau Reichert," she said quietly, "may I speak to Herr Amann for a moment?"

The housekeeper raised her eyebrows but didn't comment. "Of course." She gestured to the telephone receiver lying on its side on the hallway table, then retreated toward the servants' quarters on the other end of the apartment.

Gretchen snatched up the receiver. "Herr Amann? This is Fräulein Müller."

"Yes?" The voice sounded weak.

She listened to the chatter from the parlor. Still talking and laughing. But Reinhard might come out at any second. She'd have to be quick. "Herr Hitler wants you to rest and not worry about the accounts right now," she said in a rush. "I beg your pardon for bothering you at such a difficult time, but—" *God, she couldn't think of an excuse to ask the question!* "—I miss my father terribly, and anything I can learn about him eases my grief. You were with him, weren't you, the night before he died?"

"Yes." The word came out as a sigh. She pictured him lying in bed, propped up on pillows, his shoulder and what remained of his injured arm wrapped in bandages. She shouldn't burden him now, and yet she had to ask.

"Your father made a tremendous sacrifice." Amann sounded stronger, as if he had caught his breath.

A floorboard creaked. Gretchen whirled around. The hallway was still empty. But someone was coming.

"My poor papa." She tried to sound tearful. If Amann was anything like the other SA fellows she knew, her tears would make him so uncomfortable, he would eagerly answers any questions just to get her to stop crying. "I understand the auto ride was upsetting for him."

"He kept cautioning the Führer not to let his nerves get overwrought again," Amann snapped. "We were all so sick of him yammering on that I'm not sure who first told him to shut his mouth." He hesitated. "No mind. That time is best buried."

Reinhard stepped into the hall. He glanced at Gretchen, his eyes questioning. Had he heard anything? Surely not or he'd already be asking her what the conversation was about.

"I hope you feel well soon," Gretchen said hurriedly, and hung up. The smile she plastered on her lips probably looked ghastly. "I wished to give Herr Amann my wishes for a quick recovery," she said to Reinhard.

He shrugged and ruffled her hair as he passed. It took all of her strength not to wince. She didn't watch him leave but traced the sound of his whistling down the hallway and out the apartment door, when it abruptly faded. Whistling. A couple of hours after he had killed a man.

She steeled herself and walked back to the parlor to thank Uncle Dolf and Geli for the lovely dinner.

Later, on the streetcar ride home, she watched the buildings crawl past, trying not to see her reflection in the window, milk-pale and frightened. Trying not to remember Reinhard raising the pistol and firing, his face unchanging as the bullet bit into the man's chest. Trying not to think about Papa's comrades yelling at him, when he had only been attempting to soothe Hitler. Trying not to ask the questions torturing her mind.

# 30

ALL THROUGH THE NEXT DAY, GRETCHEN thought about the papers under the floorboard in Reinhard's room. Clippings from the *Munich Post* and the index card she hadn't had the chance to read. What other secrets did her brother have?

But Mama kept her busy—Mass in the morning, then endless chores in the afternoon: scrubbing the bathtubs, beating the carpets, hanging laundry on the lines between the walnut trees in the courtyard. It wasn't until the next night, after supper was over and Reinhard had ambled out, calling over his shoulder something about a beer hall with the fellows, that Gretchen saw her opportunity.

She crept up the stairs and fitted a hairpin into his door lock. A few careful twists and she was inside. The room seemed unchanged: a blank canvas instead of a proper bedchamber, the only clue to its resident's personality an SA uniform hanging in the open armoire, its shirt damp from a recent sponge cleaning.

The floorboard lifted easily. Below lay the stack of newspaper clippings and the index card. The articles stretched back over two months in time, the first dated 22 June 1931. She flipped through them rapidly. All came from the *Munich Post*.

What possible reason could her brother have for cutting out stories from the newspaper Hitler hated most in the world? Reinhard certainly didn't read it.

Each clipping showed an ever-higher number in bold, black print. Someone, presumably Reinhard, had circled the numbers in red ink and written, *Work of Cell G*.

She'd never heard of Cell G before the other night, but she knew what those numbers meant. They were called "the murder column." The figure, printed in every *Post* issue, was the running total of all of the murders unofficially credited to the National Socialist Party.

Carefully, she tidied the clippings and laid them down. *Filthy propaganda*, Uncle Dolf had said to her so many times, *false numbers, the poisonous lies of poisoned minds*. These murdered men might be the NSDAP's political opponents, but their deaths had nothing to do with *him*. They were beaten in beer hall brawls, stabbed outside bars, shot in alleys, unfortunate victims of street violence.

She knew better now.

Names written in Reinhard's quick, left-leaning script covered the index card. Each name had been crossed through with a black line. The last read, *Dieter Adler Bogenhausen Munich 12 September*.

Two days ago, and the location where Reinhard and Kurt had shot that poor man. Nerves prickled the back of her neck. She was looking at a death list.

As she fitted the floorboard in place, memories flashed through her mind. Kurt and an older SA man in the Senators' Chamber saying Reinhard had been approached and had accepted, and would give them no trouble, for he had ice in his veins. Reinhard declaring he had important work for the Party. Leaving for an overnight trip, not telling where he was going or why.

Even though the air was warm, she shivered as though she stood in a rainstorm. A death squad, organized and run by SA men, operated in accordance with Hitler's wishes. He *must* know. She had heard him make the same boast so many times: *Nothing happens in the Party without my knowledge. Even more, nothing happens without my wish.*

She closed Reinhard's door with trembling hands. With her hairpin, she jiggled the lock back into place. Half past nine. Daniel might be home by now. She crept downstairs, slowly so she could skip the stairs that creaked.

By the time she reached the street, she was running.

Stars lay scattered across the sky like a handful of coins. Beneath their soft glow, Gretchen and Daniel sat on the straw mat he had unrolled on his apartment terrace's cold stone floor.

"I didn't want you to learn about Cell G in this way," Daniel said at last. "It must have been an awful shock."

The street below was dark and empty. She stared at it with dull, dry eyes.

"How long have you known?" she asked.

"About a week." His tone was apologetic. "I'm sorry I didn't tell you. My editor, Martin Gruber, swore me to silence, and it wasn't my secret to tell. We've got a source within the SA who's been slowly feeding us information. Once we've verified everything, we'll break the story." He took her hand, turning it over, tracing the lines in her palm. "I had no idea your brother was involved. Perhaps I should have suspected."

She bowed her head. Suddenly, it felt too heavy for her neck to support. "I'm sure Reinhard has been an ideal recruit. They can turn him into a killing machine with scarcely any effort."

Her brother, who had played jacks with her on the pavement when they were children. Who had stolen peppermint sticks from the corner druggist's and given her half—when their father's pay hadn't bought enough bread to last the week. Who had lain beside her on the divan they shared as a bed, silent, unmoving but awake, after one of Papa's beatings.

Her throat tightened. Who had ripped apart her paper dolls after she beat him at jacks. Who had insisted she write out his mathematics homework in payment for the peppermints. Who had said she should shut her mouth when she asked if he needed bandages or salve.

How desperately she had wanted to love him. And how long she had wondered if something was wrong with *her* because she couldn't.

Daniel's lips brushed her temple. "Gretchen, you should stay here. You shouldn't go back to the boardinghouse."

When she shook her head, he said, "You're living with an assassin. He has already beaten you with barely any provocation.

Imagine what he would do if he knew that you've come to me tonight with this information."

"I know." She leaned against his comforting warmth. "But you said it will take some time for you and the other reporters to substantiate the story about Cell G before you can print it. And I must learn what happened to my father. I can't live with these lies any longer.

"I leave for Herr Hitler's mountain home with Geli in the morning. I believe—I hope—I can learn more about him from his sister, who is the housekeeper there. Hitler's secrets are buried in the past, and if I can find out what happened in that hospital, I will be closer to knowing what happened to my father." When he said nothing, she went on, "You must see that I have to do this. There is no other way. Not for me."

For a moment, he stayed silent.

"I know," he said at last, and because he did, because he understood her as no one else ever had, Gretchen leaned forward and kissed him.

Her heart raced. Never had she been so bold. Her mother's admonition ran through her head—*once a girl's reputation is tarnished, it is tarnished forever*—but she threw the warning aside, and let Daniel's arms come around her back and gently guide her down to the straw mat.

She lay beside him in the silver-lined darkness, feeling his lips touch her cheeks, her eyes, her throat, tasting the warm saltiness of his mouth. When he drew back, her eyes snapped open. His face hovered above hers. Even in the dimness, he looked shaken. As though they had done far more than he intended. Then he grinned ruefully.

"I'd best get you back to the boardinghouse," he said. He stood up, extending a hand to help her to her feet. "While you're out of town, I'll try to track down the doctor who treated your father and Hitler during the war. In the letter, your father said he was a consultant from Berlin, so perhaps I'll locate him there."

Gently, he tucked a strand of hair behind her ear. "I don't think I told you how much I like your haircut."

She tried to conceal her sudden shyness under a flippant tone. "Thanks. I look quite different, don't I?"

"No." He rolled up the mat. "You look like yourself."

For an instant, she stared at the top of his dark head, at his shoulders moving as he wound a tie around the mat. If he had written her reams of poetry, he couldn't have said anything more beautiful.

When they reached the street, they didn't speak, walking along in easy silence, hands clasped. On the streetcar, they stood next to each other, smiling, ignoring the drunks clustered at the back. At the Königinstrasse, Daniel walked several paces behind, in case her brother or the boarders happened to see them.

As she unlocked the front door, she felt his gaze, and she turned to find his lone figure, a familiar shadow, standing across the avenue, near the garden entrance. She waved a hand in farewell and went inside, hurrying to her bedroom so she could watch him walk back alone in the direction from which he had come.

# PART FOUR

## THE INFERNAL MACHINE

The great masses of the people will
more easily fall victims to a big lie than
to a small one.
—*Adolf Hitler,* MEIN KAMPF

# 31

THE HAUS WACHENFELD STOOD AMONG THE rolling green mountains, a modest-size rustic villa of dark wood and plateglass windows. Somehow, it wasn't what Gretchen had expected, although she didn't know what she had thought she would see: a country home as spartan and bare as Hitler's old room on the Thierschstrasse, perhaps, or a mansion as stunning and luxurious as his apartment on the Prinzregentenplatz.

But this pleasant and plain house rested between the two extremes of his Munich homes. It wasn't large, his elder half sister, Frau Raubal, had said apologetically as she led Gretchen and Geli to the chamber they would share, but to Gretchen, who was accustomed to a cramped boardinghouse, the place seemed sizable, with a dining room, a parlor, and three bedrooms.

After unpacking and having tea, Gretchen followed Geli and her little sister Elfriede on a hike in the direction of Berchtesgaden, the nearest village. Dirt tracks meandered down the mountains into the valleys below, where the buildings of brick, beige, and gray lay scattered about like toys that a child had tossed down in a fit of pique.

As far as Gretchen could see, the mountains undulated on and on. Some of the peaks were already covered with snow, and as she watched, they seemed to disappear behind a patch of sunset-tinted clouds. Seconds later, they emerged again.

"The magic mountains," Geli said. "Because of the high altitude, the snow there never melts."

By squinting hard, Gretchen could make out the jagged shape of the Untersberg. Sunlight glittered on its snow-capped peak. According to legend, Emperor Charlemagne still slept inside the mountain, and one day he would rise again to restore the old glory of the German Empire. Uncle Dolf always said it was no coincidence his country home stood opposite it.

Long grasses whispered against the girls' legs as they wandered off the path to pick wildflowers for the dinner table. From the corner of her eye, Gretchen watched the Raubal sisters, both tall, dark-haired, round-faced, chattering in their Linz accents. In the spring, Friedl was saying, the flowers were so plentiful—primroses, bluebells, yellow-eyed daisies, pink clover. But now, in the autumn, there were few blooms on the ground. Gretchen picked Bavarian blue fairy thimbles, thinking.

So often she had heard Uncle Dolf say how much he longed to live among the mountains and clouds forever. Someday, when his work was finally done, he planned on retiring to Haus Wachenfeld.

Her gaze swept down the grassy mountain to the valleys, then back up to the dark wooden house. Harsh autumnal sunlight flashed off its plateglass windows. Spare and simple, the house reminded her of an owl perched in a tree, studying the forest for prey, or a king settled on a throne, surveying the kingdom spread out below him. Removed and remote, for the house's isolation separated its occupants from the rest of the world. Apart from the villages below and the farms dotting the mountain. Alone. Like Uncle Dolf.

As they ambled along the dirt trail, Gretchen asked about Hitler's childhood, but nothing Geli or Friedl said told her much. Crowded rooms, sickly babies, a distant and rigid father, a meek and subservient mother, frequent moves because of his father Alois's job as a customs official. None of the poisonous ingredients Whitestone had led her to expect.

She wished Daniel were with her. Maybe he would catch a crucial detail she had missed. Later, as she lay in the spare room beside Geli, listening to her friend's shallow breathing, she watched moonlight pushing through the curtains and filled her mind with him.

What would he think of this bourgeois mountain retreat? She pictured his dark eyes, intent and focused, as they swept over the kitsch-filled parlor, and his mouth, curling in derision, as he peered through the windows at the valleys so far below. *Playing the part of the genial country host, now, is he?* she could hear him say, and her dry eyes ached. How clearly he saw things. And how long it had taken her to see anything but shadows. Shame weighed her down, until finally she closed her eyes and escaped into sleep.

❧

The next morning, Frau Raubal taught them how to make one of Hitler's favorite Austrian desserts, poppy-seed strudel. As she punched the dough, she explained she had learned to be a good cook when her husband died young and she'd found work in a Jewish students' hostel, in the kitchen.

"Adolf was living in Vienna with a boyhood friend." Frau Raubal rolled the dough on the counter until the pastry was paper thin. Gretchen's dough tore as she tried rolling it out, and she formed it into a ball again. "But he came back when his mother—my stepmother—was dying from cancer of the breast. He cared for her like a good son. He moved her into the kitchen, since that was the only room they could afford to heat. He prepared her food, scolded our little sister Paula over her poor marks. He was eighteen when she died, making us all orphans, for our father was already gone. The doctor—Doktor Bloch, a Jew but still a very good doctor—said he had never seen anyone so prostrate with grief as my little brother. Then Adolf returned to Vienna, to apply for the second time to the Academy of Fine Arts."

There his life faded to a sheet of white until he volunteered for the Germany army when war was declared. Sometime during that period he had moved to Munich, the place he called the city of his heart. Gretchen reached for the rolling pin. Seven years of nothing, carefully hidden. She pressed the pin into the dough, flattening it.

There were no answers. He remained a mystery.

But an answer came in the afternoon. They had gathered in the parlor. Frau Raubal had slipped off her customary flour-stained apron and sat beside her daughters on the faded sofa, sewing an eternal-sun motif on a handkerchief for her younger brother.

Pillows embroidered with swastikas and rising suns clustered on every available surface, and Frau Raubal laughed, saying Adolf often complained that elderly ladies wouldn't stop making him hideous pillows he couldn't throw away, so he sent them here, where at least he wouldn't have to see them often.

The room was crammed with cheap-looking sofas and spindly chairs, and tacky decorations, including a brass canary cage, a cactus, and a rubber plant. Ugly and provincial, so unlike Uncle Dolf's old rented room and his current posh apartment that Gretchen couldn't reconcile the three.

While Geli and Elfriede pasted dried flowers in a book, Gretchen flipped through an old photograph album, studying the photos: Uncle Dolf as a baby, with thick, dark hair and round cheeks, his little feet encased in white booties, and then a school photo of Hitler at about ten, whip thin with a fall of hair pushed off his forehead, arms crossed, chin raised defiantly, the obvious leader in the back row.

"That was taken during Adolf's naughty days." Frau Raubal nodded toward the picture. "What a little scamp he was! Not even his mother could make him listen to reason, sometimes. But she had one trick for him that always worked. When we were children and he refused to get out of bed, which he often did, mind you, she would tell me to wake up my baby brother with a kiss. And if he didn't shoot out of bed at hearing those words!"

The girls laughed politely, and the Raubal sisters went back to pasting their flowers. A wisp of smoke rose in Gretchen's mind, so faint she couldn't reach it. Naughtiness, and an unwillingness to be touched . . .

She tried to sound casual. "How was he naughty?"

"Oh my, where do I begin?" Frau Raubal patted her ample bosom, chuckling. In her broad cheeks, smiling mouth, and dark hair, Gretchen tried to find the same features that might brand Frau Raubal and Uncle Dolf as half siblings. Something about the bone structure, perhaps, but the woman's ordinary, good-natured appearance divided her from her younger brother.

"He was a terrible hellion." Affection warmed Frau Raubal's words. "Quite the leader in all the village boys' games, always dashing off to play cowboys and Indians and ripping and dirtying his clothes.

"He did all manner of mischief—he stole pears from the neighbor's orchard and was caught smoking, and at night, Adolf used to shoot rats in the nearby cemetery."

Gretchen tried to calm the rush of blood to her brain. The photo album slipped from her fingers, landing hard in her lap. "I beg your pardon?"

"Rats," said Frau Raubal, picking up her embroidery again. "Adolf liked to shoot at the foul little things. With a pellet gun, I believe. Oh, how he laughed!" She shrugged. "It caused his mother some distress, for she didn't like the thought of anything being in pain. But Adolf always did what he wanted."

Gretchen looked at the picture of ten-year-old Hitler, slender, pale-faced, arms crossed, head tilted arrogantly to the side. *Adolf used to shoot rats.* She fell back through the last eight years, to the day she, Mama, and Reinhard had visited Uncle Dolf in prison, where he awaited his trial.

She had never been to Landsberg before; it lay nestled in a deep valley like a bird in a nest. Looming over the small village was the prison. The interconnecting series of grayish-white stone buildings looked like an ancient fortress and had been divided into two sections, one for ordinary criminals and one for political prisoners.

Hitler had gone on a hunger strike, the prison doctor warned as he led them along the long corridors, and they would find their friend much changed.

When they entered the cell, Hitler slowly turned from the barred window to stare at them. He had lost a great deal of weight, and his clothes hung loosely on his skinny frame. His eyes had sunken back into their sockets, and his skin was stretched so tightly across his cheekbones, it looked as though it might rip if he smiled.

"My friends," he said quietly, "it is very good of you to come."

Mama started crying. "Herr Hitler, you mustn't go on in this way! You'll die if you don't eat!"

"Perhaps it would be better," he murmured as Gretchen came forward to be kissed. His lips felt cold and cracked against her cheek.

She had imagined a stark cell and Uncle Dolf in prison coveralls and rations of bread and water. But Uncle Dolf wore his own suit, and she heard him say that he took his meals in the cafeteria with his imprisoned comrades, and every day they were permitted to exercise outdoors in the prison courtyard.

The cell was quite small, but it contained a pretty white iron bed. Sunshine poured through the barred window, sending slats of gold and shadows across the floor.

"My goodness, Uncle Dolf, this is much nicer than your room on the Thierschstrasse," she said.

A stunned silence stretched until Uncle Dolf started laughing.

"Come to me, my sunshine," he said. She went to him obediently and didn't move as he tipped her face back so he could look into her eyes. He smiled. "Such a pretty girl, all sweetness and light. If only all the world could be like you, there would be no need of a man such as me. And I have become a joke, a laughingstock around the world. The newspapers say the putsch has ruined all my future chances."

"Your trial hasn't started yet," Mama said. She stepped forward, her gloved hands twisting anxiously. "There are many in Germany who are sympathetic to you, Herr Hitler."

A small crunching sound spun them around. Reinhard knelt on the floor. With his thumb, he was methodically crushing ants crawling in a line.

"Stop that this instant!" Mama snapped. "Don't you remember what the doctor said? You aren't supposed to touch animals anymore—"

Uncle Dolf interrupted with a dry, dusty chuckle. "He's simply being a boy, Frau Müller." And he smiled at Gretchen and Reinhard, patting their cheeks as he always did. "The future," he murmured. "What do I care for adults when I have their children?"

Now, eight years later, as fading afternoon sunshine filled the little parlor, Gretchen saw the first glimmers of light rimming the edges of the dark.

At last, she understood. Franzl, the family cat that had gone missing the month before her father died, hadn't run away. Her brother had killed him. Just as he'd killed Striped Peterl.

Perhaps Reinhard had wanted to know what it felt like to

snuff out a life. The reason hardly mattered now. But her father had recognized the danger in Reinhard. That must be why he had found another cat for her so quickly, so she wouldn't figure out what had happened to the first one. That was why he circled Reinhard nervously, like a man confronting a wild beast.

"Excuse me," Gretchen murmured. "Some fresh air . . ."

She walked out onto the terrace. Pine trees rose like black spears into the sky. *Adolf used to shoot rats.* And Reinhard had liked to kill animals, too, when he was a boy. . . .

Sightlessly, she gripped the terrace railing. She had thought Reinhard and Hitler were nothing alike. But Herr Doktor Whitestone had said they were twisted reflections of each other. . . .

The door slapped shut and Geli joined her at the railing.

"Does your uncle like doctors?" Gretchen asked.

"What? No, he hates them. But—"

"Why?"

"I don't know." Geli looked bewildered. "I suppose because he's like most hypochondriacs. He always imagines he's ill but dreads a doctor finding something truly is the matter with him. What does that have to do with anything?"

"Everything," Gretchen said, and she saw the long hospital corridor as her father had described it in his letter—two doctors conferring in hurried whispers while her father stood nearby and a young Austrian corporal sobbed brokenly in his bunk. In her mind, she heard Herr Doktor Whitestone saying in his schoolboy German that one of the distinguishing characteristics of a psychopath was his childhood interest in torturing animals. She whirled to face Geli. "How soon can I get back to Munich?"

❦

Five minutes later, she was standing in the parlor, trying to convince Frau Raubal that she was having a perfectly lovely time but had remembered pressing business in Munich that would compel her to leave tonight, when a knock sounded on the door.

"Who on earth can that be?" Frau Raubal asked. "We have so few visitors. . . ."

She started walking toward the front hall, but Friedl came in, followed by Reinhard and Kurt.

Both boys wore brownshirt uniforms. Reinhard caught her eye and grinned. He extended his arm in the National Socialist salute, saying "*Heil Hitler!*" to Frau Raubal.

She didn't return the salute. "If you're looking for my brother, he isn't here."

"No, Frau Raubal," Reinhard said, "we have come to fetch my sister." He flashed Gretchen one of his wide, careless grins. "Uncle Dolf is anxious to see you again."

# 32

THE BRAUNES HAUS WAS MOSTLY DARK WHEN Kurt's automobile coasted to a stop along the Briennerstrasse; only the windows on the second story were lit. A shape paused before the glass, and Gretchen's throat closed in panic. Hitler was waiting for her.

What was he going to do to her, now that he must suspect her disloyalty? Reinhard and Kurt hadn't spoken to her during the drive—they had talked to each other, laughing about some chorus girls they'd seen in a cabaret—but they *must* know, or else Hitler wouldn't have sent for her.

The two guards positioned outside the massive bronze doors were gone, no doubt dismissed for the night. From the backseat, Gretchen glanced up and down the avenue. A couple walking arm in arm, yards away, and a single car gliding past. No one she could run to before Reinhard would catch up with her.

He opened the car door and grabbed her suitcase off the floor, grinning easily. "Mustn't keep Uncle Dolf waiting. You know how impatient he gets."

She got out. Reinhard slung an arm across her shoulders, pulling her close. Kurt walked on her other side as they climbed the front steps.

Inside, a lone adjutant was crossing the great hall. He barely glanced their way, but Kurt whispered, "Not a word," and Gretchen nodded.

She doubted she could have spoken. A band had encircled her chest, squeezing tighter and tighter until she could scarcely breathe. It took all of her concentration to mount the grand staircase without falling.

Rudolf Hess stood when they entered Hitler's anteroom. He had been reading through a sheaf of papers, which he now tucked into a manila folder and set on the desk. His deep-set eyes flickered over Gretchen, but his expression didn't change from its habitually mournful one. "Thank you for fetching Fräulein Müller, gentlemen. The Führer is grateful for your prompt service. You're dismissed for the night."

Somehow, Gretchen half expected Reinhard to object—she had never heard him take orders from someone other than Hitler or Röhm before—but he saluted, dumped her suitcase on the floor, and spun on his heel, Kurt at his side. The door banged shut behind them. She glanced at the closed door to Hitler's office. What was he waiting for?

Hess gestured toward a chair. "Some tea, Fräulein Müller? Or do you prefer coffee?"

"I . . . Tea, please." She calculated the number of steps to the corridor. She could never make it. She sank into a chair and watched while Hess fetched a silver tray from a nearby table. Perhaps he was coddling her to lull her into a false sense of safety. "I don't understand why I was summoned."

"The Führer had need of you."

Her hands shook as Hess handed her a white porcelain cup.

"The Führer is lonely," Hess went on, settling into a chair across from her. "It is not easy for a man in his position, with so much resting on his shoulders. You are a balm to his soul, Fräulein Müller; I have heard him say it many times."

Hope drifted like a plume of smoke through her chest. Maybe they knew nothing; maybe she was still safe. She shot a nervous glance at Hitler's shut door. Why was he making her wait so long? Was it possible he had figured things out and was enjoying letting her dangle at the end of a long chain, twisting and turning until he finally snapped it?

The office door swung open, a long shaft of lamplight falling into the dim anteroom. Hitler stood in the doorframe, feathered by the golden glow. Tonight he wore his usual plain brown uniform. His face was calm, his hair slicked back with brilliantine except for the front strands that flopped over his forehead and irritated him.

"I thought I heard voices," he said. "Did you enjoy your time in the mountains, my sunshine?"

"Yes, I—I—" *For God's sake, say something normal before he suspects!* "Yes, thank you, Herr Hitler. You have a beautiful home."

He raised his eyebrows. "Herr Hitler, Gretchen? I thought we had moved beyond such formalities long ago."

"Uncle Dolf." She forced the words out, and he smiled as he

ushered her into the office. The door shut, leaving Hess alone in the anteroom. "Perhaps it's no longer seemly for me to address you so casually. I am getting older now—"

"Yes," he interrupted. "I know."

Something in his tone made her look at him. He appeared as he always did: a half-starved face softened by the office's lamplight, a slight figure starting to round at the waist, heavy-lidded eyes that fastened her in place when they focused on her, as they did now.

"You are growing up, Gretchen."

There was no mistaking the measuring look in his gaze. She recognized the way his eyes swept up and down her body. Her face burned with embarrassment.

"Herr Hitler—Uncle Dolf," she corrected quickly, "I have known you for many years. Since I was a young child—"

"Yes, yes," he interrupted. "You shall keep me company tonight and distract me from my worries." He led her to the red upholstered chairs lining the wall.

What if this was all an elaborate trap? How he would enjoy toying with her, watching her wonder if he suspected the truth. The muscles in her arms tensed, ready to yank her hand free from his.

She glanced at his chest. Through the brown jacket, she saw the unmistakable ridges of a cartridge belt. If he wanted to shoot her, he wouldn't miss. He was one of the best marksmen in Munich. Her fingers, still wrapped in Hitler's, convulsed.

He squeezed hers back. Shock froze her in place. He thought she was *flirting* with him.

There was almost a laugh in his voice when he said, "You

have saved me from listening to Hess's interminable complaints about his health. Once he was *mein Rudi, mein Hessrl,* but now spending time with the man is torture. Yet," he went on, sounding almost shy, "I cannot bear solitude. I prefer the company of a pretty woman over a thousand men, but . . ."

He lifted his free hand helplessly. "A man in my position cannot choose the little pleasures that make life bearable. I must think only of the good of the Fatherland."

Hitler's knee brushed hers, but for once he didn't spring back as though the unexpected contact repulsed him. He began to talk, a steady stream of words that widened and deepened to a river. The upcoming presidential elections; the campaign trip throughout Bavaria he would commence in a few days with Hess and Hoffmann; filthy Communist swine; beloved president Paul von Hindenburg, who was slowly turning to dust and would surely die before the year was out; and the tremendous burden that lay on his, Adolf Hitler's, shoulders, for he had such a mighty task ahead of him to right all the wrongs . . .

"Do you see why I summoned you tonight?" he asked suddenly. His eyes met hers with such force that she nearly lost her breath. The bright blue reminded her of snapping live electrical wires, downed in a storm, sizzling in the darkness. "In the midst of all this, I find I am alone, quite alone. A yawning chasm seems to greet me at the end of the day, and the only thing that draws it closed is the company of a pretty young girl."

It was clear what was expected of her. Unconsciously, she had been filling this role for Hitler for years, and she saw that now—the giggling, cheerful child who had demanded nothing more from him than an occasional kindness, indulgent smiles, presents of chocolates at Christmas, cheap jewelry at birthdays, praise over her school marks. Easy and meaningless.

His fingers slipped from hers. He wiped his hand on his jacket, as though scrubbing away her touch. *Thank God.* Maybe he had grown tired of her company and would send her back to the boardinghouse.

But he leaned so close, she saw the tiny flakes of dandruff dusting his shoulders. "Cheer me with your chatter, my child."

"Your home on the Obersalzburg is so lovely," she began haltingly, and he nodded eagerly, encouraging her to go on. She prattled about the beautiful mountains and the long hikes and his sister's delicious cooking, and underneath the chatter, she heard the steady ticking of the desk clock.

Her mind worked furiously. Herr Doktor Whitestone had been wrong. Hitler and Reinhard were not alike. Reinhard could never comprehend loneliness, and Hitler seemed to ache from it.

Bewilderment caused her to stumble over her words and drop the string of what she had been saying, but Uncle Dolf reminded her gently about Charlemagne sleeping within the mountain, and she went on, talking about the snow that never melted. About the cold that never disappeared into warmth, so the ice and snow always remained.

Herr Doktor Whitestone had said psychopaths could not experience loneliness, because they could not feel love or yearn for companionship. Was it possible he had been so deeply mistaken about Hitler? Or did Uncle Dolf have a new kind of mental disease, one that doctors hadn't encountered before?

Hitler rose, and she stopped in midsentence, afraid she had somehow angered him. She stood, too, mentally counting the steps to the door. Sixteen. She could make it, but she might not get past Hess.

The room fell into blackness.

Hitler stood at the wall, his hand on the light switch. Moonlight spilling through the long windows painted his face silver. He watched her quietly, then said, "Aren't you going to come to me, Gretchen?"

She couldn't move. *My God.* He couldn't want from her what she suspected. . . .

A floorboard creaked. Hess. He was still out there. Listening, perhaps, or waiting for her to come out. There was nowhere for her to go.

Like a swimmer walking underwater, she crossed the room. The darkness was so complete that she stumbled into a side table, even though she knew the location of every stick of furniture, since she had been in here so often. A tiny gasp of pain burst from her lips, but Hitler didn't ask if she was hurt. Unmoving, he continued to watch her.

When she reached for a lamp, Hitler caught her wrist.

"No," he said. "I prefer the dark."

Slowly, almost hesitantly, his hand brushed the side of her face. He smelled like toothpaste and sugar. "You are so lovely, Gretchen."

He moved closer now, a collection of shadows that somehow combined to form a man, arms and legs and head made up of wispy darkness. She couldn't see him at all, but heard his breath, loud and ragged.

"Gretchen," he said, "may I kiss you?"

Everything within her recoiled at the words. *No.* She couldn't do it. She stumbled backward. In the darkness, she saw the whites of his eyes, which were following her. Fear shot through her veins like adrenaline; she was terrified to say no but unwilling to live with herself if she said yes.

They stared at each other. His expression did not change, remaining impassive. She could not guess what he was thinking. Even now, he had retreated within himself, keeping his thoughts hidden from her.

The silence stretched between them, broken only by his harsh breathing. Then he reached for the leather whip tucked into his belt. It whined through the air as he drew it free.

Her heart lurched. He was going to beat her, here, while Hess waited right outside. Fear locked her in place.

But the whip smacked into his open palm, so loudly that she shuddered.

Agony flashed across his face. Gretchen took a shaky step back, her hands curling into fists. She would fight him. She might not stop him, but she would rake her nails across his face and blacken his eyes, so everywhere he went people would wonder what had happened to him. They would whisper about him, and she knew nothing wounded him as deeply as stares and snickers. He would feel punished.

He stepped closer, clutching his injured hand in his other hand. Blood, black in the darkness, trickled between his fingers. The whip had sliced into his skin. The pain must have been excruciating, but his expression had become calm, detached. Revulsion coursed up her throat. He had hurt himself on purpose, and he didn't seem to care.

With slow, measured movements, he tucked the whip into his belt.

"Good night," he said, and walked away.

When he opened the office door, lamplight from the anteroom illuminated him for an instant, one bloody hand gripped in the other, the shoulders hunched with pain, the face placid.

And then he was gone, and her legs softened to water.

There was no way out except through the anteroom, and she felt herself stumbling forward. Hitler and Hess glanced at her when she came in, Hitler looking vaguely annoyed.

She heard her voice whispering good evening and felt her hands gripping her suitcase handle, and then she was hurtling down the staircase and into the front hall. It was empty now. For an instant, she wondered if Reinhard and Kurt were waiting for her outside, but then remembered they had been dismissed and were surely gone for the night.

She pushed the heavy doors open. The street was deserted. She took off at a run, the suitcase bumping against her leg, glancing back at the Braunes Haus growing smaller and smaller behind her, shrinking from a mansion to a house to a speck. Finally, she whipped her head around and concentrated on the street ahead. She was free.

# 33

THREE FLIGHTS UP, TWO WINDOWS FROM THE left. Gretchen counted before flinging the pebble. It hit the glass with a solid *clink*. A face pressed against the pane, and her insides slowly loosened with relief. *Daniel.* She hadn't realized how desperately she needed him until she saw him now.

He held up a staying hand, and she nodded. For a moment, she stood in the street, listening to the far-off purr of an automobile. The front door opened, and Daniel stood in the entrance—dark hair mussed, suit jacket tossed on haphazardly over a white shirt, scuffed leather shoes on his feet—so reassuringly solid and normal, and yet not normal at all, but talented and clever and open-eyed and determined, and so wonderfully unlike the shadowy men she had known all her life that she felt grateful tears well up.

"Daniel—" she began, and suddenly they were embracing,

his arms warm around her.

"Are you all right?" he asked. His voice was muffled against her hair.

"Yes, I'm fine."

But that wasn't true.

"I didn't think you were due back in the city for another two days," Daniel said as they stepped apart. Over his shoulder, she saw a suitcase at the foot of the stairs.

"Are you going somewhere?"

Now he smiled. "A lot has happened in the past couple of days. I can't take time to explain or I'll miss the night express to Berlin, so I'll ask instead—do you trust me?"

She had never trusted anyone more. "Yes."

He kissed her, hard and quick. "Then come with me now, and I'll explain everything on the ride."

She didn't hesitate, but interlaced her fingers with his, and together they stepped into the night.

The central train station stretched out its metal tracks like an octopus spreading its tentacles. At this late hour, the place was nearly empty except for a few bleary-eyed travelers, and Gretchen and Daniel had a third-class compartment to themselves. As the train gathered speed, the lights of Munich fell away, turning first into a twinkling necklace, then into shimmering dots in the distance.

They talked late into the night. Gretchen told Daniel everything that had happened in the mountains. When she spoke of meeting Hitler in his office, she stared out the glass, watching the darkened fields rushing past, too embarrassed to look at Daniel.

He took her hand in his. How different his touch felt from Hitler's, strong and warm, not hesitant and cool.

"I don't know what Herr Hitler is, exactly," she said. "A different sort of psychopath from Reinhard, that's clear. My brother thinks only of himself, and feels nothing. But Hitler . . . It's as though he feels *too much.* And he yearns so deeply to touch the mind of everyone he meets."

She blinked back tears. She wouldn't cry for their splintered friendship. She wouldn't cry for Hitler ever again.

After they ordered tea in the dining car, Daniel told her quietly what he had accomplished while she had been away. He had tracked down Herr Doktor Edmund Forster, the neurologist who had treated her father and Hitler at the end of the Great War. Forster now served as the clinic head and psychiatry department chair at Greifswald University, in a small city by the sea, hundreds of miles from Munich.

Gretchen gripped the teacup with freezing fingers. They could switch trains at Berlin, she supposed, but she couldn't imagine how long it would take them to reach Greifswald, or even if the trains left regularly for such a remote location. "It's so far. . . ."

Daniel grinned. "He's already responded to my telegram. He's staying at the Hotel Adlon in Berlin through the end of the week for a medical conference. He's agreed to meet with me."

Gretchen exhaled in relief. A piece of luck, at last.

The *Munich Post*, Daniel told her, had made good headway with its investigation into the National Socialists' plans for the Jews. Their SA source had supplied additional information, and they hoped to break the story soon.

Finally, Gretchen and Daniel turned to her father's murder. He had been killed at about noon on November 9. The leaders had decided to march through Munich at eleven thirty. Barely a half hour had elapsed between that decision and her father's death, but somehow, during those thirty minutes, someone had lured Klaus Müller into the front line and murdered him.

She pictured the men in the front line during the march. Papa hadn't really known the Munich SA head, or the army colonel. Hermann Göring had been too far away. Hitler's bodyguard had been intent on protecting his employer, and had been nearly killed. The army general had walked upright through the whizzing bullets, too proud to hit the ground; he was such a famous war hero that many of the bystanders never took their eyes off him. None had had the chance to kill her father.

Neither had Max Scheubner-Richter. He'd been shot through the lung and died instantly. Minutes before the shooting started, he'd linked arms with Hitler, and when he collapsed, he dragged his leader down to the ground with such force that Hitler's shoulder was wrenched from its socket. That was the story she'd always heard.

Her eyes narrowed. "Herr Scheubner-Richter stood on Uncle Dolf's right, didn't he?"

Daniel's forehead wrinkled in concentration. "Yes."

Gretchen shot him a swift, searching look. "Then why was Hitler's *left* shoulder dislocated?"

Comprehension flashed over Daniel's face. "Someone else grabbed him. But who? And why?"

"That," Gretchen said, "is one of the things we must find out."

⁂

Berlin was a polished diamond. Broad boulevards lined with massive buildings stretched in all directions; sleek automobiles and streetcars wound along the roads without any of the horse-drawn carts that Gretchen was accustomed to seeing in Munich. Pedestrians swarmed along the sidewalks, the ladies smart in their dresses and gloves, the men professional in business suits and hats, all hurrying to their midmorning destinations. At a corner, two dark-skinned men waited for their turn to cross the street, and Gretchen stared because she had never seen Negroes except in the cinema.

Everywhere she looked was evidence supporting Berlin's reputation as a liberal, progressive city: Cubist paintings hanging in the front windows of art galleries; cabarets featuring political comedians whose work would earn them a beating back in Munich; sidewalk cafés where bohemian types sipped tea together, their mix of fine and shabby clothing proclaiming that members of different social classes mingled in this city.

Gretchen had never seen anything like it, and suddenly Daniel made complete sense to her: his openness, his fierce desire to learn the truth, his insistence that others see with their own eyes. He had come from another world. Although Berlin and Munich were only a few hundred miles apart, they might have been on separate continents.

Gretchen and Daniel changed clothes in a tearoom's lavatories, he into his best dark suit, she into a pale blue linen frock dotted with flowers. The dress was the fanciest thing she had in her suitcase, but she worried it wouldn't conform to the hotel's dress code.

Apparently it did, for the waiter only ran a brief disapproving glance over her outfit before leading them to a table where a middle-aged man sat alone, chasing peas with his fork. He didn't notice them until the waiter cleared his throat and said, "Pardon me, Herr Professor Forster, but this lady and gentleman wished to meet with you."

The man looked up, blinking as though waking from a deep dream. He was a pleasant, ordinary-looking fellow of around fifty. He peered at them through small, round spectacles. "Yes?"

Daniel extended his hand for the fellow to shake. "My name is Daniel Cohen, and this is Fräulein Müller. I sent you a telegram a few days ago. We're very interested in your work."

"Ah, yes, I remember." Smiling now, the man rose and bowed slightly. "Please, sit and join me. You haven't eaten luncheon yet, have you? A couple of menus, waiter."

"Just tea for us," Daniel said as they sat down, and one glance around the large dining room told Gretchen why he didn't want to order lunch. Ladies in silk and men in fine suits lounged about the tables, and waiters in full livery carried heavy silver platters. She couldn't even guess how much a single meal would cost.

"It isn't often I meet someone not in the medical field who's aware of my work," Forster said as the waiter poured them cups of steaming, fragrant tea. He pushed aside his plate. "Particularly a young lady."

Gretchen met his gaze. "I find the study of mental disorders fascinating. I plan to become a psychoanalyst."

A trio of ladies in silk frocks walked past, trailing a waiter. Their flowery scent wafted over Gretchen, and she felt again that she had stepped into another world, one made of fine clothes and gourmet meals and pearls and perfume. Munich, with its grimy cobblestones and tobacco-choked beer halls and streets teeming with brown and black and red and green and yellow political uniforms, seemed far away.

"Indeed?" Forster picked up his teacup and studied her over its rim. "A worthy but difficult ambition."

"I've always wanted to be a doctor, ever since my father died when I was a child." Gretchen set her cup on its saucer on the damask tablecloth. Although her throat was painfully dry, she wasn't sure she could swallow a single sip. "But we didn't come to discuss psychology with you. We need to know what happened at the end of the war in the military hospital in Pasewalk, when you treated my father, Klaus Müller, and his friend Adolf Hitler."

"Ah." Behind his spectacles, the doctor's eyes narrowed. He studied her with the same intentness that she had often witnessed in Herr Doktor Whitestone. As though he could dissect her with a look, slice beneath the skin to the beating heart and learn all her secrets with an unblinking stare.

"You look like him," he said at last.

"You remember him." *Thank God.*

"Of course. But I can tell you nothing about his treatment. The medical field's code of ethics requires my silence."

Gretchen glanced at Daniel. He nodded in silent understanding. They must tell the doctor everything.

She leaned across the table, pitching her voice low. "I understand, Herr Professor Forster. But I'm not a weepy, sentimental girl trying to pry into her father's secrets. I'm trying to solve his murder."

"Murder?" Forster's eyebrows rose. "Your father was the

sainted Nazi martyr, I believe."

"That is what everyone believes," Daniel cut in, "but her father was shot from both the front and the back." He paused as Forster's forehead creased in surprise. "We believe something crucial happened in the military hospital in Pasewalk, Herr Professor Forster, and you might be the only person who can tell us what it was."

Forster sat very still.

Gretchen rose. She bent close to Forster's ear, whispering so the diners at the next table wouldn't overhear. "I'm beginning to realize I barely knew my father. But he was kind and good to me, and he didn't deserve to die in the street like a dog." When he didn't answer, she moved slightly, trying to meet his gaze. "Please. If something happened in the hospital that led to my father's death, I need to know what it was."

The doctor sat motionless. Then he looked her hard in the face. "Very well," he said at last. "I shall tell you all you need to know."

# 34

AS THEY WALKED TOWARD THE BRANDENBURG Gate, Daniel kept his hand lightly on Gretchen's arm. On her other side, Forster moved jerkily, as though at any moment he might turn around and go back to the hotel, and Gretchen feared he was reconsidering his offer to help them.

Ahead, the massive triumphal arch loomed like a great, hulking mountain of stone. It should have looked beautiful to her, but she remembered Daniel's words in the restaurant—*You never know who might be listening; let us walk in the Tiergarten, where we may be assured of privacy*—and she shivered.

Beyond the gate, the Tiergarten stretched out for miles. Leafy trees clustered together on tidy lawns intersected by long paths. The doctor took the nearest one, striding so quickly they had to hurry to keep pace. Gretchen heard the voices of small children, playing somewhere nearby, beyond the trees, their gleeful giggles the sound of a separate world.

In silence, Gretchen walked with Daniel and the doctor until the trees formed a protective green tunnel over their heads. Enclosed in this verdant passage, she felt safe enough to speak.

"Herr Professor," she began, "my father overheard you talking with another doctor about Herr Hitler when he was a patient in your hospital. You used a word he didn't understand. I realize this was a long time ago, but it occurred on a momentous day, when the patients learned about our surrender. Perhaps you can remember—"

Forster looked sharply at her. Sunlight pushed through the overarching trees, sending panels of shadow and gold across his quiet face.

"Then you don't know," he said. "Of course, you wouldn't. I'm sure your parents wished to keep the truth from you."

Daniel's hand tightened on her arm; she was glad of the steady pressure, a tangible reminder he was there. "I don't know what you mean."

"The Pasewalk hospital wasn't an ordinary military hospital. It contained seven different clinics and sick bays."

But that still didn't explain . . .

"For treating hysterical soldiers," Forster added.

"Hysterical . . ." She remembered Whitestone's teachings. "You mean mentally diseased."

Ahead, the path arrowed forward in a straight line. A breeze shivered through the trees. As she walked, she saw a few early leaves on the ground; colored red and orange, crackling like paper beneath her feet, they were already dead.

"Neurotics unfit for duty," Forster corrected. He spoke so

quickly, she had to concentrate to snatch hold of each word, or they risked running together in a stream of sound. "Not through any physical injury, you understand, but from their weak constitutions. There were so many of them that the Berlin War Ministry had to pass a law, quarantining the hysterics from the able-minded soldiers in hospitals. Eventually, different facilities were set up to treat them."

What the doctor said couldn't be correct. Gretchen's throat closed. She felt her legs moving, propelling her forward on the path, but they seemed disconnected from her body. *Hysterics. Mentally diseased. Neurotics. Not Papa.*

"Why were they quarantined?" Daniel asked.

"My dear young man." Forster looked astonished. "Hysterics *had* to be separated from other soldiers in the hospital for fear of their hysteria infecting entire wards and rendering hundreds more men unfit for battle. Their weak nerves were contagious, you see."

A woman pushed a baby carriage toward them. They waited until she had passed, cooing to the screaming infant. Beneath the carriage's canopy, Gretchen had seen the baby's tiny red face, screwed up in rage. Quickly, she looked away.

Forster continued. "Naturally, Hitler and Müller were sent to a different hospital than the rest of their regiment. There was no question they had been gassed, but the other soldiers had already recovered their sight. Those two still claimed to be blinded."

Gretchen stiffened. Her father had been a war hero, not a coward hiding behind a pretend injury. "How could you possibly know they weren't truly blinded?"

Forster stopped walking. His body seemed coiled tightly as

a spring when he burst forth, "Because that was my job! I saw hundreds, perhaps thousands, of soldiers during the war. In a moment, I could determine who was genuinely wounded and who was faking.

"Neither Hitler nor Müller had any of the physical characteristics of men still suffering from gas poisoning." Forster pointed a finger at her. "Hitler's eyes were reddened, probably from conjunctivitis; Müller's eyes were clear. Their eyes had none of the dead tissue or milky-gray appearance that would have resulted from a blinding gas attack. They were what we called malingerers—clear cases of hysteria."

Gretchen bowed her head. The nights Papa spent sobbing, alone, in the bedroom while Mama slept with her and Reinhard in the parlor. The times he beat Reinhard with his fists or his belt, finally sagging in exhaustion against the wall.

"Shell shock," she whispered. "That's what it was called, wasn't it?"

"Yes," Forster said. "The trauma of warfare can be devastating. Some men improve after treatment. Others never recover."

Daniel began walking again, Gretchen and Forster falling in step beside him. "How did you treat hysterics?" he asked. "With electrical shocks?"

"As a last resort," Forster said. "My preferred method is what I call 'the enlightening technique.' I spoke to the men as though they were naughty, disobedient children, told them their behavior was shameful for a German soldier. Most hysterics were cured quickly and sent back to the battlefield. Fräulein Müller's father responded well to talk therapy, and if the war hadn't ended, he would have returned to the front. But Hitler was most resistant to treatment."

Gretchen could hardly bear to ask, but she had to know. "What did he do?"

They continued walking, veering off the path and plunging deep into the gardens. Grass murmured under their feet.

"Sometimes he was furious," Forster said, "and sometimes he cried inconsolably, like a small child left alone in the dark. To the layperson, he would have appeared as a typical malingerer, recalcitrant and moody, to be sure, but typical."

He paused. "Not to me. I immediately suspected what he was, and when Müller came to me, saying Hitler had lost his sight again, I knew I was right. Hitler could not bear to see because he couldn't bear to see his beloved Germany defeated."

Gretchen's heart throbbed through her dress's thin fabric. "What happened next?"

"Hitler had chosen blindness again," Forster said. "As we walked to the dormitories, I ran into one of the neurologists and stopped to consult with him about Hitler's case."

At last, he looked directly at her. "Although I diagnosed Hitler when he was in my care, I have watched his career since and I have been forced to concede that he is utterly unlike anyone I have encountered in all my years of medical practice. He exhibits traits of a certain type of personality, but he also appears to be a narcissist and swings wildly from high to low moods with dizzying speed. He is a volcanic eruption, a lightning strike in the desert, a man perhaps with several different mentally diseased conditions. By all rights, he should be impossible. And yet he exists."

The doctor raised his hands, then let them fall helplessly to his sides. "What I originally diagnosed him to be, and what I said to the other doctor that day in the corridor, is that Hitler is a classic psychopath. And I'm very much afraid your father heard me say it."

The trip back to the train station was silent. Gretchen and Daniel didn't speak until the railway car lurched forward, going faster and faster until the brightly lit buildings of Berlin fell away and the green fields stretched out, the long grasses brightened by late-afternoon sunlight.

Their third-class compartment was crowded and noisy. A group of grimy-faced children and their exhausted-looking mother had claimed the seats opposite, but they were so busy teasing and scolding one another that Gretchen and Daniel could talk quietly.

"I'm sorry you didn't get a chance to see your family," Gretchen said.

Daniel looked startled, then smiled. "That isn't why we came here. But yes, I would have liked to see them." He hesitated, then took her hand in his, turning it over and twining their fingers together. "I would have liked to introduce them to the girl I've fallen in love with."

She didn't want to cry but couldn't help it. The moment should have felt like a miracle, but it was sad instead, like broken bootlaces, cracked glass, missing buttons on a blouse, everything once whole but now damaged. How could she and Daniel hope to stay together in Munich, whose cobblestone streets were slowly turning the National Socialist colors of brown and red and black?

"You and I are impossible," she said.

"No." Gently, he brushed the hair back from her face. "We are what's real and true."

And even though the children in their compartment started to shriek with laughter, he leaned closer, pressing his lips lightly to hers.

It didn't feel like a kiss; it felt like sharing a breath. Somehow, everything tumbled away, the giggling children, the train's monotonous rocking, the smells of burned coffee and yeasty bread from the food trolley rolling down the corridor. Nothing existed except Daniel and the steady pressure of his mouth.

Even as his lips touched hers, she felt tears tightening her throat. This boy, whom she had feared and despised. This boy, whose hands were supposed to press an infectious virus beneath her skin.

This boy, whom she loved. Even if she couldn't bring herself to say it yet.

When they pulled apart, Daniel ran his fingers beneath her eyes, wiping away the tears. "I'm sorry, too, for what you had to hear today."

She looked at the mother and children, but now they were busily scarfing down currant buns. "My father didn't deserve to be shot in the street. My parents' friends always said that he came back from the war much changed, as though part of him had been blasted away by the shells. I wonder . . . if he hadn't had shell shock, if he would have followed Hitler."

Sadness softened his face. "We'll never know."

Beyond the glass, the darkened fields flew past, tangled grasses in the darkness. Somewhere in France, in fields like these, her father had crouched in trenches and waited to die. He had watched the dirt-packed tunnels fill with smoke; he had watched as his comrades didn't put on their gas masks fast enough and died on the spot. He had sat beside Hitler, soaked with rain, dirty from mud, hungry from low rations, shaking with fear. Desperate.

"Daniel," Gretchen said softly, "I think my father may have said something about Hitler's diagnosis during the ride to the beer hall. He kept mentioning Hitler's overwrought nerves until everyone told him to be quiet."

They looked at each other. Blood thundered in her head. No. It was impossible. Papa couldn't have been cut down by his dearest comrade. . . .

The children had finished their currant buns and were watching them curiously. Gretchen and Daniel went into the little corridor that ran along the compartments. Through the windows across the way, a steady blur of shadows flashed past. At the end of the corridor stood a man in a dark conductor's uniform, glancing over a handful of ticket stubs.

Gretchen turned her back to him and stood close to Daniel. The train's wheels rumbled rhythmically, nearly drowning out her voice.

"But it couldn't have been Hitler," she said. "He's always said how grateful he is for my father's sacrifice, and he has kept my family close to him all these years. Perhaps it was Amann. He fought along with them in the war, and he would have known they were quarantined from their regiment. Maybe he wanted to protect Hitler's reputation. If the diagnosis got out, the Party would be destroyed, since Hitler and the Party are one and the same."

Daniel nodded. "Yes, but how can we know for certain *what* got your father killed? And Forster won't discuss Hitler's diagnosis publicly. He said his position as a physician prevents him from speaking about a former patient's condition. Besides, he has a family and won't put them in danger."

Gretchen started to speak, then froze. In her mind, she saw the potato bins and her mother's old trunk in the boardinghouse cellar. The trunk filled with old letters and dusty photographs, an album of dried wildflowers, hers and Reinhard's school marks. *And a doctor's report.*

A piece of paper, stamped with a doctor's name and address, covered with his scrawling handwriting. At the time, she had tossed it aside, intent on finding her father's old letters. Now she realized how strange the note was. The Müllers never went to doctors; they couldn't afford the fees. Could Reinhard's increasingly disturbing behavior have convinced their parents to take him to a doctor?

She clutched Daniel's hand. "I think I know where we might find medical information about my brother. And there's one person whom my father would have told about Hitler's treatment. If I'm right, she'll tell us everything. She has to."

His eyes met hers. "Your mother."

# 35

FOG BLANKETED THE CITY LIKE VELVET. IT HUNG in thick patches as Gretchen walked along the Amalienstrasse. Grimly, she focused on the sidewalk before her, trying not to think of riding back into Munich last night on the express train, reaching Daniel's apartment at dawn and lying alone on the sofa, falling into a gray, dreamless sleep while Daniel and his cousins slumbered in their rooms. Opening her eyes to find light from the noonday sun flooding the tiny parlor and a heavy silence hovering over the apartment. Glancing into the bedchamber the boys shared and seeing only Daniel's dark head on his pillow, the sheets rising and falling with his steady breaths, the other bed empty. Ruth and Aaron were probably at the university.

She had left a note for Daniel on the kitchen table, explaining she would be back soon, and crept out. Thank God, he hadn't woken. He would have tried to stop her. But he couldn't understand how tightly the years of friendship bound her to Eva. Not even Herr Braun's disapproval could keep her away.

The street was busy at half past twelve, the sidewalks brisk with shoppers and businessmen and storekeepers. A new collection of photographs perched in the front window of Heinrich Hoffmann's photography shop, gilt frames gleaming against the black cloth backdrops, pictures of apples and flowers and Hitler—the lover of Bavarian culture in traditional leather shorts and a cap with edelweiss tucked in the brim; the father of Germany smiling at a group of schoolgirls presenting him with a bouquet of daisies; the friend of all animals, standing beside his favorite German shepherd, Muck, his pale hand resting on the beast's head.

Gretchen ripped her gaze away and pushed the door open. Eva stood behind the counter, fiddling with her bracelet and looking bored. A young man, probably a new camera apprentice, was hanging photographs along the wall.

"Gretl!" Eva gasped. "Where have you been? Your mother rang me last night, looking for you. She said you never returned from Herr Hitler's mountain house!"

Somehow, Gretchen stretched her lips into a smile she hoped looked reassuring. "Is there someplace private we can talk?"

"The boss and his friends are in the back courtyard," Eva said. "Discussing some campaigning trip that he's leaving on with Herr Hitler tonight. We could speak in his office." She glanced at the young man. "Watch the counter for a moment, won't you?"

Eva didn't bother waiting for a reply. Together, she and Gretchen hurried down the corridor into Herr Hoffmann's office. Through the open window, Gretchen heard men's voices. The low, rich chocolate of Uncle Dolf, mingled with the harsh sandpaper of Herr Hoffmann. They were so close, only feet away. They might come inside at any instant.

She seized Eva's hands. "I'm so sorry my mother got you this job. If it hadn't been for us, you wouldn't have met any of these people. And I'm sorry I kept so much from you, but I didn't want to get you in trouble, too. But you need to know the truth."

Eva's mouth dropped open in an O of surprise. "Good heavens! Whatever is the matter?"

The men's voices rumbled through the window. Someone was talking about the upcoming elections. They would push that lily-livered Chancellor Brüning out of office, and President Hindenburg couldn't live much longer. Soon everything they had worked so hard for would come to pass. . . .

Gretchen pulled Eva out of the office, into the dim corridor, away from the men's conversation. "You can't trust anyone in the Party! Eva, I know you don't care about politics, but you must listen to what Herr Hitler is truly saying. He's dangerous and he's a fraud."

Eva shrank back. In the gray light, Gretchen saw her skin beneath the rouge, pale and child-soft, and the shape of her mouth, slender and small, beneath the lipstick. She realized with a jolt how little her friend resembled her old self, the girl she had been when she returned from convent school two years ago. As though she were burying herself beneath the cosmetics.

"Gretchen, how can you speak so about him?" Eva sounded scandalized. "He loves you as a daughter—"

"No." In her mind, Gretchen saw him moving closer in the darkness and heard the whip whistling through the air. "He doesn't love anyone."

Eva tore her hands from Gretchen's grasp. "That's a lie. He loves *me.*"

Gretchen froze. She couldn't have heard right. Eva couldn't care for him. They barely knew each other, beyond chatting casually in the photography shop. It couldn't be true. They couldn't have concealed such a secret from her.

Tears glittered in Eva's eyes. "He loves me," she said again, a plaintive note creeping into her voice. "And I will adore him forever."

"Eva," Gretchen breathed.

Eva beamed, but tears slid down her face, cutting lines through the rouge. "I met him two years ago when he came by the shop after closing. Afterward, he often dropped by with flowers and candy. Sometimes, he took me out, but he said we could only go to places where no one would see us."

The words rushed out, as though she had been storing them inside for a long time. Gretchen stumbled a step back. *Two years.* Two years this had been going on, and she had never had any idea. How skillfully he wrapped parts of his life in separate compartments. How easily he must have manipulated Eva, so she would keep secrets for him. A low cry of pain tore from Gretchen's throat. So easily that Eva had even kept secrets from her.

Horror stopped her heart for a beat. "The Jew in the alley . . . That's how Uncle Dolf knew I had protected him! *You* told!"

"Of course," Eva said. "He wanted to know why we hadn't come with the boys to the Carleton Tea Room."

"Have you told him everything?" Gretchen could barely choke the words out. "Does he know I'm investigating my father's death?"

Eva looked startled. "That ancient history? Why should I bother him with inconsequential news like that when he must devote all his attention to the Party and the elections?"

Somewhere, a door banged open and shut. The men were coming inside. Gretchen hurried back into the front room. The young man behind the counter glanced at her, his smile falling from his lips. She rushed past him, out the door, into the streams of people flowing up and down the pavement. A hand fastened on her wrist, jerking her to a stop. Eva, pale-faced and crying.

"Why can't you be happy for me?" she said. Other Müncheners walked around them, barely breaking their stride, too wrapped in their own lives to notice two upset girls. "I've never had a beau before!" She paused. "I love him."

Gretchen found her voice. "If you think love means secrecy, then you don't understand what love is at all."

Eva dashed a hand at her brimming eyes. "If you honestly believe that, go and never come back!"

There was nothing else Gretchen could do. She turned and started to walk. Her movements felt awkward, as though she were a wooden doll. She thought of her and Eva as little girls, sitting in adjoining pews during Mass. Another step, faster. Eva at the convent school in Simbach and she at the Gymnasium here, their weekly letters to each other. Another step, faster still. Giggling over film magazines, stretched out on Eva's bed while the cats purred at their feet. She started to run. Chattering about their goals to become a doctor and either a world-famous photographer or an actress. Her breath came hard and quick. The charcoal drawings of her and Geli and Eva, the girls Hitler wanted.

She tore around the corner, the Amalienstrasse slipping away behind her. Eva was gone to her. Hitler had taken her, too. Silent sobs filled Gretchen's chest. She pushed Eva's tear-streaked face out of her head and pulled forward the image of Geli standing among the sloe trees along the shore, murmuring that her uncle was watching her again. Eva had made her choice. Geli still had a chance to make one.

She didn't stop running until she reached a hotel and slid into one of the telephone boxes in the lobby, closing the accordion doors and breathing hard in the sudden silence. For a moment, she rested her forehead against the wall, letting the smooth feel of the wood tether her to the world.

With shaking fingers, she dialed the exchange for Hitler's apartment, hoping Geli had returned from the mountains by now.

She had. "Gretchen! How are you, darling? What a splendid time I had with you at Haus Wachenfeld!"

"I must speak with you." The words tumbled out. "It's about your uncle. He's dating—"

"Sorry, darling, I can't hear a thing." Geli's silvery laugh rang out. "Uncle Alf's coming through the door now and making a tremendous racket." She paused. "He's angry about something. But it can't be me."

Geli sounded anxious. "He ordered me back yesterday afternoon, and I barely argued, even though my brother had come all the way from Austria to visit, and now Uncle Alf is leaving tonight anyway on one of his silly campaigning trips."

Through the telephone wire, Gretchen heard muffled shouting. Something about dancing. "Geli, what's happening—"

Geli sighed. "Uncle Alf's merely raging again because I want to go to a dance. Like any ordinary girl my age, I might add!" She nearly shouted the last words, and Gretchen imagined her aiming them at Hitler as he came into the room. "Uncle Alf, I shall be along for luncheon in a moment."

A pause. Then Gretchen heard harsh, labored breathing mingling with Geli's shallow intakes of air. *Hitler.* He was listening. There had been no click of a separate extension being picked up. He must be pressing his head against Geli's, straining to share the earpiece so he could eavesdrop on their conversation.

She didn't know what to say. "I—I thought—"

"We could go to the shops tomorrow morning?" Geli finished. "Splendid. I'll take you around to my favorite hat store on the Maximilianstrasse. Shall we say at eleven?"

The tension in Gretchen's shoulders eased. Geli had understood. They could speak freely in the shops, without the chaperones Hitler often insisted accompany his half niece. By tomorrow, Hitler would be in Nuremberg, giving Geli enough time to learn about Eva and get out of the city, away from him.

"I'll see you tomorrow." She listened to Geli's murmured good-bye, the words mixing with Uncle Dolf's breathing. And when she rang off, she couldn't stop shivering, even as she stepped into the warm, fog-filled air and headed back to Isarvorstadt.

# 36

GRETCHEN SPENT THE AFTERNOON IN DANIEL'S apartment, listening to the ticking of her wristwatch, waiting for the cover of darkness. Finally, night laid itself across the city, and she and Daniel ventured to the boardinghouse, creeping into the back courtyard through an alley on the adjacent street.

She watched the lights in the boardinghouse blink out, one by one. Stones bit into her knees, and she half rose from her crouched position next to a walnut tree. A shadow was moving behind the kitchen windows. For an instant, it paused, and Gretchen could trace its profile in the air if she wished, for she knew it so well: long, narrow nose, full lips, smooth forehead, broad jaw. *Reinhard.*

Beside her, she sensed Daniel moving in the darkness. She felt his hand touch the small of her back. "He can't see you, Gretchen."

She nodded, not trusting herself to speak. But her fingers tightened on her knife's hilt anyway.

Through the window, she saw Reinhard open the door into the front hall, his shape outlined by harsh electric light. Then the door swung shut, and the light filling the slivers of space around the door went out. He must be going upstairs. It was time.

Gretchen and Daniel ran forward lightly. The back door was locked, but a few turns of her wrist forced the locking mechanism to slip out of place.

The kitchen was dark and empty. Beside the pantry stood the door leading to the cellar, and on the top step sat the lantern and a box of matches, just as she had left them a few days ago. Together, she and Daniel moved cautiously down the rickety steps.

When they reached the packed-dirt floor, Gretchen slipped the knife into her skirt pocket and Daniel held the lantern aloft, its tiny circle of gold battling the gloom. In the corner loomed the enormous coal furnace, a sleeping monster, silent and unlit. Vegetable bins lined the opposite wall, and the boarders' trunks and boxes sat in the cellar's far corner.

She flung open Mama's trunk and pawed through the jumble of junk: old letters, photo albums, the book of dried wildflowers, a sachet of potpourri that had lost its scent long ago. There it was, at the bottom. Her heart pounded as she lifted the paper out. The paper's stamp bore the words DOKTOR BAUER CLINIC OF PSYCHOANALYTICAL TREATMENT 56 SENDLINGERSTRASSE MÜNCHEN, and someone had added the date, 3 October 1923. A month, almost to the day, before the putsch and Papa's death.

Daniel brought the lantern closer to the paper. In silence,

they scanned the medical report. Doktor Bauer had seen Reinhard Müller, age ten, on the preceding day. After interviewing the child, and speaking with both parents regarding the child's past behavior, the doctor wrote, it was his expert opinion that Reinhard Müller displayed the symptoms of a developing psychopath.

Gretchen let out a small cry. Her mother had gone to the doctor's appointment, too. Her mother had known *and had kept them in the same house.*

Daniel touched her shoulder. "Are you all right?"

She shook her head, unable to speak. But Daniel seemed to understand her need to go on. He squeezed her shoulder, and they turned back to the report.

It was his opinion, the doctor continued in his looping handwriting, that the child had not developed the ability to bond with others during his infant years. Without treatment, such as talk therapy or electric shock therapy, the child's behavior would worsen. Violent outbursts would increase in frequency. Lack of empathy would grow more pronounced. Without proper intervention, the child would eventually progress from playing tricks on others to brutal forms of retribution.

Gretchen folded the paper with shaking hands. Now she understood why Mama hadn't taken Reinhard in for treatment. After Papa's death, they could have afforded a physician's fees—someone in the Party would have given them money for the therapy.

But Mama loved Reinhard. She couldn't bear to see him locked away in an asylum.

Gretchen had to swallow twice before she could speak. "It's

almost ten o'clock. In a few minutes, my mother should check the first floor one final time before bed. We can wait for her in the kitchen."

Daniel kissed her cheek. "You aren't alone," he said. "Not anymore. I'll be with you."

She nodded, blinking hard. She could withstand anything, as long as Daniel was with her. She watched as he closed the trunk, and they turned to go.

A door opened in the darkness above them. Reinhard stood at the top of the stairs. He had turned on the light in the kitchen, and the yellow glow lit his back and the sides of his face, leaving most of him in shadow. Gretchen saw his eyes gleaming, watching them.

She couldn't move. Beside her, she heard Daniel's quick intake of breath. His hand brushed hers, a silent warning. They must be careful.

"I thought I heard something," Reinhard said. "What are you doing, mucking about down here?" His eyes flicked over Daniel. "Who's this?"

Gretchen found her voice. "He's my friend." Even to her ears, her voice sounded unnaturally high. "We—we just wanted to talk to Mama."

"In the cellar?" Reinhard laughed. In his careless way, he loped down the steps, leaving the door open. He glanced at Daniel again. "You look so familiar. . . . I'd swear I've seen you somewhere before."

"We haven't met." Daniel's voice was hard. His hand patted his breast pocket, searching for something.

*Oh, God*, another minute and Reinhard might remember that

he'd seen Daniel at Hitler's speeches at the Circus Krone, or sitting with the other *Munich Post* reporters at Café Heck, watching Hitler and his cronies at their regular table.

Reinhard smiled. His teeth were a white slash. "Where have you been, Gretchen? Mama and I have been wondering where you went after Uncle Dolf summoned you back to Munich. Have you been with him all this time?" He paused. "Shall we start calling you Frau Hitler?"

The steps creaked. "Reinhard?" Mama called. "Who are you talking to?"

She appeared on the stairs, wraithlike in a white nightgown and robe. Barefoot, she hurried down the steps, stopping when she saw Gretchen. "My God, where have you been? I've been worried sick!"

She flew the rest of the way and wrapped trembling arms around Gretchen. "Who is this with you?" she asked, pulling back to look at Daniel. "Don't tell me you've been with a *boy* for the last two days! And what's this?" She snatched the paper out of Gretchen's hand.

"No!" Gretchen darted forward. Her mother mustn't see the paper now, while Reinhard watched. But it was too late. One glance had been enough. Slowly, her mother's arms fell to her sides. Her eyes were dull.

"You know about Reinhard," Mama said.

"Yes." Gretchen felt Daniel take her hand. His presence steadied her enough so she could ask. There could be no more caution. She might never have another chance. "Papa knew Uncle Dolf had received the same diagnosis, didn't he?"

Reinhard moved closer. "What the devil are you talking about?"

"You don't understand." Mama stretched out her hands, palms up, pleading. "Papa and I knew the doctor had to be wrong! Herr Hitler was the leader of a new political party, not a raving madman! So we knew our Reinhard wasn't a monster either."

Daniel brought his mouth to Gretchen's ear. "We must get out. Your brother . . ."

Reinhard stood, motionless, at the bottom of the stairs. Blocking the exit. Smiling in that blank, easy way of his. He rocked back on his heels, hands in his pockets. But Gretchen knew how quickly he could move if he wanted. How would they ever get away from here? Through her skirt, she touched the cool metal knife in her pocket. That was one way. She prayed she wouldn't have to use it.

"I don't like people speaking in riddles," Reinhard said.

"I'm sorry, Reinhard." Mama went to him, reaching up to stroke his cheek, but he stepped away, his feet hitting the back of the bottom step. He nearly fell. As he regained his balance, his eyes flashed with fury. Gretchen lost her breath. For an instant, he had looked so different. So enraged. As though the mask he wore had slipped out of place.

"Please, Reinhard, darling," Mama cried. "Don't be angry! I have kept secrets for your sake, so you wouldn't be sent away. I have loved and protected you always!"

Reinhard glanced at Gretchen over their mother's shaking shoulders. "At least I can depend on you not to dissolve into hysterics. What does she mean?"

"Don't," Daniel said, gripping Gretchen's hand, and she understood. If they hoped to get out of the cellar, they mustn't upset her brother.

"It's nothing—" she was starting to say when her mother interrupted, sobbing.

"How could I abandon him when I had made him what he was?"

In one swift motion, Reinhard cupped his mother's chin, tipping her head back so their eyes met. "Explain yourself."

"It was my fault." Mama kept crying. "The psychoanalyst we took you to—he said I didn't hold you enough when you were a baby. But I was pregnant with Gretchen, and so ill and exhausted all the time, and I let you lie in your crib for hours so I could sleep. At first, you used to cry all the time. And then you never did. *Ever.* It was unnatural. You didn't seem to feel anything at all. I would try to hug you, and you would push me away. . . ."

Gretchen glanced at Daniel. He shook his head slightly, in silent understanding. They shouldn't try to run past Reinhard. There was no way both of them would make it up the stairs.

"And then Papa came home from the war, so horribly changed," Mama choked out. "So sad and so angry and unable to control himself. And the peculiar things you used to do—pushing Gretchen into a wall and laughing, or throwing stray animals into rain barrels—they confused us so much. Herr Hitler always said you were just high-spirited, but we weren't certain."

Mama trailed off. Reinhard's expression remained calm, quiet. His eyes darted back and forth, as they always did when he was thinking. Gretchen slipped the knife from her pocket. From the corner of her vision, she saw Daniel pull something from an inner pocket in his suit. Something metal, gleaming dully in the pale light washing down the steps from the kitchen. A pistol.

Their eyes met. He held his right arm against his body,

waiting. Her fingers tightened on the knife handle. They both might manage to get out. But what about Mama? They couldn't leave her here with Reinhard.

Her mother's sobs had subsided. "Papa tried to beat you into submission, but you would stand there and watch him without saying a word. We kept hoping you would turn into a normal little boy. Then one day I found the cat, strangled and left on the kitchen windowsill."

A wave of nausea rolled over Gretchen. She had been right.

Reinhard's hands dropped from Mama's face. "Why are you upset?" He sounded confused. "It was only a cat."

Mama didn't seem to hear him. Misery had woven itself into the fine wrinkles around her eyes and the slender slope of her shoulders. Suddenly, she looked far older than her thirty-eight years. "It was *an animal*, not a piece of garbage to be thrown away! We took you to a doctor, to see what he recommended. And then Papa died a few weeks later, and I knew I must keep the three of us together, however I could."

Reinhard sighed and looked at Daniel again. "I know I've seen you before—"

"Why don't we go upstairs," Daniel cut in quickly, "where we can be more comfortable?"

Shrugging, Reinhard turned and started up the steps. *Thank God.* He hadn't gotten angry. Gretchen's legs wobbled beneath her as she climbed the stairs beside her mother, Daniel just behind. In a few minutes, they could be outside.

"Wait." Reinhard spun around on the top stair. His eyes fastened on Daniel. "*You*," he said, loading the single word with venom. His face had changed, hardening into granite. At his sides, his hands curled into fists. "You're that reporter from the Poison Kitchen. The Yid."

Gretchen raised her knife. Below her, she sensed Daniel swinging his arm up, pointing the pistol directly at Reinhard. Dimly, she heard her mother gasp.

"We prefer that our newspaper be referred to by its proper name." Daniel sounded cool. "Not the ridiculous appellation Hitler has given it. Now let your sister and mother pass."

Reinhard's lips twisted in disgust. Then he turned and ran. Gretchen saw him race across the kitchen and hit the door hard with outstretched hands. The door swung open and shut, open and shut behind him. She heard him pound across the hall and wrench the front door open, the hinges rasping in protest. He thudded down the steps and into the street. Then all that was left of him was the echo of his running footsteps, growing fainter.

With a small moan, her mother lowered herself to the steps. She sat, hugging her knees to her chest, sobbing.

Gretchen knelt beside her mother. "Mama, you shouldn't stay here. Reinhard might come back tonight."

Her mother lifted a tear-blotched face. "I can't leave him. He's my child. All I've tried to do is love and protect you both."

Pity stirred in Gretchen's heart. How young and alone her mother must have felt, after Papa died, without any money or relatives willing to shelter her if she took Reinhard, too. How could a mother choose between her children? Then she thought of Reinhard, throwing her to the floor, looming over her in the darkness, and she felt sick. There were always choices.

"I won't leave my son," Mama said. "I'll be fine. Go where you will be safe, Gretl."

Daniel seized Gretchen's hand, pulling her upright. "Come," he implored, and she followed him through the kitchen and outside. They scaled the back wall, dropping easily into the courtyard of the building behind the boardinghouse. When they reached the street, they broke into a run and didn't stop for several blocks until they saw a streetcar grinding to a halt on the corner.

Inside, they stood close together, breathing hard, trying to ignore the curious gazes of the other passengers. A few young men, university students perhaps, and a couple of middle-aged fellows in patched trousers and jackets, slurring, probably heading home from a beer hall. Gretchen turned away from them, resting her forehead on Daniel's shoulder, breathing him in. How long did they have before Reinhard tracked them down?

"He doesn't know my name," Daniel said. He had guessed at her thoughts. "Even if he remembers it, he won't be able to find us tonight. My cousins are listed in the city address directory, not me. I've moved too recently to be included in the current edition. We're safe, for tonight at least."

"For tonight," she repeated, and fell silent. She could not even guess what might await them in the morning.

# 37

DANIEL'S COUSINS HAD GONE TO FRANKFURT AM Main for the weekend to visit their parents. Without them, the apartment felt large and quiet. From Daniel's doorway, Gretchen watched him light the candle on his nightstand. Its golden warmth touched his face, softening its angles and planes.

She had never been inside his room before. There were two narrow beds, one wedged beneath a window, the other shoved against a whitewashed wall. Plain cambric curtains framed the window, and an ancient-looking armoire stood in the corner. Stacks of books covered the writing table, and beneath lay a pile of clothes she suspected were desperately in need of laundering. Cheap reproductions were tacked on the walls. She recognized the sharp Cubist shapes of Picasso and the wild colors of Klimt—two artists Hitler loathed.

"I shouldn't be in here," she said.

Daniel looked at her. "Shouldn't? Or don't want to?"

He stood so close, she felt the warmth emanating from his skin. "I want to be here."

His gaze locked on hers. "With a Jew?"

Once she had seen him as nothing more than that. She moved nearer, keeping her eyes on his. Not a caricature, but a person, whole and wonderfully complex and unique. Love for him welled in her heart. "With Daniel."

"We are one and the same," he said, looking serious. "My faith is part of me, Gretchen. If we wish to be together, we must accept every part of each other."

Hesitantly, she placed her hands on his shoulders, felt the muscles flexing beneath her fingers. "I accept every part of you."

He smiled and cupped the back of her neck, propelling her closer until they kissed. Everywhere his lips touched, she felt circles of sparks revolving under her skin. He kissed her mouth and her neck and her temple, and she kissed him back, his mouth, and the delicate curve where his neck met his shoulder, and the warm flesh beneath his ear, and she felt the blood in her veins soften and smooth into liquid honey.

"You are so beautiful," he murmured. "So lovely, my Gretchen."

She drew back. *Beautiful*. How could she be pretty, when her family was mired in such ugliness and secrecy? She sank onto the bed's edge, staring at the unevenly varnished floorboards. What must Daniel think, when he looked at her? What must he *see*?

"Gretchen?" The mattress sank under his added weight. His knee brushed hers. "What is it?"

"I'm not beautiful. My family . . ." She forced the words out.

"My family is twisted into such ugliness."

For a moment, he was quiet. "You are your own person, separate from your brother and your parents. Do you really think you're responsible for what they became? These are ties of blood, nothing more. You have chosen who you want to be."

Her throat tightened. "I'm so ashamed of them."

For an instant, he said nothing. "Do you think I don't understand shame?" he asked at last. "I'm a Jew. All my life, I've been hated and mocked."

He stretched himself out on the bed, pillowing his head on his interlocked hands. Scarcely believing her nerve, she lay down beside him. She rolled onto her side, resting her head on his chest.

He told her a story she had never heard before. Last December his father had taken him to the Mozartsaal theater on the Nollendorfplatz in Berlin. The American version of the film *All Quiet on the Western Front* was playing for its second night. Automatically, Gretchen stilled, for she knew its plot. She had read the book last year, even though Hitler despised it, as he despised all books that portrayed the Germans' experiences in the Great War in a critical light. But she had been curious, and had hidden it beneath her stack of library books.

The evening was supposed to be a grand treat, Daniel said. As the film began, hordes of men poured into the darkened theater, screaming, "Jews, get out!" Missiles flew off the balcony, falling onto the seats below, where Daniel and his father were sitting. The missiles exploded on impact, filling the air with a hideous smell.

*Stink bombs*, Daniel had realized, even as people started screaming, and he got up, shouting at his father to escape. Then he heard mice squeaking—the sound was horribly magnified, as though countless numbers were rushing toward them—and he felt their sharp claws digging into his shoes and saw their little eyes shining in the darkness, dozens—no, *hundreds*—of white mice, swarming across the floor.

He pulled on his father's arm, urging him to hurry. But his father shrank back, murmuring if they stayed silent they would be left alone. SA brownshirts raced up and down the aisles, grabbing men at random and punching them in the face, shouting, "Jews, get out!"

Daniel felt hands gripping his arms and spinning him around. Light from the flickering movie screen illuminated the SA man's face. Grinning.

Daniel's hand clenched into a fist. But before he could land a punch, the other man hit him squarely in the jaw. Daniel fell back, half collapsing from the sudden white-hot pain. His father seized him, dragging him down into the seats. "Not a word," his father said, and the man went on, searching for more victims as police whistles blasted.

Daniel couldn't look at his father. Papa had done nothing. He had watched as that man hit his son. Because he thought silence and acceptance meant survival. In that moment, as police officers started pouring into the cinema and the SA hordes ran out, Daniel resolved never again to feel ashamed. Never to submit. He would fight until his last breath. Only death would stop him.

When he had finished, he and Gretchen lay quietly for a moment. Her beautiful Daniel, passionate and loyal and true to himself. She had never known anyone like him. Like sunlight sparkling on clear water, not the fog and shadows she had known all her life.

She sat up, so she could look him squarely in the face when she said the words she had so longed to say back to him on the train ride from Berlin.

"I love you, Daniel."

He smiled. The candlelight reflected in his eyes, glimmers of gold in the brown. "I love you, too."

Warmth pooled in her chest. She couldn't stop smiling as she lay down beside him again. Through their clothes, she felt his heart thudding into her back. Listening to his soft, even breathing lulled her into dreams, and she surrendered to their welcome oblivion.

In the morning, they had hard rolls with cheese and coffee for breakfast. Gretchen checked her watch. Half past nine. They had slept terribly late.

"I must hurry." She drained her cup. "I'm due to meet Geli at eleven."

Daniel stared at her. "You're still planning on going to Hitler's apartment?"

She carried her dishes into the kitchen and set them in the sink. "Herr Hitler left for Nuremberg last night. He's gone on a campaigning trip he's been planning for quite some time, so he won't miss it. Sometimes he insists on Geli's having chaperones, but not if she's going shopping with a girlfriend. There will be no one at the apartment except for Geli and the servants."

She filled a pot with water and set it on a burner to boil. Daniel dumped his plate and cup into the sink. His face was dark.

"I must, don't you see?" Gretchen asked. "Geli needs to

know that he's dating"—Eva's name stuck in her throat, and she hurried on—"someone else, and she's free of him. Daniel," she added when he said nothing, and took his hands in hers, "you didn't see her face at the picnic, when she whispered that her uncle was watching her again. She loves him, I think, but she feels trapped."

He sighed. "You have a good heart, Gretchen. Please, be careful."

The pot started to boil, and Daniel reached past her to pick it up. "I've got to get to the office. There's talk there will be a Communist demonstration on the Odeonsplatz tonight. If there is, the brownshirts are sure to be there to start a fight. My editor wants me to cover it."

"Can I come with you?"

He poured the boiling water into the sink. Steam floated up, hiding him from her for an instant. "Your brother might be there. He's one of the SA's best brawlers."

She raised her chin. "It's a small city. I'll have to see him again sooner or later."

Daniel had started to scrub the dishes, but he stopped to look at her. "That sounds as though you plan to stay in Munich. It isn't safe for you here anymore. Not now that your brother has seen us together."

"I know." She felt suddenly shy and busied herself with tidying the table. She picked up the bread knife and her pocketbook. "I'm not leaving until I can learn what happened to my father. But I must get out at some point. There's nothing else here for me but you."

His expression was so remote she couldn't guess what he was

thinking. "You'd like Berlin," he said at last. "And my parents would like having me closer again."

Was he suggesting what she thought? She wasn't sure how to ask him, and before she could say anything, he resumed washing the dishes. He hadn't put on his suit jacket yet, and she saw the muscles moving beneath his white shirt as he scrubbed the plates in circular motions. A boy who washed dishes.

His lopsided grin pulled the left corner of his mouth higher than the right. "Are you going to watch or help?"

"Oh. Sorry." She snatched up a dishtowel and dried a plate. "It's just . . . I've never seen a boy wash dishes before. It's wonderful."

He surprised her by catching her hand in his wet one and kissing the knuckles, every one.

After they finished cleaning, she left quickly, before she could change her mind. Jews and Eastern European immigrants walked past—some of the ladies in all black, some of the men in traditional Hasidic dress, and other men and women wearing ordinary suits and dresses, plain and much mended—and everywhere she heard them talking to one another, German, Yiddish, Russian, Polish, all these unfamiliar words wrapping around her like a cloak. She might have been in a different world from the Munich she had always known.

She watched her reflection in storefront windows. No one was following her, but a few of the pedestrians glanced at her in obvious fear. They must have noticed her necklace. In another section of Munich, she would have seemed an ordinary girl. Here, her black skirt and green blouse and heels marked her as not one of Isarvorstadt's typical residents. And the *Hakenkreuz*, gleaming gold around her neck, identified her as one of the district's enemies. She touched the charm, its sharp edges biting into her fingers. No, she wouldn't take it off. Not until she had learned once and for all who had killed her father, and she could cut the chains linking her to National Socialism forever.

# 38

HITLER'S HOUSEKEEPER ANSWERED THE DOOR after one knock.

"Oh, Fräulein Müller, it's you." A handkerchief fluttered in Frau Reichert's hands. Her normally placid face looked pale and drawn. "I was expecting the police."

Gretchen started. "The police? What's happened?"

Frau Reichert hesitated. "It's—it's Geli." She held the handkerchief to her mouth, as though she wished she could muffle the words. "Herr Hitler will be so brokenhearted when he gets back."

Fear squeezed Gretchen's heart. Geli must be hurt. She had to get to her at once. Quickly, she pushed past the housekeeper. From the front hall, she heard men's low murmurs, but not the silvery tinkle of Geli's voice.

Four men sat in the parlor, ranged in a circle, leaning forward and talking so intently none noticed her approach. From the doorway, she watched them for an instant. Even from the back, she recognized the thin slope of Rudolf Hess's shoulders and the cloud of his dark hair. She didn't know the others: a baby-faced brown-haired man; an older fellow with a long, heavy face; and a fourth gentleman, who seemed familiar, middle-aged, thin, black-spectacled, balding.

Sweat beaded this man's upper lip as he said, "The bad publicity will be devastating."

"Can't be helped," the older man growled. He pointed at the baby-faced man. "Do it." The fellow bent over the telephone and dialed. "Listen, you're to tell the press it was an accident, not a suicide."

Gretchen froze. *Suicide?*

The baby-faced man exclaimed into the telephone, "What! You didn't! You're awfully quick off the mark. It's only been twenty minutes since I last rang you!" He ran a hand through his hair, his forehead furrowed in concentration as he listened. "No, it isn't your fault, naturally not. Good-bye."

He hung up and groaned. "We're too late. The Braunes Haus has already released a statement to the press. What a disaster."

Gretchen gripped the doorframe so hard her fingers went numb. *No.* They couldn't be talking about Geli.

The old man sighed. "All right, let's think. After Hitler and Hoffmann left last night, Geli succumbed to her growing fears regarding her future as a professional singer. She committed suicide last night."

Geli was dead.

Gretchen cried out before she could stop herself.

All four swung around to stare at her.

"What the devil is she doing here?" Hess surged to his feet.

She staggered backward. *Impossible.* Geli would never kill herself. Not laughing, sweet, merry Geli. She had been too alive to seek death.

"Fräulein Müller, come here." Hess extended his hand toward her.

She spun away from him and raced through the sprawling apartment to the long corridor where Hitler's and Geli's bedrooms sat side by side. She wouldn't believe it. Not until she had seen for herself.

Geli's door had been broken down. The doorframe's hinges hung drunkenly, and wooden splinters lined the gaping hole. Gretchen skidded to a stop in the doorway and stared.

In the room, Geli lay facedown on the floor. Blood had pooled beneath her chest and spread out on either side of her body. It had faded to the color of rust. She must have been dead for hours. One arm stretched across the carpet, as if reaching for the gun lying on the sofa.

Gretchen knew that gun so well—it was the Walther 6.35 that Hitler kept on a shelf in his bedroom. Nausea hit her like a strong wave, and she had to brace herself on the doorframe so she didn't sink to her knees.

She snatched a quick impression of the room. It was as she remembered: the dainty vanity table crowded with pots of powder and bottles of scent; the prettily made bed; Hitler's landscape painting on the wall; the framed photograph of Muck on the desk. Today, there was a sheet of paper on the table. If she squinted, she could make out the final sentence. *When I come to Vienna—I hope very soon—we'll drive together to Semmering an . . .*

The sentence stopped in the middle of a word. Not a suicide note.

Hands gripped her shoulders and pulled her back.

"You mustn't see this, Fräulein Müller. It's too upsetting for a young girl—"

She ripped herself out of the man's grasp. It was Hess. His deep-set eyes seemed hooded beneath his thick brows.

"What happened to her?" she cried.

"Fräulein Raubal was distraught," he said in his slow, deep voice. "Or perhaps she was playing with the Führer's gun and it went off."

Geli would *never* hurt herself. Gretchen felt her insides turn to water. Unless she had been driven to it. Even then, Gretchen knew who must be responsible.

Hess took her arm, guiding her along the corridor. Gretchen moved like a sleepwalker. Each thought seemed to travel miles before surfacing in her brain. If only she could break through this haze and think. . . .

"It's such a terrible tragedy," Hess said. "The Führer's grieved beyond measure. I telephoned him myself at the hotel in Nuremberg only minutes ago. I have never heard him scream like that. He's in such a state that we all fear he may do himself a mischief."

Gretchen stumbled. Geli lay dead on the floor, and Hess was worried about *Hitler's* well-being. Because he was the only one who counted.

The older man appeared at the end of the corridor. "Herr Hess, you must leave. The police should be here any minute. Herr Schwarz shall remain. He's a city councilman," he added as Hess opened his mouth, probably to protest. "It's best for the

Party if a prominent citizen can deal with the inspectors before Herr Hitler returns."

"Very well. But I should prefer to remain for the Führer's sake."

"You can best serve him by leaving." The man stared at Gretchen while Hess strode away.

Panic swamped her chest. What was this stranger going to do to her? As she backed away, his hand shot out and fastened on her wrist. "I'll say this only once, so listen well. Herr Hitler and Herr Hoffmann left yesterday evening on their campaign trip. Afterward, Fräulein Raubal went into her room. She must have shot herself sometime during the night. This morning, the servants were concerned when she didn't appear for breakfast, and they broke into her locked room. Do you understand?"

She understood nothing. She tried to pull away from him, but his grip remained firm.

"Let go of me!"

A doorbell jangled. "The police," he muttered. "Come."

She wouldn't go anywhere with him. She tore her arm free and raced headlong down the corridor.

Another man stepped out from the entryway. She was going too fast to stop herself, and she collided with him. She heard the air push out of his chest in a sudden gasp. In the dim light, his spectacles looked like blank discs, concealing his eyes from her. The fourth man from the parlor. She remembered him now, from countless dull evenings at Café Heck. Franz Xaver Schwarz, the Party treasurer. She could count on no help from him.

"Ah, Herr Schwarz," the older man said behind her. "Take the young lady to Frau Reichert's room. I don't think we can depend on her discretion, so there's no need to alert the police to her presence."

"Very good." The slender man glanced at her. Perspiration wet his high, pale forehead. "Please, Fräulein Müller, your presence could prove difficult to explain to the police. We must avoid any potential embarrassment for the Führer."

Was it safer to break free and find the policemen or follow the men's instructions? She thought of the fellow she had bribed so easily at the central station, and remembered Hitler laughing, saying the Party had little to fear from the police as many officers were becoming loyal National Socialists. There was no guarantee she could trust the officers entering the apartment.

Quietly, she followed Schwarz through the parlor. From the front hall, she heard a man talking to Frau Reichert, saying he and his partner had arrived to investigate the young lady's death.

Gretchen and Schwarz reached the far end of the apartment. Maybe she should go to the police. Perhaps they were honest men. She started to turn, but Schwarz grabbed her arm and shoved her into a small room. The door slammed shut. She heard the scrape of a key in the lock, then the whisper of fading footsteps.

She sat on a chair and took several deep, steadying breaths. Then she glanced around the small, plain room. No telephone. No way to get word to Daniel. Even if she shouted, the policemen might not hear her because the apartment was so large. And Hitler's men or servants might be standing nearby, keeping watch. Listening for her. She was trapped.

A memory swam into her mind. Sitting in the parlor, clutching a teacup in bruised hands, trying to see through a blackened eye. Geli's casual words: *Henny and I felt like characters out of a Western film.*

Awareness shot through her. Geli and Henny Hoffman had been receiving weapons training at a shooting range outside Munich. Geli had shot Walthers before. She knew how to take them apart, clean them, and fire them properly.

Gretchen stilled. How could Geli have accidentally shot herself? It seemed impossible. . . .

A creaking floorboard pulled her into the present. The door opened. Frau Reichert peered inside.

"Are you all right, Fräulein Müller?" she asked. "Would you like luncheon? The cook is preparing sausage."

Gretchen's stomach revolted at the thought of food. Something must have shown in her face, for Frau Reichert stepped into the room and closed the door. "It is a terrible thing, Fräulein Raubal's death," she said quickly. "The investigation should soon be over, and you may return home. I hope you'll be comfortable in my room for the time being."

Then she was gone, the door snicking shut. Gretchen heard the tumblers click. She was locked in again.

One. Then two o'clock. Finally a quarter to three. She must have paced the room a hundred times by now. The door opened again. Schwarz stepped inside.

His quiet eyes blinked behind his spectacles. "The detectives have left," he said. "They will return around three thirty to interview the Führer, who should have arrived by then. You're free to leave, Fräulein Müller. And thank you for staying quiet. Your concealment could have proven difficult to explain to the police."

She didn't bother replying. There was nothing safe to say.

Schwarz ushered her into the corridor. All around them, the apartment breathed, silent and still. This was all wrong. There should have been people weeping in the parlor, servants preparing food for mourners, policemen searching Geli's bedroom for clues. The apartment should have been busy as a train station at rush hour. Instead, it was a grave.

She stopped so abruptly that Schwarz ran into her. She mustn't be afraid; Geli needed her friends now more than she ever had in life. "Tell me what the inspectors said."

"Fräulein Müller, surely some matters are not proper for a young girl's ears." A faint flush tinged his cheeks. "It's far better that you return home."

"No, it's far better that we honor Geli's memory by ensuring the police are adequately investigating her death." She watched as his narrow lips firmed. There was nothing he could say without losing face. "What did the inspectors say?"

"Not very much. There's exceedingly little for them to do in clear cases of suicide. Clear cases, Fräulein Müller," he repeated, still blinking owlishly behind his glasses. "The police doctor has come and gone, and he has confirmed that Fräulein Raubal died yesterday evening."

"But how can he be so sure?"

"Rigor mortis set in several hours ago," Schwarz said, and suddenly she felt sick, thinking of Geli's body hardening and changing. "The single, fatal shot penetrated through her clothes to pass directly above her heart. It never exited her body, but remained lodged above her left hip, where it can be felt through the skin. Are you satisfied, Fräulein Müller?"

*No.* She would never be satisfied now that Geli was dead. What else could she do? Somehow, she forced one foot forward, then the next. It seemed so wrong to leave, but she didn't know how to help.

They had reached the parlor. Gently, Schwarz took her arm as if to guide her toward the front hall, when they heard the sound of a doorknob turning, loud in the quiet. They looked at each other.

"It's Herr Hitler," Schwarz said. "He's back."

# 39

SHE HEARD THE SHOUTING FIRST.

*"Where is she?"* From the front hall, Hitler's voice seemed to fill the entire apartment. He sounded panicked. "Where is my Geli?"

"The Führer needs privacy in his grief," Schwarz said, and he pushed Gretchen through a door just as four men charged into the parlor. She caught a glimpse of their pale faces—Hitler, Hoffmann, the chauffeur, and her brother—before she stumbled backward into the kitchen and the door slapped shut.

The servants stared at her. Frau Reichert and the butler were seated at the table, and the cook stood over the sink, peeling carrots.

"Herr Hitler has returned," Gretchen said. Through the door, she heard his frantic cries. *Not my beautiful princess*, he was sobbing, and someone else, perhaps Hoffmann, murmured soothingly, like a mother to a sick and fretful child.

"He will need assistance." Frau Reichert rose. "Herr Hess said the telephone disconnected before he finished delivering the message of Fräulein Raubal's death, so Herr Hitler doesn't know yet that she's dead. He'll be in a terrible state."

Like drivers unable to look away from a bad auto accident, the other servants drifted after her, leaving the kitchen empty. This might be Gretchen's only chance. She tucked her pocketbook under her arm and dashed to the telephone to dial the exchange for the *Munich Post*. But the door opened, and Reinhard peered in. She slammed the earpiece onto its hooked handle, her heart racing.

"What the devil are you doing here?" he asked.

She met his stare. "I could ask you the same thing."

He stepped into the kitchen and leaned against the wall. He wore his brownshirt uniform. When he shoved his hands in his pockets, a ridge of muscle undulated along his shoulders and down his arms, pushing against the plain khaki-colored fabric. She had to swallow the nausea rising in her throat.

"I left for Nuremberg last night," Reinhard said, "to inform Uncle Dolf about the traitor in our midst." He paused. "The blood traitor."

That could only mean her. The Aryan who had polluted her own blood with a Jew's, for that was how Hitler would see it.

"I told him his beloved little sunshine has dirtied herself with a Jew." Reinhard pushed himself off the wall, sliding his hands from his pockets. "He was most displeased."

She felt numb. "That was unwise. Don't you realize this could destroy you, too?"

"How? I've proven my loyalty by turning you in, and you've

shown that you're a race defiler."

"Yes, you would see it that way, but *he* won't. He'll view the entire family as tainted by their association with me; he'll secretly despise all of the Müllers and—"

"No, he won't," Reinhard said scornfully. "Haven't you ever heard him talk about the Jew doctor who treated his mother for cancer? He's still grateful to the fellow, more than twenty years later. Uncle Dolf can put his feelings into separate boxes when he needs to."

Gretchen stared at him. *Feelings. Separate boxes.* The *Günstlingjude*, Hitler's "favored Jew," the doctor who had cared for his mother. Crumbling letters and an old newspaper photo. Dead cats and a dislocated shoulder and the men's positions in the front line. The psychiatric diagnosis that only her father and Uncle Dolf had known about. Papa trailing after Hitler into the beer hall, desperately unhappy, and confiding to Gerlich that his old wartime memories were troubling him. Dying at the front line when he should have been in the rear unit. Only one person would have had the authority to order her father to march with the leaders. The same person who had known about the wartime diagnosis and wanted to shut her father up before he spilled the damaging secret. The man who could seal his hatred for Papa into a box and smile at her for years. Hitler himself.

At last, she knew who had killed her father.

She had to escape. Pushing past Reinhard, she threw the door open and raced into the parlor, staggering to a stop when Hitler appeared in the doorway. He moved like an old man, his shoulders rounded, his steps slow and unsteady, his face pale as paper.

"Gretchen," he said hoarsely.

She couldn't look at him; she couldn't speak or he would guess the truth, that she finally knew what had happened on that November morning eight years ago. She must act ordinary; a few whispered words of condolence and she could be out the door.

"I'm so sorry about Geli—" she began, but Hitler shouted, "*Do not speak her name!* You are not fit to say it!"

Schwarz appeared behind him. "Herr Hitler, you must rest before the police return. We shall explain to them it was a terrible tragedy—that, of course, Fräulein Raubal's death was an unfortunate accident."

"Yes, an accident, yes, thank you!" Hitler sobbed, practically falling into Schwarz's arms. "My beautiful Geli . . ."

Now was her chance. She sidled along the wall, toward the doorway leading to the front hall. Quickly, quietly, so they didn't notice. Another second and she could run for the door. They wouldn't dare stop her once she reached the street, she was sure.

A hand clapped over her wrist and jerked her back into the parlor. "Where do you think you're going?" Reinhard breathed in her ear. "Uncle isn't done with you. Uncle Dolf," he said more loudly, "I believe you have my sister to deal with."

Like a man awaking from a dream, Hitler swiveled out of Schwarz's awkward embrace. "Yes." A strange expression Gretchen had never seen before tightened his features. It might have been hurt.

Reinhard released her and walked away, joining the other men at the opposite end of the parlor. She stood alone before Hitler.

"You're too trusting, Gretchen," he said. "Everywhere, the Jew disguises himself to seduce pure German maidens. But he cannot transform his true self."

There was nothing she could say, nothing that he could hear. Shaking, she raised her head so she could look at him—sheet-white and sweating, his eyes bloodshot and focused on the wall instead of her. No, there was one thing she could say to him.

"You're wrong," she said.

It was as though a switch had been thrown. He sprang forward. "Someday I shall have gallows upon gallows erected, and the Jews shall hang from them! All save for a few, who I shall keep alive so they may see that their race has been annihilated from the face of the earth."

His face had flushed. Sweat had turned the strands of hair at his temples from brown to damp black. His eyes, that wild, piercing blue, fastened on her.

She stepped closer to him, so near she could smell his scents of sugar and toothpaste and hair pomade. The other men ranged about the far side of the parlor, Hoffmann, Schwarz, and the chauffeur shuffling their feet, clearly ill at ease, Reinhard perched on a chair's arm, looking bored. They couldn't hear her if she spoke quietly.

She looked at Hitler. They were eye to eye.

# 40

SOFTLY, SHE SAID, "I KNOW WHAT YOU DID TO MY father."

"What are you talking about?" Hitler stared at her. A tic pulled at the left side of his face—such a quick motion she nearly missed it.

"You killed him. He knew about the diagnosis you received at the hospital in Pomerania. He brought it up during the auto ride to the beer hall, cautioning you not to let your nerves become too overwrought again. That was why he was so upset that night. Because you were angry with him, and he couldn't bear your disapproval."

Her heart hammered against her ribs, so loudly she could scarcely hear her own hushed voice. Hitler continued staring at her, but he didn't even open his mouth. He was speechless. She hadn't known it was possible. She rushed on, the words tumbling out.

"You summoned him to the front line—it must have been you because no one else would have had the authority to move him from the back. I don't think you planned on shooting him, for no one could have predicted you would walk directly into the waiting police." She grabbed a quick breath, and Hitler remained silent, watching her. Glaring. "Perhaps you wanted your old war comrade near you again. It doesn't matter. He marched with you until you reached the Residenzstrasse. The street is so narrow that you couldn't walk together, so he stepped a little in front of the first line. When the bullets started, you saw your chance to eliminate an inconvenience."

Hitler's left cheek rippled from the tic. Above the undulating skin, his eyes were stone, as though the parts of his face belonged to different people.

"He was right in front of you," Gretchen said. She kept her gaze locked on his. "It was easy to shoot him in the back. The force of the bullet made him fall into your path, taking the shots meant for you. The only man who knew you'd fired at my father was Max Scheubner-Richter, because his arm was linked with yours. But in the next second, he was shot, too. He died instantly, and your secret was safe. Everyone said that your shoulder was dislocated when Scheubner-Richter collapsed, pulling you down with him. But he was on your right side. It was your left shoulder that was injured. My father must have grabbed at you when he fell. Perhaps he realized what you had done, and was attacking you. Maybe he was reaching out for help. He seized your left arm, yanking you down with such force that your shoulder was wrenched from its socket. As usual, you were lucky—no one noticed the discrepancy in your story."

Still Hitler said nothing. The tic had transformed his face, pulling so hard on the skin that she scarcely recognized him. At his sides, his arms hung tensely, the hands convulsing into fists. Behind him, the other men clustered together at the parlor's far end, talking quietly to one another, obviously unaware of what was happening.

"It was your misfortune that he was credited with saving your life," Gretchen said. "You had to honor his memory or your followers would wonder why you refused to acknowledge the martyr who protected you. By the time you were released from prison and the ban on your speaking in public had been lifted, the story of my father's death had grown into legend. I'm certain you realized you could use the story to your advantage and show that you were someone worth dying for. But how it must have galled you, all these years, to pay homage to the man you had murdered."

His eyes bulged. He stepped forward, his cheek still rippling. "You foolish girl."

She turned and ran.

"You foul, loathsome liar!" Hitler shouted. She heard his footsteps thudding as he followed her into the front hall. She was moving so fast, she nearly tumbled over the chair in the corner, where he usually kept his cartridge belt and weapons. Her shin banged into the chair's seat. Empty now. Which meant he was still wearing a whip and a gun. He could kill her right here.

"Somebody stop her!" Hitler screamed. "Get the Müller girl!"

She spun away from the chair and raced across the front hall. Behind her she heard the whine of Hitler's whip, drawing free from his belt, and the other men's shouts and pounding footsteps. She flung open the door.

The tiled staircase spiraled below her. She ran down. She heard the men above her, and risked a glance over her shoulder. Reinhard and the chauffeur were following her. Hitler stood at the stairway landing, clutching his whip, sweat-darkened hair hanging over his forehead, shouting something unintelligible.

She whipped her head around. Down, down into the front lobby. She skidded across the polished floor, ankles wobbling in high heels. Something touched her back—Reinhard, she was sure of it, she could tell by his cologne—and she swung her arm back, connecting hard with something soft and fleshy—she heard his startled gasp—and then she was twisting the door handle and shooting across the front steps, heading into the Prinzregentenstrasse, startling a flock of doves that shot toward the skies in a flutter of wings and cooing voices.

She raced down the street, legs pumping, ignoring the surprised pedestrians leaping out of her way, heading toward the river, running until she thought her lungs would explode, and every time she glanced over her shoulder, she saw Reinhard following her, his face grim with purpose.

Gretchen jumped onto a streetcar as it lurched forward. While she walked down the center aisle, past the seated housewives and children and burghers, she watched through the windows as Reinhard ran closer, shouting and waving his arms.

*Don't stop, don't stop,* she silently begged the driver, and her legs shook from relief when the car trundled on, picking up speed, leaving Reinhard behind.

She sank onto a seat. Hitler now knew they were enemies. She might die now. And yet she couldn't regret what she had said.

Hitler deserved to know that she had seen through him.

But she wouldn't be frozen out or ignored, like other National Socialists who had fallen from favor. It would be different for her, Hitler's adored sunshine. She had committed the worst crime imaginable. She had seen his true self.

The streetcar stopped. She took another, heading north to the Golden Phoenix, where no one would think to look for her and she could telephone Daniel at the newspaper. She didn't dare go to his office. Not now that Reinhard knew about Daniel and where he worked. It was possible he'd sent an SA comrade to keep a lookout for her at the *Munich Post* building.

Dread sat in her stomach like stones. Through the streetcar's smeared window, she watched the fine houses of the Leopoldstrasse slowly shrink into crumbling two- and three-story structures. Marquee lights, dimmed now in the fading daylight, announced comedians and musical acts and GIRLS! GIRLS! She was almost at the nightclub. Soon she would speak to Daniel, and it would be all right, somehow. She would get out of this city and never return.

She exited the streetcar at its next stop. The Golden Phoenix was nearly deserted. Only half past four—an hour and a half before the day laborers' quitting time, and far too early for university students to stop by.

Gretchen stood at the bar. The cavernous dance hall's chandeliers were unlit, and the orchestra stand was empty. A single gas lamp burned above the bar. Nursing their drinks, a few men and women in ancient-looking, patched clothes slumped at the round tables. The bartender wiped a tired-looking dishrag over the counter, watching her.

"What it'll be?" he asked, draping the rag over his shoulder and speaking around the cigarette hanging from his lips. "You aren't allowed to stand in here for free, Fräulein."

"I need to use the telephone—"

"There's a public exchange box down the street."

"Please, may I use yours?" Unease dragged cold fingers along her back. This was taking too long. "I promise to pay you for the call—"

Footsteps clicked on the scuffed wooden floor. She spun around. A tall figure was crossing the dimly lit room. *Reinhard.* How had he known where to find her?

She whirled on the bartender. "Is there another way out of here?"

He stubbed the smoldering cigarette out in an ashtray. "For customers who buy drinks, maybe."

The restrooms! She could kick out a window and escape that way.

She ran toward the corridor leading to the lavatories. As she seized the doorknob for the women's restroom an arm whipped around her shoulders, pulling her close. She forced a breath, feeling the smooth, hot skin of Reinhard's face pressed against hers.

"How did you find me?" she whispered.

His cheek moved on hers as he smiled. "I followed your streetcar in a taxi. It was worth the expense." He jerked her backward a step, toward the bar. "Hesitate and your Jew dies. Let's go."

He couldn't have gotten to Daniel already. He must be bluffing.

She looked at Reinhard. "You're lying. You haven't had enough time to find Daniel."

He raised his eyebrows. "Calling the Yid by his first name? How cozy. And I didn't say *I* had him." His arm tightened around her shoulders. "But Kurt should have, by now."

Then she was too late to warn Daniel. He might be hurt already or kidnapped, and she had no way to help him.

She didn't fight her brother because there was no choice to make. Together, Reinhard's arm draped over her shoulders, they walked down the corridor, back into the dance hall. He nudged her into a chair and strode toward the bar.

He passed a few coins to the bartender, his teeth flashing white in his careless grin as the man handed him the telephone receiver from the set hanging on the wall. Gretchen felt a hot spurt of outrage. How easily Reinhard charmed others into doing what he wanted, when her desperation had left the bartender unmoved.

Her legs tensed, wanting to run, but she didn't move. Her acquiescence might mean Daniel's life.

Who could her brother be talking to? If only she could make out the shape of his words, but the room was too dim.

Still grinning, he ambled back to her. "Want a drink?"

What was he planning? She couldn't even guess.

Fear rendered her mute, and she shook her head while Reinhard waved to the bartender, calling for a beer. Silently, clutching her pocketbook so she had something to hold on to, Gretchen watched her brother lift the stein to his lips, the muscles in his throat working as he gulped the drink. He thumped the table, shouting for another, and drank that down just as quickly.

What were they waiting for? She could hardly bear the tension. Daniel was somewhere out there, perhaps already beaten and bloodied. While she sat here and did nothing.

Trembling, she got to her feet. "I demand you take me to Daniel."

Reinhard's pale eyes flickered over her face. As usual, his face held nothing but a calm blankness. "Very well. We've probably given Kurt enough time to get here."

"What—"

"Aren't you ever quiet?" he snapped and grabbed her arm, yanking her outside into the warm September evening. Uncertain what was happening, Gretchen stood beside him at the curb while traffic streamed past, the usual motley collection of private automobiles and horse-drawn carts and streetcars. A Daimler coasted to a stop in front of them. Kurt sat behind the driver's wheel. There was no sign of Daniel. Terror curled inside of Gretchen. What had they done to him?

"Ready to see your Jew?" Reinhard laughed, shoving Gretchen forward.

She opened the car door. The backseat was empty.

The realization hit her like an ocean wave: They didn't have Daniel. They had tricked her.

She started to whirl on her brother, but he pushed her so hard that she fell across the backseat. Gasping, she scrambled upright, but he had already climbed in after her and slammed the door shut. The car shot away from the curb. Horns blared behind them as Kurt maneuvered into a lane.

Frantically, Gretchen looked out the window. The large stone buildings of the Leopoldstrasse rose all around them. They were heading south. Back into the city's heart. The car turned left, then right, merging onto the Königinstrasse.

"You'd better have a good reason for summoning me," Kurt said, glancing back at Reinhard.

Her brother smiled faintly. "I have the best reason of all. We're going Jew hunting."

# 41

AS THEY DROVE SOUTH, GRETCHEN WATCHED the familiar sights rise up and pass away: the stretch of redbrick row houses with thatch roofs, the silent stone-faced boardinghouse, the square of pavement where she had skipped rope as a little girl, the places she had known so well and that fear had rendered unreal.

Daniel's name drummed in her head. Probably he was still at work, or preparing to leave and have a quick supper before heading to the Odeonsplatz to cover the Communist demonstration. He might not have heard yet about Geli's death. For him, it was still an ordinary day. Determination made her sit straighter. She would do everything in her power to keep him safe. She would never tell Reinhard and Kurt where to find him.

They drove on, pushing farther south, their progress slow. As the automobile bucked to a sudden stop, Gretchen tensed, eyeing the car door and wondering if she dared to fling herself outside and cry for help.

"No you don't," said Reinhard.

"Please," she said. Perhaps she could find the right words to appeal to him. "Don't you understand? Uncle Dolf killed our father."

Reinhard blinked, his lids lowering and rising over his lake-still eyes. "Was that why he was so upset with you? What a stupid thing for you to say to him. Now you've ruined all my chances for advancement."

He lunged toward her across the seat—his fist connecting so hard with her head that she was thrown against the door. A thousand stars blazed into brilliance and then faded into tiny pinpricks in her mind.

Nausea crested in her mouth, gagging her. Dimly, behind her, she sensed someone fiddling with the car-door handle. Before she could sit up, the door was wrenched open, its hinges squealing in protest. She tumbled backward toward the pavement.

Arms caught her around the waist. She turned her head. Kurt. So close, she saw the dusting of freckles across his nose and the smooth flesh of his chin, unmarked by stubble.

"Go." He set her onto her feet, giving her a small push. Around them, car horns honked and small children darted along the pavement, shrieking with laughter. So close and yet a separate world.

"Where are you ta—" she tried to ask, but Kurt wrapped his arm around her neck and pulled her near. A black curtain fell over her eyes.

"Reinhard's going after the Jew himself." Kurt spoke in her ear, so low she could scarcely hear him above her jagged breaths. "His newspaper office isn't too far from here. Within an hour, we'll be together again at the location your brother and I have agreed upon. But if you and I aren't there when they arrive, your brother will slit the Jew's throat from ear to ear. Is that understood?"

His grip was so tight she couldn't nod. This was her fault; she had brought Daniel into danger. She had failed him so badly.

Kurt squeezed harder, muttering that he needed an answer. She managed a wheezing "Yes" and he loosened his hold. Gray patches filled her vision. She heard the car's engine thrum into life behind them, and the slow purr as the car glided into traffic, carrying Reinhard away. She blinked several times, the grayness receding.

"Good," Kurt said, and began walking. There was nothing she could do but follow him. Hopelessness washed over her as she broke into a jog to keep up.

He brought them to the Englischer Garten. A flattish expanse of grass, dotted with chestnuts and weeping willows, unfurled on either side of the path. She didn't know this section of the park well, and wasn't sure where they were going.

They kept walking, past housewives in kerchiefs carrying shopping bags and mothers pushing prams and workers returning home. No one noticed them. Gretchen wanted to scream at each person they passed, *Help me! Stop him!* But her silence meant Daniel's life.

Up ahead, a lake gleamed pink in the fading afternoon

sunlight. They stopped near the water's edge, and Gretchen risked a glance at Kurt, but his grim expression told her nothing.

She didn't know where she had expected they would end up—an abandoned building, an empty auto garage, a desolate stretch of forest—but it wasn't the shore of the Kleinhesseloher See.

The lake had three miniature islands. Right now they were quiet, private, far from curious gazes. During summer, the lake would be dotted with rowboats, but now the cool breeze shivered the surface. Only geese and ducks paddled across the water. She shuddered. It was an ideal place to conceal a body.

"Now we wait," Kurt said. "We'll row to the Königinsel together." He gestured to a stone monument behind them. "Sit there. It shouldn't be long now."

Slowly, she sat down, resting her back against the flat stone. Why couldn't she figure out what to do? Her mind was dulled by fear. Again, she clutched her pocketbook, so she had something tangible to hold on to and wouldn't fly apart. Through the leather, she felt a long, hard shape. The bread knife! She had absentmindedly taken it with her this morning.

She peeked at Kurt. He had sat down a few feet away, keeping his eyes trained on her, his hands on the dagger clipped to his belt. She might be able to attack him before he retrieved his weapon. One sickening slice and Kurt would be gone. But Reinhard and Daniel would see them across the flat stretch of grass; even from a distance, they would see Kurt's crumpled form on the ground, and Reinhard wouldn't hesitate to act. One arc of his arm and Daniel would be dead.

No, she couldn't risk it. So she watched and waited.

⁂

The minute hand on her wristwatch ticked slowly. Each of its motions felt like an hour. A few boys ran past, whooping, chasing a rubber ball. Quarter past six now. Gretchen shifted uneasily, the stone monument pressing like ice into her back. The sun was starting to slide down the sky in a wash of pink and orange.

Half past. A group of men walked by, talking in booming voices, probably going to the beer garden at the Chinese Tower. Gretchen listened to their footsteps fade, charting their progress in her mind until she couldn't hear them anymore. Somewhere, a woman started laughing and whispering that they mustn't, not out here in the open like this, until her murmurs, too, slipped away. Gretchen and Kurt were alone again.

It was nearly seven. For two hours they had sat and waited here. She could scarcely believe Kurt was waiting so long, until she looked at his nervous hands, patting the knife sheath clipped to his belt, and she understood: He knew how to follow orders, but not how to think on his own. The unexpected paralyzed him.

The air felt sharp and cool, tinged with the smoky bite of autumn. The sky was washed in red and orange, turning the lake to flame. In the west, the sun hovered on the horizon. A few more moments and it would tip below the surface, a giant, blazing ball extinguished by night.

A few more moments and she would run.

She had to confront the truth: For whatever reason, Daniel and Reinhard weren't coming. Although there were dozens of possible explanations, she refused to consider a single one. Daniel was still alive. That single shining thought she must cling to with both hands.

Trying to steady herself, she closed her eyes. But Geli's image loomed against her lids: stretched across the floor, her dress stained with rusty blood. *Geli.* For a second, the pain was so immediate and so raw, she couldn't breathe. But there was nothing she could do for Geli now; all she could concentrate on was her own survival.

She opened her eyes. In the thickening darkness, a man walked along the shore. The sunset's red light flooded his face. Her lungs seized up. God, it couldn't be—but it was, she recognized his lumbering walk and the heavy belly straining his SA uniform's shirt. Ernst Röhm.

She could scarcely breathe as he drew nearer. Beneath his cap's brim, Röhm's eyes were small and dark like stones.

"Fräulein Müller," he said, "I regret to inform you that your brother has been in an accident."

Her mouth opened and shut. She didn't trust herself to say a single word. *Daniel—*

Röhm's gaze flickered to her companion. "I'm afraid he's smashed up your automobile, Jaeger. But that's what you get for handing over your keys to a fellow who can't drive." He laughed—a harsh, rasping sound.

"That's all right." Kurt spoke calmly, but his eyes darted around the lake, across the water and along the shoreline and then back over the fields. He looked afraid. Gretchen's fingers curled, the nails cutting into her palms. If *he* was frightened, then what lay before her?

Both men looked at her; they were waiting for her to say something. She had to clear her throat twice before she could speak. "What's happened to him?"

"Müller refused to go to the hospital." Röhm walked closer.

The scents of oil and leather and tobacco smoke wafted over her. "When I got word that one of my best men had been injured, I went to see him at home."

Röhm watched her steadily now, and she had to concentrate on breathing gently, in and out, and forcing her eyes to stay on his, so he wouldn't see how frightened she was.

"He was raving by the time I arrived," Röhm continued. "Shouting about a Jew that he needed to hunt down and punish for his sister's blood sin." Röhm brought his face so near she could smell his breath, flavored with beer and sauerkraut. "Now, why would he say that?"

Relief arrowed through her: Reinhard had gotten into an accident before he'd reached the newspaper office. Daniel was still safe. Now she would withstand anything.

The pocketbook lay heavy on her lap. Even if she opened it and got the knife out before either of the men attacked her, how could she defend herself against them both?

"No idea? No inkling at all why your brother would say such a disgusting thing about his own sister?" He clucked his tongue when she shook her head. "Strange. But it doesn't matter. Your brother, in his feverish ramblings, mentioned several items of interest, among them your current location. I am pleased to see I arrived before he did."

She started. Wasn't Reinhard still at the boardinghouse, tending to his wounds?

"I was most annoyed when your brother excused himself to use the lavatory and never returned, as though he suspected something," Röhm went on. He hooked his thumbs into the belt straining around his portly torso. Next to his hand hung a sheath for a knife. She saw the carved handle and swallowed hard.

She gripped her pocketbook. The clasp bit into her hand. If only she could twist it open without Röhm noticing. . . .

He hauled her upright. Beside her, Kurt scrambled to his feet. "We'll find him together," Röhm said. "I have my orders from the Führer." He held her by the arms. Even in the reddish light, she saw the thick gouges shrapnel had left in his cheeks. She tried not to shiver. She wouldn't give him the satisfaction of her fear.

He released her so suddenly that she fell back a step, and he turned toward Kurt. "Jaeger, how much of this untidy mess did Müller pull you into?"

"Very little, SA-Stabschef Röhm."

"Good." Röhm patted Kurt on the shoulder as if pleased. Gretchen caught the gleam of something in his hand, and before she had registered what it was, Röhm had dragged the knife across Kurt's throat and jumped aside to avoid the blood spraying out. Stunned, Gretchen staggered back, choking on the bile coursing up her throat. "Now it will stay that way."

Horribly, Kurt wasn't dead. He clutched his throat, blood pumping red between his fingers. He was trying to say something, but he couldn't get the words up his torn throat, and he fell to his knees and then sank facedown on the ground. Even in the growing darkness, Gretchen saw his blood seeping across the grass, in a widening circle of black.

Röhm wiped his blade clean on the grass. He looked regretfully at the reddish flecks on his shirt. She started to back away, and he straightened. "I wouldn't think of running, Fräulein Müller. If you do, I've a pistol I won't hesitate to use. I'd prefer to avoid the noise, though, as you can see."

With a fleshy hand, he gestured toward Kurt's motionless body. Gretchen fought the wave of revulsion rising within her.

Röhm tucked his knife into its sheath at his belt. "The Führer may be leaving right now for a country retreat to grieve for his beloved niece, but there are many remaining in Munich who are eager to fulfill his demands. And he was quite clear about your family's future, when we spoke by telephone a few minutes ago. Your mother has already been persuaded to leave Munich for her parents' home in Dachau. But you and your brother remain."

She balanced on the balls of her feet, ready to run. Perhaps Röhm had been fast once, but the years had piled flesh and flab onto him. She could outpace him. She was sure of it.

He placed his hand on the bulge beneath his brown shirt. A bulge the shape of a pistol in a shoulder holster. "As I already mentioned, your brother had several interesting things to say when I met him at your boardinghouse. One was a cry that his uncle Dolf could not have killed his father. Imagine the Führer's displeasure when I repeated such a peculiar statement to him.

"The Führer said," Röhm went on, watching her face with a malicious pleasure, "he has grown tired of the Müller family and the National Socialists will be a stronger party without their continued presence. None of us are so naive that we do not understand him." He stopped, clearly waiting for a reply.

Her fingers tightened on her pocketbook. "No. None of us are that naive."

"Good." Röhm kicked Kurt's body, checking that the boy was dead. Gretchen slipped her hand into her purse. Her fingers scrambled over the junk she habitually stored in there. Handkerchiefs, old postcards, marks, a tube of lipstick . . .

Röhm looked up. "Then we comprehend each other perfectly."

A comb with half of its teeth missing, an empty pillbox Eva had given her because she had admired its tortoiseshell top, a pen . . . There it was! She felt the cold metal of the knife and ran a finger along its serrated edge. It was dull, but it would have to be good enough.

"You shall come with me," Röhm said. "You'll show me all the places where your brother might be hiding. We shall smoke him out together," Röhm added, and then his face hardened. "What are you doing? Get your hand out of your purse!"

She gripped the knife. She had to do it. She leapt at him, bringing the bread knife down with one swift motion. She felt the knife's teeth bite into the soft, doughy part of his neck, and his hands came up, knocking the blade away. She turned and ran as hard as she could into the darkness that had spread across the park.

# 42

GRETCHEN GRABBED A BICYCLE THAT SOMEONE had tossed on the grass by the park's entrance. From the muffled giggles coming from a clump of trees, she guessed that two lovers had hastily left it behind. It was old and rickety, but it held her weight when she swung herself on.

The Leopoldstrasse was nearly empty now. The occasional car glided past, and in the distance a streetcar clanged, but there was little traffic. She pedaled hard, her breath coming in gasps, and tried to ignore the aching exhaustion in her legs.

Soon she would be at the Odeonsplatz. Chances were, Daniel had no idea yet what had happened to Geli or that Reinhard was looking for him. Probably he was already in the square, scribbling in his spiral-bound notebook or snapping pictures with his Leica, imagining that tonight's work entailed an ordinary newspaper assignment. With no inkling that Reinhard was hunting him down right now. She had to get to him right away.

Her legs shook so badly that the bicycle wobbled. She knew she was operating on pure adrenaline. At some point, her energy would fail, but she must push on until she found Daniel.

Abruptly, the Odeonsplatz opened up before her. She dropped the bicycle by the side of the road and stopped for an instant to get her bearings.

The Odeonsplatz was massive. Lining its western edges was the Theatinerkirche, an enormous Baroque church. In the gathering blue darkness, its pale yellow stone walls looked white, and its two towers were small shadows in the night sky. Directly ahead stood the Feldherrnhalle, an immense stone hall with three arches. A staircase at the central arch led to the entrance, which was flanked by two stone statues.

Tonight the square was filled with men, endless lines of dark figures parading around its center. They kept shouting something she couldn't quite make out—something about Lenin and Marx—and some carried flaming torches, the light flickering across their faces. Most of them were scarcely older than she: university students, probably, in their late teens and early twenties. They wore the standard black shirts and red bow ties of the Communists and they looked both excited and defiant.

And then she saw why.

Brownshirts lined the square. A couple of hundred men, perhaps, standing motionless, arms folded across their chests in the prescribed position, ready to strike at any instant. All of them stood motionless, as if waiting for an order.

The Communists started chanting louder. Now she heard the words. "Death to National Socialism! Long live Lenin!"

Again her gaze traveled over the hundreds of men choking the square. But there were so many. . . . How could she ever find Daniel?

She must. She had to.

She skirted the square's periphery, scanning the Communists as they swung by. Perhaps he had concealed himself among them, for he could never hope to hide in the uniformed SA ranks. Even if they didn't recognize him as one of the reporters who attended Hitler's speeches, his ordinary suit would give him away.

On and on she crept, keeping behind the line of SA men. She raised one hand, half covering her face, hoping no one looked at her. They might know her as Hitler's pet or Reinhard's little sister, and perhaps they had already been told that Röhm was looking for her. She had picked the most dangerous place in the city to be tonight.

Far ahead, a figure hurried up the stairs of the Feldherrnhalle. A man on the landing extended his hand, urging the newcomer on. As Gretchen looked again, she recognized the line of the figure's shoulders and the tilt of his head. *Daniel.*

She broke into a run, keeping her hand raised to her face. Through her fingers, she saw the brownshirts, their gaze trained on the Communists circling the square. Menace hung in the air like smoke. All it would take was one match and the Odeonsplatz would be afire.

She reached the Feldherrnhalle steps. Daniel stood on the landing, a notebook tucked under his arm, a camera strap slung over his shoulder, talking urgently to an older man. Reflected torchlight flashed off the man's round spectacles. *Fritz Gerlich.*

Somehow she managed not to scream Daniel's name, yet as

she raced up the steps, he turned toward her. She knew the exact instant he saw her, for it was as if his face came alive again; all the fear fled, leaving his features relaxed and softer, his lips saying her name.

They ran to each other. It took all of her self-control not to throw herself into his arms, but they couldn't waste a second. He clasped her hand, saying, "You're all right! I've been looking for you everywhere. There's a rumor going around that Fräulein Raubal is hurt or dead, and I didn't know what had happened to you—"

"There's no time to explain. We have to get out of here—" she started to say as Herr Gerlich rushed to them.

"That's what I've been trying to tell Herr Cohen," Gerlich said. "I heard from one of my sources that Röhm's looking for the Müller brother and sister. I don't see how you can escape from this square alive."

"I'm not leaving without Gretchen." Daniel squeezed her hand.

Fear had transformed Gerlich's usually calm face into a frozen mask. "Perhaps if you leave separately you'll attract less attention—"

"No," Daniel cut in. "We escape together."

The shouts had grown louder and the brownshirts were shifting their weight from foot to foot and muttering to one another. They looked restless and ready to fight.

One of the men glanced around the square, his gaze stopping when it reached her. Gretchen felt the flicker of recognition in his eyes like a punch. He knew who she was. Although they were too far apart for her to hear what he said, she saw him grab his companion's sleeve and his lips form her name. The other man looked at her and nodded, then turned to the fellow next to him and spoke rapidly. Comprehension shot along the brownshirts like a line of fire. Another moment and all two hundred men would know exactly where she was.

There was no place to go. The flight of steps led directly into the square and hundreds of waiting brownshirts.

Gerlich frowned at the marching men. "What a mess. Reminds me of the putsch all over again."

His words struck a match in Gretchen's brain. In her mind's eye, she saw the National Socialists marching through the snow, looking uneasily at the waiting police officers.

"I know what to do," she said, almost to herself, and then, more loudly, she said again, "I know what to do!" She spun to face Daniel. "We create a riot and flee during the chaos."

To her relief, Daniel nodded in immediate understanding. The same basic tactic had allowed Hitler to disguise a murder and get out of the city. Perhaps it would work again.

In the square below, the brownshirts had begun moving toward the Feldherrnhalle steps. Even the Communists had noticed that they no longer interested the National Socialists, and they, too, stared up at Gretchen, Daniel, and Gerlich.

"Good-bye, Herr Gerlich." Daniel clasped the man's hand for an instant. "We haven't known each other long, but I've learned much from you."

"Stay alive," Gerlich said. "I shall expect great things from you both."

He stepped back, letting Gretchen and Daniel move forward on the landing. Below, a few hundred faces had turned to watch them. Along the square's edges, SA men started walking toward the Feldherrnhalle, like a quickly moving brown stream.

Gretchen and Daniel gripped hands. His fingers felt slick with sweat, but his voice was steady when he said, "Here we go," and together they walked down the Feldherrnhalle steps, directly into the waiting crowd.

# 43

TORCHLIGHT FLICKERED OVER THE MEN IN THE square, turning them into reddish shadows. The SA men along the back of the square watched Gretchen and Daniel, most likely waiting for a signal to attack. But the brownshirts clustered at the Feldherrnhalle's base weren't paying them any attention; the whispers must not have reached them yet. It was Gretchen and Daniel's first piece of luck and the one thing that might save their lives.

They descended into the square. The nearest Communists marched past, shouting, "Death to National Socialism!" They walked four abreast, their arms linked, their eyes darting toward the brownshirts surrounding the Odeonsplatz. The SA men said nothing, but their restless shifting and grim faces must have warned the Communists of the danger. They were itching to fight. They reminded Gretchen of an infernal machine—working so perfectly in unison they had become an automaton, each man a separate gear that clicked together with the others to form a relentless army.

It had to be now. Gretchen slipped her hand from Daniel's.

"Stick close," he said. "If we lose each other in this crowd, we may never find each other again."

She nodded, then let herself stumble into the closest line of brownshirts. Awkwardly, they caught her in a tangle of limbs, and she smelled warm flesh and cigarette smoke and damp linen.

Quickly, she pushed herself away. "One of them pinched me!" she shouted, throwing her voice as far as she could. "One of those loathsome boys laid his hands on me!"

"No!" some of them cried. "She fell into us—"

Their words were swallowed by the crowd's sudden roar. She had been right—the insult to a girl's honor was all the encouragement the men needed. The Communists' shouts swelled against her ears like an onrushing wave. The men broke ranks and ran toward the brownshirts.

Fists met flesh with sickening crunches. Clenched hands rammed into faces and stomachs, and everywhere the air filled with cries and shouts. In an instant, the milling crowds had transformed into a mass of twisting bodies.

Someone slammed into her, knocking her away from Daniel. She tried to see him through the fighting men, but they seemed to form a wall surrounding her. Each man was intent on destroying the other; their limbs flailed as they struck at one another, their flinging arms and torsos acting like a screen, separating her and Daniel. She could see nothing but an endless whirl of moving bodies, the colors of their clothes blurring like a child's swirling paints on paper, black, red, and brown sliding together.

Hands gripped her shoulders. *Daniel.* She spun around and found herself staring at a neck encircled by a familiar khaki collar. Her heart kicked against her ribs like a mule's legs. *No.* He couldn't have found her. He couldn't have known where she would be. She let her eyes travel up to his face and nearly cried aloud. *Reinhard.*

A long gash started at Reinhard's hairline and continued diagonally across his face, tracing a red line across his nose, ending at his jaw. Both of his eyes were black and one had swelled shut. He stood unsteadily, so hunched over that his shoulders were at different heights. Bandages covered both of his hands, but he must have torn at the wrappings, for strips of gauze fluttered from his wrists.

A fresh circle of blood blossomed through his plain brown shirt. As she watched, the circle widened on the right side of his chest. Either he had never stopped bleeding or he was bleeding again.

"Gretchen," he said. Saying her name tugged at his facial cut; the puckered skin seemed to stretch and fresh drops of blood appeared at the laceration's edges. Tiny, crystalline specks fell from the cut. For a dazed instant, she thought they were diamonds, and then she realized they were glass. He must have been thrown through the windshield.

"Gretchen," he said again, and swayed. Automatically, she reached out to steady him. Even through his clothes, she felt heat pumping off his body. He was dangerously hot. "I knew you would want to find the Jew," he said, spraying blood with each word. "And where else would a reporter like him be tonight but here, to write about the next fight between us and the Communists?"

Blood had turned his teeth red. He must be bleeding internally. When he spoke, the cut across his face tugged again, showering more glass specks. "I'll redeem myself for your sin by delivering you to Röhm. He's already here for you."

Panic flooded her heart. Over Reinhard's hunched shoulder, she saw Röhm through the spinning bodies. Although a clump of men fought between them, she recognized his large, flat face. A short, jagged cut wrinkled the smooth skin of his neck; blood had run down from it and dried, leaving behind a dozen little lines. He hadn't even stopped to bandage or clean the wound.

She whirled and tried to push her way through the warring bodies, getting away. An arm jabbed her side, and she caught a fist in the face, but she kept shoving against the others, attempting to carve a path for herself.

"No," Reinhard said, and she saw he was right beside her, stumbling, half bent over. He grabbed her wrist, but she pulled herself away and found herself facing a man's massive chest. There were bloody flecks across the khaki-colored shirt—*God, no*—and she raised her gaze to meet Röhm's.

He said nothing. Something pressed against her breast. She looked down, even though she could guess what it was. A pistol. Its barrel felt cold through her blouse. She didn't dare move.

"Herr Röhm," Reinhard said behind her, "you see, I've brought her to you."

"Yes. Thank you." Röhm cocked the trigger. Gretchen let out a tiny choking gasp and flung herself away, into the swirling mass of bodies, and even as she moved, she saw Röhm's arm swing to the right, toward her brother, and then she fell into a bunch of fighting men. Behind her, she heard a sound like a firecracker exploding.

Someone slid against her, his shoulder hitting hers, then his hand brushing her leg, and she turned to see Reinhard crumple noiselessly to the ground. He landed on his side and didn't move again. A second bloody circle seeped through his shirt; somehow that blood looked alive while he did not.

His face seemed relaxed, all the tension and anger finally gone. Even through the blood and glass and bruises, Gretchen could see how handsome he had been: the perfectly formed bones, the long sweep of jaw, the narrow nose, all of the features that Hitler had praised as Aryan.

A scream burst from her throat. She fell to her knees, as though she had been cut down, and reached for him. Beneath her fingers, his cheek felt sticky with blood and warm, but his eyes were glazed over. What she had half wanted, and hated herself for wanting for so long, had finally happened: He was gone. But not just out of Munich and out of her life. Gone forever. She made a noise deep in her throat, and couldn't say a word.

Then she heard how silent the square had become. She tore her gaze from her brother's face. Dozens—no, *hundreds*—of men had turned in her direction. Some still clutched their opponents' arms, their hands frozen in midpunch. Others had released their enemies, and their arms were hanging limply at their sides. Torchlight flickered over their faces. Some had gone slack from shock; others were tight from fear, still others hard from anger. They were all watching Röhm.

The instant seemed to stretch out. Gretchen jumped up, her

eyes fastening on Röhm's hand as he raised the pistol again; she rocked onto the balls of her feet as Röhm rotated his arm in a wide arc toward her, torchlight gleaming off the weapon's barrel, and her legs tensed as she sprang toward the nearest group of men—

"He has a gun!" someone shouted.

Everything began happening at once. The men unfroze and started running, scrambling to get away, shoving others out of the way in their haste to escape. The air filled with shouts and cries. Gretchen ran as hard as she could. There were so many people in such a small space, they all squeezed against one another as they struggled to flee. Men's bodies pressed into hers, propelling her forward, their arms and legs knocking into her as she ran, but she didn't even register the pain. Somewhere, behind her, she heard Röhm's voice through the men's cries, screaming her name, but she didn't look back.

The men pushed and pulled against her, and it took all of her strength to remain upright. She tried to run, but so did everyone else, and they stumbled and fell into one another like blind people. The air was so heavy with screams she couldn't hear her own breathing.

She tripped over a man's foot and almost fell, but someone else's arms pulled her up, and she stumbled forward, trying to regain her balance, but the men behind her were pushing so hard that she couldn't.

"Gretchen Müller!" Röhm shouted. "Someone, stop her!"

Nobody grabbed her. No one was paying attention to her; they were all too eager to get away. She staggered on, tripping and swaying, and had nearly fallen headlong again when fingers fastened around her wrist and jerked up so hard that her shoulder nearly popped out of place. She had to bite her lips so she wouldn't scream from the sudden, sharp pain.

"Sorry," said a voice in her ear. "But you mustn't fall or you'll be trampled."

She knew the voice and turned to see Daniel stumbling beside her, his face white and blood-streaked and his eyes dark and feverish with pain. He looked badly hurt. She cried out his name and grabbed his hand. Sweat nearly slid their fingers apart, but she held on as hard as she could.

They reached the edge of the square. The pressure from hundreds of straining bodies pushed them into the street that was rapidly filling with Communists and brownshirts, and Gretchen and Daniel popped like wine corks into the suddenly loosened air. They ran a few yards down the street, and then Daniel stopped. He bent at the waist, breathing hard and cradling his left arm tight against his chest.

"Go." He gritted the words out between lips turning white. "I'm slowing you down. *Go*, Gretchen!"

She would never leave him. Instead of replying, she scanned the street. The Theatinerstrasse reminded her of a scene from Dante's *Inferno*, the glimmering torchlight transforming the running men into shadows made of red and black. More and more men spilled into the street, the Communists and brownshirts still punching and kicking. Howls of pain sliced through the night. In the distance, police whistles tweeted, a silver sound that seemed pitifully weak against the hordes of men streaming into the street.

"The police are coming," she said. She and Daniel shared a

look, making further words unnecessary—the police's presence was no guarantee that help had arrived.

"We must get out of the city," he said.

"Can you make it to the train station—"

"Yes," he cut in. "Come on."

Gretchen snatched up Daniel's good hand, and together they half walked, half stumbled through the darkness toward the train station. At this late hour, the shops were closed, their fronts concealed by metal grilles, their awnings rolled up. Along the apartments in the upper stories, faces appeared at the windows, their expressions worried.

Gretchen and Daniel followed the narrow, twisting streets. They would take a few steps along one avenue before darting down a side street, zigzagging as frequently as they could to confuse anyone who might be following them. But the screams and running feet were fading away, softening like the night all around them. They were almost there.

Gretchen looked at Daniel. They had slowed to a walk, and each step seemed to require tremendous effort from him. The cords stuck out in his neck, tight as ropes. He walked with a shuffling gait, his injured arm dangling at his side. It hung at such an unnatural angle, she knew it must be broken, or seriously damaged. A thin sheen of sweat gleamed on his skin. The National Socialists must have beaten him with the truncheons she'd seen them carrying.

Daniel stopped to lean against a building. She doubted he could go on much longer, and her heart twisted. He had wanted so badly to become a reporter in Munich, and now his friendship with her had ripped that dream away.

"We can probably never come back to Munich," she said, willing her voice to stay steady. He looked at her, blinking hard to force his eyes to focus, but they kept blurring. She knew he should be in a hospital, but surrendering to a doctor's care would be only a temporary reprieve before the NSDAP found him and murdered him. If he wanted to live, he would have to keep running.

With his good hand, he gestured toward his battered body and almost smiled. "I know."

"And that means . . . you can either go home to Berlin or continue on with me." She took a deep breath like a swimmer bracing herself before plunging into icy water. The only nearby sound was the purr of a car engine, and a sleek black automobile swung past, its headlights cutting across them for an instant.

"No place in Germany is safe for me anymore," she went on. "Wherever I go, the Party will find me. I know we haven't made any plans to leave, but I see now I must go. I have a friend in England"—her voice cracked, but she went on—"the psychoanalyst I told you about, and he's a good man, Daniel, who sees the truth about Hitler. He said he would help me, and I'm sure he would extend the offer to you as well. Getting there will be difficult—we haven't any money or proper identification papers with us, but I know we could find a way. You needn't come with me. If you don't want to, I'll understand."

He reached out with his good hand, cupping her chin. "Gretchen, don't you realize by now I would give up everything to be with you?"

The sound of screeching tires ripped through the air. The car they had just seen had circled around and skidded to a stop. A man peered at them through the open window.

"It's them!" the man shouted. "Alert Röhm and spread the word to the others! It's the Müller girl and the Jew!"

They ran.

The central train station was a few minutes away. Gretchen glanced at Daniel, but the moment's rest seemed to have done him good, for he kept pace beside her, running hard. They rounded a corner and the Munich Hauptbahnhof rose before them.

"Stop, stop!" cried a man behind them. His footsteps thudded on the pavement, and suddenly the sound multiplied and Gretchen glanced over her shoulder. Several men had joined their pursuer and more were flooding in from the pockets of darkness spread along the street. About twenty brownshirts followed them now.

The train station grew nearer, a pile of stone and glass that even from a distance seemed deserted. Perhaps during the bustle of midday they could have blended into the crowds, but there would be few people in the station now, a businessman heading to one of the neighboring towns, a family on holiday, but no commuters, no throngs of Müncheners clogging the platforms. There would be few witnesses to watch whatever the brownshirts would do to them.

Gretchen and Daniel flung themselves at the entrance. She caught a glimpse of the lobby—a flat stretch of floor spreading out in all directions to the various platforms—

"This way!" Daniel shouted, and they ran to the right. This was the city's main train station, with lines to places like Landshut, Nuremberg, and Rosenheim. But both Nuremberg and Landshut were National Socialist strongholds. Wherever they went, there would be Party men waiting for them.

A train's whistle blasted. Gretchen whirled, trying to locate the sound. There it was, the only train in the station, slowing to a stop two platforms away.

"Go." Daniel nodded toward the train.

Adrenaline surged through her veins so fiercely that she felt as though all of her cells were jumping beneath her skin. The only way to reach the train was to go back the way they had come. They would head straight to the men who were rushing toward them now. The brownshirts now numbered nearly thirty and more streamed through the station's entrance. They pounded across the lobby, calling her name, telling her to stop.

Indecision locked her in place. How could they possibly escape? There was no place to go.

Röhm stepped through the front doors. He didn't bother to run, as though confident his men would easily retrieve her and Daniel, but he moved quickly, one hand resting on the knife at his belt.

"There's no escape," she cried, and Daniel tugged her around to face the train platforms.

"Yes, there is."

And then she saw it. The only way to reach the other platform was to jump into the little well where the railway lines ran, clamber over the tracks, and then pull themselves up onto the adjacent platform.

Daniel ran across the platform and flung himself off. She raced to the edge and watched him land about four feet below. He winced, but didn't stop to absorb the momentary pain;

immediately, he started scrambling across the thick metal rails, toward the opposite side.

Gretchen dropped down after him. She landed between the rails just as a loud, metallic scream rent the air. A single halo of light appeared far off in the railway tunnel; in the space of a second, it sharpened into a headlamp. It was a train, hurtling down the track toward them.

"Gretchen!" Daniel shouted. She looked up. He had reached the opposite platform and was reaching toward her with his good arm, his face pale and shiny with sweat. "Take my hand!"

A rush of wind whooshed over her. The train was slowing, but still shooting closer, its brakes squealing. She saw the engineer's surprised face through the window, saw him jerking on the controls, but she already knew it was no use; he wouldn't be able to stop soon enough. There was no time to step carefully over the tracks and pull herself up onto the platform. She would have to jump.

She sprang as hard as she could. For an instant, she was suspended in the air, the wind pushed by the oncoming train dragging at her clothes, and then Daniel's arms closed around her.

Her feet knocked hard against the well's lip, and she and Daniel fell onto the platform, Daniel landing on his back, she on top of him. The air slammed out of her lungs.

"Come on," Daniel panted.

They scrambled to their feet. Behind them, the brownshirts' frustrated shouts mingled with the train's screeching brakes, a wave of sound washing over them. The other train's doors started to close.

"Go!"

They raced across the platform, throwing themselves onto the train. The doors shut with a hiss. The train lurched forward, and Daniel nearly fell. Gretchen swung her arm around his waist, supporting him as they limped to the nearest compartment. She eased Daniel onto a seat, hearing his low moan of pain as he touched his injured arm. Suddenly, her legs turned to water, and she sank down beside him, shaking all over.

The train gathered speed. They hurtled around a curve, emerging into the city. Through the window, Gretchen saw the street, now swarming with brownshirts. Superimposed on them were her and Daniel's own reflections, their faces pale as milk, their eyes ringed with exhaustion. The images lasted for a second before the train pulled away, dragging them deeper into the dark night.

She turned to Daniel. He sat back in the seat, breathing hard. Sweat slicked his hair back from his face.

"Are you all right?" she asked, even though she knew he wasn't, and he managed a weak grin.

"Not bad when I think how furious Röhm must be that we got away from him." He grimaced. "The worst of it's my arm. I can move it, so I don't think it's broken, but it feels like it's on fire."

He glanced at Gretchen. "We need to figure out where this train is going. I'm sure Röhm and your brother are already racing to intercept us at the next stop."

Pain arrowed through her chest, so swift and sharp she had to close her eyes for an instant. "Then you didn't see what happened, back in the square." She plowed on before he could reply.

"Röhm shot Reinhard. He's dead."

There was a beat of silence. With his good hand, Daniel took hers, turning it over so he could lace their dirty, blood-stained fingers together. "I'm sorry."

Her dry eyes ached. She was still too numb to know how she felt. There was only this blank emptiness in her heart for the brother she had feared and had wanted so badly to love.

They had entered a third-class compartment, so the seats were crowded closely together, but it didn't matter because they were alone and there was no one to hear them. It was so dark outside that she couldn't tell what direction they were headed in, and she had no idea what their destination might be.

A conductor stepped into their car and peered at them disapprovingly. "Tickets?" he asked dubiously, as if two filthy and battered-looking teenagers couldn't possibly have tickets.

Which, of course, they didn't. Daniel paid for them with the last of his pocket change. At some point, Gretchen had lost her pocketbook, so they had no possessions at all. As the conductor turned to leave, Gretchen asked him where their train was going.

"Dachau," he sniffed, and retreated to another car.

She almost laughed. It was their second piece of luck tonight. Dachau was a scant thirty minutes' train ride from Munich—not very much time for Daniel to recover his strength or to form a plan, but the short trip could work in their favor as it didn't give the brownshirts much time to catch up to them.

"We have about fifteen more minutes until we reach Dachau," Gretchen said. "I doubt Röhm and his men could have beaten us there, but . . ."

"We mustn't take the chance," Daniel finished. He touched

Gretchen's face. "I'll be all right," he said, and she realized he must have guessed her idea. "I can make the jump. Sitting here has given me a decent rest. But Dachau is a small village—we can't possibly hope to conceal ourselves among the locals."

"We won't need to. My grandparents live there. Mama will be with them, since Röhm persuaded her to leave Munich. They'll help us. By the time the SA guess where we've gone, we'll have left long ago."

"But will your family assist a Jew—" He cut himself off. "There's no time to argue. The train's starting to slow down."

Together, they made their way along the narrow corridor. Through the windows, the trees and countryside whipped past, little more than blurred shadows.

She wrenched the door open. For an instant, she stood in the doorway, the wind tearing at her clothes and flinging her hair like a curtain over her eyes. The train was still moving so fast she had to hold on to the doorframe so she didn't lose her balance.

She shook her hair out of her eyes. There, farther along the rail line, she saw a faint glimmer in the darkness—the station's lighted windows, and beyond them, the steeply pitched roofs of the little village.

*Now*, she thought, and flung herself into the darkness.

# 44

SHE LANDED HARD, WITH A SICKENING CRUNCH of bone. The instant her feet touched the ground, she tucked herself into a ball and rolled down the hill. She tasted grass and dirt and wildflowers.

Somewhere nearby she heard Daniel rolling through the tall grasses, the hard sound of a body slamming against dirt over and over. When she stopped, the world tilted drunkenly on its axis for an instant, the stars spinning overhead, and she staggered to her feet, throwing out her arms for balance. A few feet away, Daniel sat up, bracing his good hand on his knee. He spat out a clump of earth and cursed.

"Are you all right?" she asked. The stars stopped wheeling in the sky, but her stomach still pitched.

"Fine. You?"

"Fine."

He got up. "How far is your grandparents' home from here?"

They stood in the midst of a field, its tall grasses rippling in the wind. Here, the stars hung low in the sky and looked like nail-heads that had been hammered through black velvet, so immense and so bright that they stained the field silver. She hadn't taken the train to Dachau in two years, so she couldn't immediately picture their location on a map.

Through the tall pine trees, she saw the cluster of red-roofed buildings that made up the town square. In the darkness, their stone facades were ghostly white. The dozens of buildings looked like children's toys. To the right, the river Wurm shone like silver.

On the eastern side of Dachau, she knew, stood a massive concrete wall encircling an abandoned munitions factory.

Gretchen pointed. "West of the old powder factory. My grandparents have a farmhouse near the church."

"They're not in the village proper, then." Daniel exhaled sharply. "That's a small point for us."

"There's another one," she told him as they began walking, the long grasses slapping against their legs. "My grandfather keeps a car."

They had walked for several minutes when Gretchen noticed a change coming over Daniel. Gradually, his steps had grown faster, his footing surer, his breathing deeper. He held his injured arm in his good one and the sweat had dried on his face. He didn't look as exhausted.

The whispery sound of grasses bending and then rubbing against something interrupted her thoughts. She stopped. They had drawn closer to the old factory, and it was difficult to see anything now because the immense wall seemed to blot out the stars, extinguishing what little light there was.

The sound came again, and then Gretchen saw the outline of shoulders, a slim torso, long legs, a flowered housedress. *Mama.*

How had she known where to find them?

"Gretchen?" her mother said. She moved forward, into a patch of moonlight, and saw Gretchen and Daniel standing motionless. She ran to Gretchen, opening her arms for an embrace, then seemed to think better of it and stopped, her arms sliding to her sides. "Are you all right?"

Gretchen ignored the question. "Why have you come out here, Mama? Hoping to deliver us to Röhm yourself and weasel your way back into Uncle Dolf's good favor?"

Her mother winced. Although her gaze flickered over Daniel, she said nothing to him. "Two SA men drove up to my parents' door a few moments ago. Your grandfather snuck me out the back, and I came straight here, hoping to intercept you on the way. You mustn't go there, Gretchen. They're waiting for you."

Gretchen hesitated. She didn't know what to do now.

She looked at her mother. The pain in Mama's eyes was unmistakable. She wished she could despise her mother, or feel indifferent—anything but this endless back-and-forth between pity and anger. "Mama, Reinhard's dead."

Her mother let out a soft cry, like a newborn kitten. "I knew this day would come." She spoke almost to herself. "How did it happen?"

Gretchen couldn't tell her the truth. Misery was etched in every inch of her mother's body, from the dejected slope of her shoulders to her hands knitted tightly together. She wanted to give her mother something, at least some tiny piece of solace to hang on to. "He died protecting me," she said, and it was almost the truth, for his death had prevented hers, giving her precious seconds to hide herself among the crowd. At her side, Daniel squeezed her hand. She saw the pride on his face, and relaxed a little. He understood what she had done.

Mama sighed. "Thank God. Thank God for that." She reached into her pocket and withdrew a leather wallet. "This is for you. It's all the money I possess in the world. I want you to have it."

It must be the extra money from the household accounts, and whatever savings Mama had managed to squirrel away. Gretchen looked at the wallet, but didn't move to take it. "How will you live?"

"It doesn't matter." Her mother pressed the wallet into Gretchen's hand. "All I care about is that *you* do." At last, her mother looked at Daniel. Something seemed to change in her face, a barely perceptible loosening of muscles as though she had unclamped her jaw.

"You love my daughter," her mother said.

Daniel nodded. "Yes. With all of my soul."

"I can't pretend to understand it." Her mother studied Daniel. "It isn't natural. Just promise," she said to Daniel, reaching out as if to touch him, then shrinking back as if she'd suddenly remembered herself, "just promise you'll treat my daughter well."

Daniel looked solemn. "I will, Frau Müller."

To Gretchen's shock, her mother pulled her close in a hard embrace. "I love you, my little girl," she murmured, then released her suddenly and strode away into the darkness. For an instant, she was a silver-edged figure in the shadows, then she was nothing more than the whispers of tall grasses and wind. Gretchen swallowed against the welling emotion in her throat.

"We must go," Gretchen said, and they headed north, keeping close to the river as they skirted Dachau's outer edges.

The nearest village with a decent-sized train station was nearly forty miles away, a few days' hike, since they stopped frequently to forage for berries or drink from streams.

At Ingolstadt, they caught a train that carried them southwest. A few bills from her mother's wallet convinced the conductor not to ask for their passports. Their good luck couldn't hold out for long, and they would have to find a forger to make them false papers so that they could continue to England.

Dawn had lightened the sky to a pale pink when they reached Switzerland. The train curved around a hill and a small village lay beneath them, gray stone buildings tucked among the towering evergreens. It looked like Germany.

But it wasn't, and Gretchen knew she might never again see her home, the land that reminded her of fairy tales for its dark beauty and cunning cruelties, its crystalline lakes she had swum with Hitler, its pine forests she had walked with her father, its city of stone and stained glass where she had met Daniel.

"We may never go back," Gretchen said.

Daniel looked at her. He had slept on and off throughout the night's train ride, and though his face was still tight with pain and his arm still lay crumpled over his chest, he looked far better. His skin felt soft and warm to the touch; the danger had passed. Every time she looked at him, her heart seemed to burst out of her chest with gladness and gratitude.

"No," Daniel agreed. He leaned closer, brushing her lips with his. "We may not. But I think we will, Gretchen. Somehow, someday, Hitler will fail. And we'll have been part of the force that brought him to his knees."

She hoped he was right. Her mother's money would get them to England, and there they would tell everyone they could the truth about Hitler; they would shout about the danger in Munich to everyone who could hear. And somehow they would survive together—she would live the life she had chosen for herself. For now, that was what mattered. And it had to be enough.

She looked at Daniel—so solid and dependable and real, not like the figures of smoke and shadow she had known her whole life. "I'm ready," she said. The train hesitated at the top of the hill, then slowly started sliding down, picking up speed until they were hurtling toward the village and whatever lay beyond.

# Author's Note

ALTHOUGH *PRISONER OF NIGHT AND FOG* IS A WORK of fiction, much of it is rooted in fact. Please note that this section contains major plot spoilers, so read no further if you haven't finished the book!

Gretchen, her family, Daniel, Dr. Whitestone, the boarding-house residents, Kurt Jaeger, Gretchen's classmate Erika, Lars and Stefan Dearstyne, and Cell G's victim Dieter Adler are fictitious characters. Everyone else was a real person.

I wove a fictitious murder around two of the most devastating real events in Hitler's life: Germany's surrender while he was being treated for "hysterical blindness" and the "Beer Hall Putsch."

During the final weeks of World War One, Hitler's regiment suffered a poison-gas attack. While other temporarily blinded soldiers recovered their eyesight fairly soon, Hitler didn't and was labeled a "hysteric." According to a Berlin War Ministry decree, all "hysterical soldiers" had to be quarantined because their nervous condition was thought to be contagious. Accordingly, Hitler was separated from his regiment and sent to a military hospital in Pasewalk, Pomerania. There he proved to be such a difficult patient that doctors called in a consulting specialist named Edmund Forster, who diagnosed Hitler as a "classic psychopath."

Austrian-born Hitler was starting to see again when he received news of Germany's surrender. The knowledge that his beloved adopted country had been defeated was more than he could bear, and he temporarily lost his sight again.

He recovered by the end of November. Without any job prospects, he decided to remain in the army, originally working as a guard at a prisoner-of-war camp. By spring 1919, he was a *V-Mann*, an informant designed to keep track of anti-German and anti-Bolshevik sentiments brewing within the army. In the autumn, he was ordered to attend a meeting of one of the countless new political parties that were sprouting up in Munich like mushrooms. The group was the German Workers' Party, and although Hitler agreed with many of their patriotic principles, he discovered something even more important when he became involved with its members—he had a gift for public speaking.

This organization morphed into the National Socialist German Workers' (Nazi) Party, and Hitler easily maneuvered himself to become its new leader. The *real* putsch went down as follows: Hitler decided the fledgling party was ready to overthrow Munich's government, Nazis stormed the Bürgerbräukeller, and took the city's top three leaders hostage. By the next morning, state police troops and National Defense soldiers had been mobilized, and the would-be putschists faced imminent arrest.

In an effort to go down swinging, they marched across the city to rescue Ernst Röhm and his men, who had taken control of the Reichswehr (National Defense) building during the night but were now surrounded. Unfortunately for the Nazis, they took a wrong turn down the Residenzstrasse and marched directly into a waiting cadre of state police troopers. To this day, no one knows who fired the first shot. A furious thirty-second gun battle ensued, leaving four policemen and fourteen Nazis dead (sixteen in this book because of the fictional additions Klaus Müller and Lars Dearstyne).

Right before the shootout, Hitler had linked arms with his comrade Max Scheubner-Richter, who was one of the first to die. As Scheubner-Richter collapsed, he pulled Hitler down with him. Simultaneously, Hitler's personal bodyguard, Ulrich Graf, flung his body in front of his leader's, shielding him from the bullets, then yanked him down to a safer position on the ground, dislocating Hitler's shoulder in the process. For the purposes of my story, Gretchen's father appears to assume Graf's lifesaving role. In real life, Graf was grievously wounded, but survived.

A couple of Nazis hustled Hitler into a getaway car, and they rushed to Ernst Hanfstaengl's country house in nearby Uffing, where the future Führer was arrested a few days later. He was convicted of high treason and sentenced to serve five years in Landsberg Prison, where he wrote his autobiography/political manifesto *Mein Kampf*. After a mere nine months, a sympathetic judiciary let him out, although they banned him from public speaking for an additional three years. His political career should have been over.

But, as was often the case with Adolf Hitler, what should have been the end was only the start of a new chapter.

Although many historians have recounted his life in minute detail, there is little consensus on his personality. Many believe he was simply evil. Some, such as Dr. Forster, think he was a psychopath. Others think he was a misguided monster who was convinced that wiping out the world's Jewish population was right and just. Still others portray Hitler as a fraud, someone who had decided that creating an enemy was the best way to consolidate his power base and catapult himself into office. For readers who'd like to learn more about Hitler, I recommend the biographies by Alan Bullock, Joachim Fest, John Toland, and especially Ian Kershaw, whose three-volume biography of Hitler is nothing short of masterly.

The *Munich Post* was run by heroic journalists. Their experiences inspired me to create Daniel, who loves the truth and seeks it as aggressively and bravely as they did. These reporters—notably Edmund Goldschagg, Erhard Auer, Julius Zerfass, and editor Martin Gruber—spent the 1920s and early '30s investigating Hitler and the Nazi Party. In their eyes, he was a gangster determined to seize power and destroy the Jewish population.

In 1931, the paper broke the stories about the Nazis' death squad known as Cell G and their eventual plan for the Jews. Everything that Gretchen and Daniel overhear in a cigarette house was reported in a *Munich Post* article published in December 1931, including Hitler's insistence on secrecy because he feared his plan would have a negative effect on Germany's relations with other countries. If you're interested in learning more about the *Munich Post*, anti-Nazi journalist Fritz Gerlich, or various theories about

Hitler's personality, read Ron Rosenbaum's excellent and insightful *Explaining Hitler* (Random House, 1998; Harper Perennial, 1999).

For those who'd like to know about the real people who appeared in this book, here's a brief roundup of their lives until 1933, when Hitler became chancellor and the forthcoming sequel to *Prisoner of Night and Fog* begins.

Angela "Geli" Raubal, Hitler's half niece, is often referred to as the only love of his life. Although her death was classified as a suicide, inconsistencies in the story have fueled dozens of conspiracy theories over the years. She was buried at the Central Cemetery in Vienna. Hitler kept her bedroom as a shrine, and on the anniversary of her death, he would sit in there alone for hours.

Eva Braun was a seventeen-year-old camera apprentice in Heinrich Hoffmann's studio when she first met Hitler in 1929. Although they flirted and dated occasionally for two years, she didn't become his mistress until a few months after Geli's death.

Ernst "Putzi" Hanfstaengl came from prominent German and American families. During the 1920s and early '30s, he helped the Nazi Party in many ways, lending money and introducing Hitler to members of high society. Eventually, he became the Party's foreign-press chief.

Max Amann, also known as "Hitler's business dwarf" and personal banker, benefited more financially from the Third Reich than any other person. Under his guidance, Eher Verlag, the Nazi publishing house, grew to gargantuan proportions, and Amann became a millionaire. After the war, he was arrested by the Allies and stripped of his personal fortune. He died in Munich in 1957.

Rudolf Hess, Hitler's personal secretary, became the deputy Führer. During World War Two, he secretly flew his own airplane to England, intending to speak with Prime Minister Winston Churchill about the possibility of a truce. Instead he crash-landed in Scotland and was promptly captured. After the war, he was sentenced to life imprisonment and incarcerated in Spandau Prison, a facility reserved for Nazi war criminals. He died in 1987.

Ernst Röhm, the head of the SA, first met Hitler during World War One. He was executed on Hitler's orders in July 1934 during the "Night of the Long Knives," an attempt by Hitler and his top lieutenants to clean out the unruly and unpredictable SA troops.

Heinrich Hoffmann was a respected photographer who joined the Nazi Party in its early days. After the war, he was arrested by the Allies and served four years for war profiteering. His daughter Henriette, nicknamed "Henny," was a particular favorite of Hitler's; she married Nazi youth leader Baldur von Schirach in 1932.

The men who marched with Hitler in the front line before gunfire ended their disastrous putsch were Erich von Ludendorff, a famous general who later severed his ties with the Nazi Party; Hermann Göring, an ace World War One pilot who became the second-most-powerful leader in Nazi Germany; Hermann Kriebel, a retired lieutenant colonel, who remained in minor political posts under the Nazi regime; Ulrich Graf, Hitler's bodyguard; and Max Scheubner-Richter, an early leading Nazi.

The unidentified men who convened for a top-level meeting in Hitler's apartment after the discovery of Geli's body were

Henny's future husband, Baldur von Schirach, Nazi youth leader and later Reich governor of Vienna who spent twenty years in Spandau Prison for war crimes, and Gregor Strasser, a pharmacist and early prominent Nazi who frequently clashed with Hitler. Strasser was killed during the Night of the Long Knives, on Hitler's orders. Hitler's unnamed chauffeur was Julius Schreck, who died of meningitis in 1936.

Fritz Gerlich was a conservative journalist who often tangled with Hitler during the tumultuous 1920s. In 1932, he assumed leadership of a weekly newspaper he renamed *Der Gerade Weg* (*The Straight Path*), and wrote many articles condemning Nazism, anti-Semitism, and Communism.

Edmund Forster, the neurologist who treated and diagnosed Hitler at the end of World War One, later became chair of the Psychiatry Department and director of the Neurological Clinic at Greisfwald University. In 1933, about eight months after Hitler became chancellor, Forster was denounced by Nazi coworkers as a Communist, a criminal, and a "Jew lover." He was forced to resign. A week later, he was found dead in his home, shot through the head. His death was ruled a suicide.

Dr. Eduard Bloch, who treated Hitler's mother for breast cancer, remained at his medical practice in Austria until 1938. He emigrated to the United States, settling in New York City, and later admitted that Hitler had granted him special favors because of their past relationship.

The ideas Hitler expresses in *Prisoner of Night and Fog* are based on things he said in real life, and the talk he gives in Osteria Bavaria touches upon themes he discussed in speeches early in his career. The idea for this book's title came from the infamous

"Night and Fog" decree of 1941, which permitted Nazis to arrest resistance agents in occupied countries and bring them immediately to special courts in Germany, circumventing due process and procedures for treatment of prisoners. In essence, Nazis could spirit away their enemies into "the night and the fog," just as the supernatural being abducts the boy in Johann Wolfgang von Goethe's famous literary ballad "Der Erlkönig."

Now that you're caught up, I'll meet you again in 1933, right after a certain Austrian politician has been named Germany's newest chancellor. . . .

# Selected Bibliography


"Adolf Hitler, Millionaire." *Ken*. March 9, 1939: 28.

Bartoletti, Susan Campbell. *Hitler Youth: Growing up in Hitler's Shadow*. New York: Scholastic, 2005.

Brown, Cyril. "Hitler Organization Declared Illegal." *New York Times*: March 17, 1923: 2–3.

Bullock, Alan. *Hitler: A Study in Tyranny*. New York: Harper & Row, 1971.

Bytwerk, Randall L. *Julius Streicher*: *Nazi Editor of the Notorious Anti-Semitic Newspaper Der Stürmer*. New York: Cooper Square Press, 1983, 2001.

Evans, Richard J. *The Coming of the Third Reich*. New York: Penguin, 2004.

Fest, Joachim C. *Hitler*. Translated by Richard and Clara Winston. New York: Harcourt Brace & Company, 1974.

Hale, Oron J. *The Captive Press in the Third Reich*. Princeton, NJ:

Princeton University Press, 1964.

Hancock, Eleanor. *Ernst Röhm: Hitler's SA Chief of Staff.* New York: Palgrave Macmillan, 2008.

Hanfstaengl, Ernst. *Hitler: The Missing Years*. New York: Arcade Publishing, 1957, 1994.

Hanisch, Reinhold. "I Was Hitler's Buddy." *New Republic,* April 5, 12, 19, 1939.

Hayman, Ronald. *Hitler & Geli*. New York: Bloomsbury Publishing, 1997.

Hitler, Adolf. *Mein Kampf.* Mumbai: Jaico Publishing House, 2008.

Hunt, Irmgard A. *On Hitler's Mountain: Overcoming the Legacy of a Nazi Childhood*. New York: Harper Perennial, 2005.

Junge, Traudl. *Until the Final Hour: Hitler's Last Secretary.* Edited by Melissa Müller. London: Weidenfeld & Nicolson, 2003.

Kershaw, Ian. *Hitler, 1889–1936: Hubris*. New York: W.W. Norton & Company, 1998.

———. *Hitler, 1936–1945: Nemesis*. New York: W.W. Norton & Company, 2000.

Koehn, Ilse. *Mischling, Second Degree: My Childhood in Nazi Germany*. New York: Puffin Books, 1977.

Kubizek, August. *The Young Hitler I Knew*. Westport, CT: Greenwood Press, 1976.

Lambert, Angela. *The Lost Life of Eva Braun*. New York: St. Martin's Press, 2006.

Large, David Clay. *Where Ghosts Walked: Munich's Road to the Third Reich*. New York: W.W. Norton & Company, 1996.

Lebert, Stephan, and Norbert Lebert. *My Father's Keeper: Children of Nazi Leaders—An Intimate History of Damage and Denial.* Translated by Julian Evans. Boston: Little, Brown and

Company, 2000, 2001.

Lewis, David. *The Man Who Invented Hitler.* London: Bounty Books, 2005.

Longerich, Peter. *Heinrich Himmler.* Translated by Jeremy Noakes and Lesley Sharpe. Oxford: Oxford University Press, 2012.

Manvell, Roger, and Heinrich Fraenkel. *Hess: A Biography.* New York: Drake Publishers Inc., 1973.

Padfield, Peter. *Himmler.* New York: Henry Holt and Company, 1990.

Read, Anthony. *The Devil's Disciples: Hitler's Inner Circle.* New York: W.W. Norton & Company, 2003, 2005.

Redlich, Fritz. *Hitler: Diagnosis of a Destructive Prophet.* Oxford: Oxford University Press, 1998.

Rosenbaum, Ron. *Explaining Hitler.* New York: Harper Perennial, 1998.

Schirach, Henriette von. *The Price of Glory.* Translated by Willi Frischauer. London: Frederick Muller Limited, 1960.

Shirer, William L. *The Rise and Fall of the Third Reich: A History of Nazi Germany.* New York: Ballantine Books, 1960.

Speer, Albert. *Inside the Third Reich.* Translated by Richard and Clara Winston. New York: Galahad Books, 1970.

Strasser, Otto. *Hitler and I.* Boston: Houghton Mifflin Company, 1940.

Toland, John. *Adolf Hitler.* New York: Doubleday & Company, Inc., 1976.

Whetton, Cris. *Hitler's Fortune.* Barnsley, South Yorkshire: Pen & Sword Books Limited, 2004.

# Acknowledgments

FIRST AND FOREMOST, THANKS TO MY AMAZING editor, Kristin Daly Rens, for her enthusiasm, careful reading, and guidance. Kristin, you asked all the right questions and helped me turn *Prisoner of Night and Fog* into the story I wanted it to be. Thank you.

I owe a big thanks to the rest of the Balzer + Bray/Harper-Collins team, including Alessandra Balzer, Donna Bray, assistant editor Sara Sargent, designer Michelle Taormina for a beautiful cover, Emilie Polster and Stefanie Hoffman in marketing, and Caroline Sun in publicity. I'm especially grateful to copy editor Kathryn Silsand, who went above and beyond the call of duty.

Many thanks to everyone at Adams Literary, including Josh Adams for his ninjalike business savvy, and especially my agent, Tracey Adams. Tracey, I'll always cherish my memory of meeting you at the Mid-Atlantic SCBWI Conference ("Whew, Daniel is sexy!"). You believed in this book, and that has changed my life.

Thanks to my mom, Lynn Brostrom Blankman, for telling me I needed to write this story and for helping me whip an unwieldy 540-page manuscript into submission-ready shape. To my husband, Mike Cizenski, for his encouragement and computer expertise. I'll never forget acting out Klaus Müller's death with you. To my daughter, Kirsten, for disproving the myths about the terrible twos and happily taking naps so I could write. Thanks also to my dad, Peter Blankman, for taking me to the public library to show me the section on World War Two when I was twelve and devastated after reading Anne Frank's diary. And to my brother, Paul Blankman, for reading my stories when we were kids and not making fun of them, although you must have been tempted. For the record, Paul is nothing like Reinhard.

I am grateful to Esther Benoit, PhD, LPC, for teaching me so much about abnormal psychology. I'd also like to acknowledge my coworkers at the York County, Virginia, Public Library System, especially Pat Riter, better known as the ILL goddess, who not only retrieved every item I requested but did so in record time.

Many thanks to the librarians, teachers, booksellers, and bloggers. And especially to the readers.